JAPANESE HOLLYWOOD CAST

"Hey, I've got a great idea!" Kelly said suddenly. "Instead of just telling everyone in town through the typical tradepaper announcements, let's show them by staging a spectacular press party—on the back lot! We'll turn the studio into a small city for the night, with neon lights, shooting fountains, skyscrapers, music, food . . ."

Takashima eyed her with new respect. "That is an excellent idea, Kelly-san. But we must make the city Tokyo, recreated all over our Constellation lot."

Kelly smiled broadly as she turned to Robert. Even he seemed to like the idea. "Perfect, Mr. Takashima," she said. "The town won't stop talking about us for months."

Takashima beamed, charged up with the idea of being able to see every important movie star before he slowly began to eliminate them. "No cost will be spared. I am very pleased with your idea, Kelly-san, very pleased. . . ."

① SIGNET   **(0451)**

SENSATIONAL BESTSELLERS!

- [ ] **FAME AND FORTUNE by Kate Coscarelli.** Beautiful women ... glittering Beverly Hills ... the boutiques ... the bedrooms ... the names you drop and the ones you whisper ... all in the irresistible novel that has everyone reading ... "From the opening, the reader is off and turning the pages!"—*Los Angeles Times* (160290—$4.95)

- [ ] **PERFECT ORDER by Kate Coscarelli.** Glamorous Manhattan forms the backdrop for the sensational story of Cake, Vanessa, and Millie—three beauties who move into high gear in the most super-rich, super-sexy, super-powerful city in the world ... "Every woman over the age of twenty ought to have three copies."—*Los Angeles Times* (400038—$3.95)

- [ ] **LIVING COLOR by Kate Coscarelli.** From the highest reaches of posh society to the lower depths of Hollywood and betrayal, this dazzling novel traces the lives of twin sisters separated in infancy but drawn together by an indestructible bond. (400828—$4.50)

- [ ] **A MORNING AFFAIR by Janice Kaplan.** A sexy, glamorous novel about a young woman's rise to the top of the world of morning television—where the only sin is coming in second. "Great fun to read ... what its like behind the scenes."—Joan Lunden, "Good Morning America" (164288—$4.95)

- [ ] **BABY DREAMS—A Novel by Maxine Paetro.** Georgeous and talented Stephanie Weinberger is going to all the right places, but there is something wrong with her seemingly perfect life. What do other women have that she wants? What is the dream for which she might risk everything to make come true? "*BABY BOOM, thirtysomething, BROADCAST NEWS* rolled into one ... hip, thought-provoking great reading!"—*Los Angeles Times Book Review* (165683—$4.95)

Prices slightly higher in Canada

Buy them at your local bookstore or use this convenient coupon for ordering.

NEW AMERICAN LIBRARY
P.O. Box 999, Bergenfield, New Jersey 07621

Please send me the books I have checked above. I am enclosing $_____
(please add $1.00 to this order to cover postage and handling). Send check or money order—no cash or C.O.D.'s. Prices and numbers are subject to change without notice.

Name_____

Address_____

City _____ State _____ Zip Code _____

Allow 4-6 weeks for delivery.
This offer is subject to withdrawal without notice.

AVENUE OF THE STARS

Jina Bacarr and Ellis A. Cohen

A SIGNET BOOK

SIGNET
Published by the Penguin Group
Penguin Books USA Inc., 375 Hudson Street,
New York, New York 10014, U.S.A.
Penguin Books Ltd, 27 Wrights Lane, London W8 5TZ, England
Penguin Books Australia Ltd, Ringwood, Victoria, Australia
Penguin Books Canada Ltd, 10 Alcorn Avenue,
Toronto, Ontario, Canada M4V 3B2
Penguin Books (N.Z.) Ltd, 182–190 Wairau Road,
Auckland 10, New Zealand

Penguin Books Ltd, Registered Offices:
Harmondsworth, Middlesex, England

Published by Signet, an imprint of New American Library,
a division of Penguin Books USA Inc. Previously published
in a Dutton edition.

First Signet Printing, November, 1991
10 9 8 7 6 5 4 3 2 1

Copyright © Jina Bacarr and Ellis A. Cohen, 1990
All rights reserved

REGISTERED TRADEMARK—MARCA REGISTRADA

Printed in the United States of America

Without limiting the rights under copyright reserved above, no part of this publication may be reproduced, stored in or introduced into a retrieval system, or transmitted, in any form, or by any means (electronic, mechanical, photocopying, recording, or otherwise), without the prior written permission of both the copyright owner and the above publisher of this book.

PUBLISHER'S NOTE
This book is a work of fiction. The characters are fictional and created out of the imagination of the authors. When reference is made to individuals whose names are identifiable and recognizable by the public, it is because they are prominent in their respected fields and mentioning them is intended to convey a sense of verisimilitude to this fictional work.

BOOKS ARE AVAILABLE AT QUANTITY DISCOUNTS WHEN USED TO PROMOTE PRODUCTS OR SERVICES. FOR INFORMATION PLEASE WRITE TO PREMIUM MARKETING DIVISION, PENGUIN BOOKS USA INC., 375 HUDSON STREET, NEW YORK, NEW YORK 10014.

If you purchased this book without a cover you should be aware that this book is stolen property. It was reported as "unsold and destroyed" to the publisher and neither the author nor the publisher has received any payment for this "stripped book."

For LEN LaBRAE—
My husband, my lover,
and my best friend,
who makes all my dreams
come true

>   —Love always,
>   Jina

To my wonderful parents,
Leonard and Selma
"FOR ALL WE SHARE"

>   —Love,
>   Ellis

Foreword

They say there's a story behind every story, and this book is no exception.

It all started during the 1988 Writers Guild Strike, when virtually all of Hollywood came to a standstill. The two of us were introduced to each other by author Ara John Movsesian at the American Booksellers Convention in Anaheim, California. We decided to collaborate on a novel, and *Avenue of the Stars* was born.

We brought the best of our abilities to the project:

Jina, a multifaceted writer, has written numerous scripts for both U.S. and Japanese television. She has also been a commercial spokesperson for a major Japanese food company. In addition, she has studied the Japanese language and culture for several years, and her invaluable expertise was crucial in the shaping of this side of our story: *Japan*.

Ellis, an award-winning producer-writer of CBS-TV movies, contributed his twenty-five years of insightful knowledge of working between New York and Hollywood—as an exec at the William Morris Agency, to editor-in-chief of a national television magazine, to Hollywood press agent—in the shaping of this side of our story: *Hollywood*.

When we began the creative process, our story was fiction. During the summer of 1988, the climate in Hollywood was more concerned with the studio takeovers than the making of movies. As we developed our novel, stories about Japan made the evening news almost every day. If it wasn't some Japanese conglomerate rumored as buying such-and-such studio, then it was their leaders who were being besieged by political turmoil.

Call it coincidence or luck, but some of our original story touched on similarities to this reality. In fact, our novel was purchased a few days before Sony bought Columbia Pictures. That's why we now refer to our novel as a work of "faction."

Many terrific people helped us along the way, but one in particular gets a standing ovation and a special thanks from us: our wonderful editor, Hilary Ross, who made a major impact on our novel with her creative and intuitive guidance. We also thank her for her patience and tolerance. We also applaud and thank our manuscript editor, John Paine, for all his valuable suggestions. We thank literary agent Richard Curtis for selling our book.

Special thanks and bravos to Army Archerd (*Daily Variety*), Gary Craig (Associated Press), and Michio Katsumata (*Nihon Keizai Shimbun*), for first telling Hollywood, the United States, and Japan, respectively, about our story. We are also very grateful and appreciative to the various government officials of the United States, Japan, and Fiji for lending their assistance and technical advice. In addition, a special thanks to both Kelly A. Rose of Ernst & Young and to Captain John R. Deakin of Japan Air Lines for lending technical assistance and advice. Finally, thanks to Vickie Mackenzie for all her terrific assistance.

Well, that's the story. The rest is, as they say, history. And they say it only happens in the movies.

—JINA BACARR AND ELLIS A. COHEN
Hollywood, California
March 15, 1990

Acknowledgments

I wish to thank Danny Simon, J. Michael Straczynski, and Alan Brennert, who always had the time as well as an encouraging word for a fellow writer over the years. Also, Sidney Iwanter, who taught me that the written word never dies, it is just rewritten.

—JINA BACARR

I would like to express my sincerest gratitude and appreciation to the following individuals who became my personal "cheer-leaders" during the arduous writing of this novel: my brother Jerry, Heidi Wall, Gunther Schiff, Sid Lyons, Victoria Morales, John Gemmill, Chris Kreyer, Stan Sarniske, Jeff Rose, Tom Lackey, Peter Young, Ursula Johnson, Alan and Sonja of The Script Center, Henry Cordova, the soda and pizza ladies of Farmers Market, Dyonne, L.J., and Gus from Federal Express, and a special thanks to my good friend and fellow writer Rod Browning, who always had an extra moment to answer my questions.

A special thanks to Marie Anne Jorgensen for always seeing every day as sunny and bright.

In conclusion, through my checkerboard career, I am forever indebted to some very special people who, as mentors, teachers, and friends, gave me the insight, knowledge, and support to effect my contributions to this novel: Bob Day, Lee Solters, Susan Silver, Don

King, Larry Holmes, Burt Prelutsky, Alan Gansberg, Steve Mills, Bob Silberling, Jane Rosenthal, Peter Frankovich, Casey Clair, Neil Pilson, Hilary Hartman, Peter Werner, John Cannon, David Braun, Jack Valenti, George Chapman, Ken Leedom, Major Ron McNeil, Ken Wilson, Ellen Muir, Lee Polk, Sylvia Schwartz, Andy Gottlieb, Frank Holston, Muriel Durand, Angela DiPene, Bill Cunningham, Flo Gaines, Melvin Van Peebles, Steve Shagan, Joseph Heller, Steve Yeager, Elliott and Marsha Hersh, Ron Rubin, Aunt Rose and Uncle Moe, Gary Myers, John Leino, Robert Evans, Frank Yablans, Brandon Tartikoff, Mayor Abraham D. Beame, Eve Lapolla, Susan Bernard, Michael Jaffe, Gerry Abrams, Marvin Katz, Joseph Wershba, Alan King, Jean Stapleton, Jim Sikking, Bill Carter, Michael Hill, Richard Berger, Sherry Lansing, Dawn Steel, Robert Lee, Lisa Hills, Lisa Mackey, Jana Gladstone, Julie Smith, Big George Robeson, Lindsey and Lola Scott, Dr. Jerrold Petrofsky, Dr. Mary Groda-Lewis, Dr. Michael DeBakey, Astronaut Alan B. Shepard, Betty Skelton, Bill Bateman, Bill Sullivan, Carl Spielvogel, Michael Fuchs, Chick Hyman, Joe O'Kane, Bill Lindstrom, Fran Needle, Betty Gomes, Suzanne Gordon, Dorothy Pendergast, Richard Lewis, Donald March, Ambassador Angier Biddle Duke, and Tony Cerkvenik.

And in loving memory of the following people who inspired and enriched my life: Paddy Chayefsky, Tennessee Williams, Nat Lefkowitz, Lee Stevens, Lori Jackson, Aunt Mary Dobkin, Stan Hough, Adele Kenyon, Huck Katzen, Michelle Levin, Bob Wood, Sammy Davis Jr., and Lucille Ball. And Finster and Buffy.

—ELLIS A. COHEN

*I am one, my liege,
Whom the vile blows and buffets of the world
Have so incensed that I am reckless what
I do to spite the world.*

    —WILLIAM SHAKESPEARE, *Macbeth*

Patriotism is the last revenge of a scoundrel.
      —SAMUEL JOHNSON

Prologue

NOVEMBER 9, 1988

Every time a patron pushed open the ornately carved steel doors of the crowded Tokyo club, a preview of the winter west wind would sneak inside. But no one in the Juraku-dai, the Palace of Gathered Pleasures, seemed to notice. The men had their eyes riveted on the blond *gaijin*, or foreigner, slinking around on the small stage. She squeezed her nipples, then ran her hands lightly over her naked breasts in time to the raucous stripper music provided by a three-piece combo in the background.

"Here's something for your *mamasan*," she teased them over the jazzy sounds of the sax, but the audience did not hear her. They were going crazy, yelling and jumping up and down.

This was Tokyo at night, where company men arrived in steady groups, to unwind after the long days at the office before catching the last train home at midnight.

As the drummer gave her an enthusiastic drumroll, the fair-skinned dancer seductively wiggled out of her see-through panties. As she twirled them around on her finger, she looked out at the audience and licked her hot wet tongue over her lips. Wearing only a G-string, she threw her discarded underwear into the audience. Her message was loud and clear.

But all was quiet in the hidden room concealed near the stage, where a lone man watched the show in privacy. As the *gaijin* taunted the audience with her gyrations, the dark-eyed man anxiously pacing back and forth narrowed his eyes in pleasure.

Each stripper possessed her own style, but this woman was exceptional. Nearly six feet tall, she was even taller in her clear plastic stiletto pumps with sprigs of wild purple feathers at the heels. He noticed her round, firm buttocks, then the large breasts, just begging to be pinched. The girl would easily fulfill his customers' sexual needs. *Hai*, he thought, she was exceptional. But then, everything Hiroshi Takashima owned was exceptional.

He had paid a small fortune to buy out the top Danish model's contract from a Copenhagen show, but it had not been a mistake. He had been certain the businessmen would be willing to pay double the usual drink rate of twenty-five hundred yen per cocktail to see his gorgeous *gaijin*. Like other Asian businessmen, Takashima despised anything acquired too cheaply and used too freely. The girl was worth the price.

His club, like no other in the world-famous Ginza district, was now booked for two years' advance business. He had an unbreakable contract with the beautiful stripper, although he would make it a point to make sure she understood her duties included more than performing onstage. Takashima expected complete obedience from his employees.

He continued watching her through the one-way mirror separating his luxurious playroom from the noisy club. Takashima took no chances; he believed that spying on his patrons was simply good business tactics.

He focused his eyes on the naked girl as she slid her slim fingers up and down her body, and he began to perspire, even in his air-conditioned room. The collar of his pristine white shirt felt tight around his neck. Even the lightweight platinum frames of his gray-tinted aviator glasses felt heavy on his well-shaped nose. He breathed in deeply as he watched the blond bend over and jiggle her pale fanny naughtily.

In the club, the patrons nearly fell out of the low-to-the-floor red plastic divans. Their eyes rolled back wildly in their heads, their voices rising to a screaming pitch as the beautiful *gaijin* tore off her flower headpiece and pulled out a dildo. She caressed it lovingly between her large breasts, then slid it down her nude body and began fondling it between her legs.

From his hidden vantage point, Takashima lit a cigarette, his excitement growing. He grunted loudly as his hard penis pressed against his pants.

"Takashima-san, important news."

Annoyed, Takashima spun around as his short, sturdily built accountant bustled in. Wearing shirtsleeves rolled up, his glasses sliding to the end of his nose, the intruder stopped short and bowed apologetically several times. Takashima restrained himself from voicing his anger. No one else would have dared interrupt him, but Michio Noda was his most trusted employee. In fact, the brilliant young accountant was the heir apparent to Takashima's organization.

Noda turned on the big-screen television and a life-size image of George Bush, the new American leader, was waving to a cheering crowd.

". . . and read my lips, no new taxes."

Takashima eyed the tall, skinny President-elect, unimpressed. Bush looked like a common peasant to him, with no backbone, no daring. He had no use for that type of person. He was just another American politician, like those responsible for destroying his people in 1945.

As the CNN newscaster continued to detail the highlights of Bush's acceptance speech, Takashima, with the remote control at his fingertips, turned off the television.

"Enough, Noda-san. His election does not change our plans."

"Do you believe he will do what he has promised, Takashima-san?"

Takashima crushed his cigarette into a golden shell ashtray by way of a reply. "He is weak, like the one before him. America will continue to be an easy mark for our people."

Takashima nodded toward the naked girl on the stage and asked Noda, "What do you think of my new *gaijin*?"

Embarrassed, Noda refused to look at her. He did not share his mentor's salacious interest in the flesh. He turned his head, hoping Takashima would not see him blush.

Takashima grunted his displeasure at his accountant's embarrassment. The young man spent too much time with his books and numbers. Then Takashima smiled. After all, they were his empire's business books.

"It's time to go." Takashima clapped his hands, and instantly a hulking character in a tight dark suit appeared. His black hair was permed, and he wore flashy alligator loafers. Then a second, bigger man appeared, dressed similarly, in the traditional uniform of a bodyguard: dark blue double-breasted suit, white shirt, black tie, and dark sunglasses.

They were Takashima's Yakuza bodyguards. They hovered around him like presidential Secret Service agents, but with a difference—both men were minus the little fingers on their right hands, a symbol of their devotion to their master.

Even among his business associates, the Asian Octopus was noted for his strong-arm muscle. He often joked that his Yakuza were merely a symbolic image of his strength. And, most of the time they did stay in the background, since Takashima was very careful not to allow them to tarnish his businessman image. But he did not think twice about using them when necessary.

Without uttering a word, the bodyguards followed Takashima and Noda through the invisible sliding door and into the nightclub.

The combo had stopped playing, and piped-in rock-and-roll blared through the club. As Takashima walked through the sweaty, inflamed crowd, a man drunkenly bumped into him.

Takashima's chief Yakuza, Minoru, immediately grabbed the man by his collar. The poor man nearly fainted as he looked up into the Yakuza's menacing bloodshot eyes, then at the deep scar crisscrossing over his mouth. Minoru was raising his fist, ready to splatter the man's pale face all over the velvet paper walls, when Takashima boomed, *"Stop!"*

The man is a customer, he thought, and should be treated with courtesy.

"He has tasted enough pleasure for one night. Put him on his train and make sure he arrives home safely . . . so he may return another night."

Abruptly Minoru nodded, then bowed low. *"Hai,* master."

A slim woman in a dragon-fire-red kimono slid open the paper doors, then called out, "Kakue-san, where are you?" No one answered. How dare the girl leave the floor covered with tea leaves? Chisako thought. Cursing under her breath, she bent down and sifted through the black, murky residue with her fingers. The floor must be cleaned, and there was not a moment to lose. Tonight's dinner was of the utmost importance.

Without hesitation Chisako grabbed a broom and began sweeping the floor until it shone with a deep, glossy sheen. Everything had to be perfect. I should beat her with a bamboo stick, Chisako thought. Then she shuddered. She could not do that. How many times had she felt the stinging blow of her master's wrath? *Buriburi*, the beating with many sticks, was the horror of every woman who ever displeased her master. As Chisako continued sweeping, she promised herself that she would speak to the girl about *giri*. Duty to one's master must be upheld at all cost.

"Chisako-san, he is here!" A petite girl in a rose-pink kimono stumbled into the room, tripping on her trailing sash.

"Kakue-san," Chisako warned, "slow down. A geisha does not move so quickly. She takes slow, graceful steps. Like this." Chisako proceeded to demonstrate, arching her long, graceful body in a swanlike position as she glided across the floor in her white stocking feet as quietly as cat's paws.

"I am sorry," the young girl said, remembering her training as she lowered her head and hid her face behind her fan.

Chisako shook her head. "You have much to learn, young one," she said. "A geisha must always be aware of her appearance as well as her demeanor."

Chisako looked at the young girl and saw her own sweet moon face of long ago. Kakue's big eyes were sparkling with excitement, while her tiny nose wiggled. Her black hair was piled high on her head, making her look like a baby doll. Was I ever as innocent as this child? Chisako wondered. She had seen so much of life since being enrolled at twelve as an apprentice. For a moment she remembered those days: the quiet moments of meditation in the garden, the hours of flower arranging and learning the rituals of the tea ceremony. Then she sighed. That had been years ago, before she had met the Asian Octopus.

Chisako carefully arranged the child's long, flowing sash into a proper train—a symbol of Kakue's training period. Then she picked up two finely carved cherry-wood combs and placed them in Kakue's hair. "Remember, it is the illusion that pleases the most."

Chisako smoothed down her long kimono sleeves in an effort to compose herself, then picked up the ivory-handled mirror and studied her own reflection. Bright black eyes stared back at her. At thirty, she was more beautiful than she had been as a child. Heavy lashes drooped under her small, finely arched brows, giving her an air of submission when lowered. Her skin was white and transparent, and her lips were the perfect shape of a cherry, but only to delight the eye of her admirers. When she smiled, two tiny dimples appeared. But tonight she was not smiling. She was straining to remember what she had learned so many years ago in the Gion district of Kyoto.

She had whitened her face with nightingale droppings as tradition dictated, and her kimono was subtly arranged to reveal the nape of her neck and just a hint of shoulder, the traditional erotic focus of geisha custom. A far cry from the skintight dresses and skimpy lace undergarments she usually wore when she entertained her master. Tonight she was to play the role of a traditional geisha.

A dark-suited Yakuza quietly entered. He glared at her, then bowed slowly and presented her with a gift of willows from Takashima. The gift was merely a way of letting Chisako know that he completely dominated her life. In his fanatical way of thinking, Takashima considered himself a reincarnation of the old *daimyo*, or feudal lords, the upper class who ruled Japan hundreds of years ago. "The Master is waiting for you."

Chisako nodded, not showing her surprise. Bowing, she handed the willows to Kakue, who took them and arranged them in a vase. As Chisako waited for her to finish, she kept her eyes lowered. She had learned not to show fear in the presence of her master's Yakuza, although they made her shudder with their leering looks, but she could not help fidgeting with the rich satin of her sash as it slid through her fingers.

With a brave smile Chisako motioned for Kakue to follow her. The young girl did so dutifully, careful to keep her head down. Chisako said nothing. It would be easier for Kakue if she knew nothing of what would be expected of her.

Silently the two women walked past the closed door of the garden room with their heads bowed low. Chisako bit her lip to keep from smiling. What would the American say if he knew why he was being kept waiting?

* * *

Stephen Resnick was nervous. Nothing had gone right for the tall, good-looking blond attorney with surfer looks since he had left Los Angeles. And now the man he was supposed to meet wasn't even here. He had already been offered some foul-smelling green tea but had politely refused a cup, although he could have used something for his nerves. All this waiting was just making him more antsy.

Shit, he thought, I wouldn't even be in this mess if I hadn't missed that point spread on the Rams game. Then he grimaced. The boys in Vegas were upset over a lot more than one game. Because of them, he now found himself in a strange country about to betray the one person who had given him everything: Jake Baron, his stepfather and the owner of the legendary Constellation Studios.

As Stephen cracked his knuckles, he prayed under his breath. God help him if Jake ever found out. He'd be through in Hollywood, New York, everywhere.

He looked at his gold Rolex: nearly eight o'clock. He had been planning to catch a return flight home first thing in the morning. He wanted to get this meeting over with and get the hell out. After all, the longer he hung around here, the more dangerous it would be for him.

Stephen played with the clasp on his briefcase, opening and closing it many times. He tried to keep his shoulder from twitching, a nervous tic that occurred when he was tense.

"Shit," he cursed under his breath. Where was he?

Chisako closed her eyes as she put her master's penis into her mouth, then licked it lovingly with her tongue. She no longer felt embarrassed performing the act in front of his Yakuza, but she did wonder what was going through Kakue's mind as the young girl watched her open her kimono, then fall to her knees at Takashima's feet.

She pushed away her knee-length black hair, shining like rich onyx, over her shoulders. Her slim, sensual body moved with the grace of a tigress. When she spoke words of desire, her voice was low and sensual, with none of the coarseness of many of her trade.

Takashima grunted, his black eyes flashing. His stomach ached with anticipation. He rubbed his hands together. They were sweaty, yet cold. He could feel his heart beating fast, like the wings of a bird trapped in a dark cave.

He was seated on a black velvet cushion, wearing his white shirt, tie, and socks, but nothing else. Next to him, a steaming cup of tea rested on a tiny mother-of-pearl-inlaid table. Lanterns softly glowed around the room. Tender, melancholy notes of recorded traditional music could be heard in the background. The smell of burning incense filled the air. The walls were filled with erotica: Asian women with wild manes of hair posed in stylized sexual positions. On a black lacquered tripod rose a vase of fresh white camellias, their purity a strange contrast to the scene.

The apprentice geisha, Kakue, had never seen anything like this.

"Please, may I go?" she asked softly, bowing low to Takashima, while interrupting his pleasure. She was afraid to show her embarrassment.

"Stay, Kakue-san," he grumbled, without missing a moment of the pleasure he enjoyed of having Chisako suck him off. Yet from the corner of his eye he glanced over at Kakue.

Kakue raised her head and looked into his eyes. She must not refuse Takashima, even if she wanted to leave. Chisako had taught her to fear his wrath, and like other geisha who had preceded her, she also found herself mesmerized by his dominating presence. She wanted to ask him why she must stay and watch, but decided to keep silent. Indeed, although frightened and naive, she was also strangely aroused by the sights and smells around her.

Embarrassed by her own thoughts, she lowered her gaze to the floor, but a nearby Yakuza lifted her chin with his hand. A warm flush seeped over her. She had no choice but to continue to watch the sexual ritual unfolding before her eyes.

Chisako looked over at Kakue from under her heavy lashes. She knew what was happening. This would be the first part of Kakue's initiation into Takashima's pleasure circle. She too had been put through the same ordeal. She grimaced as she flicked her tongue over the soft skin of Takashima's penis. She prayed that her destitute mother had never known what had befallen her eldest daughter, whom she had sold her to the *okāsan*, proprietress, in charge of the geisha house.

"Good," Takashima said loudly, the signal for her to stop. She slowly opened her eyes, then gracefully let her kimono slip to the floor. She felt a small chill, but she did not hesitate; the act had to be completed.

Sitting on Takashima's erect penis, Chisako began rhythmically rising and falling. The more she did, the more she had to control her own sexual desire. It would be incorrect for her to show pleasure before her master. To her horror, she could not stop herself, and a soft moan escaped from her lips.

Suddenly Takashima grabbed her hips, pressing his fingers into her warm flesh. *"Banzai!"* he yelled like a war cry, shouting his victory into the still room. No one moved, no one breathed.

Then it was over.

"You will now greet our American guest," he ordered as he lifted her off and wrapped a house kimono around himself. "Quickly."

As Chisako hurriedly bent down to pick up her kimono, shivering from the coolness, she inadvertently bumped into the tiny table next to Takashima.

"Oh!" she cried, trying to grab the cup of tea, but it was too late. The fiery liquid splashed onto the bare flesh on his arm. He did not cry out, though, for he believed that physical pain was merely a state of mind, one he had hardened himself against many years ago. Instead, he spat at Chisako, "Whore!"

As he angrily continued to scream obscenities at her for being so clumsy, he allowed Kakue to tend to his arm with a cool, wet cloth that one of the attending Yakuza had rushed in.

Chisako cowered as the Yakuza threw her kimono at her. Quickly she put it on and ran from the room. She was shaking so hard she could not speak. She did not look back. She prayed her master would be too busy this evening to beat her. Summoning all her strength, she begged the gods to get her through the rest of the evening.

She hid in a small alcove in the adjoining garden. The west wind was blowing the trees tonight. Still trembling, Chisako hesitantly felt for the thin gold box in her kimono sleeve. Her craving for opium was very strong, but she must resist. She had started to use the drug when her master had compelled her to smoke it during a night of pleasure. Soon it had become a necessary part of the arduous nights she had spent pleasing him . . . and his friends.

Finally her compulsion overcame her will, and she pulled out her small bamboo pipe. Soon she was no longer shaking. Her hand was steady; her mind was at peace as she entered the space of dreams where her search for lost happiness was fulfilled.

Chisako slowly walked from the garden to the area where the American guest awaited them. The room with woven mats overlooked a tea garden with glowing stone lanterns. The sound of trickling water from a running stream masked their footsteps. An occasional turtle ambled along the pathway, completely in harmony with the rustic peace of the garden.

Behind Chisako, Kakue, prettily dressed in a pink kimono with a butterfly design, followed, her head demurely lowered, her steps small and hesitant. But Chisako walked proudly, head high. She was the hostess.

Stephen, sensing someone approaching, suddenly turned around. He forgot his irritation while adjusting his necktie as he saw two Japanese women slowly walking toward him.

"Please bring Mr. Resnick some whiskey, Chisako," he heard a man's voice order one of the women as he clapped his hands twice.

Stephen observed the Japanese man as he approached him, surrounded by menacing-looking bodyguards. The attorney hadn't realized he was being observed from across the room, but he wasn't surprised. The smug-looking man with the dark glasses had to be Takashima. Stephen didn't take his eyes off him, but the man didn't flinch under his scrutiny. He was lean, broad-shouldered, and although there were streaks of gray at his temples, he appeared to be much younger than Stephen had been led to believe.

"Mr. Takashima, I have brought—"

"At the correct time, Mr. Resnick. First, you must enjoy my best whiskey." Takashima bowed curtly as he purposely interrupted his guest. He then presented the American with his gold business card. Taken aback, Stephen also bowed. He had no more than a moment to glance at the card, engraved on one side in Japanese and in English on the other.

Takashima's Yakuza, flanking him on either side, escorted him into the dining area of the four-star restaurant. Stephen eyed them uneasily, knowing their reputation for unpleasantness. He just wanted to get his money and get out.

As Takashima signaled Chisako to present their guest with one of his new hi-tech electronic mini-cameras as a courtesy gift, Stephen was openly surprised.

"Thank you, Mr. Takashima, for your generosity."

Takashima returned Resnick's compliment with a slight bow, then grinned broadly as Chisako served more whiskey. She sank slowly to her knees, touching her forehead to the floor as she proffered the drink to their guest. Stephen took the drink and tasted it slowly.

It was very strong, yet pleasing. He gulped it down all at once. He had a feeling he was going to need it.

Takashima watched the American with distaste as he drank. Quick. Everything, always quick! he thought. Yet they rarely arrived anywhere on time. He had much more to learn about these people, but that would come in time. For now, he was anxious to receive the information that Resnick had brought with him.

"Kakue will take you to a private dining room, where we will discuss our business." Takashima clapped his hands, and Kakue gracefully indicated with a slow sway of her head for Stephen to follow her.

The small private dining room was different from the rest of the restaurant. Stephen was surprised to see two small padded chairs for them to sit on. And the bright lights overhead shone starkly on the white walls, bare of any decoration. This was quite a contrast from the dimly lit room they'd just left.

Stephen sat down nervously and extended the files to Takashima, but his Japanese host waved them away as Chisako appeared, holding a tray filled with several dishes.

"First we will enjoy a traditional *cha kaiseki* dinner," Takashima said, smiling.

Before Stephen could protest, Chisako began naming the dishes on the tray. "For appetizers, *Natto-Tofu*, fermented soybeans and soybean curd and *Uni*, fresh sea urchin; then soup, sashimi, *Yakihamaguri*, broiled Cherrystone Clams on Sea Salt, rice, pickles—"

Takashima raised his hand. "Enough. Our guest is hungry after his long trip and is ready to eat."

"No, thanks," Stephen began, looking at the strange food distastefully on the lacquered table in front of him, as he again picked up his files.

Takashima looked at him sternly, then said in an authoritative voice, "As is our custom, you will begin eating first."

Realizing he had no choice but to comply, Stephen positioned his chopsticks and reluctantly sampled a bite. He couldn't figure out what he was eating, but it didn't matter anyway. He just wanted to get this thing over with.

"Thanks, but I'm not really hungry," he said flatly, putting down the chopsticks as the sweet taste of ginger lingered on his tongue. Then curiosity overtook him as he pointed to a dish. "What is this?"

Takashima shook his head at the American. "It is not necessary, Resnick-san, to know what ingredients have been used. It is more important to transform the food into art—pleasure for the eye as well as the palate."

Reluctantly, Stephen gulped down the food quickly.

The two men remained silent until Takashima burped loudly, signaling his enjoyment and the end of the meal. Then he indicated with a nod to Stephen that he was ready to discuss business.

Quickly Stephen handed him the files, one at a time, from inside his briefcase. The Asian Octopus merely grunted as he went through each of them.

Everything seemed to be there, as promised, and in order. Constellation's financial reports, bank drafts, profit-and-loss sheets, the private world of Jake Baron's business. There was even a memo from Baron's controller reminding him that the studio's insurance policy would soon lapse unless he authorized the premium to be paid.

Smiling broadly, Takashima closed the files and handed them over to one of his Yakuza. He was certain that the contents would supply him with the missing intelligence he needed to complete his plan to buy the studio as a cover. That would make it appear that he was serious about producing films. "I am most pleased, Mr. Resnick," Takashima said, taking out a thick envelope.

As Stephen began to reach for it, Takashima held it firmly in his grip over Stephen's head. He winced with an evil delight. The American was too eager for his reward, like a lazy house dog who sought only the pleasure of the fresh meat and not the hunt itself.

Takashima had to be sure. "Mr. Resnick, have you been careful not to allow knowledge of your trip here to reach the ears of your employer, Mr. Baron?"

Stephen looked at him in puzzlement. Did Takashima know that Jake was his stepfather? Was he just playing him for a sucker? For a moment he also suspected a double cross. Maybe he wasn't going to be paid after all.

"Yeah, sure. Everything is okay," he answered swiftly. "I'm covered."

Takashima nodded. "You must remember, Mr. Resnick, the love of money is like a tiny leech; it does not suck out all the blood at once, but a little at a time until death claims the victim."

Stephen rubbed his sweaty hands together and felt his shoulder twitch. "Excuse me, I'm not sure what you're talking about."

Takashima raised his right hand, and a Yakuza handed Stephen a file. For a moment he thought Takashima was returning his information and the deal was now off.

"What the fuck . . . ?" Stephen said until he saw his name on the file. He opened it and saw a long profile on himself as well as a red-lined ledger with his gambling debts meticulously entered with dates, times, and places.

He was astonished. "Where did you get this?" he asked nervously, handing the file back to Takashima. Is he going to blackmail me? he wondered.

"It does not matter. Be advised that you must continue to be more careful in the future, Mr. Resnick, now that we are doing business. One false move, and you might . . . like a deer, be eaten by a hungry wolf." Takashima then handed the envelope to Stephen. "I have enjoyed our chat together."

He relaxed his grip on the envelope. It was not the pittance in dollars he was worried about. He had to be sure the American attorney would not cross him. Now that Stephen knew of the file on him, Takashima was willing to trust him. He had built his empire on such risks.

Stephen, even more tense than before, nodded as he ripped open the envelope and quickly counted out the large bills: one hundred thousand dollars, plus expenses. He breathed easier. Not bad, he thought, for a few duplicate files that Jake would never know about. He ignored the guilt beginning to eat away at his insides. At least he was saved again from the Vegas bookies, and that was all that counted.

Suddenly, to his surprise, Takashima pulled out another envelope with Stephen's name written in English on the front.

"What's this?" asked Resnick, while wondering if he really had a trick up his sleeve.

"Mr. Resnick, please open this extra envelope."

As Stephen cautiously tore the edge of the surprise envelope, he looked in amazement at a stack of hundreds. Takashima quietly informed him that this was the first of many bonus envelopes he would receive routinely if he continued to cooperate.

Takashima said nothing more. Neither did Resnick. Takashima sat still and smirked while Resnick counted the money. The Yakuza continued to stare at Resnick while the geisha removed the dinner plates.

Takashima's game of revenge had just begun.

PART ONE

1

Whoosh! White snow exploded in twin walls of powder as a gorgeous blond raced her snowmobile down the mountain at more than a hundred miles an hour. Chasing after her was a man in a second snowmobile, a high-powered rifle slung over his shoulder. He was in hot pursuit and gaining fast. Recklessly the girl steered her snowmobile down the steep corniche of Aspen Mountain. Under no circumstances would she allow herself to be caught.

The air was fearfully still. Only the sound of the runners on her snowmobile slicing cleanly through the snow could be heard. It was unusually cold and the girl shivered as she noticed snow starting to fall. She had to lose him now.

The young woman shifted into high gear, then braced herself for the long run down the back of the mountain toward Little Annie Basin. The man followed, but veered off course when he struck some exposed rocks in the thinning snow. He steered quickly to the right to avoid tipping over, but didn't slow down. He was nearly upon her now. . . .

"I didn't think he was going to make that turn."

"You don't know Erik. He's one of the best."

A man and a woman continued to comment as they watched the action, a few miles away, on a closed-circuit TV monitor, seated in plush-velvet swivel chairs. Their eyes were riveted to the screen.

As the snow fell faster, the girl wiped her helmet visor clean and looked around. The man pursuing her was closing in. In seconds she would be within rifle range.

The girl raced her snowmobile into the oncoming icy white tunnel.

But the man wouldn't give up the chase. Confidently he followed the course of the tunnel, keeping close along the ridge of the mountain until he reached the edge; then he sailed off the ridge and through the air. After a few seconds airborne, he landed on the snow just a split second after the blond bolted from the other end of the tunnel in her snowmobile. She was so close he could almost touch her. The man put his hand on his rifle . . .

Blindly the girl tried to steer her vehicle, but the mountain run suddenly curved. She didn't see the boulders ahead until it was too late. The man would overtake her in seconds. Panicking, she tried to stop, but the brakes wouldn't grab. Her arms ached with racking pain, but she continued twisting the steering wheel from side to side in an attempt to avoid hitting the boulders. Suddenly one of her runners caught on a protruding tree root, propelling her snowmobile into the air and straight for the rocks. She tried to shield her face with her arms, but she knew it was all over.

As she crashed head first, the snowmobile burst into red-hot flames. Her frozen screams, however, continued to echo through the cold air. . . .

"Cut!" yelled Academy Award-winning director Terrence Taylor through the amplified bullhorn of the helicopter hovering overhead.

"That was one of the best stunts I've ever seen, Kelly!" the man in the swivel chair said, turning off the TV monitor.

The woman smiled her acknowledgment as they walked out of her trailer. Jumping onto their individual snowmobiles, they took off down the mountain.

About two miles away, the bright orange-striped

copter circled around the area as an ambulance below raced to the scene of the crash. A fire truck was close behind. Next a nine-person Sno-Cat sped onto the scene, and out jumped the first assistant director, the producer, and the rest of the main crew, all wearing black snow parkas with the name of the film, *Criminal Intent*, inscribed in red letters on the back. They watched anxiously as the paramedics pulled the stuntwoman to safety and the fire fighters put out the flames.

As the helicopter landed nearby, Taylor leapt out with his handsome face aglow. Dressed in a multicolored parka and wearing yellow-lensed goggles, he was immediately flanked by an arriving pair on snowmobiles.

The woman jumped off her snowmobile and smiled at him.

"That was sensational, Terry," Kelly said, taking off her snow glasses. She blinked her light green eyes a couple of times against the glaring sun. "Right, Jake?" she asked the man standing next to her.

She was Kelly Kristopher, the president of Constellation Studios, and she looked younger than her thirty-three years. Twitching her thick braid of strawberry-blond hair so that it dropped back over her shoulder, she revealed a slightly snowburned face that glowed with her natural beauty. She had a slightly turned-up nose with smooth skin that bore only a trace of powder and a few freckles, with laughing lips outlined in her favorite red lipstick. Her trim figure complimented the cool blue snowsuit she wore, zipped up the front and trimmed with white lamb's wool. The entire package was stunning.

"A terrific ending," Jake said breathlessly, directing his comment to Taylor but smiling at Kelly. "Best fuckin' one I've seen in years," he finished, slapping the director on the back.

Kelly smiled back. Jake Baron was her boss and mentor. He was the owner of Constellation, the last privately owned Hollywood movie studio.

At fifty, Jake was tall, lean, and muscular. His longish salt-and-pepper hair curled at the bottom of his neck under his blue wool cap, and he had stone-gray eyes and a pronounced dimple in his chin that became more striking when he smiled, something he did often. He had big strong hands, weathered from years of working around the studio lot. He wasn't the type who went in for Gucci loafers or two-carat-diamond pinky rings. Instead, he was a rugged individualist who was more at home in jeans and scuffed cowboy boots. In fact, there was a standing joke around the studio that the only time he ever sat still was to sign checks.

Kelly continued to look enthusiastically at Jake while Taylor made some notes. She knew Jake needed this film to be a blockbuster. Ever since he had appointed her president, five years ago, she had been determined to make Constellation continue as one of the great Hollywood studios. So far it hadn't been easy.

She turned and studied Terry's face. He looked more relaxed now that the shot was over. She knew the time was right to interrupt his thoughts. "What do you think, Terry?"

"Well, Kelly, we've got another hour and a half of daylight," Taylor said, glancing at the watch in his hand and then pensively up at the sky.

"Time for one more shot?" Jake asked hopefully.

Taylor nodded as he started walking away. "Sure. All right, round up Harrison and Michelle for their close-ups," he said to his first assistant director. "I'll be in my trailer looking at the board."

Before Kelly and Jake had a chance to get back on their snowmobiles, a robust woman with black hair pulled tightly into a knot on the top of her head rushed toward them. Rose Kaufman, Constellation's first lady of publicity, was legendary for getting great mileage for a film, even when a star broke a fingernail. Though an older woman, she always walked faster than anyone twenty years her junior. But it was her curious, oversize brown eyes, which lit up her face with a glow, that people always remembered about her.

"Kelly, great news," she said, huffing and puffing. She paused, catching her breath. "Hi, Jake," she said quickly, handing him some mail.

"Where's today's *Variety*?" he asked, shuffling through the stack of letters and papers.

Rose took a freshly folded copy of the Hollywood trade paper out of her briefcase and handed it to him. "Been keeping it warm for you, Jake," she said with a cheery grin. She always had a big smile for her favorite fellow. She had known Jake since he was a kid making his first one-reeler on the back lot. Rose, who had been a fixture at Constellation since the late fifties, considered herself a member of the immediate family.

She put on her bifocals, and with an air of excitement read from her notes: "*Good Morning America* is interested in doing a location segment for *Criminal Intent* . . ."

Jake acknowledged her with a special wink and a hug. "That's great news, Rosey."

"We can always use some free publicity," Kelly said, putting her snowglasses back on. "Anything else?"

"Operation: Children has asked you once again to participate in their annual Christmas toy fair." Rose waited for Kelly's answer, but she already knew what it would be. That's why she'd already confirmed the pretty president's acceptance. Kelly had been a perennial volunteer for many charitable causes since her mother had become terminally ill several years ago.

"Sure, Rose, you know I'll be there," Kelly said enthusiastically. "Anything else?"

"No," Rose said, shivering as she pulled up her collar. "It's getting too cold for these old bones. You know, we've been using that plastic dreck so long, I'd forgotten what real snow feels like."

As Rose said her good-byes, she flipped through her briefcase. All of a sudden she remembered the sealed letter from their head of production.

"Kel, wait, I almost forgot this letter from Ortega. Cynthia sounded excited when she gave this to me. She'll be out of her office until later this afternoon, but she'd like you to call her." Then with a quick wave she was gone.

Kelly's face lit up as she opened the note and quickly skimmed it. "Jake, you know that Levinson property that's in turnaround at Columbia. Well, Cynthia may have convinced that agent she's dating at CAA to move it to us!"

Beaming, Jake raised his dark eyebrows in surprise. "Son of a bitch, that's great. What else?"

Kelly continued: "Cynthia also has heard that Robin Williams loves Barry's script and wants to work with him again. She thinks he'll be available. Now, if we can just make that deal fly . . ."

Jake was so excited he kissed her on the cheek. A Barry Levinson film on top of Taylor's *Criminal Intent* would start bringing top directors back to Constellation. "Sounds good, Kelly, Barry's really hot now. I'd bet he'll win the Oscar for *Rain Man*." Then he added sarcastically, "But please keep your husband from fucking up this deal. Really, try to keep him out of this loop. Just don't tell him about this project, okay?"

Kelly bit her lip, thinking: Here we go again with Robert. Jake never wasted a moment in making clear his position about her agent-husband in very certain terms. Somehow, when Robert learned of an impending Constellation project, he'd always persuade Kelly to think of one of his clients. Jake hated Robert so much, he didn't want him to have any part of their films.

As a few glistening snowflakes fell on her hair, then on the tip of her nose, she looked into Jake's eyes. "Please, Jake, give him a chance. Maybe he'll have a good idea for some talent."

"I have, Kelly. Ten years ago I gave him his chance when I let you go, and I've regretted it ever since."

Kelly put Cynthia's note back into her pocket. "Jake," she said, trying to project her voice over the loud start of her snowmobile, "what happened a decade ago between you and me is over, you know that." She looked him straight in the eye as she turned the key off. "I thought we agreed on that."

"We did, Kel. I admit I made a mistake with you back then," he said. "And Robert was smart enough to snatch you from me. But that doesn't change my opinion of him one fuckin' bit. He's still an underhanded dealmaker." Suddenly Jake stopped short. For Kelly's sake, he wouldn't go on and relate the rumors of Robert's extramarital affairs, even though most of the town seemed to buzz about them. He wondered what Kelly saw in the asshole anyway.

"Please, Jake, that's enough. Robert isn't here to defend himself."

Jake snorted contemptuously.

"Jake, for once, please forget he's my husband and see him as a creative agent." Kelly raised her voice sharply as she looked away.

Jake couldn't forget it, no matter how hard he tried. "Someday, Kel, you'll know I'm right about that putz husband of yours," he stated firmly. "And then I'll be waiting."

Hidden in a small crowd lined up outside a sex club, Takashima and Noda waited patiently while a smiling customer paid the fee of thirty-seven thousand yen at the front door. Flashing pink neon lights strobed the entryway, shielding them from view. They would not have long to wait, since Takashima was a welcomed VIP guest. In any case, several Yakuza guarded them, keeping their eyes open for any trouble.

Takashima kept his hands in the pockets of his long overcoat while Noda grabbed his scarf tighter around his neck as the freezing west wind blew past them and down the small alleyway nearby.

Careful to stay hidden in the shadows, they entered the whorehouse. Takashima received a polite bow from the rugged-looking doorman, and the Yakuza discreetly followed behind Noda. Immediately a beautiful hostess showed them into the main room. They followed behind a customer and a nubile young woman in a silver fishnet bikini to a large reception area, divided into other rooms by nearly transparent paper partitions.

Any erotic experience imaginable could be had in the Kabuki-cho, the Japanese pleasure center, where anyone could come and indulge his fantasy in this sexual amusement park. Takashima and Noda stood behind tall black onyx screens so they could watch unobserved. The Yakuza kept their distance behind a partition. They all could see the empty coffin in the middle of the room.

The girl in the fishnet bikini smiled at the customer as he bowed respectfully to her. "Please," she said, bowing, then motioned for him to get into the coffin.

The man took off his shoes and clambered in. As he lay down in the coffin, the girl closed the lid and told him to close his eyes. His face was exposed through a small open window. He waited patiently while the young woman unlocked the hinged door farther down on the coffin. Without hesitation she quickly found his penis and began slowly fondling him with her silky hands, adorned with long scarlet fingernails. She took her time in arousing him, giving him his money's worth.

The only light came from a red-and-black paper lantern swaying silently back and forth overhead, casting seductive shadows on the partition and beckoning them to indulge further in their lusty game.

Takashima was watching the scene with great interest, when he heard a commotion behind him. He turned around and saw that his Yakuza were arguing among themselves. They could wait no longer. He smiled with a sadistic look of pleasure on his face. Why not give them what they wanted?

"Go now!" he said loudly to his men, clapping his hands.

Without any ceremony, the Yakuza knocked down the partition separating them from the customer in the coffin. While one of them picked up the girl and slung her over his back, another picked up the coffin with the customer still inside and carried him outside. The others went off in search of other girls.

Takashima could not help but laugh. Noda cringed, however, as he watched silently. He knew better than to say anything.

"What are you doing? Who are you?" yelled a hunchbacked old woman who appeared out of nowhere.

"*Okāsan*, control yourself. My men have earned their sport," said Takashima, taking out a huge roll of yen and counting out a small fortune to the proprietress.

"*Domo, domo,*" chanted the proprietress many times over as she took the paper money and disappeared again.

The Yakuza returned with their booty—eacn one had a girl or two flung over his shoulders—and bowed low to Takashima, silently expressing their gratitude.

"I will see you later," Takashima said. "Enjoy yourselves, in honor of our people's victory at Pearl Harbor. *Banzai, banzai.*"

Takashima and Noda then walked quickly through the room and into the rest of the establishment, filled with other erotic pleasures—phone sex in a lighted red telephone booth, peep shows, and a suds dance performed on the customer by a nude girl. Takashima hardly noticed now; it was time for the important business of the evening.

He led Noda down a steep flight of wooden stairs, used by seventeenth-century serving wenches who also acted as prostitutes to weary travelers. The earth was bulging through the old walls, and the smell of mold and rot filled their nostrils as the stairs led them deeper and deeper into the bowels of the ancient building. As they came to the bottom, Takashima pushed a hidden button and they entered a cramped, open elevator. Immediately it plunged downward.

When they finally stopped and the door opened, Takashima headed for a steel door cut into limestone. Two footprints were molded in the flooring. Takashima put his feet into the prints and waited.

Noda stared up at the futuristic door. Each time he came with Takashima, he was amazed. Who would have thought that the heart of Takashima's entire organization lay under a whorehouse in the old Shinjuku district?

Noda took off his glasses and pinched the perspiration from his nose. He always felt tense coming here, for the men inside had never liked him. He shivered slightly as he remembered what had happened to him the first time Takashima had brought him here.

"Noda-san, I have a great secret to share with you," Takashima had said. "This enterprise is a secret corporation that I have been funding since I became a wealthy businessman. No one in my Takashima Group knows of its existence but you, Noda-san."

Takashima had quickly explained they were meeting with the Ronin no Zaibatsu, his group of spies, unknown to the public and responsible to no one but him. The insider information the Ronin amassed, not to mention the misinformation they spread, gave Takashima the edge in almost any business venture he wanted to enter. They were the best in the world at what they did, which included the American CIA and the Russian KGB.

As a child, Noda had believed they were merely a myth, not a real group. They had derived their name from the famous tale of the forty-seven Ronin, or outlaw knights, who had devoted their lives to avenging their murdered master before each systematically took his own life. The word *Zaibatsu* referred to the crafty world of underground big business that was often said to control the Japanese government.

Noda watched as a garish yellow light glowed around Takashima's feet; then the door slowly opened. Takashima walked through, and Noda followed. The door clanged shut behind them.

As Noda stepped forward into the darkened annex, he asked timidly, "Takashima-san, where are you?" He reached out, but felt nothing ahead.

As if on cue, he heard footsteps all around him. He looked to his left, then to his right, but he could see nothing in the dark.

Suddenly spotlights filled the room with brilliance. Noda shielded his face with his arms and blinked several times to adjust his eyes.

The room was as he remembered: huge white computer terminals were lined up in several rows, their keyboards controlled by unseen hands. Some kind of remote control, Noda figured. He looked around and saw large screens and printers spewing out computer printouts at a frantic speed. On a white topographical map of the world on the wall, jeweled colored lights signaling different countries and cities blinked on and off. Different areas of the room were sectioned off, each representing a different part of the world—Asia, North America, Europe, South America, Africa—and various businesses were highlighted within each of those countries: oil, superconductors, stocks, weaponry, foodstuffs, computers, communications.

Noda walked cautiously on the floor, made out of glassy black marble. He marveled at how it seemed to disappear, giving the whole room a floating sensation. Dizzily he looked around, but he could barely see the black silhouettes of the dozen or so men stationed around the round-shaped room at strategic positions. They stood so still, the only noise in the room seemed to be the sound of his own breathing.

"Welcome, Takashima-san," a somber voice said from somewhere behind the lights. The Ronin paused, allowing the silence to communicate his displeasure at seeing the younger man with him. All of them knew Noda's story, but that did not soften their irritation.

Takashima had raised him since childhood, when his mother, Takashima's mistress, committed hara-kiri. Following Japanese tradition, he had taken the boy as his own. He became the son Takashima had never had, and Noda had not disappointed him. Noda excelled in education, which culminated with his graduation from the Wharton Business School. While in America, though, he had become very western in his way of thinking. Instead of prolonged deliberation, the Japanese custom before making a final decision, he would often jump to make a deal, in the process becoming an unsung giant in the Tokyo stock market. However absentminded he might be in his personal life, Noda was now Takashima's right-hand man.

That was why the Ronin disliked him. The straightforward young man was a threat. Like the Yakuza, these men were outcasts, members of the Buraku-Min, or untouchables. Some of mixed parentage, others merely self-styled individuals, they had made their way by sheer guts and deception. Takashima appreciated their craftiness; Noda did not.

"We are honored by your presence," a different voice said somberly from another part of the room.

Takashima bowed and Noda did the same.

"Takashima-san, your ingenious suggestion in honor of our ancestors' glorious victory at Pearl Harbor forty-seven years ago today has been implemented." The Ronin paused, checking his watch. "Your first specialist in terrorism is now making the journey to America. Others will continue to follow in advance of your arrival."

"Good. However, let us now proceed with our business for tonight," Takashima said. "I must review the confidential data on all the major Hollywood entertainment people. It is extremely important that I see the most up-to-date information available on several specific executives."

Reading from a prepared list, Takashima continued: "Lew Wasserman, Peter Guber and Jon Peters, Michael Eisner, Barry Diller, Aaron Spelling, Dawn Steel, Michael Ovitz, Steve Ross, Martin Davis . . . plus the additional information on Jake Baron and Constellation Studios that I previously requested."

Takashima stared calmly into the darkness. It did not matter that he could not see his shadowy technicians. It was traditional that one would not look his fellow conspirator in the eye. "I await your information with patience."

"But first, Takashima-san," a voice replied, "let us inform you that the secretive file you had delivered from the American attorney was correct with its information. We have updated this business venture of yours and we will give you that with certain recommendations in the red file." As several computer printouts began whirring louder than the others, the voice continued, "Most important, we are devising a foolproof money-laundering scheme that will allow you to move lots of cash from your pachinko parlors in and out of your recently purchased Beverly-Rodeo Bank."

"Hai," Takashima said, bowing his appreciation. Then he turned to Noda and smiled. The Beverly-Rodeo Bank held a loan to Constellation Studios.

The darkened screening room was quiet except for the rattle-clapping sound of the projector. No one moved, for the action on the screen was riveting. Dinner would wait. So would this last night in Aspen. No one wanted to miss a single frame.

Jake put a cigarette into his mouth, although he didn't light it. He turned to Kelly, who had put her notes from dailies back into her briefcase and whispered, "Damn, what I wouldn't give to get a copy of this on cassette." Jake had known the film was good, but he hadn't realized it was that hot. This might be the bait for the further loan he so desperately needed.

Criminal Intent, adapted from the novel by Pulitzer Prize writer P. J. Thompson, was a mystery-thriller starring Harrison Ford and Michelle Pfeiffer. With its sensational action scenes and special effects, this movie was destined to be their box-office hit next Christmas.

The final snowmobile chase scene raced across the screen like a hot fireball. It didn't stop until the exciting climax filled the screen with brilliant yellow-red flames.

The lights went on, followed by enthusiastic applause.

"Fabulous, Terry."

"Brilliant photography."

"Your best work."

Harrison and Michelle gathered around Taylor, along with the producer and the director of photography. Everyone was excited, especially Taylor, who had just finished duplicating the same scenes today as a just-in-case backup to yesterday's footage.

"How soon do you want it, Jake?" Kelly asked nonchalantly as the room started to empty.

Before Jake could answer, Taylor came over and patted his shoulder. "Looks good, don't you think?" Kelly kissed Terry's cheek as her acknowledgment.

"Terrific, Terry," Jake said, grinning.

Taylor smiled widely at both of them before going back to his two stars.

Jake turned to Kelly. "You weren't kidding about getting me that cassette, were you?"

"The cassette will be here before you leave tonight," she said with certainty. "I've talked to the lab and passed a note on to my assistant. As soon as it's ready, Geoffrey will run right over and get it to you."

"You're terrific, Kelly!" Jake said, then impulsively kissed her on the lips. She tasted sweet, like he always remembered. He looked at her pretty face and chuckled. Her lipstick was now smudged from his kiss.

"Guess I owe you a new lipstick," Jake said, laughing as he handed her his handkerchief.

"Jungle red." Kelly smiled, wiping it off.

He winced as she reapplied her lipstick. "Jungle red" had been a private joke of theirs back when . . .

Suddenly Kelly glanced about, making sure the others had left. Quietly she asked, "By the way, what're your chances in New York?"

Jake hesitated. Only Kelly and his controller, Max Gerstein, knew of his intentions to see some investment bankers to raise capital. He didn't want to furnish any gossip about his financial troubles to the Hollywood trade papers, so he kept it from the other key players at the studio. He couldn't take any chances on someone leaking about his desperate straits.

"Not the best," he said as they left the screening room together. "But we do have a great film on our hands." Jake paused as loud music and high-pitched giggling filtered in from outside, making it difficult to talk.

Since that black October day of the year before, when the stock market had crashed and Jake had lost millions of his personal fortune, he had been in serious trouble. He had taken out a collateral bank loan against his studio to help finance *Criminal Intent*, as well as to reduce Constellation's negative cash flow of $250 million. But now the interest on the note was coming due, and he wasn't sure where they would get the cash to pay it. The figures Max had just faxed him that afternoon made the situation look even bleaker.

"It's my job to convince the Wall Street investors just how good our film is. Who knows? Maybe I will," he finished, his voice a hoarse whisper.

Kelly looked up in surprise at this lapse of self-confidence. Jake Baron afraid? She had great faith in him. In an era when every other Hollywood studio was publicly owned and controlled by large corporations that cared more about stock leveraging than moviemaking, Jake was now the last of the dinosaurs: the sole owner of a major private studio.

Squeezing his hand, she said, "You've always been able to convince me." She put her arm through his and smiled. "You'll do it, Jake."

Jake tried to return her smile, but couldn't.

As they walked slowly along the path, glancing over at the night skiers racing down ramps flooded with lights, Jake winced at the loud commotion from the large outdoor hot tub. He hoped it wasn't anyone from his crew making that infernal racket. Shit, he thought, glancing at his watch, it was now almost nine-thirty. They should all be getting packed and ready to leave early in the morning.

A girl's voice begged sweetly, getting louder as they got closer. She giggled in delight.

Jake stopped suddenly. He had thought that giggling sounded familiar. His beautiful blue-eyed daughter, Mistica, clad in a skimpy chartreuse rubber bikini displaying her deep cleavage, was spashing around in the hot tub with Erik, the stuntman who doubled for Harrison Ford. Jake sighed as he watched her twirl her bleached blond hair around her finger and pout her lips. She used to do the same thing, he thought, when she was a little girl sitting on his lap listening to him read scripts. She hadn't changed.

Jake felt his blood pressure going up. When would she grow up? She was twenty-six, but still irresponsible at times.

He stopped a waiter carrying a tray of dirty dishes. "Got a pen?"

"Sure, Mr. Baron." He placed the tray down on the frozen walkway.

Jake scribbled, "You're driving me to the airport, so get moving," on the back of the day's call sheet, then pulled a five-dollar bill out of his pocket as a tip. "Take this to the girl in the hot tub."

* * *

The spit-shined Mercedes limo sped like a black bullet through the nighttime Ginza district. A mosaic blur of reds and yellows and blues lit up the signs advertising anything from Coca-Cola, in both English and Japanese characters, to the seductive faces of young schoolgirls in sailor suits on billboards.

Upscale pachinko parlors were crowded onto every street. Tiny love hotels—small rooms, all with the amenities of TV, porno tapes, velvet cushions, and, of course, beds—could be rented for as little as an hour or for the whole night by would-be sinners. Many *udon* shops offering a quick meal of steaming hot noodles tempted late-night diners.

While taxi drivers drove crazily through the nameless Tokyo streets, even veering onto the sidewalks as their passengers yelled "*Hayaku*, go faster!," pedestrians stood patiently on the curbs, waiting for the traffic lights to change.

Takashima took no notice of any of these things as his limo headed for a seedy part of town where the smell of freshly cured leather instead of noodle soup filled the air. This was where the outcasts of Japanese society had set up their shops centuries ago and still practiced the inferior trade of leather making.

When the Mercedes finally pulled up at a ramshackle pachinko parlor, Takashima jumped out.

With his Yakuza at his side, he walked through the parlor, looking straight ahead. As tradition dictated, he had Koreans fronting the establishment for him. Even though he was the sole owner, he did not want to disturb his *wa* by looking too closely at the rundown place. All he cared about was that every seat at the fifty pin-tables was taken.

This was one of his busiest pachinko parlors in Tokyo, and his profits were a large share of the hefty thirteen trillion yen collected yearly by these establishments. In addition, this filthy place provided perfect cover for his many secretive business meetings.

With a permanent haze of cigarette smoke clouding

the huge game room, no one took notice of the flow of men in dark suits who had walked through the parlor. The noise was deafening, like that of a large factory of printing presses at work. With bells, buzzers, even rock music, filling their heads, the patrons, from housewives to salarymen to students, sat in front of the numerous pinball machines, pressing the levers, then waiting for the steel balls to favor them with a win for soap, sweets, fruit, or toys.

Although pachinko was a legal form of gambling, it was also a drug of the mind, often likened to the Buddhist state of attaining illumination in order to cope with the everyday world. The repetitive motion of the pachinko game with its tiny steel-and-chrome balls bouncing off nails and dropping into holes provided the desired level of consciousness.

Takashima noted with disgust the peeling paper on the walls, the dirt on the floor, the cracks in the old ceiling. To top it all off, a woman sitting in the corner looked up eagerly from nibbling on cold boiled rice with chopsticks broken off at the ends. She was not really old, perhaps in her early thirties, but her addiction to opium had aged her badly. Still holding her bowl of rice, she got up from her small tattered cushion and quickly walked over to intercept the Asian Octopus.

Wrapping her dirty kimono tighter around herself and raising her head, she stood defiantly in front of him with her sunken eyes, daring him to pass. But Takashima looked away in revulsion as he motioned to his Yakuza to clear the way.

With a cutting blow, Minoru knocked the bowl of rice from her hand. It splattered to the floor and cut her leg, but she did not cry out. Instead she continued to stand defiantly in front of him as the blood began to drip down her leg.

"Takashima-san, do you not know me?" she asked, her voice crackling with emotion.

"Out of my way, whore," he yelled, then clapped

his hands. He could not remember every female who had bedded him, especially this smelly addict. The Yakuza grabbed her and yanked her by the hair, then dragged her away. Takashima never gave her a second glance.

Quickly he wiped his hands with a towel handed to him by another Yakuza, then disappeared into the cloakroom and through a secret door. He pushed aside the curtains and entered a concealed room furnished with a large round table, carved from onyx and low to the floor. Pearl and jade screens showing the graceful dance of several geisha, along with a peaceful garden with a ring of small stepping stones in a perpetual circle of oneness, completed the simple furnishings. Several lighted stone lanterns provided a shadowy blue light, casting a strange glow in the room, while fresh water slowly dripped from a bamboo pipe into a stone cistern.

Seated on a red-and-gold brocade mat, Chisako watched Takashima enter through the hidden entrance. She bowed until her forehead touched the floor. He was the last one to arrive. The others had already taken their places on the dark blue and black velvet cushions.

Some of the presidents of the biggest companies in Japan were members of Takashima's financial group. Noda sat with them, having already passed out duplicate files detailing the information on newly targeted companies, including the one that the American movie attorney had brought with him. As the men looked over the various files, they drank from bowls of thick green tea to stimulate their appetite before dinner.

These investors could not deny the fact that if Takashima was successful with the purchase of the Hollywood movie studio, he would preempt the ambition of Morita of the Sony Corporation, and others like him, in becoming the first Japanese to enter the American film industry as a studio owner. Like the feuding lords of centuries ago, these powerful businessmen had not lost their conquering spirit. They applauded, somewhat cautiously, Takashima's efforts.

It was well known that Takashima was one of the top five billionaires in the world. His steel company rivaled Nippon Steel. His companies manufactured video games, vending machines, VCRs, and automobiles. He was one of the largest real-estate investors, and he had recently bought into Climatic, a proposed Japanese subterranean city to be built by the year 2000. He also owned the GlobeTel Hotel Corporation, auto dealerships worldwide, real estate in the South Pacific, a winery in northern California, and his recently purchased bank in Beverly Hills.

Takashima was known as a *tochi-richi*, one who had grown rich on land sales in recent years. Part of this was due to the fact that, like most of his countrymen, he saw no shame in hiding much of his income from the tax collectors.

Takashima was certainly not a carbon copy of other Japanese businessmen. Usually dressed in a blue-gray pin-striped suit and wing-tipped shoes, he was the personification of regality—like a warrior prince. As all the men in the room knew well, Takashima had never forgotten the terrible suffering of his childhood. He always wore tinted glasses to mask his pain from the outside world, and it was that pain that had sparked the streak of individualism he possessed that was so foreign to the rest of his group as well as his countrymen.

Though he kept his public image very guarded, the stories about his opulent lifestyle and generosity with his employees were legendary. There was even a popular *manga*, or comic-book, character loosely based on Takashima and his sensational rise from the bombed-out rice paddies of Nagasaki to become a modern samurai warrior. But as much as he was admired, Takashima was also feared. A number of rivals had mysteriously disappeared over the years, never to be found again. And even though he was a prime suspect,

Takashima had too many influential political friends to actually be charged with a crime. He was also known to show no mercy to anyone who even thought of betraying him, including the beautiful women attracted to him by his ruthlessness.

Takashima took his place at the table and looked at each member of his group, bowing courteously to them, their eyes cast downward, their minds silently computing the business plan presented for their scrutiny. He grunted with impatience.

One man sneezed and grabbed his handkerchief, barely taking his eyes off the papers in front of him. Another coughed. But no one said a word. Takashima would have liked to move forward on his own, but that was not possible. He remembered the old Japanese proverb: "The stake that sticks up gets hammered down." He could afford no mistakes. The group always took their time, as was expected.

Finally Takashima could wait no longer. He spoke first:

"We must not delay any longer. First we will discuss the movie studio. According to these reports, the American movie studio is in danger of collapsing very soon."

"But what will happen, Takashima-san, if the owner of the company is able to pull together his resources and save his studio?" one of the group members asked.

Takashima stared straight ahead, while under the table he clenched his fists so tightly that his bones almost stuck through his skin. The question was irrelevant. He had his contacts everywhere. They had to agree with him tonight. There was no way the American could save his company.

"I am certain he will fail at every turn," Takashima said simply. His eyes revealed rage as furious as a midnight storm, but he merely smiled at his group. They must believe that he wanted to purchase the studio for legitimate reasons and not for revenge. Furthermore, he thought, already in one week, three additional well-trained Yakuza arsonists had entered the

U.S. via his Honolulu immigration contact, and more were on the way.

The group member nodded, accepting Takashima's word, but then merely turned back to perusing the files.

An hour passed. Noda looked over at Takashima as he pulled his white handkerchief out of his back pocket to wipe the sweat from his face. Takashima's face was expressionless, but his breathing was harder, his face pale under his tan. His lips were tightly pressed together into a thin line on his face. Noda had seen that look before. His foster father loathed the Japanese tradition that dictated that one of them must consult with business associates before taking any formal action to acquire any company, especially an American one. All determinations must be reached by using this *ringi* process of group decision making.

"We have reached our decision," the *sempai*, senior member of the group, said.

Straining to keep his face devoid of expression, Takashima said coolly, "I await our honorable group's decision with infinite patience." He bowed slightly, as a courtesy, but he was now certain of what they would say. He surmised that if they had not agreed with him, the members would have silently left the table without argument rather than disturb the harmony.

The vote was now quickly taken around the table: "*Hai . . . hai . . . hai . . .*

Takashima was exuberant. He would now be able to put his plan of revenge into operation, thanks to his group's ignorance of the truth.

He allowed himself a moment of pleasure as his face lit up with a victorious smile. He raised his arm high and called out in a clear voice: *"Banzai!"* A thousand years!

The others joined in the yell, cheering so loudly the walls of the room echoed their voices many times over. Takashima bowed his head as the others continued to yell, and at long last he raised his head. As the cheering stopped, he looked around for Chisako. Minoru pulled her up from her mat and pushed her to Takashima's side. She dropped to the ground and bowed, her forehead touching the floor.

"*Dozo*, Chisako-san, please begin the tea ceremony," Takashima requested with dignity.

It was time to relax and enjoy his group's support.

2

The sleek black Jaguar ran the red light at Santa Monica Boulevard and Beverly Glen, but the motorcycle cop chasing after it turned off his flashing light, waving him on, when he read the license plate: "AV STARS."

Stephen Resnick looked into his rearview mirror and smiled. Picking up his ringing car phone, he continued cruising down the boulevard at the same speed. The cops wouldn't give him a citation. He was well known as the guy who hired off-duty police officers as bodyguards for Constellation's many movie premieres at twice the going rate.

As Stephen turned onto Century City's Avenue of the Stars, he opened up his sun roof and let the morning rays caress his blond hair. He put on a pair of black-framed Porsche Carrera sunglasses, then picked up a second ringing phone and began talking on two car phones at once.

"Haven't you gotten hold of my father yet?" he asked angrily into one phone.

"No, sir, Mr. Resnick—"

"Well, dammit, try his private line now!" Stephen switched to his other phone, never missing a beat, and said to his law-office secretary, "Rita, has what's-her-name been calling? You know, the chick I took to the black-tie dinner last week . . . she probably thinks I'm still in London."

"That's exactly what I told her, Mr. Resnick," the voice at the other end answered.

"Good. Thanks, Rita."

Stephen slowed at the pedestrian bridge arching over the street, noticing a couple of cute secretaries on their lunch break leaning over the bridge and smiling at him. He smiled back. His masculine pride allowed him that much. But he didn't have enough time for an affair with some local secretary. Women cost money, and that's just what he didn't have right now. His big payoff from Takashima had made only a dent in his losses. A light sweat made his deeply tanned face gleam as he thought about the rest of the dough he owed. But at least he was okay for now.

As he stopped at the traffic light at Constellation Boulevard, he unconsciously patted the bulge of the last of the cash from the Tokyo trip in his breast pocket. He had decided to hold off depositing everything at one time; he never knew when he might be audited, and this newfound money would be hard to explain. At least he was able to pay off some of his back losses to his bookmaker. And once Takashima came on board, he thought, I won't have a thing to worry about. He could still play the ponies, as he was now guaranteed at least ten thousand a month to do some bullshit favors for Takashima. He gritted his teeth. Now he wouldn't be totally under Jake's thumb anymore—something he had hated from the day he first met his stepfather.

Stephen had just turned ten when his mother married the bachelor movie studio owner Jake Baron. At first Jake hadn't known what to do with the shy, handsome little boy who spent more time hanging around the movie crews than in school. Jake made it clear that he had envisioned his relationship with Stephen as being the same as the one the boy had enjoyed with his dad, but it had never worked out that way. Stephen resented Jake. He missed his real father, who had suddenly died one day from a massive heart attack. He felt Jake and his mother had time for him only between studio functions.

As Stephen grew up, he began to compromise. He went into entertainment law as a way to get closer to Jake. But somehow that didn't change anything. There was always tension between him and his stepfather, especially after Stephen's mother died. Stephen knew that she had asked Jake to promise her that he would always look after him. And Jake did.

He looked up through the sun roof. The warm sun beating down on his face actually gave him a little courage. He thought about dropping in on Jake around the corner at the studio. But just as quickly he scrapped the idea. Come to think of it, he wasn't really in the mood for a face-to-face meeting with his stepfather at all today.

Suddenly the car phone rang. Stephen picked it up quickly.

"Yep."

"Mr. Resnick. I have you connected with Mr. Baron's secretary."

"Hello, Mr. Resnick—"

"I need to speak with Jake right away."

The voice at the other end hesitated, then said, "I'm sorry, Mr. Resnick, Mr. Baron is still out of town. I'll leave word." Click.

What the hell was going on? He'd get to the bottom of this fast. He dialed another number.

Kelly's assistant, Geoffrey Norton, answered. "Ms. Kristopher's office."

"Get Kelly right away," Stephen barked in his most obnoxious, pissed-off voice, "or you won't have a job five minutes from now."

There was a slight pause; then: "One moment please, Mr. Resnick."

"Stephen, what's the problem?"

He decided to play it safe by sounding like he was in control. "No problem, Kelly. I've just been trying to get hold of Jake, and his secretary says he's out of town. What gives?"

"Stephen, if I knew where Jake Baron was always off to, I wouldn't have any time for my work. I'm sure if you leave word, he'll get your message and get back to you. Sorry, I gotta run now. There's a production meeting that I have to join."

Stephen had to accept her sarcastic answer, although he was certain she wasn't telling him the whole truth. She always knew where to reach Jake.

"Mr. Resnick." It was Rita on the other phone again, and she sounded concerned. "There's an interesting item about that judge friend of yours in Orange County in Liz Smith's column today. Do you want to hear it now?"

Stephen thought about it for a moment. He knew the judge, but the item couldn't have anything to do with him, so it could wait. "Hold on to it, Rita. I'll look at it when I get in. By the way, any calls from Vegas? . . . No? Terrific."

As the light turned green, Stephen, hearing horns honking behind him, continued driving down Avenue of the Stars toward Fox Plaza. He clicked off the phones as he drove around a stalled truck, past the ABC Entertainment Center on the left, with the *Les Miz* banner in front greeting him and the familiar Century Plaza Hotel on the right.

He should feel great, but he didn't. His gambling debts were on hold for a while—that was a break—but where was Jake?

Suddenly Stephen felt a surge of fear. His shoulder began twitching. He wondered, as he had asked himself continually for a week: had Jake found out about his Tokyo trip?

The unseasonably warm breeze blew in Kelly's face as she drove her custom-made golf cart around the studio lot. Stephen's phone call earlier had left her uneasy. At times his paranoia got to her and even to Jake. She loosened the scarf around her neck, trying to relieve the tightness in her throat. But there was nothing she could do about Stephen. Kelly sensed that Jake had made some deathbed commitment to his first wife, but she had never been quite sure. It didn't matter. Jake had made it clear that Stephen's role as principal counsel would last as long as he owned Constellation.

Kelly turned the corner in front of a large blue-gray soundstage and picked up Rose and her own personal assistant, Geoffrey. Tall and lean, with a shock of ash-blond hair falling over his forehead, Geoffrey had been with Kelly since her first days at Constellation. His efficiency and dedication to the job were legendary around the studio. He prided himself on being there whenever Kelly needed him.

Geoffrey was preoccupied with development meetings scheduled for later in the day. Rose, on the other hand, had noticed that Kelly looked troubled, but she kept any personal comments to herself.

Kelly drove her cart—a fifth-anniversary gift from her staff—across the main quadrant of the studio. Today interiors were being shot for two feature films on Stage 12 and Stage 15, and as a part of Kelly's normal routine, she would often show her presence to the various movie crews. However, she had learned from Jake never to intrude. "And meddle only if necessary," he would say firmly.

Her mind, however, was far away today. Since that last night in Aspen at dailies with Jake, she still couldn't stop thinking about the past. It was almost haunting her now.

As she honked her cart's rubber horn in greeting to the teamsters working in front of the commissary, she felt another moment of nostalgia. The teamster men and women were unloading a twenty-five-foot fir tree from one of the large flatbed trucks. Had it been ten years already since she was with Jake watching that first Christmas tree going up on the studio lot? she wondered.

"How's it going, Miss Kristopher?" one of the men with a full beard yelled over to her.

"Great, Mack," she answered, waving back.

Besides being occupied with hopeful thoughts for Jake's last-ditch quest for financing in New York, Kelly's mind was also on studio business. She was praying that Geoffrey's hand-held portable cellular phone would ring at any minute confirming a sit-down meeting with Peter Guber and Jon Peters, two of the hottest producers in today's Hollywood, regarding a movie project that was not part of their deal with Warner Brothers.

Just the idea that Constellation might make a Guber-Peters film would add excitement to their current lineup of projected films. Wall Street obviously would be very impressed, and that could only help Jake in his fund-raising efforts.

Kelly turned to Rose. "I'm sorry I've been a little distant with you this morning. I have a lot on my mind," she said apologetically as she pushed some stray hair away from her eyes.

"Kelly, if I didn't know that Jake Baron was your chief mentor," Rose began with her infectious laugh, "I'd think you were serious about an apology. Listen, sweetie, in the great tradition of the Barons, you're doing a superb job. So stop worrying so much. Things will work out."

Impatiently Jake raced out of the elevator into the serene lobby of the Sherry-Netherland Hotel. Dammit, he thought, where is that guy? After several days of making the rounds of the major New York City investment bankers, he had finally convinced a sour-faced Morgan Stanley representative to take a look at the cassette of the unedited raw footage of *Criminal Intent*. Jake couldn't contain his excitement. Now he was waiting for the representative to discuss the matter over lunch at La Reserve and, he hoped, give a thumbs-up response.

He paused before the lobby newsstand and glanced

around at the magazines on the rack. He had to get his mind off his frustration. He eyed the covers of *People, Spy,* then a couple he hadn't seen in a while: *Paris-Match, Elle.* Jake picked one up and flipped idly through the pages, trying to admire the nubile young fashion models. It was no use, though. The fate of his studio—his lifeblood—hung in the balance. Goddammit! he thought, glancing around. Where is that stuffy prick?

Shaking his head, he lit up a cigarette and continued to scan the rack of magazines. He passed on *Variety* and the *L.A. Times*. He would catch up with them back home. Then he saw the grisly headline "COP SLASHED" on the front page of the *Daily News*. Picking up the rag, he leafed through it and stopped at Liz Smith's column. She seemed to always be on top of the latest Hollywood news, even before his daughter, Mistica, who swore by *The National Enquirer*.

As he scanned the Smith column, one item in particular made him pause. He read it again. It concerned a certain California Superior Court judge indicted for fraud and pandering who had decided to drop names for one of the sleazy tabloid shows, naming a pretty Hollywood exec among his conquests. Sounds like an interesting idea for a film, Jake thought.

"Good afternoon, Mr. Baron."

Jake looked up from the paper. His gray eyes clouded over as he stared at the staid young man in a tailored navy-blue pin-striped suit. He glanced down at his own rumpled suit, splattered with dried mud drops from a taxi that had splashed him earlier that morning. Then he noticed the banker doubtfully eyeing the *Daily News* and remembered these types read only the *New York Times*. Hurriedly he slapped the paper down on the stack. "Well, shall we go?"

It was crowded when they arrived at La Reserve. The tiny foyer was filled with lunchgoers chatting noisily as they shook the rain off their wet umbrellas.

Jake watched questioningly as the man whispered something to the stern-faced maître d', who nodded and motioned for them to follow. Jake was impressed. If this guy had pull at La Reserve, maybe his luck was changing after all.

"The film footage looks terrific, Mr. Baron, but . . ." The Morgan Stanley banker pulled the cassette out of his briefcase and handed it back to Jake with a polite smile on his face.

"But what?" Jake asked hesitantly.

"Money is very tight right now, Mr. Baron."

Stalling for a moment, Jake looked around the restaurant, fumbling with an empty pack of Marlboros. "Look, doesn't the fact that it's a Terry Taylor movie and we have both Harrison Ford and Michelle Pfeiffer starring . . ."

The Morgan Stanley rep nodded politely as he scanned the menu. "Have you tried the swordfish here?" he asked nonchalantly. "I hear it's quite good."

Jake didn't even pick up his menu. He ordered coffee and another pack of cigarettes. No matter what he said, he decided, the representative could only repeat a management decision that was already made.

Jake glanced at his watch. Shit, he thought, time was running out.

"I'm sure Meryl will be your lead. She not only loved the script, but when I told her that Kevin had already signed to play the husband, that became the clincher," Robert said, finishing his spiel to his wife, Kelly, seated across the table from him. He winked, and she laughed back.

Robert Zinman, co-owner of one of the town's most successful boutique talent agencies, personified the very best of everything: he had the best office, the best-looking secretary, the best clients, and most of all, the best wife.

"What's so funny?" he asked curiously. He wasn't used to seeing her in such a playful mood.

"Oh, nothing much. My mind was just wandering for a moment," Kelly said while she flirted back at him. They had such few good times together anymore. Either she was too busy at the studio or with some charity, or he was away on business.

She'd never forgotten the first time she had seen her husband, sitting behind a small secretary's desk with some funny-looking earpiece sticking out of his right ear. He had then been an agent trainee with the William Morris Agency in Beverly Hills. Except for the pained look on his face, he was quite handsome, with short black hair, flirtatious lazy brown eyes, and high cheekbones.

He is even more handsome now, Kelly thought as she reached out and grabbed Robert's hand. In a town where women spent more time with their hairdressers or agents than with their husbands, she considered herself very lucky to be able to see Robert as much as she did, even if it was almost always regarding business.

After a frustrating few years as a motion-picture talent agent with the Morris office, Robert had had a severe personality clash with management. Even though he was bright and very active, his superiors—who were feeling the losses over the past years from many defecting high-powered clients to their new chief rival, Creative Artists Agency—continually rode Robert and other agents very hard to be more aggressive. In addition, they also felt that he had become biased toward Constellation once his wife was hired to run the studio, and thus caused friction with other studios, such as Warners, Columbia, and Paramount.

After many interoffice battles, and after consulting with Kelly, Robert had decided that if he had to put out so much extra effort, why not let the profits come back into his own wallet?

So with Kelly quietly investing some seed money—she was now earning a mid-six-figure salary—Robert formed Worldwide Artists Agency the day he quit the Morris office. Two other agents also resigned to join him as partners.

The three decided that occupying the penthouse

suite of a pricey address wasn't good enough for their new image. Instead, they built their own three-story red brick building in the heart of the famous Beverly Hills shopping district near Rodeo Drive.

On the top floor, overlooking the fancy designer shops of Beverly Hills, was Robert's huge corner office. It was decorated in the art-deco style of the Hollywood moguls of the thirties, but he had added his own personal touch: hats he had collected from various professional and college teams hung on the wall, along with pennants and pictures of him with all the greats: Magic Johnson, Pete Rose, Sugar Ray Leonard, Kirk Gibson.

As Kelly grabbed her briefcase, she saw that Robert had finally finished reading a deal memo. "If you can sign Meryl to the project, I'll love you forever," she said, a little embarrassed at her show of affection.

Gracefully she got up from the table, tossing her head back. During the long morning, her hairdo had lost most of its curl. She had to get back to the studio. Jake had arranged a meeting for her with his old buddy Norman Jewison about some script that really excited him.

"You mean you only love me for the meantime?" Robert played back her cute remark his way as he sat back and admired her. "If Meryl and Kevin sign, I want you to give me a lifetime no-cut contract," he said, pretending to be writing down his words.

Kelly laughed, but she suddenly felt fatigued. She had spent most of the morning listening to Robert and his other agents discussing some of their new projects.

"Time to close up for today, Robert—"

"Hold on, Kel, I've got one more thing I want to discuss," he gently interrupted her as he sat her back down again.

Kelly looked up at her husband, not hiding her surprise. "Okay, Zinman, what's up now?"

"I've just signed a hot new client, a writer named Rod Browning. Kel, his newest script is on fire. Both

Sydney Pollack and Oliver Stone would give their nuts to direct it. In fact, I've already had calls from their CAA agent."

Kelly shook her head, disappointed. The moment of shared tenderness was gone. After almost nine years of marriage, she should have known better. Robert would talk about scripts in bed if she'd let him. But on the other hand, that's what made him the successful agent he was.

"Give me the script and I'll take a look at it later," Kelly said, stifling a sigh and glancing at her watch, trying not to show he had hurt her. Anyway, she had to get back to her office.

Robert looked at his notes, ignoring her anxiousness to leave. He still had several more projects to discuss.

"Hold on, Kel, there's another project here," he began, then noticed the funny look on his wife's face.

She was tired, he realized. She hadn't been sleeping well recently. More than once he had the feeling she was hiding something. Oh, God, what if she was pregnant! he thought in alarm. That would ruin everything. There was definitely no room in his life now for a family. The last thing he imagined himself doing was sitting in a sandbox or pushing a kid on a swing in Roxbury Park on Sunday afternoons.

"Hello, you two." A handsome older man with a head of Ronald Reagan-style dyed black hair popped into the office. Kelly and Robert looked up at Sol Goldberg, one of Robert's partners. He always had a big line to go along with his even bigger ego.

"How many deals have Hollywood's most successful couple closed today?" he said with smirking envy. His wife was a typical Beverly Hills housewife: she changed houses everytime she decided to change her hair color.

"Sol, you're just in time to tell Kelly about your new project with Warren."

Kelly shook her head. She wasn't going to be sidetracked again. She stood up and buttoned her Bob

Mackie suit jacket. The bronze-gold wool crepe suit with military gold buttons set off her slim shape.

"Sorry, guys, I've really got to be leaving." She smiled at the two of them.

"But, Kelly, you just got here," Sol quipped.

Kelly shook her head, ignoring his little joke. "You know, Sol, someday I'm going to steal my husband away from you and keep his talents all to myself."

Goldberg smiled as he reached for a cigar from the open humidor on Robert's desk. "He's too busy, Kelly. He's constantly got us all coming and going. Did he tell you that he insisted that WAA buy two tables for your luncheon next week?"

Kelly laughed. "And I'll bet you and your wife dinner that he also conned you into buying a couple of thousand-dollar raffle tickets for our Save the Environment fund-raiser."

Goldberg nodded as he chewed off the tip of his cigar. "Three tickets, in fact. Anyway, I think I'd better get out of here before it costs me any more money," he said, backing out of the room as Robert's cute secretary inched around him. The shapely girl smiled at Goldberg, then at Robert.

"Oh, excuse me, Mr. Zinman," she announced in her affected British accent, "there's a call on line one from Dr. Buss about some Laker tickets you wanted." She finally smiled at Kelly.

"Good afternoon, Ms. Kristopher," she continued. "Your office just called to remind you that you have a meeting following lunch."

Kelly acknowledged the message with a forced smile. *Little Miss Whatever-her-name-was doesn't leave much to the imagination, does she?* she thought, looking down at the girl's visible cleavage. She often wondered about Robert gazing at his knockout secretary every day. She knew there were stories about Robert and his casting couch, but she had believed in his fidelity since their marriage. At least she thought she had. Sometimes, like now, she wasn't so sure.

"I'll take it in a minute," Robert said to his secretary.

Kelly picked up her briefcase. "Dinner tonight, Robert?" she asked casually. They hadn't seen much of each other the past few weeks. Besides, she thought tenderly, maybe tonight they could recapture what she had felt moments earlier with him.

"Sure, Kel—" Then he stopped, snapping his fingers. "Shit, I almost forgot . . ." How could he tell her something else was cooking tonight? Something tall, brunette, and with double digits in all the right places.

"Uh, I can't make it, Kel," he said, his brown eyes flirting with her. "John asked me to go over to the Improv and catch this new comic's act. The talk is, he's the next Billy Crystal." He nuzzled her cheek and gave her a little kiss, then whispered in her ear, "I hope you don't mind."

"You know how I feel about John," Kelly said, trying to keep the edge out of her voice. She wished Robert wouldn't hang around with that guy. He was notorious for "Polaroid parties" at his condo, which always involved plenty of alcohol, women, and dirty gossip.

"C'mon, Kel, it's just business," Robert said glibly. "I promise I'll be right home after the show."

"Sure, maybe dinner tomorrow," she said, trying to smile. She felt a headache coming on. It wasn't just her relationship with Robert; all the problems at Constellation were starting to catch up with her. She couldn't help but think of Jake. Maybe he would call her tonight with some news. It would be just as well if Robert wasn't at home, so she could talk more freely. She had decided not to burden Robert with the studio's problems or Jake's most recent trip to New York. Robert had his own business to worry about, she thought. Trying to read his face to see if he realized she was hiding something from him, she frowned. He was so handsome, yet there was something artificial about him at times.

"Sure, Kel," Robert said, giving her a quick kiss on the cheek and handing her a stack of WAA scripts that they had talked about earlier.

Kelly nodded as she took the scripts and left his office.

Breathing a sigh of relief, Robert didn't even sit down as he picked up the phone. The weekend was coming up and he had to make sure he was set for Saturday night. He punched in his blinking private line. "Dr. B., old pal. Yeah, sure, great, two seats behind Nicholson for the Golden State game."

As the curtain fell on the final act of *Don Giovanni*, the standing-room crowd clapped and roared their approval of the accomplished visiting opera troupe from Munich. Many of those in the audience then began to rise to their feet, following the lead of Crown Prince Akihito and Crown Princess Michiko in the royal box. Standing next to them was Hiroshi Takashima, looking resplendent in a black tuxedo. The well-known and beautiful actress Hana Sha, Takashima's escort for the evening, stood in the back of the box. She knew when not to take center stage.

After several curtain calls, the formally attired crowd emptied from the Tokyo Bunka Kaikan, where they were greeted with a full moon in the midnight sky. The streets were crowded with fans who waited anxiously for a peek at the famous first-nighters now spilling out of the theater. The crown prince and his princess waved to the crowd, but it was Takashima's lady, the popular film star, who drew the most attention.

As the photographers' flash bulbs went off, the fans clamored for Hana Sha's autograph. For his part, Takashima and his Yakuza quietly watched the street beyond the crowd as a black limo drove up on schedule and double-parked. Without a word, a Yakuza opened the passenger door and Takashima stepped inside. A Ronin was inside waiting for him.

"Good evening. Is everything arranged?" Takashima

asked, lowering the shade. He had no desire to be disturbed or to be seen by anyone.

"*Hai*," the Ronin answered, excited. "I have most important news for you."

Takashima raised his hand. This was the information he had been waiting for regarding their final departure plans. "Wait, we will speak on the way."

The Ronin nodded.

Takashima looked out the window. The noisy crowd of teenagers and gawking men around Hana had increased. The exotic beauty glowed as she signed one autograph after another. She chatted with several people in the crowd, especially the men, and smiled while she savored every minute of attention.

Takashima, however, was getting impatient. The stupid woman was beginning to irritate him. Not because of the attention she was receiving, but because she was acting like some silly American soap-opera queen.

He quickly got out of the limo and slammed the door behind him, not waiting for his bodyguard. He remained still as he snapped his fingers impatiently a couple of times. "Gekijo-san, Minoru-san." The two Yakuza needed no further instructions.

Hana suddenly appeared in front of Takashima, flanked by the Yakuza. She was still smiling. "Takashima-san, I have never signed so many autographs in one night! I am so excited."

Takashima did not answer, but looked at her with a critical eye. The girl had disappointed him. Obviously, since she had appeared in a couple of American-produced films, she had lost her sense of traditional Japanese womanhood, something he always demanded.

He continued to stand impatiently, tapping his forefingers together. This would definitely be his last evening with her.

All the same, she still looked very pretty in her long black gown, beaded with thousands of sparkling sequins, like a black swan, wet and glistening all over like the morning dew. She was tall for an Asian woman (perhaps one of her ancestors had dallied for an evening with a Portuguese sailor.) Her skin was white and transparent, like the shimmer of a full moon. She used makeup expertly: red, glossed lips, westernized eyes lined heavily in black kohl like the American girls who posed for the Coca-Cola ads. Her full breasts, enlarged with silicon, swelled over her dress, inviting his touch.

Perhaps he should not end the evening so hastily, Takashima thought as he studied her. It was still early enough to complete his business later. After all, the woman must be taught a lesson.

As he slipped his hand around her bare shoulder, he motioned to a Yakuza seated in a second black limo to drive up to them. One of Takashima's bodyguards jumped out and opened the door for the smiling actress.

"Where are we going, Takashima-san?" she asked as he slipped in beside her.

"We are already here," he said firmly as his eyes began to undress her.

She instinctively put her hand on his inner thigh and ran her fingers up and down his leg, while he gently took her face in his hands and kissed her lips: sweet, and very willing. Good, he thought as he unzipped the back of her gown and slowly pulled it down to her waist, exposing her perfectly shaped breasts. He fondled them for a few minutes, then forced himself to break away from her. He was anxious to get on with the evening. This would not take long.

"Hana-san, you are most beautiful," he said, then kissed her hand, his lips lingering on her soft ivory skin. "I await your pleasure, dear one."

Hana smiled knowingly as she unzipped his pants. Her hands had already begun to fondle his penis, and now she was prepared to give him what he wanted. Careful not to smear her lipstick, she teasingly put her fingers into her mouth, one at a time, then sucked them slowly with her tongue. Her eyes never left his as she rolled her tongue over her finger, promising the same kind of pleasure for him. This was a game they had played before. She knew her part well. She watched him become straight and hard. Then, bending down, Hana put her red lips around his penis and began to suck on it.

He grunted as he felt his blood rushing hurriedly throughout his body. She was performing well, but he had a different game in mind tonight. He intended to show her his power, not only over her but also over his own physical self.

"That is enough," he said gruffly, pulling her head back by the hair so hard she cried out.

"What?" Hana screamed, stunned.

Takashima zipped up his pants, pushing against his throbbing penis. "I am finished with you."

"Wait. Please," she began, her eyes beginning to tear, but Takashima got out and slammed the limo door shut. A Yakuza immediately jumped into the back seat from the other side.

"Takashima-san," Hana pleaded, leaning out the half-open window while she tried to cover her naked breasts with her gown. "What is wrong?"

"You have become very much like your ugly American friends, Hana-san. I believe you prefer their ways to ours." He paused. "Their ways are not mine," he finished, spitting out his last words with hatred.

He ignored her muffled cries as he turned on his heel and walked back to the other limo. He had no use for such a stupid whore. Instead he left with the Ronin, speeding through the crowded streets of Tokyo.

3

Kelly raced her Mercedes 450 SL convertible onto the studio lot, having no time today to stop and chat with the veteran studio guard as she often did. She had to get ready for her big luncheon and she was already running late. She checked her makeup in the rearview mirror while holding the steering wheel with her left hand. "Oh, shit." She had forgotten her earrings. She remembered taking them out of her jewelry case and laying them on the marble counter in her bathroom when the phone rang.

She kept her eyes focused straight ahead as she drove toward her office. She was being honored by the Ecological Media Organization with their first annual Humanitarian Award for her many years as a volunteer with various environmental organizations.

She tugged on her ear. Damn, she couldn't go to the luncheon without her trademark earrings: big golden round ones. Her mother had always said, "Never face an audience without your jewelry, baby. It'll give you confidence." Well, this was one time she needed all the confidence she could get.

As she pulled into her personalized parking place, she looked at the digital clock on her console: 11 A.M. She was really late now.

"Geoffrey, we're going to Neiman's."

"Kelly, you're crazy! There's no time," he shouted back to Kelly as she ran by him and into her office.

She didn't even notice that he was holding two dozen long-stemmed red roses. And she didn't even stop to say hello to his two assistants.

Geoffrey followed behind her, his arms still filled with the roses.

She was quickly on her phone at her magnificent desk, which had once belonged to Jake's dad, founder Bunky Baron. The large old-fashioned desk, replete with lions' feet, even had a secret drawer. It still bore the original nicks and stains from Bunky's years of studio wars, and Kelly would often swear she could still smell the lingering cigar smoke from his stogie every now and then.

Across the room, where she would hold court for informal meetings, two plush cream-colored sofas faced each other, while a round walnut table with chairs stood on the other side. They were known as Kelly's serious, heavy-duty meeting seats.

Her walls were filled with scores of pictures: President Reagan, Barbra Streisand, Jack Nicholson, Shirley MacLaine, Meryl Streep, Robert Redford, Bob Hope at one of his many charity events. There were also numerous awards and commendations, which included a plaque from Mayor Tom Bradley commemorating "Kelly Kristopher Day" in Los Angeles, on her first day as president of Constellation.

Geoffrey walked to the front of her desk, smiling, still holding the roses as he waited for her to hang up the phone.

"I still say you're crazy," he said a second time, trying to shake his hair out of his eyes.

"Earrings are important to me, Geoffrey. I want to look my best today."

"But, Kel, you always look beautiful, with or without them."

Kelly, listening halfheartedly, glanced at the Hollywood trade papers as she leaned back in her high swivel chair. A curious smile crossed her lips. "Thanks

... but tell me, Geoffrey, would you go to lunch half-dressed?"

Geoffrey raised his eyebrows. He knew when to give up. Kelly always had an answer for everything. Even in the toughest meetings with agents, producers, directors, writers, and fellow studio execs, he was continually surprised at her perseverance in not giving up until she got what she wanted. Suddenly he remembered the roses. "Oh, I almost forgot. These came a little while ago from Mr. Baron." He put the vase of roses in front of her.

Pleasantly surprised, Kelly looked at the card. Well, he was still in New York. Her heart skipped a beat as she read the short message. There was only a congratulatory phrase, no hint of how things were going with the investors. Hopefully she'd hear from him later.

Kelly bit her lip. She would miss Jake terribly today. She owed him so much. He had taken a big risk when he hired her as president, and she wanted to publicly acknowledge her thanks to him today in front of the celebrity audience.

After arranging his flowers on her desk, Kelly checked her mail, but there was nothing important. "Any urgent messages?" she asked, glancing up.

Geoffrey's handsome face lit up as he showed her his open Gucci briefcase filled with telegrams and pink phone slips. "Any other questions?"

Kelly was overwhelmed. "Read them to me on the way," she said, already running for her limo. "Let's go."

As they passed through the outer office, one of the other assistants blurted, "Ms. Kristopher, Mr. Zinman rang to say he'll be late."

"Thanks, Jana," Kelly said, dashing out the door and hopping into the limo. She didn't have time to figure out why Robert would be late. Probably some last-minute business at his agency, but that was nothing new.

Geoffrey followed her, grabbing his clipboard. He checked his watch. Not a minute to lose.

They were off to Neiman's.

The last of the lunch crowd had just started to leave. Three empty shot glasses sat on the bar at the Friars Club in front of Jake. Turning away, he signaled the bartender to bring him another double as he spoke into the phone to his secretary.

"I'll be here a couple more days, Paula." Pause. "Yeah, I've got some other appointments. I'll check in for messages. Would you switch me to Max? I'll wait."

Jake drummed his fingers on the bar. What was taking her so long? Finally he heard Max's familiar voice.

"Yeah, listen, Max, things aren't going so great here. . . . Yeah, the Big Apple's full of worms. . . . No, don't do anything until I get back. Save those people. I'm not giving up yet."

As he hung up the phone, he eyed the whiskey, then pushed it aside. He had changed his mind. That wasn't going to solve his problems.

Damn, he wondered, what would Bunky say if he knew his studio was so deep in hock? And his son so desperate to save it.

Al Baron, affectionately known as Bunky, even to Jake, had built Constellation from scratch. He was a man who cared more about what was on the screen than in the bank. He had started out as a one-man studio, shooting one-reelers back during the Depression, through earthquakes, heat, downpours, all the while he was a button salesman. Over the years, he rubbed shoulders with all the legendary founding fathers of Hollywood—Mayer, Goldwyn, Cohn—as well as all the memorable screen stars: Harlow, Bogart, Gable, Davis. But as Bunky would say to his young son, Jake, "You can give them all the stars in the heavens, but without a good story, you ain't giving them nothing but strained eyes and sore butts."

Remembering this advice, Jake slammed a fist down

onto the bar, oblivious of the heads that turned his way. That was the whole problem, he mused; he had never pinched pennies. He had taken over the studio in the early 1960's when his father had retired, and successfully turned the sagging, depressed Constellation into a blockbuster enterprise with a series of money-making hit movies—the envy of all his Hollywood competitors. This winning streak had lasted through the end of the seventies.

However, during the late eighties some of Constellation's high-cost movies became major box-office flops. Jake flared with anger as he thought of them, then of the smug bankers who had rejected him the past few days. And according to the rumors, some Wall Street analysts had already predicted that Constellation was on the verge of going belly-up.

Yet Jake had refused many substantial offers to sell his studio, especially after last year's stock-market crash. Over and over again he also rejected the idea of going public to some of the world's giant media barons who would have been prepared to bankroll him for shared control. He even said no when a major soft-drink company offered to buy him out for an outrageous sum. Jake was proud and stubborn. He had sworn he would never sell his studio. It was all he or his family had ever known. Besides, he thought, smiling, he did have fun with an occasional box-office hit.

"Well, well, well," said a smiling Milton Berle, coming up behind him. "Look who's here: Bunky's little boy."

Jake tried to smile. "How's it going, Unc?" he said, using his own pet name for the famous comedian.

Henny Youngman was right behind. "J.B., how 'bout joining Miltie and me for a *schvitz*?" he asked. "I've got some new jokes I want you to hear."

Jake shook his head as he got up from the bar. He'd had enough. He didn't feel much like laughing today.

And besides, he had already heard Henny's new jokes twenty years ago.

* * *

"They look beautiful, Miss Kristopher," the Neiman's saleswoman said approvingly as Kelly fastened the boldly styled gold earrings onto her ears.

Kelly looked into the hand mirror the saleswoman held up for her. She wasn't sure. They were elegant, but not her usual style. She turned to Geoffrey. "What do you think?"

"I hate to admit it, Kel, but you were right," he said honestly while checking his watch. "You look even more sensational. But we've got to go. We're already late."

"I'll take them," Kelly said, signing the credit slip. Then she rushed out, barely noticing the extravagant holiday decorations adding to the already glitzy look of the expensive store.

As they got back into the limo and took off for the Century Plaza Hotel, Kelly tried to keep her mind on today's luncheon. But it was impossible. She was more concerned with Jake and the studio.

Kelly tried to listen while Geoffrey read off congratulatory telegrams—from Hoffman, Streep, and Nicholson, among others—but as she looked out the limousine window, she hardly heard a word. In fact, she didn't even notice the heavy traffic along little Santa Monica Boulevard as they inched along. It was all a blur to her.

In a couple of weeks, the entertainment industry would be closing down for the Christmas holidays. Jake hoped he would have Constellation's money problems solved by then. The studio needed a hit in the worst way. Until *Criminal Intent* completed principal photography and postproduction, Jake was doubtful about putting too many other features into the works. It was up to her now to keep the studio's good name out in front of the public and to quash any rumors about their financial problems that had been circulating since her return last month from Aspen. She had to put on a good show today.

As the limo came to a momentary stop, Kelly tapped the window button and watched the window lower. The street was so jammed with cars, it might have been midtown Manhattan. Too much new construction, she thought angrily.

It was warm for a December day, especially with the hot fumes rising from cars stuck in traffic around them. Damn, she'd really be late now. She prayed that Robert had finished his last-minute business—whatever it was—and would already be there waiting for her. She needed him at her side.

She owed him a lot, especially after the roof had caved in on her in the early eighties.

Sherry Lansing, the first female president of any Hollywood studio, had hired her as a production exec at Twentieth Century-Fox. With her recent marriage to Robert, at the time a hot agent with the Morris office, Kelly had had the extra stability that she craved.

She had been proud to be a member of the all-woman creative team at Fox. Production had been in high gear. But all that changed when Denver oil magnate Marvin Davis bought the studio. Sherry Lansing was replaced, as was most of her team, including Kelly. That's when she had needed Robert the most, and he had come through.

He beat his agent's drum into every Hollywood corner about her, hyping her talent and experience everywhere. Kelly was seen doing lunch at Ma Maison with Paramount's Don Simpson and Michael Eisner. She went to all the major studio screenings with Robert, who touted her capabilities to the press as well as to the brass. Her photo was seen frequently in the papers with the top directors, including Sydney Pollack and Steven Spielberg. She continued her charity work with local organizations like About Children, as well as working relentlessly with the hospitals and environmental causes. Soon everyone in town thought she was being signed by everyone else. No one doubted that she would be the next woman studio president.

Robert, on a tip, had advance word that Constellation's current president, Dan Golden, was leaving the post to accept a three-picture deal as an independent producer at Columbia. The studio had been having some problems, and studio owner Jake Baron was looking around for a new president who could reinvigorate them.

Kelly had never dreamed that she would cross paths again with Jake. She hadn't seen him since their break-up a few years before. But to her surprise, Robert, who winced at the merest mention of her former lover, had insisted she talk to him.

One fall day, Robert brought Kelly into his WAA office. "Now, remember, Kel," he had said, squeezing her hand, "this is the opportunity we've both worked hard for. Be cool, and don't accept his first offer under any circumstances."

Kelly remembered that she only nodded back to Robert, unable to answer. She was more afraid of seeing Jake again than of not getting the job. She was worried that she would still feel the same toward him.

"Good to see you, Kelly," she had heard him say as he walked into Robert's office. He smiled at her, and suddenly she knew nothing had changed for her. But instead of turning away from him, she had embraced the opportunity to work with him when he offered her the job.

"We're about fifteen minutes behind schedule," Geoffrey said, breaking into her thoughts.

"Well, they'll just have to wait for me," she answered wistfully as the traffic began to move slowly.

As the white stretch limo pulled up in front of the Century Plaza Hotel, she held her breath. There were reporters and photographers everywhere to cover the star-studded event, not to mention the society and movie crowd arriving in white limos, black limos, and even a few Rolls-Royces.

As Kelly got out and waved to the crowd of reporters, she looked around for Robert's red Ferrari, but she didn't see it.

She was quickly circled by the advance publicity people from the studio, but all she could think was: Where in the hell is he?

In a fiery rage, his dark eyes burning like hot black

coals, Takashima stood over his huge desk and pushed the entire stack of computer printouts onto the floor. "*Bakayaro!*" he cursed. "I want answers, not printouts. Where is Noda-san?" he shouted loudly in his plush high-rise office in the center of the Ginza district, not caring who heard him. Immediately three secretaries in blue skirts and white blouses ran in and began cleaning up the mess.

Several large Tokyo banks were buying millions of U.S. dollars as the dollar fell to a postwar low against the yen. Takashima gritted his teeth as he blamed the new American President. Already the investors were running scared.

He paced up and down, paying the secretaries no more attention than if they were insects to be stomped on. He nearly crushed one of their hands, but the woman kept her pain to herself. If she did not, she would be fired.

The frightened women eyed each other helplessly. No one knew where Noda was, but they dared not admit it. In self-defense, the secretaries bowed low, touching their foreheads to the ground. They had never seen him in such a rage before. Nothing could quell his vicious words, not even his Yakuza, who hovered around him protectively.

His eyes fell on the crossed samurai swords, presented to him by the Emperor, hanging on the far wall. Pacing back and forth, he took a moment to compose himself before returning to his Yakuza. Something had to be done. And now. "Bring Noda-san here immediately!"

Turning to his secretaries, he barked, "Get me today's closing numbers on both the New York and Nikkei exchanges. Then tell my Prudential-Bache brokers to buy American companies with assets of more than fifty million dollars." He paused momentarily as he stepped over the mess of computer paper, then said, "But only those whose stock is undervalued at this time."

"*Hai*, Takashima-san," the secretaries answered in unison, bowing again as they stood up.

His Yakuza entered with Noda huddled between them.

"You have heard the news about the dollar falling to just over one hundred and twenty-two yen, Noda-san?"

He nodded while completing his courteous bow. "Do not worry, Takashima-san, that will not change your plans to buy the American studio. All is in readiness." He handed Takashima a sealed file from the Ronin.

Noda was pleased that he had finally been summoned. Since he knew Takashima respected his judgment, he was never afraid to oppose a wrong decision made by him. He took special pride in knowing that only he could calm Takashima.

Takashima grunted as he took the pages from the file and began reading. His recent rage was now gone. As he laid down the pages, a strong sense of spiritual peace began to overtake him instead. The fabricated business story that he had just read would be the perfect charade, just as his Ronin group had suggested. Only Noda would ever know the truth: that this was a made-up motive, while revenge was still his true reason for wanting the Hollywood studio.

"Noda-san, please let me discuss the elements of the proposed cover story," he said with his smile becoming more and more sinister. "All of the research from the Ronin has suggested that our competitors, like Morita-san, have a growing need for software for both here and in Japan and around the world. We will also say that we need this software for cable, pay TV, home video, and satellite transmissions that we will be buying into. We must also pretend to our Takashima Group that our motives are to keep Japan's hold on the international marketplace, while we discuss global synergy with our American enemy. Finally, as the Ronin have advised, we will move quickly and pretend there is no more time to lose, especially with Europe becoming one unified community in 1992." He paused, looking for his heir's reaction. "Does that not sound convincing, Noda-san?"

Noda smiled while he politely applauded the master's presentation. "I am certain that your story, Takashima-san, will convince even the American enemy."

Takashima acknowledged Noda's compliment with a slight bow.

"Will you and your first entourage be leaving soon for Los Angeles?"

"Hai."

Noda nodded in approval. He could not stop grinning. The excitement of his eventual move to the United States—where he hoped to reunite with some of his college friends—began to make him forget for the moment his quiet fears that they might eventually get caught with Takashima's phony venture.

But like Takashima, he felt it was no time to worry. Instead he smiled at the thought that they would soon conquer.

The grand hallway of Takashima's country estate was filled with steamer trunks, Louis Vuitton suitcases, and garment bags. Chisako, looking casually seductive in a pair of tight jeans and a white halter top, checked off the suitcases from her list. It seemed there was more luggage in front of her than was on Takashima's list. She was beginning to lose track. She stopped. She counted them again, wondering if she would ever finish the job. She still had some personal belongings to pack before they left in the morning.

"This one next," she said to the short, extremely muscular Yakuza. He was shirtless, his macho response to the cold room. Takashima liked his houses cold, even when it was pleasant outside. He believed it kept his mind and body tougher.

Chisako turned away as she eyed the guard's exposed back, showing a large tatoo of a genteel lady reclining on a fish. She had never gotten used to the strange Yakuza body art. Suddenly she realized she was sweating. She knew what that meant: she needed another fix.

Ever since that night when she had spilled hot tea on Takashima, she had feared she was smoking opium far too frequently. She had been worried that Takashima might not take her on his journey. And if that happened, she would have nothing.

Swinging the ponytail that hung down past the curve of her back, she wiped the perspiration from between her breasts and off her back as the room seemed to be getting warmer and warmer. Without any thought to modesty, she unhooked her halter top and pulled it over her head, unaware that the Yakuza was watching her from across the room with a troubled gaze. She was so used to them, she sometimes forgot they were there. She closed her eyes, enjoying the freedom of her nakedness as she wiped her breasts dry with her halter.

"*Dozo*, Chisako-san," the Yakuza snapped, advancing and tapping her on the shoulder. She opened her eyes in surprise. "Please, you must cover yourself immediately. The master will be very angry with both of us if you do not."

"Please do not tell him; I will cover myself," she answered, throwing the halter back on hurriedly. But it is a funny way of thinking, she thought, becoming cross with the man. Takashima did not mind the two of them making love in front of his entire group of bodyguards, but when she was alone, she was somehow supposed to act like a pristine Japanese woman again.

"Well, what are you waiting for?" she said loudly to the Yakuza, who had not moved since making his request.

Satisfied, he bowed and Chisako watched as he hoisted a large trunk on his shoulder.

"Take those, too, Gekijo-san," she ordered.

Gekijo nodded and picked up two heavy suitcases

along with the trunk. His muscles strained at the effort, and the elaborate chrysanthemums tatooed on his arms formed large bulges on his biceps. As he left, carrying all three pieces of luggage, a house servant entered, carrying a black dinner suit.

"*Dozo,* Chisako-san." She handed the suit to Chisako, then left quickly.

Chisako started to pack the suit, but she still felt uneasy from the lack of opium. At any moment she felt she might collapse. She had to sit down.

With Takashima's suit in her lap, she inhaled a familiar fragrance. Investigating further, she sniffed the lapels of the suit. She frowned, furrowing her finely lined brows. Bal à Versailles. French perfume. It was not her scent, but that did not surprise her.

She knew her master had many women. It was not only expected of him; it was his pleasure—young women, expensive women, famous women. But the knowledge of that did not make it any easier for her to accept.

Curiously she searched his suit pockets and she found a program from the opera. She turned it over and was dismayed to see that it was autographed by the popular actress Hana Sha. Angrily she tore it up into pieces, upset and disturbed that she was no longer able to please Takashima with the sweet flower of her youth. Worriedly she glanced around at the suitcases. This had been her home for so long. All this luxury, she mused, so unlike the wooden hut she had grown up in.

She had been raised in a small farming village. After several years of drought and no rice crop, her family had been left destitute. She had always been a quiet child, but had a curious mind, a dangerous thing for a Japanese woman, who was expected to know her place.

She had often been reminded by her mother of the custom of placing a newborn baby girl upon the ground for three days so that she might quickly know her place in the world. Women were of the earth, she would often tell her beautiful child; men were of the heavens. Any woman who wished to change that would be quickly punished.

Her mother had often said her eldest daughter was too beautiful to keep a traditional Japanese home, raise children, or fight with a mother-in-law. No traditional man would marry her because of her intelligence, but they would pay to be entertained by her. Her family knew that the life of a geisha would be more befitting. And what choice did she have? Her family did not have enough rice to feed their children.

Like all Japanese, Chisako valued parental love above all else. In order to ensure the survival of her family, she had willingly gone to the geisha house and been proud that her family would now receive an unusually large amount of money for her.

Chisako had learned to enjoy the art of the geisha, from singing traditional songs to preparing the blood of the eel to arouse the desire of the oldest of men. But when she was nearly sixteen, she had met Takashima, who had bewitched her with his strange ways. After one night with him she knew she could no longer stay in the *geisha-ya*. She had left with him and never looked back. But Chisako always knew what her place would be: part prostitute, part servant.

Shaken by this thought, she took out the thin golden box that Takashima had given her. She could not deny herself her freedom from pain any longer. Without hesitation she removed a small amount of opium and rolled it between her fingers. Next she lit the small pipe and inhaled slowly. Her head fell lazily backward. The loving peace she craved was now hers.

She floated on silk through a soft, warm mist into a space of dreams. Everything around her was subdued: sounds, colors, even the hated fragrance of the French perfume.

She walked languidly into her own quarters. Delicately she placed the torn opera program into the ivory box of secrets where she kept the other mementos of her life with Takashima. Then, without another troubled thought, she lay down on a brocade covering, the color of a bluebird with golden wings, and found peace where Takashima could not hurt her.

"Hold it, Miss Kristopher!"
"Over here, Kelly!"

Kelly turned and smiled at the many photographers, tossing her hair over her shoulder. Her bold golden earrings caught the blaze of the flashes as the cameras went off. She smiled widely, trying not to blink. Ever since she had gotten out of the limo, she had been besieged by the press. As soon as she turned around, another camera would go off.

"Hey, how about a shot of you with the mayor?" someone yelled as Tom Bradley arrived, waving and smiling at the crowd. Kelly gladly posed with her old friend while the cameras continued to go off.

All the while, she stretched her neck out over the wall of reporters, trying to see who was arriving. One limo after another pulled up and dropped off important passengers. But no red Ferrari, she noted with dismay. She wished Robert would get there. If he didn't turn up soon, people would start to notice his absence, and she didn't want any rumors starting. One snide comment from the wrong person at a function like this could distort the whole thing out of proportion. Then they'd be in the tabloids again.

As she frowned in dismay, a camera clicked. That's the photo they'll probably publish, she thought, trying to recover with a big smile and a wave.

"All right, gang, that's it. There'll be plenty of time for pictures later." Rose Kaufman's booming voice could be heard above the crowd as she made her way over to Kelly. "Come on, guys, give the lady ten feet, or else."

As the uniformed doorman held the glass door open, Kelly sighed in relief when she saw Rose and her two PR assistants paving the way for her.

"Thanks, Rose," Kelly called out, giving the reporters one final smile as she went inside the lobby. "I thought I'd have to give my speech out there on the sidewalk."

"Even if you did, those putzes would still misquote you." After three decades of handling the press for Jake, and now Kelly, Rose had hardened to many of the assholes in the fourth estate.

"Rose," Kelly said, dropping her voice low. "I have no idea where Robert is."

Rose jangled her bracelets a couple of times and pursed her lips. "Don't worry, Kelly, I'm sure he'll be here soon." Agents, like the press, were a necessary evil, but in Rose's eyes Robert was evil and not very necessary, period. She was very sympathetic to her favorite studio exec.

Kelly tried not to show her distress. With a forced smile she grabbed Rose's arm and held it tightly as they walked by the curious hotel guests.

Rose intoned with an authoritative voice, "Kel, why don't you go downstairs with my assistants. I've got to wait up here. As soon as I see Robert, I'll bring him down to you. By the way, Mary Hart and her *E.T.* crew are setting up down there to do a quick interview with you. I'll join you shortly."

"Stop wiggling, Ginger," Robert pleaded irritably. He'd never get it up if she didn't sit still. He was trying to hold on to the pretty nymphomaniac as she sat on the counter next to the black marble bathroom sink. The mirror behind her, framed with light bulbs, gave him a rear view of their every move. They were kissing passionately.

Ginger, pulling away, laughed through her shiny pink lips while she Texas-twanged her silliness back to him: "I can't help it, Bobby. It's cold sitting up here." Shifting her weight from one side to the other, she resumed her deep, wet kissing with Robert.

The girl, about eighteen, was nude except for her three-inch platform heels, gold ID ankle bracelet, and a string of pearls around her neck. Her dishwater-blond hair hung straight and long over her shoulders, reaching down to the tips of her nipples.

He held her down as he nuzzled his face between her breasts, enjoying the warm haven he found there. He flicked his tongue over her breasts, tasting the salty sweat mixed with her cheap perfume. "Time to make you real hot, baby," he said huskily.

He ignored the loud sounds of the television coming through the thin walls from the next room as he unzipped his pants. He didn't have much time left to fool around with the pug-nosed dancer who had flown in from Houston for the day. She had to be on the three-fifteen flight back to Texas to dance later that night at the private gentlemen's club where Robert's buddy John had first met her.

Robert never forgot John's call, saying: "This cowgirl gives the best head in North America, maybe in the world." Robert immediately wanted in, and had convinced John to let him know when she would be in town. Of course, Robert hadn't counted on it being the day of Kelly's luncheon. But he wasn't going to miss out on a prime piece of ass like this. Luckily, the Beverly Wilshire Hotel, where he often got a room under one of his clients' names, wasn't too far from the Century Plaza.

Ginger, jumping onto the queen-size bed, seductively invited him to join her. She smiled when she saw the size of his dick. "Wow."

That's all Robert's ego needed to hear. Soon it was long and hard and very ready.

He held her tightly, putting his arms around her. She purred contentedly. "Ummm, how 'bout another kiss, Bobby?"

"Sure, honey."

As he probed her mouth with his tongue, he heard the strains of some familiar theme music creeping into his subconscious through the walls. He realized that time was getting short, and he hadn't had a good fuck in a while, so he would give her a rain check for getting it in her face the next time. He was very horny now. His wife had been either too tired or just not in the mood lately.

He spread her legs apart as he quickly pulled on a rubber. Then he entered her, pumping all his frustrations and pent-up energy.

Unfortunately, he couldn't wait more than a few seconds. "Oooh, good . . . yes . . . yes . . ." Robert shouted as he shot his load.

Shit, why can't that asshole next door turn down that television? Robert thought as he tried to catch his breath. Then it hit him what he had been hearing: *The Young and the Restless*. Damn, he had a client on that show. Fuckin' shit, he realized, that meant it was probably way after twelve. Cocktails had already started a half-hour ago. Oh, shit.

"See you later, toots," Robert said as he hurriedly climbed off her, playfully slapping her on her bare ass. He pulled his pants up, then grabbed his coat and tie and started running out the door.

She ran into the hallway after him, waving a small hand towel around in a wild frenzy. Breathing hard, her big breasts bouncing up and down, she called out angrily. "Hey, Bobby, stop! You can't go yet. Didn't John tell you about my fee?"

Standing in front of the elevator, Robert started digging through his pockets. He'd never hear the end of it from John if he fucked up and didn't pay her. He threw her some hundred-dollar bills.

"Here, buy yourself a bigger towel," he joked as the elevator door opened.

A well-dressed woman got out as he went inside. Robert paid no attention to the shocked look on the woman's face as she watched Ginger scooping up the money. He pressed the button and the elevator door closed. It was time to play loving husband again.

As Mistica Baron and her stepbrother, Stephen, came

down the Century Plaza escalator, they looked around the huge reception area at the hundreds of people milling around. The room was packed with the familiar Hollywood faces and their familiar talk. As was typical of Stephen, he waved to someone in the distance, then made a mad dash into the throng, leaving Mistica to fend for herself. Damn him, she thought, pouting. It was just like him to abandon her like this. He probably felt he had already done his part by just bringing her.

But today Mistica would shine with or without Stephen by her side. Screw him. She lifted her chin and pushed out her chest. Once she got past the first hello, she'd be all right. Let him be weird on his own. She'd know how to play her part well today.

With her pretend straight-vodka cocktail in hand—plain water with a twist of lime—Mistica, feeling hot in her tight-fitting banana-yellow tube dress, began to move slowly through the famous and want-to-be-famous crowd with her usual ease. She knew from experience when to laugh at their corny jokes, as well as when to look concerned—like over a lost deal or a lost love. She had been to so many of these luncheons over the years with her dad, she could say hello to everyone with her eyes practically closed.

"Mr. Wasserman, nice to see you," Mistica called out, waving to MCA's legendary studio head as he chatted to smiling producer Thom Mount.

"Cher, your hair looks lovely."

Mistica swung around and a boyish Steven Spielberg hugged her. She grabbed his arm, and with a twinkle in her eye, asked, "When are you going to direct a film for my dad's studio?"

He laughed. Even Spielberg found Mistica Baron hard to resist. "When you tell me how you got the name of Mistica," he quipped.

Mistica took up his challenge. "Dad named me Miriam after his grandmother, but I never liked it," she began, pausing to take a sip of her drink. How she had hated that religious-sounding name. She had wanted to be free and independent, not some old woman. "Then one day when I was in high school, I read a book about the mystic, free-spirited sixties, and that's where I got my name."

"Hi, Steven. Oh, Mistica . . ."

Mistica turned around as producer Sherry Lansing ran up to them and gave both of them a quick hug and kiss on the cheek. Moving toward Warner Brothers' boss Bob Daly, Spielberg whispered his answer to Mistica.

"You look terrific today, Mistica," Sherry said sincerely. "Is Jake around?"

"Thanks, Sherry," she answered, hoping to divert her question. She wasn't even sure herself where her dad had been the past few days. Fortunately, Sherry's producing partner, Stanley Jaffe, entered the room at that moment and she ran off to join him.

Suddenly Stephen came up behind his stepsister. He must have noticed the high-level power people surrounding her. Now Mistica was important again. She tried to casually ignore Stephen's presence. She was doing just fine, thank you, on her own.

"Mistica, please," Stephen growled, "aren't you going to talk to me? And by the way, where in the hell is Dad? He's been gone over a week already."

Mistica eyed him curiously. This was the second time today he had brought it up. Why was it so important to him?

"There's Bette talking to Eisner," he said, already halfway across the room again. "I think I'll join them." Mistica wanted to ask him why he was so concerned about their dad, but he was already gone.

"Mistica Baron, how do you feel about Kelly's honor today?" a beaming Mary Hart of *Entertainment Tonight* asked as she shoved a mike in front of her.

"We're all very happy for Kelly," Mistica said with a big grin at the *E.T.* hostess. She kept smiling, trying to stand up taller in her new high-heeled suede pumps.

"She's a wonderful person and very deserving of this honor," she finished, although she didn't mean a word of it. She had long been jealous of the way her father confided in Kelly and not in her.

"Thanks," Mary Hart said, cutting Mistica off abruptly as she saw her main target across the room. "There's Kelly. C'mon guys."

Mistica watched as Mary Hart and her crew joined the other news media surrounding today's guest of honor. She had to admit to herself that Kelly looked beautiful and confident as always. Mistica bit her lower lip in frustration. She might as well admit it: she was only Jake Baron's daughter and nothing more. And all the hugs and kisses were because of her dad's status, not hers. She needed a real drink now. She turned around and headed for the bar.

"Do you believe the movie industry is doing all it can to help the environment?" Mary Hart asked Kelly.

The pretty president of Constellation thought a moment, then paused as she saw Robert's partners, Sol and Melinda, coming down the escalator. She lost her concentration as she noticed Robert wasn't with them. Where could he be?

Suddenly she realized she was still on camera. She tried to smile as she continued: "Uh, I'm sure the movie industry will stand behind any projects to protect our natural resources—"

Geoffrey approached his boss, interrupting her.

"Excuse me, Kelly, I have an important message . . ."

"From Robert?" she asked hopefully when the newswoman had retreated.

Geoffrey leaned closer to her ear and whispered. "No, it's from Mr. Baron."

Kelly felt her heart stop. Jake must have some news. "What is it, Geoffrey? What did he say?"

"He had intended to surprise you and be here today," Geoffrey said, pushing his hair above his forehead as his eyes darted around the room to make sure no one could overhear him. "But something came up and he caught an early flight from Kennedy to Chicago instead." He looked at Kelly for a confirmation of the message, but he asked no questions. That was also part of his job.

Kelly pulled on her earrings nervously. Jake's message could mean only one thing, she hoped: he was onto something positive from an investor.

"Thanks, Geoffrey," she said, her eyes wandering around the room. Suddenly she felt elated and angry at the same time: Robert was finally coming down the escalator.

Something stopped her from giving in to her first impulse of running over to him. Sure, she was glad to see him, but there was something about the look on his face that troubled her.

Robert quickly hurried over to her. "Kel, you look sensational. How's it going?" he asked as he kissed his wife on both cheeks.

Kelly stiffened for a moment, then warmed to his familiar touch as she stood close to him. She could smell the scent of his cologne as he hugged her. He looked happy to see her. She must have been imagining that look on his face.

"Thanks, Robert, it's been very hectic," she said, reaching for his hand. "Where have you been?"

He squeezed her hand and kissed her again. "Well, I'm here now, Kel, and you don't have anything to . . ." he said, his voice trailing off as he led her toward the cocktail bar. Then he saw Alan Ladd Jr. "Laddie, let's do lunch sometime soon," he called out.

As Robert stopped to chat with Disney Chairman Jeff Katzenberg for a few minutes, Kelly was again surrounded by people, congratulating her all at once: Dr. Armand Hammer, Oprah Winfrey, Sigourney Weaver, Whoopi Goldberg, and Tom Selleck, as well as Roseanne Barr and Marcy Carsey. Kelly smiled and said thank you so many times she thought she'd never be able to smile again. But beneath her beautiful smile, she was still troubled by Robert's late appearance.

Robert didn't waste any time working the crowd along with her, complimenting the lovely ladies surrounding him. "Seems like everyone who's important is here," he said in a low voice to Kelly. She nodded. "Everyone but Jake," he whispered, chuckling as he grabbed her around the waist.

Kelly was about to rise to Jake's defense when she realized that she had to keep mum. "Jake has been traveling around, trying to work out some advance publicity for *Criminal Intent*," she answered lightly.

Robert eyed her closely—his wife had always been terrible at lying—but he said nothing. He knew that Jake had his lackeys to do his advance work. Kelly took advantage of the situation to change the subject as the lights blinked on and off. The luncheon was ready to begin.

"C'mon, Robert, they'll be opening the doors in a minute," she said, holding his arm tightly.

Moments later, Wendy St. John said emotionally to Kelly, "I'm proud to be doing your introduction today." Seated to Kelly's right on the fifty-person dais, Wendy had always been Kelly's number-one choice for the honor. The two of them had long been close friends, ever since they had met at one of Kelly's charity affairs. Wendy was a board member of the Ecological Media Organization—the group that was honoring Kelly.

Amid the noisy chatter of the bigshots sitting around them, Wendy went on, "Kel, you've become a great credit to the entertainment industry." Tears dotted the corners of her eyes as she leaned over and impulsively hugged her friend. She quickly composed herself. "I'm really proud to know you."

Kelly winked at her, thanking her modestly.

As they chatted about Wendy's recent trip to the Orient, Kelly excitedly looked around at the other guests sitting with them on the four-tier dais. Robert was at her left. Sherry Lansing was seated two places away from her. Columbia's Dawn Steel sat next to

Michael Fuchs of HBO. Madonna and Shirley MacLaine up on the side of the second tier. Barbra Streisand was laughing with Mayor Bradley. Governor Deukmajian was directly above her, next to Bette Midler and CAA's Ron Meyer. Disney's Michael Eisner, Fox's Barry Diller, CAA's Mike Ovitz, ICM's Jeff Berg, Triad's John Kimble, William Morris' Norman Brokaw, and APA's Marty Klein filled the remaining tiers.

Kelly, now preoccupied with her acceptance speech, pulled out her notes from her purse and scanned them, trying not to think of the one person missing from the dais. She prayed that Jake was having good luck.

Suddenly, out of the corner of her eye she noticed Rose Kaufman waving frantically to her from the wings. Robert's antennae went up as he sensed something was amiss. He grabbed her hand as she started to get up from the table. "Stay here, Kel, I'll find out what she wants." He left the dais quickly.

Sitting at his Constellation table, in the center of the room, Stephen also noticed something was going on at the corner of the stage. He threw down his napkin. And hurriedly joined Robert and Rose.

Kelly watched the three of them huddled together. She wished she could hear what they were saying, especially because Rose looked like she was about to burst into tears.

Robert looked back at Kelly, his face starting to pale. Even Stephen appeared to be sweating. Kelly couldn't stand it any longer. She excused herself from Wendy and joined them.

"What is it? What's happening?" she asked rapidly.

"It's nothing we can't handle. Go back to your seat, Kelly," Robert said too urgently.

"Is it Jake? Tell me, please," Kelly pleaded as she suddenly felt cold. She couldn't bear it if anything had happened to him.

"No, it isn't Jake. Now, go back to your seat."

Stephen interrupted as his nervous twitch started acting up again. He loosened his tie. "She can't,

Zinman. They'll tear her apart in seconds, once they hear the news. We have to get her out of here."

Kelly was dumbfounded. What was going on? She had never seen her cool-and-confident husband look so upset; and Stephen seemed to be beside himself. She couldn't stand the suspense any longer.

"Who will tear me apart? Why? What's happening? Why can't you tell me what's going on?"

Robert looked directly at her with a pathetic stare. "Why don't we go to one of the side rooms where we can discuss this privately?" he said, putting his arm around Kelly's shoulders protectively.

Kelly sensed that whatever was happening, Robert was probably right. She didn't question him any further. As she walked between Robert and Stephen, with Rose following, Kelly saw many of the fifteen hundred people staring at them curiously.

Her heart was racing faster as she walked out of the room.

4

Takashima, with Noda following behind, entered a small, crowded office near the front of the Juraku-dai Club after pushing the right combination of black buttons on the side wall. The unobtrusive store room—neatly stacked with books, paintings, and draperies—was a diversion for a hidden wall safe.

Noda closed the door behind them, then double-locked it.

Asano, Takashima's managing director of business affairs, bowed to his superior and said, "Takashima-san, *konban-wa*." A highly nervous man, with eyes that seemed to disappear underneath his heavily furrowed brow, was hunched over a big marble table. He was not happy with his latest assignment: he was in charge of removing large amounts of untaxed cash from Takashima's many pachinko parlors. This money would be divided up and delivered to members of the ruling Liberal Democratic Party. It was the traditional way a businessman like Takashima remained in good favor with the political hierarchy.

Asano knew that these donations were important to Takashima's public mask of respectability. The untaxed money, or dangerous money, as the Japanese media dubbed it, was expected by the politicians. Whether they used it as donations for funerals or weddings or even for their own personal needs, it was all tied to *giri*. Duty.

"I am ready, Takashima-san," Noda said after quickly wiping his right hand clean.

Silently Takashima, then Noda, using their right thumbprints as identification, triggered the secret combination that unlocked the hidden safe.

When the safe opened, Noda took large amounts of yen from the rear of the safe. Asano then divided the money into stacks of one million yen and put them into pristine white envelopes.

Asano nervously handed them to Takashima for his verification. He never knew when his boss would check his count, and if he erred, he would personally be held responsible for making up the difference.

"*Yoi desu*," Takashima said, his eyes flashing with excitement. He handed the stack of envelopes back to Asano.

Asano nodded, then placed some zippered black velvet bags in the middle of the table. Noda picked up each bag and stuffed an envelope into it. They were now ready to be delivered.

Takashima lit another cigarette as soon as the one he was smoking went out. Turning to his foster son, he said, "Noda-san, we are ready to go to America."

Kelly looked at the blur of concerned faces staring down at her. She could see Robert's handsome face, along with Stephen's, Rose's, and others she couldn't quite make out. She closed her eyes quickly, wishing she could blot out the whole damn mess. She still couldn't believe this was happening to her.

She had almost fainted after seeing the glaring headlines of the afternoon papers. She felt like she had been kicked in the stomach a few times. Only her anger and outrage had helped her keep up her courage, but now there was a constant throbbing in her head that wouldn't stop.

"Ooh, my head," she uttered, her voice a small whisper. She just wished the pain would stop, but even if it did, there was a pain of another kind that would never go away. She had buried it years ago and now it had come back to hurt her again. This time, she wasn't sure if she could survive it.

Rose joined her on the couch and applied a cool cloth to her forehead. Seeing Kelly's face drawn and lined with worry, the older woman said soothingly, "This'll help, sweetie."

"How could they do this?" Kelly questioned no one in particular. Her voice was high-pitched, disbelieving. "How?"

Robert took her hand and gently caressed it. He had been shocked by the news story, rekindling an old wound that he and Kelly had forgotten about long ago. But always two steps ahead of a problem, Robert was already working on an angle to use it to Kelly's benefit.

"We just can't sit here and ignore this pile of shit," Stephen commented hotly, pointing to the afternoon papers. "There's a lot at stake here."

"Hold it, Stephen," Robert responded. "If Kelly leaves now, it will be an admission of guilt. She's got to face this crowd."

"But it's my decision to decide what's best for the studio, and Kelly represents the studio," Stephen said coldly. With Jake gone, he was in charge.

"Calm down, Stephen, no one's challenging you or your authority," Robert said evenly. He put his arm on Stephen's shoulder in a paternal manner, but Stephen wasn't about to take any bullshit from him, not when his own neck was also on the line.

Before Stephen could answer, there was a soft knock on the door. It was Wendy. Robert's partners, Sol and Melinda, along with Cynthia and Max, were behind her.

Wendy looked apprehensive. "What's wrong, Kelly? Is there anything I can do?"

Kelly tried to smile. "Thanks, Wendy, but I'm not sure," she said, handing her one of the newspapers. Wendy read the headlines while Cynthia and Max looked over her shoulder. Kelly knew by the looks on their faces that this was the last thing they had ever expected.

Stephen cleared his voice, then began his lawyer spiel. "Kelly is not speaking to anyone until we have time to prepare our statement for the press. And Rose will be the designated spokesperson."

Wendy ignored Stephen's pompous remark, trying instead to cheer her up. She took her hand. "Don't let this upset you, Kelly. What I said before, I really meant. You're a real credit to the entertainment industry. Don't you ever forget that."

Kelly clasped her friend's hand tightly. That was all she needed to hear. Wendy was right. Whatever she had done in the past was over, finished. She had paid her debt with hard work and sacrifice. Years of charitable work and her steadfast dedication to the studio spoke for themselves.

Her mind was made up. She took the damp cloth off her forehead and took a big breath. Holding on to Robert for support, she stood up.

"It's time for me to put an end to this once and for all," Kelly said with as much confidence as she could muster.

She turned to Wendy while grabbing a mirror to fix her face. "Get ready to introduce me, Wendy," she said in a clear voice. "I'm going on."

Jake bucked the Chicago wind as he walked down Michigan Avenue, an investment banker on either side of him. His cheeks were raw from the wintry blast off the lake, but he didn't even feel the cold. He was too excited.

"That's right, Mr. Baron, the deal is set."

Jake nodded. Best news he'd had in months. And it was just in time.

He ran his hand over the lower part of his face, covered with stubble. He hadn't shaved since yesterday morning. Even though he felt great, he knew he looked lousy. He dug his hands deeper into his thin coat pockets.

"When do we finalize the deal?" he asked, trying to keep the anticipation out of his voice.

"Within a couple of days, Mr. Baron, we'll have the papers drawn up," the second banker answered as the trio approached Marshall Field. The windows of the department store were illuminated with La Belle France decor. "The Italian investor was clear in his instructions."

Jake stopped and eyed the two men closely. "You're sure this Italian knows I have no intention of selling out? That this is strictly a money loan, preferably long-term?"

The other banker spoke slowly. "Quite sure, Mr. Baron. Our client simply wants to become an investor in Constellation, nothing more."

Jake nodded, satisfied. He needed this loan, but he didn't need it badly enough to lose control of Constellation. That was his greatest fear. After all, the studio was his whole life.

Jake picked up the pace as the trio entered the office building and took the elevator up to the bankers' offices on the top floor.

He hoped he was doing the right thing. There was so much foreign investment going on in the country right now, he wasn't exactly happy with being part of it, but what other choice did he have? Constellation wouldn't get out of its negative cash flow until after the success of *Criminal Intent*.

In more than sixty years of operations, the studio had never come this close to packing it all in. And it never would again; not if he could help it. The future of the studio meant more to him than anything else. With plans to reestablish a full television department, and with Kelly attracting more creative talent for their feature department, Jake had great hopes for Constellation in the next decade.

". . . and now, ladies and gentlemen, on behalf of the

Ecological Media Organization, I have the distinct honor and privilege of introducing our first annual Humanitarian Award recipient, the president of Hollywood's legendary studio Constellation: Kelly Kristopher."

As Wendy St. John finished her introduction, Kelly stepped to the mike. She handed the plaque that had just been presented to her back to Wendy. She kept her head high as she smiled to the many people loudly clapping. Even so, it was obvious from the loud whispers that the headline story had already begun to circulate the tables. She wouldn't back down, though.

"Ladies and gentlemen . . ." she began. There was a hush as she cleared her throat. They were anxiously waiting to hear what she would say.

Kelly was trembling as she put her sweat-glazed hands on the sides of the podium. As she thanked Wendy St. John for her kind words of introduction, she looked back at the dais. The people she dealt with every day: Spielberg, Ovitz, Brokaw, Berg. She couldn't stop now.

"I had a speech prepared," Kelly began, holding up her many note cards and trying to keep her hand from shaking, "but something has happened to change things."

With a deep breath she continued, "Some of you may have already become aware of this . . ." She held the afternoon edition of the *L.A. Times* high enough for everyone to see while she read aloud: "STUDIO PRESIDENT INVOLVED IN SEX SCANDAL WITH JUDGE."

The room, filled to capacity with more than fifteen hundred people, instantly became deadly silent. No one moved as Kelly read some excerpts, including the fact that this judge had recently been arrested for pandering and how he sold his entire kiss-and-tell story to *The National Enquirer*.

She fought back tears as she continued: "According to this story, about fifteen years ago, this judge allegedly gave me money for . . . nights of companionship.

But that's not the whole story." She ignored the frantic whispering, the shocked faces. Now was the time to reveal her secret.

Her throat was tight, and she could feel the tears welling in her eyes, but she continued: "With your indulgence, the real story began many years ago, in the summer of 1962, when I first came to California from Texas with my mother. I was six years old. On the rodeo circuit, Mama had more than her share of troubles, especially when her cowboy fiancé, my father, was killed in an accident. She stayed in Amarillo after I was born and supported us by selling perfume at a fancy department store. But Mama always dreamed about going to California. Then she met a man who claimed to be a Hollywood talent agent, and we hitched a ride with him in his red Cadillac convertible. Mama found us a one-room apartment, and the talent agent got her a part as an extra in a film over at Fox." She paused.

Her eyes panned the audience as she went on; they were listening to every word. "Things were rough in those years. Working as an extra just barely made the rent, so Mama got a job as a waitress. That's when her drinking started. It was just a couple of beers at first, but then it became a way of life for her."

Kelly felt the tears rushing down her face. Wendy stood up and handed her a tissue. As she dabbed her eyes, she wasn't sure if she could go on. She took a couple of moments to compose herself, then continued.

"After high school, I got a scholarship to a local college and worked part-time in an entertainment law office, typing contracts, answering the phones. I wanted to get an education, as well as hands-on experience in the film industry."

Kelly paused to take a sip of ice water to soothe her dry throat. "Mama had a recurring role on a soap by then, but I was so busy with school and work, I didn't know she was missing more and more days of work. Then one day she collapsed on the set. First came the long stay at the hospital, then the long rehabilitation at the nursing home."

Kelly brushed away a couple of tears. "I was in my last year of college, but I had to quit and work overtime at the law firm to pay the bills. Even that wasn't enough when Mama required an operation. We didn't have any medical insurance and I needed a lot of money quickly, so . . ."

Sweating, Stephen wiped his forehead in the air-conditioned ballroom. He left the table inconspicuously —making up some phony story for Mistica—and went to the hotel lobby. Kelly didn't seem to notice his departure.

". . . and I had met Judge Wilton socially a couple of times through my employer, but I didn't know he had taken a liking to me until he invited me aboard his private yacht moored in the harbor. He said he needed a companion to talk to; he said his marriage was in disarray. When I told him about my mother and that she had no insurance, he insisted on lending me some money. I was reluctant to take it at first, but I discovered that he often helped out other young women in need of money. As Mama's hospital and nursing-home bills continued to climb, he insisted on helping me. I took the extra money, although I considered it a loan. I should have realized that it wouldn't stop there, but I didn't."

She suddenly paused. Her pulse was racing so fast she couldn't get her breath. She finally found her voice. "I didn't know until later what kind of payment the judge demanded from anyone he helped. . . ."

Kelly closed her eyes, trying to blot out the memory of that night with the judge, when he had grabbed her and tried to make love to her—his smooth lips kissing her face, her breasts, his clammy hands boldly searching her flesh, his vacant eyes stripping her of her dignity.

She had pushed him away, refusing to have anything to do with him. She had assured him she would pay back all the loans, but he wouldn't listen. He didn't want his money back. He said he had a whole stable of impressionable young women who needed money and were desperate enough to act as hostesses and sexual partners for his friends. The other women in his "harem," as he called it, were more than willing to go to bed with him. He screamed she was a fool and indicated that he had photos of them together. He kept repeating that no one had ever refused him, and she wasn't going to be the first.

Kelly was now ready to collapse on stage. Her head was spinning and she felt weak at the knees. She gripped the sides of the lectern so tightly her hands turned white. She finished her story, giving as few details as possible about her relationship with the judge. Even though she didn't sleep with him, she did spend a lot of time with him—her only way to help her mother at the time. She had tried to pay back the money over the past few years, but the judge wouldn't even speak to her.

"I've made a contribution in this industry that I'm very proud of. Maybe I've made some mistakes along the way, but I'm still here. And I intend to be here for a long time. But I didn't do it alone.

"Without my boss, Jake Baron, who gave me my biggest opportunity to prove myself, I wouldn't be here today. Thanks, Jake." Then she looked over to her right. "Thank you, Robert, my supportive husband." Now cracking her first smile, she added, "And I'd like to thank the two women who never stopped giving me encouragement along the way, my dear friends with the 'major hair,' as all the columns say: Sherry Lansing and Dawn Steel."

Sherry and Dawn stood up and took a bow to the applause of the audience—both clapping their support for Kelly—then gave the stage back to her.

"In conclusion, let me say that I've never done anything I'm ashamed of—then or since," Kelly said, keeping her voice even. "All I ask, friends and colleagues, is that you judge me on my record. I believe it speaks for itself. Thank you all so very much. I'm truly honored to have been your award recipient today."

Exhausted, she took a step back from the lectern. She struggled not to collapse, although she could barely keep her balance. Then she heard something drumming loudly in her ears. My God, she realized, it's applause. A big smile slowly came to her lips. She couldn't believe it; the whole audience was on its feet, clapping and shouting her name.

She held her head up and stood tall. She felt like she had left the pain of those years behind her for the first time.

Robert grabbed her and gave her a hug and a kiss.

Everyone on the dais started to crowd around her—kissing her on the cheek, hugging her. She was heartened by their response, but the tightness in her throat remained. She knew that her life had changed today. She hoped she would become a better person for it, but she wasn't through yet. There was one more thing she had to do.

She glanced around at the celebrated people crowding her, but she missed the one person who wasn't there.

She had to talk to Jake.

The ringing of the phone startled the sleeping hotel guest. His head was still groggy as he answered with: "Yeah?"

"Sorry to interrupt you, Mr. Baron. This is the hotel operator. I have a Miss Kristopher calling long distance. She says it's urgent. May I put her through?"

"Yeah, sure."

"Go ahead, please. . . ."

"Kelly, hi. What's wrong?" Jake listened quietly, the horror on his face growing as her words hit him like hot lead. All he could think about was getting back to L.A. as quickly as possible.

"Sweetheart, calm down. I'll see you in my office at eleven tomorrow morning. . . . I'm proud of you. . . . Yeah, I miss you too. Now, go home and get some rest."

He hung up slowly, his hand trembling slightly as the news sank in. Kelly had turned to him in her time of need, and he wouldn't let her down. He lay back on the hotel bed and stared up at the wallpapered ceiling, letting memories of her swirl in his head. . . .

He felt his heart begin to race as he reflected on the first day he had seen her. He had rushed over to Stephen's office with an idea that couldn't wait. He believed that Constellation was missing out on an up-and-coming phenomenon and new potential revenue for the coming decade of the eighties: turning best-selling novels into mini-series for television. One of the biggest books of 1976, *Roots*, had just gone into production. He wanted Stephen to check into it pronto and see what prices were involved in tying up books for television.

He had forgotten all about it, though, when Stephen's beautiful new legal assistant walked in. He felt like he had been knocked out in the first round. She was wearing a prim-looking blue suit that only accentuated her slim figure. His eyes roamed down to her slender legs, then up to her long strawberry-blond hair, hanging in wisps around her pretty face. He hadn't been able to believe his luck when he had seen his interest returned in her eyes. But he had decided to play it cool.

That's when she had taken matters into her own hands. Thinking that he was divorced, as one of her friends had whispered to her—rather than separated—she had arranged to "accidentally" bump into him. Acting on a tip, she had shown up at the posh Beverly Hills club PIPS, where he played in a backgammon tourney every Tuesday night. He was currently reigning champ; nobody could beat him except, on occasion, the former house champ, Lucille Ball. Smiling, he recalled that Kelly had bumped into him, splashing his Scotch all over his jacket. All of a sudden he was looking at the knockout legal assistant from his stepson's office. After realizing that she must have a lot of chutzpah to want to meet him that badly, he had asked her to meet him the next day at his studio commissary.

As Jake stretched in bed, he continued smiling. The little vixen had shown some nerve going after him like that.

Then he remembered the first night that Kelly had really needed him. They had gone down to the Santa Monica Pier, where they played some carnival games, walked along the beach, and looked at the moon rising in the night sky. It had been chilly for late April, but the romantic fire between them simmered as they rode on the carousel, getting dizzier and dizzier as the calliope played.

During the last ride of the evening, he remembered he had kissed her tenderly and been surprised to feel her respond to him with a warm passion of her own. That was all he needed.

For the first time, they had made love that night. Kelly had been so scared. Her mother had recently passed away and she had needed someone to be her special friend. She had wanted to believe that he was that friend, but soon after, she had become very insecure, afraid it might never be the same again between them.

Indeed, soon thereafter it wasn't, but not because of that. That same week Kelly had learned the truth about Jake's entanglement with his second wife. She had been devastated. She absolutely refused to continue seeing him as a married man.

Not long afterward, Jake had heard about Kelly's quickie marriage—definitely on the rebound from him—to the young William Morris movie agent Robert Zinman.

Along with the rest of the industry during the next

few years, and unfortunately from the sidelines, Jake had watched her work her way up the show-business ladder through a succession of studio positions.

She had become more sophisticated along the way, learning how to dress, speak, and handle meetings, and most important, how to pick hit movies. She had become the one exec that every studio always wanted.

He had always thanked his lucky stars that he'd succeeded in getting Kelly to run Constellation. He had idly hoped he'd get Kelly to run his life as well, but that was wishful thinking.

Until now. Kelly had turned to him again.

"Kelly, everything will be all right. I'll make it all right," he whispered harshly into the darkness, his voice echoing the past memory.

It was a long time before he fell back to sleep.

Only the sound of the west wind could be heard blowing through the red wooden columns as Takashima and his small entourage passed through the *torii*, the sacred gateway, to the Temple of the Golden Pavilion in the ancient city of Kyoto. They could see the three-story pavilion, covered entirely in gold foil, up ahead. He stopped as he eyed the golden phoenix mounted on the roof and grunted in pleasure. This temple was an especially fitting one for him to visit before he left for America. The shogun Yoshimutsu had built it as a retirement villa, where he completed his days in extravagant luxury. Takashima had a similar plan in mind for himself.

The early-morning sunshine cast long shadows behind them as they stopped at the ablution basin to rinse their hands and mouths. First the master, then the Yakuza followed, and last, Chisako.

Once inside the sanctuary, they all clapped their hands three times to get the attention of the *kami*, the spirits of the gods of the shrine. Takashima was certain their prayers would be answered. He believed strongly in the old tradition that the early morning was the best time for prayer.

He bowed his head. The others did the same. They all prayed silently for the health of the ailing Emperor Hirohito. When Takashima signaled to Chisako, she stepped forward and left an offering of rice and money wrapped up in fancy paper and tied with red and white string. She bowed reverently, then returned to her place behind the praying Yakuza.

As they fanned away the smoke from the burning incense, Takashima looked up into the shapeless blaze of light overhead. He was certain the sun goddess, Amaterasu, would bless their venture. Thinking about his momentary departure, he then continued praying.

Especially for his success.

5

Takashima gazed out at the skyline. The view from his penthouse suite of offices at 1901 Avenue of the Stars pleased him very much. He could even see the Pacific Ocean from his west window. Up the street, the new Fox Plaza with its elegant architecture shadowed the sprawling Century Plaza Hotel. He could look down many stories below him and clearly make out the walking bridge, not to mention the numerous office buildings across the street, like the Twin Towers, peeking above the ABC Entertainment complex. And there was none of the smog this day that he had heard so much about. There was no doubt, as Stephen Resnick had informed him: "Century City is the hottest piece of real estate from the Pacific Ocean to Beverly Hills."

Along with his small entourage, he had entered the U.S. via his Hawaiian immigration contact, like his dozen or so Yakuza, who had preceded them over the past weeks. He wanted his group, as well as himself, to first blend in with the tourists before they all flew on his private jet into Los Angeles.

But with such a recent flow of his questionable associates—all through Hawaii—Takashima was informed to his displeasure that he would have to pay a higher bribe to the inspector so he would not become disenchanted with the scheme.

Takashima ignored the steady rhythm of banging, interspersed with the grating sound of hydraulic drilling, as he walked around inspecting his new high-rise offices. He had even chosen not to notice the fine layer of dust on everything he touched. Learning how to deal with adversity was part of his discipline.

He had immediately hired a complete staff of Japanese secretaries and assistants to fill the many offices that occupied half of the top floor, for he wanted to be operational right away.

The Asian Octopus had just begun to set up his American shop, but it didn't take the town long to discover his presence. The Hollywood trades, the *Los Angeles Times*, and the *Wall Street Journal* all mentioned his arrival as well as his fifteen-billion-dollar net worth somewhere in their stories. Hollywood was very hungry for the new development money that a Japanese businessman like Hiroshi Takashima could provide.

Already he was fast becoming the most popular luncheon guest around town. He was on everybody's list. He had an upcoming luncheon meeting scheduled with Disney's Jeff Katzenberg, then an afternoon appointment with NBC's Brandon Tartikoff. Tonight he was to be the dinner guest of Barry Diller of Rupert Murdoch's Fox Corporation.

Everything was moving according to plan. With his move to Southern California, he was now ready to start the final phase of his revenge.

He closed his eyes and tried to concentrate, but the sounds in the background began to irritate his tranquillity. He had refused to stop conducting business while construction work was still going on.

He opened his eyes and stared at the Yakuza supervising the workmen as they brought in several *shinpaku*, or juniper trees, for his garden, as well as hundreds of *suiseki* stones to create various illusions of nature. He knew this was the main reason for the noise in the next office, where the floor was being ripped up and the indoor garden was being planted.

However, the scraping and dragging made by the

workmen was nothing compared to the babbling of the frivolous French decorator that Resnick had recommended to decorate the offices. He could still hear her in the next office ranting between French and her broken English to her assistant about *quel élégance, quel style*, and other such nonsense. He had decided to completely ignore them and go back to dictating his confidential memo to the members of his Takashima Group.

His newly hired Japanese secretary, sitting in front of him with her pad and pencil, bowed her head low, hoping for the best. No one knew if he would accept the commotion or just explode at anyone in sight.

Hearing a gentle knock on the half-open door, he motioned for his secretary to open it all the way. Now he had to stop in the middle of dictating a memo to regain his *wa*. Harmony was always important to him.

"Takashima, with your permission, I am going house-shopping today," Chisako said, entering his office, her dimpled smile bright with excitement. Then, remembering her duty, she bowed low in his presence, sustaining her position of obedience for several seconds.

He ignored the unexpectedness of her visit, more intrigued by her rounded cleavage peeping above the skintight red latex designer dress she wore. With her hard nipples piercing through the material, and her very high black heels, her slim body was clearly revealed to him. Her long hair was pulled off to one side and flowed down her bare shoulder like a seductive serpent. He could feel his penis throbbing; he wanted her. He already imagined her naked at his feet here in his office, but he showed patience. There would be a better time later.

"Good morning, Mr. Takashima," a woman's voice said, interrupting his fantasy. Her low, husky tones grated on his ears.

For the first time he noticed the other woman with Chisako. He looked at her outrageous appearance, his sense of symmetry greatly disturbed. She wore a form-fitting yellow miniskirt to show off her good legs, even though she was well into her forties. Her long, stringy blond hair looked like a wig, and bright makeup and noisy bracelets completed her unusual look. She looked like an aging peacock, well past her prime.

"Eileen Singer, Mr. Takashima," the woman said, extending her hand toward him.

Takashima bowed so slightly that even to a westerner it was obviously an insult.

The woman, not in the least disturbed by his snub, retracted her hand. It was obvious the Japanese businessman had no idea who she was, even if everyone else in Beverly Hills did. Eileen Singer was the premier realtor on the West Side of town, known for her multimillion-dollar deals.

"Good day, Miss Singer. Now, if you'll excuse me, I am busy."

Known to do whatever it took to close a deal, Eileen Singer was unfazed. She had to admit she found Takashima's dark, exotic looks appealing, his broad-shouldered body very sexy, but he wasn't going to get away with his high-and-mighty attitude.

She slapped her handbag on his desk with a crack and grinned widely at him. "Mr. Takashima," she began sweetly, "Mr. Resnick assured me you were in the market for a couple of super houses." She emphasized the lawyer's name to get his attention.

The name worked. Takashima listened.

"You have something to show me?"

"I know a few estates for sale: one that once belonged to Robert Taylor when he was married to Barbara Stanwyck. There's another one in the Palisades . . ." She paused a moment to check her real-estate sheet. "And one on top of Mulholland with an absolutely spectacular view of the city. What do you think?"

Takashima, keeping his face expressionless while the woman finally finished talking, was now noticing her sexy legs as she sat down in a nearby chair. Although he was not interested in her physical pitch, he did listen to her business talk. It became obvious she knew what she was discussing.

No doubt she had earned a higher commission in Resnick's bed, as well as a few others. But it did not matter. As long as she did her job and found the houses he wanted, he would go along with it.

He smiled while he took a second look at her legs; her lace panties were showing now. As he bowed respectfully to the real-estate woman, he turned to Chisako. "I am sure Miss Singer will do her best to help us."

Chisako smiled, her pretty face lighting up with wondrous enthusiasm. "Thank you, Takashima-san."

Standing, Eileen Singer responded in her usual provocative manner. Her voice dripped with more than dollar signs. "I'll do anything I can for you, Mr. Takashima." She smiled widely, showing her perfectly capped teeth.

He ignored her obvious intent.

He was not interested in the American whore.

Jake sat in the window seat of the coach section of the United jet flying over the Los Angeles basin. But he didn't glance out at the city below. He was still pissed off that his plane had been delayed because of engine trouble. He continued to stare at the different newspapers spread out on his serving tray.

He read the *Wall Street Journal* story, quoting the judge from his now-famous first-person story that would appear in the next issue of *The National Enquirer*. He hadn't missed any opportunity to make Kelly look bad at every turn without actually coming out and saying it explicitly. What about those other women? Jake wondered irritably. His so-called "harem"? The fuckin' judge should be hung up by his balls for bringing her name into his dirty mess in the first place.

Kelly's photo continued to glare back at him. She was one beautiful, classy lady. He didn't for one moment believe she had done anything wrong. She had been just trying to help her mother. Too bad he hadn't known the fix Kelly was in after they had broken up. If he had, he would have advanced her the money without any strings.

The media, not surprisingly, were always harder on the women in these things. Somehow it was easier for a man to escape a mess like this. Some fast talk here, a quick deal there. Survival made a lot of people do things they regretted later on. And if she said there had been no "hanky-panky," Jake believed her. What was the big deal anyway? He smiled as he pondered why everyone always got so uptight about fucking. They all did it. A bunch of lousy hypocrites.

He had to get his mind off the whole sordid story. He wanted to rip apart those damn reporters as well. It was making him sick. He felt his blood pressure going up. His doctor had warned him about stress.

As he turned the pages of the newspaper, a curious item on the business page caught his attention: Sony again denied rumors about a takeover of Columbia. He crumpled up the paper in disgust. His blood suddenly grew cold. Those Japs were buying up everything. God help them if they ever tried to get their dirty fingers on his studio; it'd be World War II all over again. But this time, Jake thought, smiling, he'd Pearl Harbor them first.

"Uh, excuse me," his seatmate asked curiously, breaking into his thoughts, "do you know where Hollywood is down there?"

Surprised, Jake turned and looked at her.

The woman, in her late fifties, was dressed conservatively, with a wide-eyed look that never ages. He smiled. No doubt about it. A tourist.

"Well, let's see now," he said, rubbing his chin as he looked out the tiny window. He had no idea where Hollywood was from the air, but he pointed to a line of cars running up and down a long boulevard. "Right there, ma'am," he said so convincingly he almost believed it himself.

"Oh, it's just like I dreamed," the woman sighed, craning her neck to get a better view. She clasped her hands over her heart. "Hollywood," she sighed, almost spilling her orange juice on him.

As Jake looked out for noticeable landmarks, the plane flew over the Forum as it started to make its final approach. He wondered if he should point it out as well. Shit, she probably had never heard the names Kareem or Magic anyway.

"Have you ever met a movie star?" the woman asked, searching his face, hoping to see that magic aura of someone who has mingled with celebrities.

"A few," Jake answered as the wheels touched ground.

The woman started to question him further, but as the plane taxied over to the jetway, a voice on the cabin's P.A. system greeted the arriving passengers: "Ladies and gentlemen, welcome to Los Angeles. On behalf of the flight crew, we thank you for flying with United. The approximate local time is eleven A.M. and the temperature is a cool fifty-nine degrees . . ."

The woman looked around for Jake, but he was already halfway down the aisle.

Takashima looked at his watch as he finished dictating to his secretary. It was past noon. He had spent too much time earlier with Chisako and Miss Singer. He must move quickly.

He dismissed the secretary, then clapped his hands. Two Yakuza appeared at his side instantly. "I will be leaving shortly for a luncheon meeting at Langan's Brasserie." The bodyguards nodded, then left. Takashima buzzed his intercom, and a different secretary rushed to his side, bowing as she had been instructed, but a bit awkwardly.

"Has the agent from Creative Artists Agency arrived?" he asked, checking his watch.

"Yes, Mr. Takashima-san. He is waiting in the outer office." The girl checked her pad. "And Miss Mengers of William Morris is holding on the line." She looked up and said disbelieving, "She'll wait, no matter how long it takes."

Takashima merely smiled. Word did indeed get around that he was in town. However, he had more important business at hand. "Tell her I am busy until later this afternoon. She will have to call back."

He smiled at the girl, who continued to look at him curiously. "You have done a good job," he said sincerely.

The secretary was astounded at his complimentary smile. After all, another secretary had been fired just the day before for reacting too slowly to one of his commands. Unlike other Japanese, Takashima did not believe in lifetime employment. He did not tolerate anyone working for him who did not snap to attention the instant he called.

"Oh, thank you, Mr. Takashima . . . san, sir," she replied nervously.

She left his office, trying to walk backward and bow simultaneously. Suddenly she collided with the French decorator, bursting through the door at the same time.

"Shit," the woman cursed, then quickly composed herself when she noticed Takashima watching her. The embarrassed secretary disappeared quickly, fearing that Takashima's earlier kind words would turn to ones of rage.

"Ah, Monsieur Takashima," the woman said with a flourish, "I 'ave made beautiful feelings for you with my decorating." As she grabbed Takashima's arm, three Yakuza immediately surrounded her, one of them pushing her hand away while the other two stood defensively on either side of her. They made menacing obscene gestures in her face and grunted loudly.

The woman's face turned dead white. "What the fuck . . . ?" she cursed without her phony French accent.

Takashima signaled them to show restraint. He did not have any time for her now, but he was paying the woman to be there. With or without an accent, he did not care, as long as she did her job.

"I am ready, madame. *Allons.*"

Regaining her composure—and her accent—she took him into an empty office where samples of wallpaper were stacked up against the walls. There were no secretaries, no desks or computers, just a shelf with bowls of rice placed on top of it. In the middle of the room, surrounded by long, unwound rolls of wallpaper, the decorator's male assistant was in the process of dumping the rice into a trash bag.

"Can you believe this?" he grumbled in a singsong voice as they entered the office. "Some workers must have left their smelly old lunch in here." He held his nose delicately as he tossed the bowl into the bag as well.

Takashima felt the blood rushing to his face. He clenched his fists, trying not to lose his temper. This time he would not show restraint. The designer's effeminate assistant was desecrating his *kamidana*, or god shelf, by throwing out his rice offering.

Like most Japanese, Takashima always kept a small shrine in his office as well as in his home. Fervent in his beliefs, he followed both Shinto and Buddhism, although he had tried a couple of new religions, including Bosei-kyo, whose followers believed that sexual acts were primary healing agents. Takashima obviously enjoyed the advantages of that one.

Despite himself, though, he exploded, yelling the vilest Japanese curses he knew before switching to English. "Get out! Get out and never come back!" He banged the wall several times, and two Yakuza rushed in.

"But, Monsieur Takashima, there is so much more to do!" the French designer pleaded as the Yakuza grabbed her roughly by her suit collar, then dragged her and her assistant, by their long hair, out the door. "I 'ave such beautiful—" Takashima slammed the door behind them.

Ever since he had hired her, the woman and her assistant had cost him a fortune with her beautiful feelings. Good riddance.

Takashima returned to his office, seeking to regain his *wa*, but he was disappointed. The workmen were still banging on the walls and dragging their construction materials through the office. His secretaries were busy tapping at their computers. Two of his company men were on the international phone lines checking the Nikkei numbers in Tokyo. Only his cadre of Yakuza stood quietly at attention, waiting for his instructions. Frustrated, Takashima sat down at his desk. He closed his eyes and began to meditate. . . .

Suddenly a phone rang. It was not an ordinary ring, though, but a jerky, scratchy bell chime. Takashima immediately put his hand on the gold-plated receiver on his desk. He let it continue to ring. The few Japanese company men whom he had brought from Tokyo knew what to do. They immediately slammed down their phones without a word, bowed, and left the office. The Yakuza hustled out the workmen, as well as the secretaries. They looked bewildered, but asked no questions. Except one.

"But I've almost finished the report, Mr. Takashima, sir," his new number-two secretary moaned. A Yakuza merely picked her up and carried her out of the room over his shoulder like a sack of rice.

Takashima remained motionless as the phone continued to ring. Only when the room was completely cleared did he pick up the receiver of his secret phone.

"Moshi mosh' . . . ano-ne . . ." He listened. Suddenly his plans changed. He forgot about the luncheon meeting today and the CAA agent waiting for him. This required his urgent attention.

"Moichido itte kudasai," he said. Then he listened again. His Ronin no Zaibatsu had uncovered new information about his targeted movie studio. He could not wait. A menacing look came over his features. *"Boku-ni ikimashō."*

As he hung up the phone, he gave orders to his number-one secretary to set up an immediate meeting at his recently acquired Beverly Hills bank, while his number-two secretary was to reach Peter Guber. She was to explain to Guber that he could not make today's luncheon, with his sincerest regrets. Guber was someone that Takashima did not want to alienate.

He then left with his Yakuza through his private entrance, without another word.

"Are you sure you won't change your mind?" Jake asked, his back to her. Kelly had been in his office more than a half-hour, but he had barely looked at her in all that time. His pain was too great.

"No, Jake, I can't. I thought about it last night, and I've decided it's the best thing for Constellation." Kelly took a deep breath. She hated what she had to say. "I have no choice; I must resign immediately."

Kelly saw Jake's shoulders slump. She had never dreamed he would take it so hard. She had accepted it, why couldn't he?

Jake stared at the wall. Dammit, he thought, I don't want to lose her. There had to be another way. He remembered the first day she had walked into his office as president. Her green eyes had been shining with enthusiasm and excitement for the future. They had made such big plans for the studio, with the eagerness of two teenagers. And now she was leaving him.

She turned to face him, but he remained silent. Noticing how pale he looked, she began to pace nervously around his office. "Listen, Jake, you know this whole scandal with the judge wouldn't matter if I were a man. Remember your friend Begelman and the forged-check scandal at Columbia?"

Jake certainly did. The town had quickly forgotten the well-publicized scandal, when the former studio head had forged a check for ten thousand dollars and then tried to get away with it. He had gone on to become a very successful producer. But he was a man.

As Kelly stopped pacing, she continued: "You know how the business is, Jake. I'm a woman. If I get a run in my nylons, it's front-page news. It may not be fair, but that's the way it is." She stopped and looked up at him. Her expression begged him to listen. "I'm afraid that you could lose the support of your financial investor because of this, Jake. Please think about it."

Jake still didn't budge as he firmly requested, "I want you to stay, Kelly. Period."

Exasperated, she looked down at her watch. It was half-past one. "I've got to go, Jake. Robert is waiting."

Jake cursed under his breath. No matter what his personal feelings were, he knew she was probably right. Both the investor and the bankers could become sensitive about Kelly's adverse publicity. The future of Constellation was more important, and very much at stake now. He looked into her beautiful face, so full of pain. He realized it had taken a great deal of courage for her to face him and quit, but he still wasn't going to give in.

"Listen, Kelly, my dad always did things his way, and so do I. That's why I'm asking you to stay. Who gives a fuck what anybody in this town says? You're doing a hell of a job as our president, and that's all that counts."

Kelly had hoped to keep her composure, but now she began to cry. Damn, she thought, blinking furiously, he sure wasn't making it any easier. She took a big breath as she wiped her eyes with her hand. Crying wouldn't solve anything. "I have to leave, Jake, before people forget what a great studio this is."

"Dammit, Kelly, this is your home." Gently he put his hands on her shoulders. "Listen, why don't you take a leave of absence for a while? You know you can't just walk away from Constellation. Not now, not ever."

Kelly met Jake's gaze head-on. "You don't have to sell me on Constellation, Jake. I love it as much as you do. But I don't know if that's—"

Suddenly the buzzer on Jake's desk interrupted them. He pushed down the button as he raised his voice: "Paula, I told you to hold all my calls—"

"But it's Mistica," she said, the frustration in her voice coming across loud and clear. "She says it's important and won't take no for an answer."

Before Jake could take the call, he turned around to see Robert standing in the doorway of his office. He had come to say his piece, and neither Jake nor his wife was going to stop him.

"No one invited you, Zinman," Jake said, advancing around the desk.

"Jake, please, not now," Kelly begged.

"You'll listen to what I have to say, Baron, because you'll know I'm right." Robert stepped inside the office. "Kelly is front-page tabloid fodder right now," he stated flatly. "No matter what she does, she'll constantly be battered by the press. Every talk-show booker from Morton Downey to Geraldo Rivera already has his nose up his ass trying to get an exclusive interview for his show. She's hot."

"He's right, Jake," Kelly admitted. "I found a couple of reporters from *A Current Affair* hiding outside the studio this morning, trying to ambush me with their cameras and mikes. And this is only the afternoon after." She looked up at Jake for understanding. "Please, if I don't leave now, this kind of thing won't stop."

Jake started to put his arm around her to comfort her, but Robert stepped between them and put his hands protectively on Kelly's shoulders. "And that's nothing. There are half a dozen messages from different publishers on the answering machine down at the beach house, offering her book contracts," Robert said, squeezing her shoulders. She's mine, Baron, his look said.

Aloud he said: "Kelly needs time to think, to regroup. The story will never die if she doesn't step down now."

"You don't know what the fuck you're talking about, Zinman," Jake countered. "By staying on at the studio, Kelly will show them what she's made of."

"Don't listen to him, Kelly. I can see through his little game," Robert challenged. "He's willing to let you be dragged through the mud because of all the publicity you're bringing Constellation, not to mention the fact he can't run the studio without you."

"Jake," Kelly interrupted, "Robert doesn't mean it—"

Jake paid no attention to Kelly's plea. "You damn shit, Zinman, you're the worst kind of man there is. You're using your wife to front for you so you can make your underhanded deals. You're nothing but a double-dealing fuckin' sonofabitch—"

"Watch it, Baron," Robert said, stepping forward with his fist raised.

Jake didn't need much prodding. In his younger days he had brawled with much bigger men than Robert. "I'm ready, prick, anytime you are."

Panicking, Kelly stepped between them. "My God, you two, stop this!" she screamed. "You're both forgetting what's really at stake here."

Both Jake and Robert backed off as she continued, "For Christ's sake, Constellation needs a couple of hits right now. *Criminal Intent* could be completed in less than four months, but if there's any scandal attached, it may never be released. The whole ad campaign wouldn't be worth a damn."

Kelly couldn't bear for it to end this way. She looked back and forth at the two of them. She took Jake's arm. "Please, Jake. I just need some time to think things out."

She left the rest unsaid.

Robert tugged on her arm. "C'mon, Kel, the traffic's pretty bad on PCH this time of day. Let's go."

Impulsively Kelly grabbed Jake and hugged him. "Thanks," she whispered.

Then, without another word, they were gone.

As Kelly and Robert drove out of the main gate minutes later, Kelly tried to look back at the studio, but she couldn't.

Noda buzzed his boss's number-one secretary again—as he daydreamed—while gazing through the long picture window encompassing the length of Takashima's spacious office in Tokyo. Outside, the six-thirty-A.M. sun looked bright and welcoming, but it would probably rain by noontime, as was typical of the weather in Japan. He wondered how the sunrise would appear to Takashima in Los Angeles today.

He had been reading through the stack of morning faxes trickling in from around the world. As he began to review the lengthy fax from Italy, he nearly dropped his glasses. According to Takashima's undercover Ronin stationed in Rome, the Italian entrepreneur they had been watching had made his intentions clear: he would be pouring millions of dollars into the American entertainment business in the near future, as they had predicted. Specifically, the Italian had agreed to float their targeted studio. Takashima must be made aware of his competitor immediately.

As Noda folded up the fax, he sat down in Takashima's large, comfortable chair. He leaned back, calculating how the master could use this information from Rome to his advantage.

Since Takashima's move to America, Noda never seemed to go home anymore. He could always stay in one of the master's many houses, but for the past two days he had found it more convenient to sleep in Takashima's office, especially since the Yakuza were not around. Little by little, he had become accustomed to an around-the-clock work schedule. He did not question it; he accepted it dutifully.

Confidently he put his feet up on the boss's desk as he thought about Takashima's parting words: "I am depending on you to be one step ahead of the American enemy." But with the new information in the

Rome fax, his main concern was to have Takashima persuade the Italian not to invest his capital in their enemy's studio.

"We must send a fax off to Takashima-san immediately," he said to the master's number-one secretary.

He recommended to Takashima that he use his influence with the Italian to ensure that he uphold his financial support of the American movie studio right up until the last moment. Then the Italian would, persuaded by all kinds of future benefits from Takashima, withdraw his support.

Noda could not control his excitement. His straight hair flew wildly into his face as he spun around in circles in Takashima's large swivel chair. "Send it off immediately, and then get me the afternoon numbers on the New York exchange, as well as the Chicago futures and . . ." Noda stopped, noticing the shocked expression on the young woman's face.

Embarrassed, he calmed down, then took off his glasses and began to clean them. He must not lose face. "Bring me some tea, right away," he said in a calm, even voice.

The dazed secretary bowed and left. As soon as she was gone, Noda spun around again in the heavy chair, nonstop, like a kid on a carousel. He had more than proved his worth to the man who had taken him into his house as his son. He enjoyed his new power. Soon he would be moving up in the business world, and someday this would all be his.

He peeked outside Takashima's office. The secretary was nowhere in sight, and no Yakuza were around. The gods of fortune were with him for the moment. He closed the door.

Quickly, and as silently as a whispered wind, he began to copy down the current dates and amounts of the master's dangerous payoffs to the ruling political party in his scorecard notebook. Since he had fallen behind in his reporting in Takashima's rush to leave, this would be an ideal time to finish his work. He must be sure not only that these records were accurate but also that they did not fall into the wrong hands at any time, especially now, with the political climate so unstable in Japan. If anyone ever found out about this ledger, these entries could be used against Takashima in a criminal prosecution case. Even Takashima's cadre of Yakuza had no knowledge of these accounts, except for Minoru. Takashima, for the most part, trusted no one.

As the limousine slammed to a halt, Takashima lurched forward in his seat, his seat belt cutting into his stomach. He grunted his displeasure. "Why are we now stopping?" he asked abruptly.

"I do not know, Takashima-san. It looks like a . . . Christmas sleigh blocking the traffic." The Yakuza could not believe his eyes as the red velvet sleigh adorned with silver bells and fancy scarlet ribbons was being pulled across Wilshire Boulevard, causing a huge traffic jam in both directions. Several drivers honked their horns impatiently, while others got out of their cars and gawked at the sight.

Takashima tapped his forefingers together; he was in a hurry to get to his bank. He had to quickly finalize all of his banking plans. At the suggestion of the Ronin, after he had canceled his luncheon meeting, he had hurriedly called a brief meeting with H. A. Ross and some of his partners at the prestigious accounting firm of Black & Olden. He had learned from them about several new potential suitors for his targeted studio. He had no choice now but to move on his plan immediately.

He took a cigarette from his gold case and lighted it. He exhaled, filling the limo with smoke.

As he opened his blackened window, he now saw the silly contraption causing all the commotion. Christmas, he thought scornfully, simply another American excuse for slacking off. He had been disturbed that Christmas had become very important in Japan over the past years, and he had been appalled at discovering that one of his own Tokyo hotels planned to serve a traditional ham dinner on December 25. He had quickly quashed that idea. He also ordered that no Christmas trees would ever be allowed on any of his properties.

"Minoru-san," he said as something interesting caught his eye, "find out the asking price on that building over there."

Takashima pointed to a twelve-story black glass building rising on a very expensive piece of Beverly Hills real estate. Its modern design appealed to his aesthetic tastes.

Minoru nodded and made a note. Suddenly the black Mercedes limousine lunged forward as the traffic began to move again. Not long afterward they pulled into the underground parking lot of his bank.

Takashima and his corps of six Yakuza made a formidable sight as they entered the marble-faced building from the garage elevator. The upscale Beverly Hills customers weren't sure what to make of them. More than one clutched her Gucci pocketbook tightly, and several bank employees whispered among themselves. Even the bank's security force stood still, not knowing what might happen next.

Takashima grimaced, but underneath it all, he enjoyed the attention he was getting, even though he hated the presence of so many Americans.

"We are, uh, most pleased to have you, Mr. Takashima," the gray-haired bank manager said in a solemn voice as he welcomed the bank's new owner.

Takashima did not respond. The bank manager's cordial greeting was obviously insincere. He would not even make eye contact. He will be snapping to attention soon enough, Takashima thought grimly, or else.

As Takashima walked through the entertainment division of the bank, which catered to the superstars of the music and theatrical worlds, with the manager following behind him, he observed the frightened faces of the other employees. None was happy over the bank's acquisition by the Asian Octopus. No problem, Takashima thought. They would all soon be fired anyway.

"I am ready to do business now!" he barked in his noncommittal voice.

"Of course, Mr. Takashima. Right away." The bank manager almost tripped over himself as he led Takashima and his entourage into a large boardroom. Takashima did not take a seat or look at the various bank executives waiting for him. Instead he irritably gazed at the numerous gold and platinum framed records in between the mounted movie posters that adorned the walls of the room.

He nodded to his Yakuza and mumbled something in Japanese. To the astonishment of the group seated at the table, his bodyguards quickly removed everything from the walls.

"Hey, what are you do—" one executive said, jumping up. A Yakuza standing nearby put his hand firmly on the man's shoulder, forcing him to back down.

Takashima abhorred any visual distractions while he was conducting a business meeting, believing that the mind could not focus on what was being said if the eye was taking it elsewhere. Besides, he believed that records were a thing of the past. No one was cutting vinyl anymore, and the Hollywood movies were not the kind he would approve of anyway. Stripping the walls so deliberately had now become a clear message to the assembled board members of his future direction.

While Minoru stood behind him, Takashima finally took his seat at the end of the table, farthest from the door. Just as he was about to begin, though, a clerk entered, excused himself, and quietly approached the manager. The manager gulped as he read the note handed to him. With a polite cough he said he would be right back.

Takashima waited as several minutes passed by. No one moved. Becoming impatient, he tapped his forefingers together. Then one of his Yakuza entered and knelt beside him as he whispered something into his ear. Takashima's face showed no expression as he listened.

He stood up as the flushed manager walked in. Takashima was like a black panther attacking under the guise of twilight.

"Mr. Takashima, I am sorry, but our computer system has temporarily gone off-line—"

"Never mind your excuses," Takashima said, cutting him off. "When your cheap American computer system is on-line again, call me immediately. I would like a private office while I wait."

"Yes, sir, Mr. Takashima," the manager responded quietly, even managing a small bow as Takashima and his entourage left the boardroom.

As they walked by the computer room, Takashima looked inside. Two sloppily dressed workmen had taken out the interface boards and were trying to find out what was wrong. There were tools strewn around the small cubicle. A couple of empty plates and Coke cups were sitting on top of one of the computers. Takashima shook his head in disgust. No wonder the Americans are losing the economic war, he thought.

"You may use this office," the manager said with strained politeness. He led Takashima into a plush office and closed the door. The Yakuza took up sentry positions outside.

For the next two hours Takashima sent the manager on several errands within the building: getting him files, faxes, spread sheets. But he waited until no one was around before turning to the visitor who had sneaked in through one of the bank's fire-exit doors. The information from his newly arrived Ronin would be vital to him.

"Let us proceed. I am very interested in whatever additional information you have gathered on the holdings of Baron-san."

Suddenly the phone rang. Takashima meant to ignore it, but he reached over anyway and picked it up. He was certain his Yakuza monitoring the switchboard would not have put the call through unless it was urgent.

"*Moshi, mosh'* ... *ano-ne* ... what?" he said, switching to English. "Resnick, are you certain of what you are saying? ... The woman studio head has taken a leave of absence ... yes, I understand ..." Takashima listened intently, trying to comprehend the American attorney on the other end. "... and you are certain this woman was telling the truth. ... Yes, I see. I should have known you would be involved. ... No, you need not worry, Resnick. This does not change my plans. On the contrary, I intend to proceed with great haste ... It is no concern why I changed my plans. Please, never question me again."

Takashima hung up the phone, grinning widely at the Ronin as he discussed how Kelly Kristopher had lost face with her peers. "I want a complete file on her."

As he raised his cup of tea, Takashima paused, noticing the page-one *Times* story in front of him. He was intrigued by the courage of Kelly Kristopher to speak out as she had done in front of such an important industry gathering. But she could also lead to trouble. He must now have her watched very carefully.

6

"This is KABC Talk Radio and the phones are open for your calls. The question this morning is: What do you think about the Kelly Kristopher scandal? Do you believe in her? And did she have to quit as president of Constellation Studios?"

"I think she's a tramp."

"Send her over to my office anytime."

Takashima turned down the volume on his limo radio as the calls continued to come in to the popular *Ken and Bob Show*. He had heard enough. The Superior Court judge and his story of Kelly was the talk all over town now.

He relaxed for a moment as he stretched his legs onto the jump seat in front of him. He gazed through the open roof of his limo as it pulled up to his office at 1901 Avenue of the Stars. He loved the early-morning hours, for then his mind was the sharpest.

Silently, as he continued to view the heavens, he cheered on the transparent moon still struggling to survive against the bright curtain of the morning sunlight. He marveled at the moon's courage. It never ceased its struggle, even though it would soon disappear from the sky.

As he readjusted his tinted glasses and looked out at the city before him, he pushed a button on the console and the roof closed with a quiet electronic hum. He looked at Chisako, sleeping next to him.

Her fur cape had slipped off her bare shoulders, revealing her soft white flesh. He contemplated taking her as he ran his fingers through her long black hair. When she failed to respond, he cursed her with disgust. She could not feel the early-morning chill or even him touching her head. She felt nothing. She had drifted once again into her world of opium.

He would never acknowledge his own part in her habit. He believed that drugs were like any other pleasure in life—restraint could be learned.

Since she had come to America, her insolence occurred more and more frequently. He had become more impatient with her. She insisted on making her own decisions, and she had become increasingly reluctant to satisfy his sexual desires. He clenched his fists while he replayed over and over the scene from earlier in the evening.

Several prominent Japanese men—his dinner guests—had been waiting to watch her get fucked simultaneously by two muscular male dancers in the private room behind a fancy Sunset Strip restaurant when she had given word that she refused to allow them their sport. Highly embarrassed, then outraged, he struck her hard across the face, then ordered her to dress. He apologized to his guests, blaming her disobedience on her presumed drugged state.

Snapping out of his trance, he willed his anger to subside. He would deal with her later. He gave his Yakuza driver orders to take her back to her suite at the L'Ermitage Hotel. After she sobered up, he wanted her brought back for Noda's arrival. He had a surprise for her.

The footsteps of Takashima and his Yakuza tapped loudly on the marble floors and echoed eerily throughout the empty building as they walked to the express elevator. Takashima smiled, refusing to let his irritation with Chisako further upset his *wa*. She would soon pay for her disobedience.

* * *

"Quiet, we're going for picture," boomed the first assistant director as Jake and Stephen quickly walked out of Soundstage 8.

"I've been catching dailies the past few days," Stephen said. "*Criminal Intent* looks, er, good, Jake." His voice held a note of surprise, for he hadn't expected it. "Oh, by the way, any word on Kelly? Is she coming back?"

"What do you mean, good? It's terrific!" Jake answered enthusiastically as he closed the soundstage door behind them. The buzzer went off and the red light mounted outside the door began whirling around, signaling "keep out" to anyone until the filming was over. He purposely ignored Stephen's inquiry about Kelly. After her sudden departure, Rose Kaufman had released a terse statement to the trades that Kelly Kristopher had taken a leave of absence and that Jake Baron had taken over the reins of production chief of his studio in the interim.

As the two men walked along the dirt path leading back to the executive offices, raindrops began to sprinkle in front of them. Jake smiled at his stepson. "Listen, Stephen, *Criminal Intent* is a winner. We're going to make some money on this one, no doubt about it."

Stephen avoided looking at him as he answered, "I hope you're right."

Jake smiled confidently as he looked up at the hazy sky overhead and closed his eyes. The cool rain felt good on his face. He had recognized that look on Stephen's face: he was hiding something. No matter what Stephen's doubts were, he knew the film was great. Now, if only they were able to finish it.

As the two men strolled past the giant gray-blue soundstages, some large enough to house a 747, Jake grew pensive. Without the loan from the Italian investor, he'd be in deep trouble. But what could go wrong? The papers had been drawn up by the investment bankers; it was just a matter of waiting. But as his dad had often said: "Son, it's not a done deal till the check clears."

Nearly running to keep up with his stepfather, Stephen began to twitch slightly. He was not about to stop digging for information. If he furnished Takashima with new material, it might mean an extra bonus of thousands of dollars.

"Jake, there's a nasty little rumor around town, um, that the studio is in a real financial bind," he commented as the two stopped to allow an electric cart pulling a load of stage walls covered with plastic sheets to pass them. "Have you given any thought about looking for an investor?"

Jake's gaze turned cold. "Why do you want to know?" he asked, wiping the rain off his face with his handkerchief.

"Well, there's a new Japanese mogul in town. With plenty of ready cash," Stephen offered, wanting to test Jake's response.

So that was it, Jake thought. Stephen was looking around for another quick deal to make a few bucks. He'd probably collect a nice finder's fee. That sonofabitch. But how the hell did he get hooked up with the Japanese? Through his Vegas bookies?

"You mean this Takashima character," Jake said, fumbling through his pockets for his Marlboros while he triggered some dormant anger through his craw. Jake had never forgiven the Japanese for killing his Uncle Manny—his father's only brother, who was the national entertainment director for the USO. As Jake's dad had mentioned repeatedly over the years, Uncle Manny was an innocent civilian killed at Honolulu's Hickam Field during the Japanese surprise attack of Pearl Harbor.

Stephen breathed easier as they ducked between the corners of the giant stages to avoid the steady drizzle. Jake apparently had no idea about his connection with Takashima, but he had to make absolutely sure.

He nodded. "That's right. What do you think?"

Jake stopped to light his cigarette, cupping his hands, before answering. As they walked through a doorway into the fifty-year-old property warehouse, Jake looked around, but he was oblivious of the sights. He didn't even see any of the thousands of objects stored on the dusty shelves, everything from papier-mâché candelabra to genuine Queen Anne chairs. He was still preoccupied with figuring out Stephen's angle with the Jap.

"I'm not interested, period," Jake said, exhaling smoke in the direction of the No Smoking signs posted everywhere. "Sure, that Jap bastard's set up his offices just around the corner from us, but what's he gonna do?" Jake asked sarcastically. "Attack us in the middle of the night?"

Stephen, remembering his stepdad's hatred toward the Japanese, chose his next words carefully: "Jake, wait a minute, you don't understand what I'm suggesting. Perhaps we could work out a co-production deal with him. After all, we need a hit movie, and that takes money—"

Jake cut him off abruptly. "Where the fuck do you get off, Stephen? This is *my* studio and I don't need my half-assed stepson telling me how to run it."

Stephen pulled at his shirt collar and his shoulder twitched violently. He had to keep himself calm. "Jake, Max had a talk with me. He's really worried about Constellation's cash flow."

"That's bullshit, Stephen. Max knows better. Listen, there's nothing to worry about," Jake responded with more confidence than he felt. "I'll set Max and you, and all of the rest of the board, straight later today."

Stephen sensed something was up. "What do you mean, you'll set us straight?"

"Let's just say I've got a surprise for all of you."

Stephen was on the alert. This was something he hadn't counted on. Maybe Jake was going to sell the studio after all. Was his own deal with Takashima going up in smoke?

"Come on, what gives, Dad?"

"Stephen, I'll see you this afternoon at three," Jake answered glibly, avoiding Stephen's question. He turned and walked faster, seeking a dry area under a roof, ignoring the fine mud kicking up at his heels.

"C'mon, Jake, what's going on?" Stephen called out, but Jake wasn't listening as he stepped quickly toward the back lot.

Once his stepson was out of sight, Jake leaned against the front of an old saloon, enjoying the smell of clean air and the clear sky overhead. The sudden noontime storm was stopping, and as he bent his head and took a drag on his cigarette, the ghost wind of many forgotten sounds—hoofbeats, gunshots, a wagon master yelling at his team—echoed in his head. As he inhaled the smoke and dust at the same time, he looked around. He loved this part of the studio.

Hundreds of western two-reelers had been shot out here on the back lot. Many times, through the years when he needed to clear his head, he would walk this familiar route and reminisce.

As he wandered over old footprints in the dirt, muddied today, he could still feel the magic here. It was like new blood flowing through his veins. He could see hundreds of black-and-white films flickering before his eyes: cowboys shooting it out with the bad guys; the mob gunning down an informer; the blue and the gray in hand-to-hand combat in a battle of brother against brother. These images would never die.

Those were the days, he thought, and they lived in these old facades. He halfway expected to hear the voice of his dad yelling to the curious bystanders: "Quiet on the set!"

Jake whistled softly as he walked through the decaying old buildings: a red barn, a sheriff's office, the general store. They were still here; but where Autry, Mix, and John Wayne had ridden into the sunset, the new commissary now stood. During the past fifteen years, Jake had had no choice but to make room for expansion. All the same, tearing up the back lot had been like cutting off a part of himself, and when the Hollywood Preservation Society had approached him to request that Constellation's buildings be included in their restoration project, he had gladly given his approval. No more buildings would be torn down.

He smiled as he remembered the time he had ridden his pony behind a director filming an Indian-attack scene from a moving truck. His father had given him a whale of a licking when he rode straight through the shot and ruined it.

Lost in reverie, he nearly tripped over some decaying timbers scattered in front of an antebellum house. Jake looked up, shielding his eyes with his hand from the hot sun trying to break through the myriad of dark rain clouds. The four-pillared facade had been used in more than one Civil War film. Just around the corner were several brownstone fronts used in many gangster films and, recently, episodic television shows.

Why did everything have to change? he wondered with regret. The Golden Days of Hollywood had been something else. It didn't matter then if they had fancy special effects and camera lenses with names he couldn't even pronounce. They had the stories. And the stars.

Jake continued walking through the rubble of more memories. Nowadays, most of the exterior shooting was done on location. This part of the lot was now used mostly for storage.

He walked into a clearing with a wooden bridge that had doubled for an English countryside many times. He stopped in the middle of the old bridge and looked down. What had once been a pond—except for an occasional rainy day like today—was now caked with mud and filled with weeds. He remembered the day when the bridge had been freshly painted and clear blue water pumped into the manmade lake. He winced. Constellation had been in the black then.

If only he could turn back the clock, all his problems could be easily solved. In the old days, Bunky would have sat down with one of his movie friends in his office, offered him the very best Cuban cigar, then put his cards on the table. The two men would have worked something out.

But times had changed. Men like Bunky were long gone. They had been gods. Now lawyers, agents, and accountants ran the studios. The big corporations threatened to destroy the very essence that had made all the studios great: that spark of individuality of each man to mold and guide his own personal vision; to surround himself with the very best talent and make the best motion pictures possible.

He stomped out his cigarette in the mud with his boot. My God, he thought, what if I lose it all? What will I do?

He looked out beyond the studio walls at the gray steel structures of Century City now surrounding the lot. They were the new gods. The present was now closing in and threatening to destroy the past.

Takashima paced up and down the room, disturbed by news from Tokyo that had just come. Some of his Japanese rivals, including Nomura Babcock & Brown Co. Ltd. and JVC, were judiciously looking over several Hollywood studios at the moment. A deal could be imminent. He could not allow them to jump in before him. That would ruin his plans for revenge.

Noda stood nearby, watching him. He was bleary-eyed and exhausted from his seventeen-hour flight and wanted to unpack his bags and sleep for a while, but he knew that his fatigue was not Takashima's concern. Since his boss was still full of energy, Noda had to put on a good professional face and persevere.

As he opened the next file, Takashima noticed it was another urgent Ronin file. His plans to expand his holdings with Radio City Music Hall had been accepted by his group, but he had to hurry. His spies had learned that the giant Mitsubishi Group was also interested, not just in Radio City but in all of Rockefeller Center.

However, Takashima was dismayed to read that for the time being, his group had halted his plan to buy the Indianapolis race track. Too much, too soon, the group had decided. They wanted Takashima to take a wait-and-see approach on buying any other high-profile American institutions.

The next section brought a big smile to his face. "I see that Morita-san still has not yet had any luck with MGM or Columbia," Takashima said, almost laughing at his arch-competitor from Sony. "Now, Noda-san," Takashima barked, noting how sleepy he looked, "You must get some rest. We have a great deal to do."

Noda was too numb to express his thanks at Takashima's kindness. Instead, he merely nodded and left the room, carrying the files.

With this business concluded, Takashima summoned Chisako, who had been waiting nervously in one of the outer offices.

"*Sake-o, kudasai,*" he ordered. Chisako set down a tray of tiny cups and poured the hot rice wine. She was careful not to fill the cups too near to the top to show *yasashii*, or politeness. She hoped that during her sleep most of the effects of the opium had disappeared. She realized he was not pleased with her after last night. Bowing, she said, "*Dozo*, master."

However, he abruptly stood up and left the room without a word. Stunned, she nervously fumbled with her sash.

Then the door suddenly opened and Takashima entered with a woman on his arm. Chisako saw that she was very young and dressed in the most stylish Paris *haute couture*. A rich black velvet hat with a sweeping brim covered part of her face, and she wore an elegantly draped dress trimmed in black sable.

She walked—as Takashima had ordered—toward Chisako as silently as a cherry blossom falling from the branch to the earth. She bowed graciously to Chisako.

Chisako watched in awe, unable to understand what was happening. Frightened, she looked at Takashima for assistance. He seemed to be close to laughing. She had the feeling that he might have brought the woman here to humiliate her.

Then the young woman looked up at her, revealing her sweet moon face. Chisako was stunned, her heart fluttering like a bird caught in the grasp of a tiger. It was her own apprentice *maiko* geisha: Kakue.

Devastated, Chisako sank to the floor and uttered, "Please forgive me."

It was almost four o'clock, but it was already growing dark outside. Jake sat in his boardroom and poured himself another cup of coffee. The rain hadn't let up all afternoon. With the way the locals drove, especially with wet streets, he figured there would be traffic tie-ups all over town. So he had delayed the board meeting by one hour.

As he finished his coffee, Rose Kaufman came in. As she took her seat, she muttered to herself, "Crazy jerks, can't leave a body alone." She turned to Jake, her tired face full of worry.

"Dammit, Jake, I can't get rid of those idiot putzes over at *A Current Affair*. They keep insisting we're hiding something about Kelly." She made an angry face. "What do you want me to do?"

"Just what you've been doing, Rose," Jake said, looking at his watch. "Ignore the fuckin' bastards."

Rose smiled and made a memo, jiggling her gold bracelets as she wrote down those exact words.

Jake looked around the room. Stephen was on the phone, while Max fiddled with the accounting books, sharpening one pencil after another. Jake had briefly talked with his controller before anyone else had arrived and discovered that Stephen had conned Max into believing he had Jake's permission to discuss the studio's financial problems with him. Now Max was more nervous and apologetic than ever.

Jake's secretary, Paula, sat huddled in the corner, drinking hot tea. The poor woman was still recovering from the flu, but refused to go home until after the board meeting.

As Mistica arrived, Jake looked up at her. Her arms were filled with yellow-and-white-striped bags full of purchases from Giorgio's.

"Hi, Dad," she said, kissing him lightly on the cheek as she took her seat. She smiled at him, but that didn't change the wary look in his eyes: something was up, she could tell. "Look at what I bought," she said sweetly as she opened up one of her packages and held up a sexy black teddy.

He half-smiled back, but said nothing. He wouldn't admonish his daughter today. He had too much on his mind. Besides, the rest of the board wasn't here yet.

Michael Grey, VP of business affairs, and Chet Ellis, VP of marketing, arrived minutes later; then Cynthia Ortega, VP of production, walked in wet and tired after having been caught in a downpour on location in central L.A. Before she sat down, she removed her floppy rain hat and shook out her damp hair. "Fucking piece of shit," she murmured under her breath.

Hearing her, Jake asked, "Cynthia, what's the matter?" He knew that she cursed like a drunken sailor only when provoked.

She looked embarrassed. "It's that new director Zinman represents. He insisted we break early so that he could go to the ballet and watch his girlfriend tiptoe around."

Jake tried to hide his amused smile. He couldn't blame her. She wasn't the only one who complained about Robert's clients.

Finally Bill Forman, VP of advertising, rushed into the boardroom, all excited about the preliminary ad campaign just finished for *Criminal Intent*. Everyone gawked over the glossy ad slicks showing Michelle Pfeiffer and Harrison Ford surrounded by the beauty of Aspen Mountain with the shadow of the killer threatening them.

Mistica, however, kept looking at her watch. Finally she stood up. "If it's okay with you, Dad, I've got to go. Big party tonight at the Douglases'."

"Sit down, Mistica," Jake said firmly.

She started to say something, before the look on her father's face stopped her. She sat down and fidgeted with the metal snaps on her Gortex rain jacket. She hated these meetings, but her dad insisted she be there as a member of the Baron family

The rest of the board also quieted down. Everyone knew when the boss had something important to say.

Jake smiled at them. "You've probably all wondered where I've been over the past few weeks. Well, you might say I went Christmas shopping."

Stephen suddenly perked up from being half-asleep. He pushed on his ball-point pen and started to scribble some notes on his yellow legal pad. Takashima had stressed that he wanted any news of importance before he had dinner.

Jake went on to tell them about his hunt for financing, the turn-downs he'd had in New York, and finally, the good news in Chicago with the investment bankers and their Italian investor.

". . . and our white knight's buying quite a few companies in town, and it looks good that he's going to bail us out with a long-term deal."

Stephen, having no idea that Takashima already knew of this through his intelligence network, couldn't write fast enough.

Jake stood up and scanned the people around the table. Not one sad face in the bunch now. He glanced over at his stepson only long enough to see him quickly jotting down everything. He smiled. He thought of making up some nonsense to confuse Stephen. "The money should be in place within a few weeks."

Max Gerstein, who hadn't said a word for the past hour, stood up and walked over to Jake. Shaking his hand, he said, "Good work, Jake. This money will now guarantee the finish of *Criminal Intent*." He wiped his brow. "Mildred will be happy. Now I can finally sleep at night."

As Jake and the others on the board erupted in laughter, Stephen forced a grin. Smiling at the happy faces around him, Jake said, "I know it's getting late, and some of you have other engagements; I'll adjourn the meeting in a few minutes." He looked directly at Mistica, smiling. "But before I do, I have one final piece of business."

Stephen began to twitch his shoulder nervously, realizing that this was probably the appointment of an interim president.

"I'm sure we all feel the absence today of our president," Jake said softly, trying to keep the emotion out of his voice. "Kelly asked me to extend her regrets to all of you, but for the sake of Constellation, she felt it best to resign her position as one of our directors as well, especially while she's on a leave of absence. Even though I didn't agree . . ." He paused. He had to force himself to refrain from giving his personal opinion and keep to business.

"Jake," interrupted Ortega, "have you heard the rumors surfacing that Eisner and Katzenberg are offering Kelly a huge deal to join Disney in some production capacity?"

That must be Robert's doing, Jake decided. He shook his head. He wouldn't even think about that. "Now, for the next item on the agenda," he said, scanning his handwritten notes, "I have given careful consideration to the appointment of an interim president."

Not only was Stephen holding his breath; everyone else in the room looked up in rapt attention.

Suddenly no one thought about the homebound bumper-to-bumper traffic, the cold rain, or anything else.

"However, at this time I've decided to put off that

decision. I will continue to function in Kelly's position. Any questions?"

Before Stephen could offer a protest, Jake kept right on talking, trying to get this over with as fast as he could. "And with the Italian investor coming in, the investment bankers suggested that I not do any appointing. Kelly will be back here before you know it."

Wanting to show some optimism, he concluded, "Now, I realize Christmas and New Year's are a few weeks away," he said, "but I think we've got something to celebrate this afternoon." He buzzed the front desk, and the custodial staff brought in a couple of bottles of chilled 1979 Dom Pérignon and several glasses.

It didn't take long for everyone to get into a party mood. Mistica handed out the glasses. Stephen left the room abruptly, but no one noticed his absence. The rest of the board began laughing and talking.

As Jake popped the first cork, the chilled bubbles sprayed all over him. He laughed as he wiped the wet froth off his shirt; nothing could bother him now.

As he looked out the window, he thought: What the hell? Constellation is going to make it.

7

"This place is really a steal, Mr. Takashima," Eileen Singer murmured sweetly into his ear, holding an oversize multicolored umbrella in her hand. They were standing outside the breathtaking four-level estate on top of the famous Mulholland Drive that Chisako had convinced him to see.

Takashima peered through his dark glasses at the impressive house. The architecture, copied from a royal estate in the south of France, featured towers topped with blue cones at each corner and four chimneys that soared into the sky. It appealed to his aesthetic nature, and its massive presence made it very desirable to him.

Eileen Singer wasn't taking any chances on losing this sale, even when the cellular phone she carried in her over-the-shoulder bag began ringing. She simply ignored it and kept right on selling. "Look at this view!" she exclaimed as she pointed out the foggy coastline in the distance. She seemed so excited that for a moment Takashima thought she was going to faint.

Even as it started to rain, she and Takashima kept right on walking around the house. Suddenly she stepped into a gopher hole and almost lost one of her spiked heels. Not losing her composure, she freed her muddy foot and kept on moving. "A real bargain," she said, smiling through her poinsettia-red lips. "Look over here. See the lovely city view?"

She eyed Takashima, saying, "Only ten million dollars." She paused, testing his reaction. His expressionless face was not the response she had expected. Nervously she said, "However, if you'd like to see something else . . ."

Takashima raised his hand for silence, then shook his head. "You have done your duty well," he noted. Price was of no consequence. He did not care about the woman and her houses. All that was important was that he find the perfect showpiece for his forthcoming dominant position in Hollywood. He wanted not only grandeur but also simple elegance. He also wanted to buy another house in a different neighborhood where he could indulge in more hedonistic pursuits.

"This will do," he grunted, ignoring the increasing downpour. He turned and walked back to his waiting limo.

"Don't you want to see the inside?" Eileen asked incredulously, running after him.

Takashima snapped his fingers, and six Yakuza, Chisako, and Kakue appeared behind him immediately. They all bowed, waiting for his command. Takashima turned to Eileen. "I will have my representative go with you."

Believing this was her cue, Chisako stepped forward and bowed. She was flashing her brightest smile when one of the Yakuza put a hand on her shoulder. She looked at Takashima, stunned. His cold dark eyes did not reveal any emotion, but Chisako knew he was snubbing her once again.

He had attacked her publicly as cruelly as if he had chopped off her head with a samurai sword. If they were back in Japan, she realized, she would have immediately been removed by the Yakuza. She bowed again, even lower, silently apologizing for her disobedience. She prayed to the gods Takashima would be generous with her.

Takashima snapped his fingers again. "Kakue-san, *kudasai*."

Chisako watched from under her lowered eyes as Kakue stepped forward. She was dressed prettily, but now her fur-lined cape and boots were soaking wet. The young girl smiled and bowed in subdued obedience, and Takashima nodded his approval. Without a word she followed Eileen up the walkway toward the house. Chisako kept her head bowed low as the rain drenched her clothes.

The real-estate woman, having no idea what was going on, jumped at the opportunity to keep selling. She never stopped to take a breath as she and Kakue went inside. "You're going to love this house. There's a gourmet kitchen with a dumbwaiter, a huge stepdown living room, as well as a gorgeous pool with a cascading waterfall . . ."

Takashima stood silently in the rain, staring at Chisako. She remained with her head bowed, shoulders slumped, while water dripped off her face. She had displeased him with her new, strange ways. She must be made to understand that her *giri* to him was the most important thing in her life. Making Kakue his choice was his way of showing her his displeasure.

"Takashima-san," Minoru said, interrupting his thoughts. He pointed to a fifties Cadillac pulling up to the curb and stopping. Takashima watched as a tall silver-haired man got out. Opening a pocket-size umbrella, the man strode over to him.

He was Ben Silverberg, Eileen's boss. She had called him on his car phone and advised him to come over right away to help her close the deal.

Takashima greeted him with a bow, then waited patiently. Silverberg broke into a big smile and pointed to the large estate with all the enthusiasm of a man who would make a profit from his own mother. "Well, what do you think of the place?" he asked. "Quite a bargain, isn't it?"

He then lowered his voice and spoke conspiratorially out of the side of his mouth. "They were asking twelve-million-five, but houses haven't been moving too quickly around here since the presidential election."

Takashima smiled. In Japan when sales were slow, they raised prices, not lowered them. Now he was certain he had been correct about the new American President who looked like a peasant. The American real-estate market obviously was in a slump. The enemy had already lost confidence in their new leader.

Takashima, by way of reply, gave an order to Minoru to bring into the house the large suitcase from the limo.

Silverberg couldn't believe his eyes as Takashima opened the suitcase. It was filled with stacks of hundred-dollar bills: the entire down payment in cold cash.

"You may count it, Mr. Silverberg. One million dollars."

Silverberg was stunned. Even the oil-rich Saudis didn't carry around this much cash for down payments. "Then you're taking it?" he asked quickly.

"Hai," Takashima said, smiling. Another stupid American with a small mind. It seemed they all liked to ask too many dumb questions.

There was no doubt in Takashima's mind now—especially after this easy transaction—that someday soon Japanese citizens would own all the choicest and most expensive real estate in America. He wanted his house to outshine all the others.

Mistica sat on the window seat and peeked out through the latticed French windows, watching the raindrops pounding the brick driveway. She fiddled with the covered buttons on her scarlet silk robe, nearly pulling them off. How could it rain on New Year's Eve? She checked her Cartier watch: almost seven-thirty. She prayed it would stop by the time the guests arrived.

Suddenly she saw the van from Chasen's pull into

the driveway. Thank God they're here at all, she thought. She had been fortunate to get them to cater the party without much notice. Stephen, as usual, had waited until the last minute to ask her to hostess his party. But Maude Chasen was a good friend of her dad's, and she'd never disappoint him or one of his children.

Mistica ran into the large country kitchen, her slippers tapping gently on the Spanish tile floor. The extra help that Stephen had allowed her to hire were already setting up the dishes as the delivery boys from Chasen's unloaded the truck and trudged their portable ovens full of hot food inside.

Next she counted the table service and wondered if she had enough silver serving dishes for the caviar. Well, whatever Stephen had, it would just have to do, she decided.

With all the portable ovens cooking at the same time, the kitchen was getting hotter by the minute. Pushing her frizzy blond hair out of her eyes, she felt her hour-old makeup beginning to melt. As she walked around the room, she realized she couldn't do all this by herself.

Damn, she thought, it was getting late. Noticing the admiring glances from the food servers as she closed the opened buttons on her dressing gown, she panicked —she wasn't even dressed yet. The guys from Chuck's Valet would be here any minute, so would the guests.

Where the hell was Stephen? she wondered, heading for his library in a huff. This was his annual party, not hers. She was simply doing him a favor by hostessing again. She was beginning to wonder why she'd said yes in the first place.

"All right, three dimes on SC—" Stephen quickly stopped talking when he spotted her staring at him from the doorway.

He was sitting at his desk, dressed in his black tux. She had to admit her stepbrother did look handsome with his straight blond hair slicked back for tonight, emphasizing his high cheekbones and even tan. Of course, he was on the phone to his bookie again. She pressed her lips together and pouted.

"What is it?" he said, irritated.

Hearing the tone in his voice, Mistica realized it wouldn't do any good to get him more upset. "Oh, nothing. Just wanted to see if you're ready to greet your guests. They'll be here any minute."

Stephen nodded, then went back to his phone conversation.

Her feelings slightly hurt, she began unbuttoning her dressing robe as she ran down to the guest room to change. Because of this, she didn't see how nervous Stephen was as he hung up the phone. All she could think about was that he was acting like his rotten old self again. It would serve him right if no one showed up, but she knew that would not be the case.

Even though many people in the Hollywood community didn't like her brother, they still wouldn't dare not make at least an appearance at his annual New Year's Eve soiree. It was always a Who's Who, including all the wheeler-dealers, and movers and shakers. And for the few who still needed a reason to come, they usually showed up to say hello to Jake.

By nine-forty-five the party was in full swing, but that didn't change Stephen's moodiness. His bookie had assured him that even though his credit was bad, he would continue to cover his bets for the slew of New Year's bowl games, but only if he provided some serious collateral. But the only real collateral Stephen had left was his new Jaguar and his house. And he was reluctant to part with either.

To make matters worse, Takashima had been ignoring him lately. Stephen had left messages regarding his dad's pronouncement about the Italian investor, but he'd been told by Takashima's various yes-men that the master would summon him at the proper time. Stephen was counting on the extra bonus money in exchange for this information.

Brooding over these thoughts, Stephen walked through his party, nodding and smiling at his guests, including his good friend Candice Bergen and her husband, Louis Malle. Across the room, novelist Sidney Sheldon waved to him as he was about to sample the Chasen's caviar with Ed McMahon. At least his ability to draw the right A-crowd was still intact, Stephen thought.

He greeted a smiling Wayne and Janet Gretsky as they arrived, handing them a bag with noisemakers, streamers, and party hats. Next came Army Archerd of *Daily Variety*, with his beautiful wife, Selma. Army had a small notebook in hand for any interesting items, since this was one of the must parties for his column.

"Wonderful party, Stephen," said a popular attorney from the prestigious Wyman Bautzer law firm.

Stephen stopped—delaying his response—as he spotted a gorgeous girl he didn't recognize spilling out of her silver lamé minidress. She noticed his stare and giggled a smile back on cue.

"Yeah, sure Michelson," responded Stephen, shaking his head. He looked down at his glass, full of nothing but ice. He didn't even remember drinking whatever was in it. But what the hell, it was New Year's Eve. Time for another drink.

Stephen's house was decorated like a holiday display from Saks Fifth Avenue: beautiful red-ribbon decorations on the walls; tiny tinkling silver bells hung in the doorways; fresh fir and red poinsettia centerpieces, not to mention trays of tempting food, three bars stocked with the best liquor, formal-attired servers, holiday music playing on the intercom, and plenty of mistletoe.

"Did anyone ever tell you you're as beautiful as that star up there?" a handsome young man bullshitted to Mistica as they chatted on the front lawn. He was pointing to the clear sky. The rain had recently stopped and a rainbow of silver stars arched above the wet trees.

Wetting her lips, she smiled up flirtatiously at her guest. He was Marty Jacobs, a hotshot young exec from Columbia Pictures who had arrived with a couple of his buddies. They were making the rounds of the better parties.

"Sure, lots of times," she answered half-jokingly as she snuggled up close behind him. She twirled around so he could get just the right effect, and hopefully a little turned-on.

She looked ravishing tonight, decked out in a slinky silver gown, the sequins catching the light. She had splurged on the outrageous Jean Paul Gauthier creation. She was determined to be the star of her stepbrother's party. Being seen with Marty would help further her plan.

She decided to let the actor playing Santa Claus on the lawn handle the greetings alone. She had other plans on her mind as she escorted Marty into the large den, where one of her friends, Jamie Kilgore, was holding court with a stag, former California Governor Jerry Brown, while most of the other couples were letting it rip to the Michael Jackson hit "Billie Jean." The tiny floor was crowded with lots of hot bodies dancing or necking under the mistletoe hung everywhere.

As Mistica danced a couple of tunes with Marty, she noticed Rose Kaufman waving at her as two beautiful blonds spoke with her. Marty winked at all three women while Mistica pulled at his arm. Miffed, she said to him, "Those two blonds are old enough to be your mother."

"They are?" Marty joked back as Rose walked toward them with the two blonds: actresses Kim Novak and Tippi Hedren.

Rose sipped on some punch as she continued to reminisce with the two stars about the glorious years of Hollywood. But Mistica was not interested in any reminiscing tonight. It reminded her of her father, always comparing something to the past. She looked around for Marty, but he had sneaked away. She noticed that he was now busy in conversation with Jack Nicholson. Probably discussing the Lakers, she thought.

Leaving Marty to his stats and the older blonds to Rose, she mingled around the party, stopping to say hello to a very pregnant Cristina Ferrare and her husband Tony Thomopolous. Then she saw Jackie Collins.

She put on her brightest smile and best walk as she strolled over to the superstar novelist. "Oh, Jackie, how's your new book coming?"

"Super, darling, just super."

This was her chance to be discovered, Mistica hoped. She struck a seductive pose, wet her lips, and began her spiel. "You know, as a Baron, I grew up in the film business."

Jackie smiled graciously, but she was obviously not interested in Mistica's life story. "Excuse me, Mistica dear, but I must talk to Marvin and Laddie. You know, research for my new book, *Lady Boss*."

Mistica, frustrated, looked around for someone to talk to and saw her father hovering over the long table of food near the kitchen. She shook her head in dismay. He was wearing his old tux again with a funny-looking hat on his head. He had already untied his bow tie. He just didn't seem to care what people thought about him. She couldn't help but smile.

"What happened to all the caviar, sweetie?" Jake asked, picking up a deviled egg from the tray. His plate was already filled, but there was no drink in his hand. He was trying to stay on the wagon as a New Year's resolution.

"I warned Stephen," Mistica said, automatically checking out the food table. She picked up an empty silver platter and turned to the hired maid. "Please, fill this with more caviar," she ordered.

"Sí, señorita," the maid answered, taking the plate.

Mistica put her hand at the back of her neck, where she felt a nagging ache. This party was beginning to drag, and the one guy she was interested in was involved with his stupid buddies.

Then all of a sudden there was a great deal of commotion coming from the front entrance as a group of people came in all at once.

"I wonder who they are," Mistica said curiously to her dad, but he didn't respond. He was already busily involved fielding questions from Aaron Spelling and Frank Price regarding the future of Kelly. Rumors about her were all over the party, and Jake was tired of repeating the same answers over and over again. "Yes, she'll be back at Constellation . . . no, she hasn't resigned."

Mistica, sick of the whole thing, walked closer to the front entrance to get a better look at these strange-looking guests. They must be important, she decided, or her stepbrother wouldn't have invited them.

The newly arrived group was made up of about a half-dozen Asian men with strongly angular features. They all wore raven-black tuxedos with white silk shirts and ties. The tallest one, wearing aviator glasses, seemed to be in charge, for he tersely ordered the others to give back the bags filled with party favors. How odd, Mistica thought.

"Resnick-san, *konbanwa*," Takashima said loudly as Stephen approached.

Stephen bowed low. "Takashima-san," he said, using the Japanese form of polite address, "I . . . I am honored by your presence at my party."

Takashima stepped forward. "I have been most anxiously looking forward to this night," he said, deliberately overlooking Stephen's nervousness. When he had discovered from the Ronin that Jake Baron would be among the guests this evening, he decided this would be the place to make his grand debut into the Hollywood community.

Noda, feeling uncomfortable in his tuxedo and not certain how to participate, silently stood directly behind his master. As he awaited Takashima's command, he looked around the large room at the men, all dressed alike in the same dark formal suits, and their pretty women in their slinky, tight dresses. He wondered who all these people were.

"I have bought you a gift for the new year," Takashima said, bowing to Stephen. He did not notice the small crowd observing him.

The Asian Octopus snapped his fingers, and two of his Yakuza quickly lifted a package wrapped in gold foil. It was big and appeared to be very heavy, judging by the way his strong-arm guards grunted when they hefted it.

Stephen was taken aback by the gift, but he wasn't alone. With more and more guests gathered around the marble entryway staring at the exotic newcomers, there was a curious buzz coming from them.

Stephen watched as the Yakuza slowly fanned out and took up positions around his house, much to the distress of several nervous guests. In fact, a few partygoers, unnerved by the hulking Yakuza, walked straight out of the house, not to return.

As Stephen bowed again—this a thank-you for the mysterious gift—Jake entered from the kitchen with a producer from Columbia. Seeing his stepson bow to a Japanese stranger made him stop dead in his tracks.

"Who's that?" he whispered.

"That's Hiroshi Takashima, the Japanese billionaire," his friend commented dryly.

Stephen had invited Takashima to his party? Remembering his stepson's mention of Takashima's possibly investing in the studio, Jake was filled with questions. Stephen was a little too cozy with the Jap for his liking.

Stephen, on the other hand, was in his glory. He asked that the gift be taken into his solarium to be opened later, and then he had his best champagne brought in for Takashima and his entourage.

Increasingly suspicious, Jake watched as one of the Yakuza opened the front door and two breathtakingly beautiful dark-haired women entered. He couldn't see their faces clearly, but they walked like queens, as if they had been trained for this entrance for years. The younger one wore a long black dress dripping with black jet beads, and sported big diamond clips in her upswept hair. But it was the other one who captivated his attention. Her knee-length hair hung loose over her shoulders, and she wore a simple black velvet gown with lace net barely covering her ample cleavage. She seemed like a white pearl nestled in the folds of a black orchid.

Jake walked over to Mistica, standing nearby with her mouth open. "They're something else, aren't they?" he said, not taking his eyes off the beautiful woman with long hair.

Mistica merely nodded, fascinated by the magical aura surrounding these people. It was almost as if they were not flesh-and-blood creatures but mythical royalty from a far-off land.

As one of the women stopped to take off her shoes, Takashima asked gruffly, *"Nani-oshite imasuka?"*

The young girl, realizing her mistake, bowed low, then put her shoes back on. As she walked past Stephen, he smiled and said, "Hello, Kakue."

"*Hai*, Resnick-san," she answered with a sweet smile.

Jake was shocked. Stephen had called that Asian girl by name? Now he knew something was fishy.

As Mistica looked at her father, she saw the anger in his face. She decided to put an end to it by pulling her stepbrother off to the side. "Stephen, who are these people? They're upsetting Dad."

While Stephen eyed her with contempt, she became aware that Takashima was looking her over. When she winced, he smiled and nodded to her. It seemed as if she was the only woman in the room for him. She looked back, held by the dark, hypnotic eyes peering over his glasses like smoldering hot coals. She felt strangely warm but weak inside, and she couldn't stop looking back.

Stephen, feeling uncomfortable about Mistica's presence, was anxious to get Takashima away from her.

"Mr. Takashima, there are some people in the other rooms whom I'd like you to meet: David Geffen, Clint Eastwood, Jack Valenti of the Motion Picture Association of America . . . Gale Anne Hurd, the producer of the movies *Terminator* and *Alien*."

Takashima nodded, but he would not forget the little blond with the big breasts. He looked around the room as he followed Resnick into the large living room, nothing or no one escaping his gaze. He was followed by Noda, some Yakuza, and the two geisha.

"Are you okay, Dad?" Mistica asked, turning toward him as she watched Takashima's entourage leave. She then sat down with him on the oakwood bench, looking at her father with concern. The party had taken an odd turn. She wasn't sure what was going on, but she was certain Stephen was up to something.

"Sure, honey, your old man's just fine." He then gave her a quick hug and sent her back to the party.

But Jake's thoughts were much different. He was going to get to the bottom of this now. With the rumors around town that the Japanese were the most interested foreigners wanting to buy into Hollywood, he had become more and more xenophobic.

He wandered about, looking for Stephen, but he couldn't find him. However, he noticed the action around the resplendent Christmas tree. This was definitely the hottest corner of the party. Some of Hollywood's leading execs—Thomopolous, Daly, Melnick, Stark, Berger, Sagansky, and Laddie—had surrounded Takashima.

From a distance he stared hard at Takashima. He was taller than he would have expected, and by the way he placed himself in the middle of the group, he was obviously very confident. He also noticed a shorter, younger version of Takashima speaking to Dan Melnick. Jake's blood started to boil as he noticed that Stephen seemed to be kissing the Japanese mogul's ass: fawning over his every move while making sure his champagne glass was never empty. Jake moved closer so he could hear.

"According to the many reports we receive in Tokyo," Noda was saying to Aaron Spelling as he pushed up his glasses, "your exchange does not allow such stock arbitrage. However, it is quite commonplace on the Nikkei—"

Noda stopped, surprised to see Takashima staring hard at him. Had he overstepped his place by showing off? He bowed apologetically to Takashima and dutifully left the circle.

"What about the probable Japanese takeovers of Columbia and MCA we've been hearing about, Mr. Takashima?" one of the execs asked.

Another joined in: "That's right, Mr. Takashima, the whole town's been speculating on whether or not you or Sony's Morita will buy one of our studios . . . and how soon."

Takashima showed no expression as he took a cigarette from his gold case. "I see. And have those speculators also decided which studio?"

Both men backed away from the loaded question, while Takashima slowly gazed around the group as he went on. "With global synergy a reality, gentlemen, it's men like Murdoch, Morita, and me who will eventually control the Hollywood movie industry. According to our reports, Columbia seems to be in play, as are MGM-UA and Warner Brothers. Even Paramount and MCA-Universal may be available at some time in the future, as well as Disney. And, of course, there's the private one we have also been watching: Constellation."

That's all Jake had to hear. His studio was definitely not for sale. And not to any Jap.

"Excuse me, did I hear you say something about Constellation being up for sale?" he asked loudly, pushing his way through the group around Takashima.

Takashima looked around disapprovingly, irritated by the interruption. Then his face lit up with pleasure as he saw his enemy. Baron looked just as angry in person as he had in the secret Ronin photos he had seen.

"Mr. Baron, it is my distinguished pleasure to finally meet you. How was your recent trip to Chicago?" Takashima asked sarcastically, extending his hand for a handshake. "And how is your lovely ex-president, Miss Kristopher?"

No one breathed. Stephen nearly choked.

Curious, Chisako came forward out of the shadows and stopped between the two men. She sensed this was the man who was important to Takashima's plans.

Her eyes met Jake's briefly. They were fascinating stone-gray eyes that flicked right back to Takashima. Her heart began to beat faster as she felt a building surge of desire sweep over her. Suddenly she was afraid for this rock-solid man. She knew all too well the harshness of Takashima's wrath.

"Who told you I was in Chicago?" Jake asked, barely containing his anger.

Mistica had remained in the background. She feared her dad might get hurt. She noticed Stephen cowering off to the side. Why didn't he help? Who were these strange people?

Takashima looked directly at Jake, not skipping a beat. "It is no secret that your serious financial problems threaten Constellation's existence—"

Jake didn't wait for Takashima to finish. "I said, who told you I was in Chicago?" he shouted back, outraged by the idea of someone having him followed.

"I have my spies," Takashima said, a devilish twinkle in his eyes. "I know every move you make, Mr. Baron. It is what any prudent businessman should do when he intends to buy a company."

"You're not buying Constellation, you fuckin' prick."

As Jake stepped forward angrily, his fist raised, Takashima quickly nodded to his Yakuza. In another second Jake felt two massive bodies squeezing him along his flanks on either side. His friend Laddie quickly placed a hand on his shoulder.

"Hold on, Jake," another exec said. "That won't solve anything."

Jake turned and eyed the gloating gorillas just waiting for him to swing. He had pummeled too many street punks not to know that these men were killers.

No one in the deathly-still room moved except Army Archerd, making copious notes.

At last Mistica cautiously stepped forward and took her father's arm. Her eyes were cold as she looked at Takashima. "C'mon, Dad, let's get out of here."

"It has been a pleasure to meet you, Mr. Baron," said Takashima, bowing in his usual cool manner, motioning at the same time for his two Yakuza to back away. He then shifted his gaze, letting it linger on Mistica.

"Sorry I don't feel the same," Jake said, taking his daughter's arm protectively. He didn't like the way that Jap was leering at her. "Just remember, Constellation isn't for sale."

"We shall wait and see, Mr. Baron." Without another word, Takashima walked away, followed by his Yakuza.

Jake turned to his stepson, his blood hammering in his temples. "You've been hiding something from me—"

"Hey, everybody, it's midnight in . . . Bangkok!" Stephen loudly interrupted his stepfather, blowing on a noisemaker. "More champagne!" he called out quickly, walking into the den and motioning for a trio of servers to open the additional bottles for the guests. He also turned the volume up on his stereo console.

Jake started to follow Stephen, but then stopped. He felt his blood pressure going up. He'd deal with him later. Scowling, he headed for the kitchen.

"I think he's a horrible man," Mistica said, marching right behind her father, ready to help. "Do you want me to throw him out personally, right now?" she said more bravely than she really felt. She didn't want to admit to her father that she had been terrified when those bodyguards had moved in on him. "I'm not afraid—"

"Thanks, honey, but you'd better stay away from that asshole," Jake growled. He'd kill that Jap if he ever touched her. Looking at his pretty daughter, he noticed that her face was pale, her lips trembling. He gave her a hug. "Forget the whole thing, honey. Go back and enjoy your party."

She shook her head. She didn't want to leave her father alone. She enjoyed being needed by him. Besides, she didn't want to feel that Japanese man's eyes on her.

"No, Dad, I'll stay here with you."

"Don't worry, I'm all right. Your old man's got a bruised ego, that's all." He pushed her out of the kitchen. "Go on. Get out of here."

Reluctantly she left, determined to find Stephen and say something to him about those awful people.

Jake sat down on a bar stool and looked at the open bottle of whiskey sitting nearby on the counter. He reached for it, tempted to drink it straight out of the bottle, then stopped. He slammed his fist down on the tile with a vengeance. That damned Jap and his goons weren't going to get the better of him.

Suddenly he felt someone watching him. Expecting trouble, he slowly looked around. It was one of the Japanese women. He drew in his breath unexpectedly. He knew that female gaze. Desire . . . and lust. Hell, this was crazy, he thought. After all she was one of Takashima's tramps.

He turned away, blaming his frazzled nerves for mistaking the meaning of her look. All the same, though, her enchanting face—the full sensual lips and deep, secretive eyes—began to stir something in him. His curiosity forced him to look back. She was still watching him. He couldn't help but wonder what kind of woman would be with a man like that. He had a strange feeling there was more to her than he had first imagined.

He needed some fresh air, anything to break away from this uncomfortable encounter. He charged outside into the backyard. He looked around and finally gazed up at the sky. Digging his hands into his pockets, he closed his eyes and felt the sudden breeze. It felt good. . . .

All of a sudden he heard a noise behind him in the bushes.

"Who's there?" Jake demanded, twisting his head around as he tried to see in the dark. Sparkling white holiday lights dotted the trees, but he still couldn't see anything. He heard the noise again, then saw someone hiding behind the tall bushes. "Who is it?"

Barely making out the figure of a woman, he moved over to the swaying cypresses and grabbed her through the prickly branches. She tried to run away, but he held on to her tightly. He pulled her into the clearing. "What the fuck . . . ?" he exclaimed as he saw the beautiful but frightened face of the same Japanese woman. Well, I'll be damned, he thought.

"*Domo sumimasen*, Baron-san," she said, bowing her head. Her voice was soft, yielding.

Jake released his grip and blinked a couple of times. "You know my name, but I don't know yours," he said, tilting her chin up to see her face clearer in the moonlight. He had never seen a woman so lovely: white skin, deep dark eyes with swept-up lashes, and beautiful red lips.

"Please, what's your name?" he asked again curiously.

She trembled, but she did not struggle in his grasp. A strange yearning began to grow inside her at his touch. Finally she said bashfully, "Chisako."

Intrigued with this beautiful, sensual woman, he repeated slowly, "Chisako. Why did you follow me out here? It's very damp."

She smiled. "In my country, we say it is the *ryū*, the dragon, who controls the rain. He is the guardian of the Five Lakes and the Four Oceans. Only with the song of the *uguisu* does the nightingale bring him sleep, so the sun may shine and the plants may grow."

She bowed her head slowly. "I was looking for the nightingale."

Jake laughed. Such poetry from this she-devil. "I'd like to see the day Stephen puts nightingales in his backyard."

Chisako looked insulted but said nothing. This man did not understand the ways of her people. He was like all the others.

As she twisted away, Jake put up his hands in innocence. "Wait, don't go, I didn't mean anything." He eyed her closely. She had meant all she said about the spirits of her land. Intrigued, he chuckled. "I guess I'm just an old man with a closed mind. Really, what you said was beautiful."

Chisako, looking deeply into his eyes, saw curious flecks of fire dancing in them. She was certain Takashima had not expected this American to stand up to him as he had. Surely such a man must be strong in heart as well as in spirit.

She bowed slightly. "The song of the nightingale is also in the heart, especially in times of trouble."

She did not explain further, and Jake didn't ask. He was too fascinated by her combination of beauty and sensitivity. He looked down at her exotic face and felt his desire mount. He wanted to take her in his arms and explore her softness. For too many nights he had gone to sleep alone with only his memories of Kelly to hold on to in the dark. And now he was turned on by this mysterious woman.

"I'm sorry, I haven't had such a great evening," he said as he gently pulled her closer to him. "Perhaps we could both look for your nightingale."

As he pulled her tighter, he parted the soft petals of her rose lips with a tender kiss.

Suddenly a loud voice interrupted them.

"Hey, everybody, it's midnight in Arizona now!" they heard as the whole garden exploded into light. The harsh spotlights revealed Jake and Chisako in the shadows.

"Damn!" he said. "Let's get out of here."

"Baron-san, I cannot leave with you," the geisha pleaded, pulling back.

Jake looked at her questioningly. "But you can't stay here."

"*Dozo* . . . please," she said, pained. Yet she knew that the moment she had made the commitment to speak to the American, she would forever be in trouble with her master.

All of a sudden it did not matter. She knew that Takashima had no need for her now. The presence of Kakue was proof of that. She had never known any other life but that with Takashima, but now she wanted to taste more.

At least once.

As the large grandfather clock chimed another late hour, Takashima smiled as Stephen poured more champagne into his Waterford glass. Quickly swallowing the contents, the Asian Octopus raised his arm high in a New Year's salute, then turned to Noda and his Yakuza standing nearby.

"*Banzai! Banzai!*" he shouted loudly as he threw the crystal glass against the fireplace. It broke into tiny pieces.

Noda and the remaining Yakuza followed Takashima's lead, emptying their glasses and breaking them against the bricks as they shouted in loud voices: "*Banzai! Banzai!*" They all laughed hysterically.

Takashima, taking no notice of the shocked faces of Stephen and his guests, could think of no better way to toast the beginning of the Japanese Year of the Snake.

But moments before, the Asian Octopus had celebrated in a more sinister way as well. He had given instructions to two of his Yakuza, specializing in arson, to set the fire he had long planned. For good fortune for the coming year, Takashima had given both of these men the traditional end-of-the-year Japanese wish dolls to throw into the flames.

As he finished his toasting for the evening, Takashima looked around for his Yakuza. He ordered them to go through the motions to find Chisako, even though he was well aware she had disappeared around the same time as Jake Baron. He had even hoped the two of them would find each other before he changed their destinies forever.

"*Dozo*, Takashima-san, she is gone," Minoru said, bowing. "No one knows where she is."

Takashima nodded. His suspicions had been correct. She had left to fulfill her destiny with his enemy, as it had been decided by the gods.

"Get our limos. We will leave without the whore." He had earlier sent Kakue home with a Yakuza. Resnick's guests were less likely to notice the absence of both women than just one of them. However, that did not diminish his anger. Chisako would pay severely.

"It's been a great pleasure meeting you, Mr. Takashima," one exec after another said as they filed out, shaking his hand. Takashima merely smiled back to all of them. If these stupid Americans only knew the extent of his plans.

Stephen sat very still in the quiet of his solarium, staring at the gold-foil gift Takashima had brought him. Pale moonlight shone through the overhead skylight, making the package glitter with golden sparks.

His party had been over for a while, but he couldn't bring himself to open the heavy package. Some strange fear had come over him, and he couldn't shake it.

His curiosity finally overcame his fear. He began tearing at the golden paper, ripping it apart until it lay in shreds on the floor. All that remained was a large plain wooden box. He was perplexed. Was this some kind of joke?

He retrieved a hammer and began hacking away at the box. Quickly the slats were shredded away, revealing a large, beautifully woven basket, its perfect oval shape intertwined with a colorful exotic design. He stepped closer and carefully unhooked the simple latch on top. Curiously he removed the lid—pulling off a note taped to it—and peered inside.

A glimmering black pearl, bigger than the egg of an eagle, lay on a shiny emerald-green-and-black pillow.

It must be worth a fortune, he thought, salivating in greedy pleasure. Without hesitation he reached inside to grab the great treasure. Suddenly the pillow began to move, quickly unwinding into a long scaly creature that hissed viciously at him. He couldn't believe his eyes—a black mamba!

He pulled his hand back hastily, ready to scream from his fright as he barely escaped the bite of the venomous snake. My God, he thought in horror as it continued to unfurl, it must be more than twelve feet long. His pulse raced so quickly he could barely breathe.

He glanced at the note—a thank-you from Takashima for tampering with Constellation's insurance policy. He feared Takashima's final words: "A most unusual gift, Resnick-san. One that will not only show my gratitude but also predict your future."

Like the precious pearl guarded by the ugly snake, Stephen, too, felt he would never escape Takashima's grasp.

8

"*Kissu-o, kudasai,*" Chisako whispered silkily. She lay in Jake's arms, forgetting she was Takashima's kept woman, forgetting she was Japanese. No matter how the gods punished her, she would never regret this moment.

As he kissed her face and the nape of her neck, she sensed his need for her. She responded to him, pressing her hard nipples against his chest. A warm flush seeped through her as she held him tighter.

Cupping her breasts in his hands, he slightly tore the delicate black lace on her bodice, but he couldn't stop. He wanted to touch her, feel her softness. As he gently ripped the lace netting off her body, exposing her white breasts, she did not protest. She was naked to the waist, the lace floating in shreds around her like wisps of smoke.

"You are so beautiful," Jake said, kissing her breasts, then slowly removing her black velvet gown as if it were a shroud shielding the rest of her beauty from him. He ached for her now.

Chisako sensed his heightening passion. Her head was spinning from lust as she arched her back in submissive desire, longing for him to take her completely.

But Jake waited. He enjoyed looking at her, feasting on her beauty with his eyes. He knew she had broken tradition to be with him. She had spoken very little to him of her past, except to say that there was no escape from the closed world of the geisha in which she existed. For the first time, he envied Takashima; but he hated the thought of her being in that bastard Jap's arms.

Chisako turned away from him abruptly as the cool night air from an open window chilled her naked body. She covered herself with her long hair. "He is no more my master, Jake-san," she said with conviction. "There is only you now," she said as her own passion reached a fever pitch. She turned her face to him, pleading for Jake to take her under his protection.

Suddenly, as he caressed her shoulder, he stopped. He couldn't believe what he was seeing. "Oh, my God," he breathed, tenderly touching the discolored ugly scar that ran diagonally across her back.

He gazed deeply into her eyes. "Did he do that to you?" he asked, pointing to the scar.

She bowed her head low. Her shame forced her to tell, to let go of her final burden.

"It is the way of the *meifumado*, the world of death and the path of demons. Takashima punishes those who disobey him."

Hearing this, Jake felt very protective of this delicate flower of a woman who had risked so much to be with him. He wanted to help her, but he wasn't sure how.

He now saw a woman filled with pain, but also with a strong spirit. He knew he must possess her. Her black upswept eyes stared back at him, drawing him to her. He smiled, the dimple in his chin widening. He knew she was now his. She shivered as he slowly spread her legs apart. . . .

Chisako, wrapped in a satin sheet, lay against the pillows on Jake's bed. Her eyes closed, she hugged the covers to her naked breasts. The brocade coverlet was so soft, and the bed was still warm from the passion of their lovemaking. She sensed she was alone; she was grateful for the time to go over her thoughts. She had never felt such passion for any man before. She had never wanted it to end.

Jake-san, as she now whispered to him, was a tender lover, unlike her master. How often she had longed for moments of affection from Takashima, but he had never responded. Jake-san had now fulfilled those yearnings.

She forced herself to open her eyes. She got up from the bed and pulled aside the long draperies and looked outside. It was still dark. It must be several hours into the new year, she thought, but she thanked the gods that the night still hid the secret of her sin. She did not have much time.

She picked up her dress, but the tattered pieces fell through her fingers to the floor. She panicked as she relived Jake's rough foreplay that had torn open her fragile dress. She now needed courage more than a dress, knowing what would happen when Takashima discovered her betrayal. She grabbed her purse, removing her gold box filled with opium.

" 'Morning," Jake said casually, entering the bedroom. His voice was heavy with the blush of their lovemaking. He put down a tray filled with hot coffee, then set some woman's clothes on the bed. However, his happy expression changed rapidly when he saw her drug paraphernalia.

"What the hell is this?" he asked, picking up her pipe and strange-looking gold box.

Chisako made no attempt to disguise her habit. She would explain it to him freely. "Opium, Jake-san."

"You don't need this shit—"

"Please understand, Jake-san," she pleaded, her dark eyes opening wide in fear. "I must have it. I . . . I cannot live without it." She nervously lowered her head in shame. "Takashima addicted me to its pleasure many years ago. Now it is my only escape from his terror."

Jake looked hard at the delicate Japanese woman trembling before him. How could he judge her? She really meant it; she needed that drug to survive. The man was, without question, a monster.

"I'll leave it here," he said calmly, laying her pipe and gold box down on his dresser. "But please, let's not think about Takashima now."

He bent down and kissed her on the lips. He sensed what she needed now was a friend. "I've called the taxi already, but it will be about an hour or so before it comes. Now, here's something to cheer you up," he said, handing her the clothes he had placed in front of her. "They belong to my daughter Mistica."

Chisako felt the fine silk of the dress between her fingers, then marveled at the sheer lingerie trimmed with Belgian lace. It felt so beautiful and soft against her skin.

"Don't worry, she'll never miss them. They're last year's style," he joked. "Put them on and then we'll have a little breakfast before you have to leave."

She bowed and quickly took the clothes from him. She did not want him to see the sorrow in her eyes, now that their special night of love was over. She must not wish she could stay with the wonderful man she called Jake-san.

As she began to dress, she looked into his gray eyes, still filled with passion. She owed a debt to the man who smiled down at her. And she intended to pay in full.

"Jake-san, there are some things you must know before I leave—"

"Later, Chisako. You don't owe me any explanations." As he took her in his arms, he realized she was suddenly shaking. "You need some coffee." He poured her a cup.

"But I must speak." She wanted him to understand how important this was to her. She chose her words carefully. "For the first time, Jake-san, the women in my country have found the courage to speak aloud. I have now chosen to be united with them."

"Okay, if you insist, but please drink your coffee,"

he said, handing her the steaming cup. He had no idea what was on her mind, but he could see how determined she was to talk to him.

She nodded as she sipped the dark liquid slowly; then she began her story.

". . . and after I left the *geisha-ya* with Takashima-san, I was always at his side—Hong Kong, Singapore, Paris, Zurich.

"At first I did not understand why I was often invisible to him. He treated me as if I was not there. I soon realized that is his way. I wanted to please him, so I accepted this. I listened, and learned . . .

"For my sixteenth birthday, Takashima-san bought me a beautiful carved-ivory box. I used it to collect mementos of our trips, from theater tickets to a dried flower to a scrap of silk. But as our travels became frequent, I realized he was not only a powerful man, but a man with many enemies." She stopped, feeling faint.

"Are you okay?" he asked, holding her in his arms.

She nodded, gaining strength from his touch. If only this heaven would last, but she knew it would not. She needed more opium. She must not lose face in front of this man, but she could not take her eyes off her gold box on the dresser. She forced herself to continue:

"When he was a young man, Takashima-san spent much time with men who believed their duty was to overthrow the Japanese government. But he could see no profit in anarchy. He shunned the meetings of the communist radicals and those who demonstrated against the presence of the Americans in Japan. Instead he looked for a way to make himself rich. Very rich. He found it by taking advantage of impoverished landowners. He bought up their lands for practically nothing, then used them as collateral to borrow money. Money he used to commandeer Japan's black market, mostly in drugs and illegal arms.

"By the end of the 1960's, Takashima-san had much money to invest in railways, resorts, electronics—"

"But why are you telling me this?" Jake asked as he began to pace around the room, thinking about what she had said.

"Takashima-san is not a man of noble character. I am certain he will try to buy your studio and control it the same evil way he controls everything"—she closed her eyes tightly—"and everyone."

Jake stopped short at hearing this, suddenly concerned for this beautiful woman. "Why are you telling me this, Chisako? Do you want to get away from Takashima? If you do, I'll try to help you."

She put her finger to his lips. "Sssshh, it is already written that I will stay with Takashima-san until the end. I cannot find another protector. It is *giri*."

"I don't understand—"

"*Dozo*, I must speak quickly," she said, glancing out the window at the early signs of daylight.

"Do not depend on the Italian investor."

He was stunned. First, Takashima's statement about his Chicago trip, and now his mistress saying this. "How in the hell did you know about that?"

She hesitated for a moment. As she regrouped her thoughts, she said, "Please, trust my words, Jake-san. He has friends everywhere. Friends who will do his bidding. This Italian whom you have such faith in is not what he seems."

He grabbed her forcibly, and as the silk sheet fell away, her long black hair cascaded around her naked body. "Tell me, Chisako. Are you lying?"

"I swear it is true!" she pleaded as she began to shiver again. "Ask Resnick-san. He knows the truth as well."

"What? My own fuckin' *son*? Why should I believe you?"

"He came to Tokyo and met secretly with Takashima-san."

Jake had to sit down on the edge of his bed to gather his wits. "He what?"

"I was there, Jake-san," she said, lowering her head

slightly. I saw Resnick-san hand over your personal papers." She turned away, not wanting to reveal to him the tears that started to wash down her face.

Beep! Beep!

Jake was still inebriated from the bottle of Jack Daniel's he had belted down after Chisako left. He couldn't believe that Stephen was a traitor, even if it did all add up: Stephen questioning him about Takashima, the Jap at his party . . .

He couldn't open his eyes, no matter how hard he tried. His head felt like a cannonball, and his world was black. He moaned out loud. Shit, he thought vaguely, what a fuckin' hangover.

What the hell was this pounding sound in his head? He tried to shut it out, but the beeping still persisted.

Finally he couldn't ignore it any longer. But as he tried to lift his arm, it felt as heavy as a lead pipe. Slowly he reached for the beeper on the nightstand.

"Dammit, why's the service calling at this hour?"

He made a grab for it, but it fell to the floor.

Crawling on his hands and knees for what seemed like hours, but was only moments, he turned it off.

Pulling himself up, he opened the window. As the cool early-morning air hit him in the face, the hazy sun was peeking through the giant sycamore tree in the backyard. He began to feel his senses slowly return. He sat down on the bed, and as he dialed the number to his studio's answering service, he stared at where Chisako had been sleeping. He ran his hands over the pillow and sheets. If only he had met her under different circumstances . . .

"Yeah, Jake Baron here," he said into the phone. "What's the problem . . . *What?!* Oh, my God, I don't believe it." His hand started to shake as he let the phone drop to his side.

It seemed like an eternity before he put it to his ear again.

"Yeah, I'm okay," he said, feeling his body go

numb. "Please call both Rose Kaufman and Max Gerstein. Tell them to meet me there right away."

The old structures on Constellation's back lot were going up quicker than a tinderbox.

All Jake could see in front of him was a maze of fire trucks with heavy hoses aimed every which way. The thick smoke was terrible. It was like being in hell.

He couldn't take his eyes off the brilliant orange and scarlet flames reaching into the sky like the devil's fingers grabbing at the heavens. Unfortunately, the rain had stopped hours ago.

"How did it start?" Jake, now trembling, asked the fire-battalion chief standing next to him.

"Sorry, Mr. Baron, we don't know yet. But we believe the fire is of suspicious origin. Our arson investigators are checking the area right now. We did have an eyewitness who thought he saw a car with blackened windows speeding off the lot just minutes before the fire broke out."

"Find out who did it, do you hear me?" Jake yelled, his voice hoarse from the smoke drifting around them. Though he was tired from his night with the Japanese woman, he was supercharged from his raging adrenaline.

He ignored the nearby horde of press trying to get to him. Luckily, police barriers kept them away. One wrong question, and he'd most likely lose his temper. He waved to both Rose and Max as they arrived.

"Jake, how did it happen?" Rose asked, grabbing his shoulder. She wore no makeup, and she looked like she had just thrown on some old clothes quickly.

He only shook his head. "I don't know, Rosey. Max," he asked with new urgency, "are we covered?"

"As far as I know, we are. Those policies were drawn up by Resnick long before I came on board. Stephen has always stayed on top of them."

Jake nodded. He had no time to worry about Stephen now. What was important was saving as much of the studio as possible.

"Dad, Dad!" Mistica, who had heard the news on her car radio as she was driving home from her third party of the evening, ran through the police barricade and hugged her father tightly. "Dad, are you all right? I was so worried."

"Sure, I'm okay." He could barely reply as he held on to her tightly, while his emotions churned inside. "Where's your fuckin' brother?"

"Dad, you're hurting me," Mistica yelled, her tired-looking face tinged with pain. "I don't know. I left Stephen a few hours ago . . . and I've been running all over the place—"

"Sorry, baby." Jake glanced up and saw an official-looking man in plain clothes approaching them.

"Mr. Baron? I'm Police Detective Paul Stanley," he said, flashing his badge. "I'd like to ask you a few routine questions."

Jake was suddenly on guard, realizing he had to pull himself together. He reached for Mistica's hand. "Sure, ask whatever you want."

"Where were you earlier this evening?"

"At my son's New Year's Eve party."

"All evening?"

"Till about midnight," Jake said cautiously, not wanting his daughter or anyone in earshot to know his personal business. "Then I went home." He tried to smile. "One too many," he lied. He had no intention of bringing Chisako, his alibi, into this. For Chrissakes, he thought, she had enough trouble with Takashima.

Detective Stanley didn't acknowledge his remark or his smile. He just continued making notes. "Is there anyone who can attest to that fact?"

Jake hesitated. He had to be careful. "No, I was home alone."

"Well, that's all for now, Mr. Baron." The detective put away his pad and pencil as he handed Jake his business card. Then, in an authoritative voice he said, "Make sure you're around town the next few days. We may have some more questions for you." He looked up and down at Jake's haggard appearance, but he made no further comment.

Mistica suddenly panicked. "Dad, what's going on? Why are you being asked questions?"

Jake didn't utter another word. It was as if he never heard his daughter's words. He had nothing else to say as he walked away into the night.

Robert and Kelly pulled into the driveway of their two-story beach house. "It's good to be back, honey," he said, turning off the engine of his Jeep. It had been a long drive overnight from Mammoth, but now that he was home, he felt rejuvenated. He wasn't so sure about Kelly.

She didn't answer, but merely put her head on her husband's shoulder. Her emotions were mixed as she looked out over the horizon. It was dawn, and the sun was just beginning to rise over the ocean. It looked so peaceful now, like a watercolor painting.

When they had left two weeks before, it had been raining hard and the surf was furiously pounding the shore. Kelly remembered her inner turmoil as she had looked out at the fury from her upstairs bedroom window. The notoriety from the luncheon had greatly upset her. She knew she had to get away—from the media, from Constellation, from Jake. Now back, she hoped her storm had passed.

While skiing in Mammoth, she had put everything else aside, although Robert hadn't stopped trying to talk her into resigning from Constellation completely. "It would open new doors for you, Kel," he had said half a dozen times. He would go on trying to convince her that she would be a welcome commodity at any studio in town.

Kelly wouldn't listen to such talk. She never wanted to leave Constellation—or Jake. In five years of working for him, she had come to rely on his presence terribly.

She did have to admit that things had improved

between Robert and her during the time away. How nice it felt when Robert held on to her in the dark, whispering words of love with such fervent passion, as when they had first dated.

"Come on, Kel, let's get the skis, poles and groceries and have some breakfast."

She didn't respond to him, still deep in thought. She also hadn't said more than a few words on the drive home. Returning to L.A. had become very difficult for Kelly.

He continued talking, trying to keep the mood light. "Wasn't it great? Two weeks of no phones, no faxes. Just you and me on the ski slopes," he said, kissing her cheek as he grabbed some luggage. But still no response.

"Look, Kel," Robert said, turning her face toward him. His voice became stern, as if he were talking to a small child. "We had to come home sometime. What happened is now behind you."

She gave him a quick kiss, and started walking toward the house. "You're right, it's good to be back. And I'm hungry!"

Sneaking up behind her, he nibbled on her ear. "Me too, babe."

"I know just what you need," she said playfully, ignoring his obvious intent as she wriggled out of his grasp. "I'm going to make you the best scrambled eggs this side of Santa Monica."

Robert growled as he watched her bend down to pick up her front-door key, which had just dropped out of her bag. He felt himself getting hard, staring at her long hair hanging loose over her form-fitting snowsuit. Nice tight ass, he thought. She was sexier than the day he had met her.

He gathered up the many newspapers scattered around the porch and scanned through them, mumbling, "Why didn't we have the neighbors pick up the papers?"

Then he saw a headline from several days earlier

that made the color drain from his handsome face. "Shit, I don't believe it."

Kelly looked at him, alarmed. "What's wrong?"

Robert put his arm around her. He had to proceed cautiously or she might fold right in front of him. "Uh, look, Kel, something's happened at Constellation."

Her throat constricted as she looked into her husband's eyes. What she saw frightened her. "What are you talking about?" she asked, grabbing the paper. "Oh, my God!" she said slowly. Shocked, she put her hand to her chest, mindless of the newspaper dropping to the ground. Her knees buckled and she sank to the steps of the porch.

She didn't feel anything but a numbing pain as he read the headline story out loud.

Kelly buried her head in her hands. Like Constellation, a part of her had also been destroyed.

"Here, drink this and try to get some sleep," Robert said as he grabbed the alarm clock. Shit, it was three A.M. already. He was tired, but he couldn't sleep either.

Half-dazed, Kelly took the brandy and drank it. She felt it burning her throat as it went down, but she didn't care. She just wanted to blot out the pain.

For most of the day, she had sat alone in her room and stared at the headline. She still couldn't believe that the famous back lot of Constellation had been nearly destroyed. She kept trying to call Jake, wondering how he was holding up, but the line was continuously busy or off the hook.

Finally, still fully dressed, she began to doze off.

After first taking off all of his clothes except for his underpants, Robert gently took off her boots, then brought the blankets up to her waist. As he pulled down the front zipper on her snowsuit, he drew in his breath, tempted by the swell of her soft breasts exposed over her low-cut bra. He unhooked it, then stroked her smooth skin with his tongue while she rolled over onto her side, not protesting. Feeling her nipples harden under his touch, he knew he could take her now if he wanted to, but he decided to wait until she was completely awake. He would enjoy it more when she was alert and would have to beg for him.

He dimmed the light and started to head to the bathroom.

"Robert, don't go. Please," she called out in her half-sleepy, groggy voice. She wanted to talk.

"Kel, I'm right here." He took her hand, sitting down on her side of the bed.

"Do you remember when you told me this business would kill you if you let it?"

"Sure," he said, nodding. Back then he had just quit William Morris and his WAA was being formed.

"Well, part of me died today."

"I know, Kel, I know," he said, holding her close. He wanted to comfort her, give her strength, but he was electrified by the feel of her. He was a man first, a friend second.

Lying beside her, he began exploring her warm body with his eager hands, down over her hips, then underneath the soft silk of her bikini panties. His breathing came faster and his anticipation grew. He boldly put his hand down between her legs, inserting his finger inside her.

"Kel, oh, Kel," he cried out, wanting her more than ever. She was still one of the best lays he'd ever had, even though he felt a one night-stand with a complete stranger kept him fresh for her.

Unable to wait another minute, he pulled down his briefs. But as he began to climb on top of her, she was already dead asleep.

It hadn't been an easy morning for Jake, going around the partially burnt back lot with Rose and Max, surveying the damage while the insurance adjuster wrote down the information. The fire investigators had limited their tour, for the charred ruins still held many smoldering areas.

The worst damage was at historic WestTown. It was almost completely gone. Several other old buildings, including the first soundstage ever built on the lot, were also destroyed. Fortunately, all of the newer buildings, including Jake's office, had escaped untouched. The new commissary had been slightly damaged, but the kitchen was still intact.

When they reached their last stop, the property warehouse, Jake was relieved that the fire had left it virtually unscathed. Only paper-thin cinders lightly dusted the props. All the same, Jake shuddered as he slowly looked up at a life-size full-length portrait of a sixteenth-century Renaissance king. He squinted, dusting it off carefully with his fingers. Damn, he could swear that was his father's face looking down at him.

By the youthful expression on the painting, he guessed it must have been used as a prop for one of Bunky's films in the forties. Like his dad's buddy Alfred Hitchcock, Bunky had loved putting his personal touch on his films. Funny, Jake thought, still staring at the portrait, he had never seen the painting before today.

". . . Mr. Baron, please, I'm waiting. What was the amount of that last insurance premium you said you paid?"

"Amount?" Jake asked, flicking a glance at Max. "About six thousand."

The insurance adjuster seemed surprised as he checked the figures on his clipboard again. Rose tried to peep over his shoulder, but without much success. Max stood nearby, wiping his glasses clean of black soot.

Jake continued wandering through the building, skirting boxes and broken furniture. It was difficult to tell the difference between the real antiques and the junk. Some of this stuff had been sitting around virtually untouched for decades. If it hadn't been an antique then, Jake thought, blowing the dust off an old brass-stand lamp, it was now.

Suddenly Max's beeper went on. He flipped the switch off. "It's probably the restoration outfit. I'd better find a phone. I'll see you later, Jake, Rose," he said.

Jake nodded as he left, still too choked up to say much. He hadn't expected to feel so many emotions tearing out his insides. He looked around at the broken pieces of his past; the memories of his whole life, from his earliest boyhood through now, came flooding back to him. Was that all he had left? he wondered. A bunch of memories?

"Well, I think I have all of it," the adjuster commented as he turned over the various pages on his clipboard. "Let's go back to your office."

Rose gave the man a dirty look. "I don't like that schmuck," she whispered to Jake under her breath. "I've never seen anyone so coldhearted. I think he enjoys all this."

Jake put his arm around her. Her face looked tight, and her usually laughing eyes were full of pain. She was taking this just as hard as he was. "It'll be all right, Rosey, you'll see. Now, go home . . ."

"Check your figures again, they can't be right," Jake said, completely panicked. He paced up and down his office as the adjuster again punched in the dollar amounts on his pocket calculator.

"I'm afraid it's true, Mr. Baron," he said without emotion. "I thought the figure you gave me earlier was much too low, so I checked it out with my office. I'm sorry to say, you did not pay your recent premium . . . and you passed the allotted grace period." The adjuster nervously tugged at his skinny necktie a couple of times. "Very simply put, Mr. Baron, you're not insured."

Jake slammed his fist down on his desk. "You're a fuckin' liar!"

The adjuster methodically capped his Mark Cross pen, then snapped it onto his lapel. Next he removed his reading glasses and slowly put them into his case. "Figures do not lie, Mr. Baron," he said quietly.

Jake was ready to explode when he remembered what had happened:

With the studio in such deep financial trouble, Stephen had assured Max that it wouldn't hurt to put off paying the insurance premiums. After all, Stephen had said, it was the Christmas and New Year's holiday season, and no one would be working anyway. Hold it a second, he thought. Was it merely coincidence that the fire had occurred during the time the studio wasn't covered?

It had been arson. But who would . . . ? And why? The vague thought of Takashima flickered through his mind as he turned to more pressing matters. He had to cover the cost of rebuilding the burned-out part of the lot, and there was no insurance money to do it. Perhaps the Italian would kick in a few hundred thousand more, he thought, when all of a sudden Max Gerstein burst into the office.

"Jake, I've got to talk to you." He stopped to wipe his sweaty face with his handkerchief. He was extremely upset. "Right away."

"Can't it wait a few minutes, Max?"

"No, Jake." He waved a sheet of fax paper in his hand. "It's urgent."

The adjuster took advantage of the interruption to gather up his paperwork and put it back into his briefcase. He then made a quick exit as he said: "Sorry we couldn't do business, Mr. Baron; perhaps some other time. Good day to you both." And he was gone.

Puzzled, Max looked at Jake. "What did he mean by that?"

"Max, I've got some bad news," Jake said, opening his private liquor cabinet. He took out a bottle of Scotch, along with two glasses. Wagon or no wagon, they could both use a shot. "We're not insured."

Max turned completely white, shaking all over as he

slumped down onto a small couch. "Oh, my God," he mumbled, feeling personally responsible.

Jake poured him a double. "Here, take this."

Max shook his head. "No, you'd better take it." He handed him the fax. "This just came."

Jake put down the Scotch, then sat down at his desk and scanned the letterhead. It was from the Chicago investment bankers. As he quickly read on, the blood in his veins turned cold.

His vision began to blur as he read the words over and over again: they were sorry to say that the Italian investor he had been counting on for the bailout had decided to pull out of their deal. No reason given.

Jake crumpled the fax. Fuck the Italian and his money. The whole story was now completely clear to him. Chisako's words kept reverberating in his head: "Takashima-san has friends everywhere."

He stared at the wall, trying to fight the sick feeling of fear tearing at his insides. Trying to stay calm, he told Max to get the manager of the Beverly-Rodeo Bank on the phone pronto. "Let's plead for a two-week extension."

Max nodded quickly, then ran down the hall to his own office.

Jake paced around the room until he tired; then he sat down, completely unnerved. It just wasn't fair. The studio had been his whole life, and all of a sudden it looked like it would all be ripped away.

If he didn't get an extension on the loan, it was all over. That was the bottom line. No deal. No money. No Constellation.

Finally, after speaking to Max on the intercom for several long minutes, Jake started to laugh in frustration. He laughed so hard the tears ran down his face.

Jake strode into the private office in the Beverly-Rodeo Bank with confidence. He noticed that the room was dimly lighted, with only a sliver of morning sunshine peeping through the louver blinds, but he didn't care. Although he could barely hide his desperation to save his studio, he didn't want to appear too anxious, especially in front of the new bank owner Max had been told about last night. Jake was too excited to care about anything now except getting a two-week extension.

After Max's phone call, Jake didn't sleep the few hours he could have. Instead he had decided to meet with Max and pore over the books with him until all the paperwork was in order. He patted his leather briefcase for reassurance. It was all there, ready to be handed over in exchange for his signature.

Twenty minutes passed, but he refused to let the delay make him nervous. He lighted a cigarette. He didn't like the idea of being kept waiting, but he was certain the new owner and his minions were gathering up all the last-minute papers he'd have to sign. There is nothing to worry about, he told himself. Bankers always move slowly when they have to fork over money. Even his horoscope in today's *Times* said that a new fortune would be coming his way.

A side door opened, and to Jake's shock, four huge Asian goons entered and took up sentry positions around the office.

What's going on? he wondered in the moment before Takashima entered, a big evil smile on his face, followed by Noda. Then he saw Stephen come in the main entrance with a Japanese secretary. Jake felt like he'd been kicked in the stomach. Chisako had been right about his stepson.

"Good morning, Mr. Baron. Please take your seat," Takashima instructed as he pointed across the table. The bank manager now joined the group with a pile of legal-looking papers; the meeting was about to commence.

Still dumbfounded, Jake stared at the bank manager, who couldn't look him in the eye. Then Jake gave Stephen a dirty look. He'd been double-crossed. He'd had no idea, when Max made his desperate appeal for a two-week delay, that Takashima now owned the bank that held his studio as collateral against his loan.

Feeling the blood drain from his face, he could barely sit still. Inside, he felt dead. Not since his father had died had he felt such a gnawing hollowness in the pit of his stomach.

Takashima only smiled, then bowed slightly from the waist from his seat. His supreme moment was only seconds away, but he did not allow himself the pleasure of outward emotion. Business still must be attended to first. He would celebrate his victory later.

"Mr. Baron, I have all the papers to transfer your ownership back to the bank," the bank manager said, pulling a folder out of the pile.

"What about the two-week delay that Mr. Gerstein had requested?" Jake pleaded, his gaze riveted on Takashima.

"There will be no delay, Mr. Baron," Takashima stated firmly.

"You can't get away with this," Jake yelled back, his voice steaming with hatred. "I've been a good client of this bank for more than fifteen years."

"It is all very legal, Mr. Baron," interjected the bank manager, never once looking at Jake as he ignored his comment. "Now, if you would please sign this document here . . ."

He spread out the paperwork on the large boardroom table that would transfer the ownership of Constellation on a foreclosure to the Beverly-Rodeo Bank.

Takashima watched with delight. As soon as the deal was executed, he would immediately resell the studio to his own Takashima Group. It was all very simple, as Japanese business ethics dictated, and all very legal.

"Listen, Mr. Takashima," Jake began, keeping his voice calm. Instead of blowing up, he decided to play businessman. Surely this Jap didn't really want a movie studio. "I'll tell you what: you can charge me a few extra points, add it to my payment, and everyone will be happy. But just give me more time to pay the interest. Please, what about a few more weeks?"

Takashima shook his head. "No!" The American enemy did not know the rules of the game. He had lost. No further delays. "I am calling in your note, Mr. Baron; Constellation was your collateral," Takashima said as he pushed the paper in front of Jake. "Please sign where indicated," the Asian Octopus said, offering him a gold pen.

"You really don't care about what happens to Constellation," Jake said, realizing for the first time that what he was saying was the truth. "It's just another prize for your ego," he finished coldly.

Takashima did not dignify him with an answer.

Jake stared back at him for several seconds. Although the man didn't move, he could feel the tension between them, like a tight wire ready to snap. He knew he had hit a nerve.

Suddenly he couldn't sign it. Something wasn't right about this whole thing. Let those goons do what they wanted, he thought.

He turned around in his chair and stood up. He started to walk toward the exit, goons or no goons.

"You can't win, Dad," Stephen called out, speaking for the first time. Surprised, Jake turned around. What had that worthless schmuck said?

Stephen continued hurriedly. "Please, if you don't sign, you'll be dragged through the courts, and it'll cost you more in the long run . . ." He hesitated, his voice trailing off. "Don't make things any more difficult . . ."

No one breathed, but Jake could hear the pounding of his own heartbeat. "Don't you call me 'Dad,' you goddamn traitor," he snapped back. He realized he was now financially beaten, but the hurt from Stephen was worse.

Slowly, in defeat, Jake pulled out his own pen and sat down. He felt his stomach churn with anxiety, but he kept his hand steady. Then, with a deep reluctance, he signed all the papers. After he had finished, he looked up with hatred at Stephen and disgustedly threw the pen down on the table toward him.

Quickly, with a florid scrawl, Takashima signed his name, first in Japanese characters, then in western-style letters. Then, to make it official, he affixed his personal gold seal.

Without even a glance at Jake, Takashima put down the pen and turned to the portrait of Emperor Hirohito that one of the Yakuza had just mounted on the wall. Bowing, he said a prayer in Japanese:

"In your honor . . ." He remained bowed for several long seconds until he finished. Both the Yakuza and Noda stood quietly in respect, bowing as well.

Then they all left, including the bank manager and Stephen.

Only Jake remained seated. His life had just been ripped away.

9

The all-night celebration had been going on for hours in Takashima's 1901 Avenue of the Stars penthouse. Pink champagne flowed, pink balloons floated lazily in the air, and naked pink bodies danced.

Takashima had much to celebrate. His purchase of Constellation Studios was the most written-about item in every afternoon paper. In fact, the late edition of the *L.A. Times* had called him "the next greatest player in the entertainment industry, beating out every major Hollywood company, and a few foreign ones as well." It went on to say: "This first Japanese takeover of a Hollywood studio will now open up the floodgates for other Japanese businessmen with similar ambitions."

Tomorrow's headline story in *Daily Variety* would call it "QUITE A COUP!"; one of Tokyo's largest newspapers, *Nihon Keizai Shimbun,* would headline its morning edition with "DONE DEAL." And the morning lead story in every U.S. newspaper would run the banner "JAPAN INVADES HOLLYWOOD."

Takashima, pleased with his success and all the media attention, especially at being the first, watched the beautiful blond girls, glistening with sweat, fight over the champagne as the bubbly trickled down their bodies. He was very pleased with Stephen Resnick's choice of women for the evening; after all, he was paying Resnick bonuses of ten grand for those special favors.

But all of a sudden he had had enough of their

silliness. He forcefully clapped his hands, signaling his Yakuza to pop the balloons. A fine mist of gold dust floated down and sprinkled the girls and everything else in sight with the sparkling powder. There were more serious matters to be dealt with now.

Takashima again clapped his hands, and two Yakuza began hustling the complaining girls out of his office. It was now time for a special treat. Tonight he had decided to take possession of a very special gift.

Kakue.

She entered the room wearing only a kimono of the sheerest silk. Nothing was left to his imagination. He grunted loudly. Her youthful, virginal body pleased his eye. He stretched out his right arm horizontally, his hand palm-downward, waving inward from the wrist, silently signaling her to come forward.

Kakue walked closer, her steps tiny but certain. Though she was frightened, she wanted to please her master. This was her *giri* for the rest of her life. She had no other desire.

Slowly, on his command, she let her kimono fall to the floor.

Takashima looked at her for many minutes, his eyes never leaving her purity of form, her slimness of body. Her small but rounded breasts. Her dark, small nipples. Her slender hips. Her dark-haired triangle.

Under his scrutiny, she did not move the slightest muscle. He was most impressed with this strength of spirit. She was truly worthy of him, unlike others . . .

A Yakuza entered, interrupting his moment of tranquillity, and whispered something into the master's ear. Takashima nodded in acknowledgement.

"Take Kakue-san home," he said to the Yakuza. "I will return there shortly." Then he went into his private office.

He had old business to conclude first.

He sat down on the luxuriously brocaded couch, woven with timeless threads of pure gold. He then began tapping together his index fingers. Seconds later,

Chisako entered and stood before him proudly, her head high. She wore Western-style street clothes: a silk dress the color of a faded blue sky. Her hair was bound on top of her head, and she wore no jewelry. She refused to lower her head in submission. He was amazed at both her courage and her arrogance toward him.

"I am most displeased, Chisako-san."

She remained silent, but her eyes spoke volumes. She looked directly at him, her long lashes whipping up and down over her eyes in defiance. Angered, he stood up and turned his back to her. "You know why I have summoned you."

She did not answer. Nothing she would say would change her fate.

"You have betrayed me!" he shouted as he turned around and stared at her.

Chisako shivered. She tried to find her voice. His eyes were as dark as a panther's and his glare just as deadly. She knew if she did not admit her betrayal now, Takashima would take vengeance not only on her but also on Baron-san.

She fell to her knees and cried out, "Forgive me, Takashima-san. I did not know what I was doing. I . . . I was weak." She stumbled over her words, but she could not stop. "The opium . . . I was not myself . . ."

He spewed out his reply with the force of a dragon's breath. "I know you left the New Year's party with the American enemy. Tell me what you told him. I demand to know! Whore!"

Chisako cowered before him, frightened by his wrath, but her heart begged her to do what was right. Only then would her spirit be free. Takashima was an evil man, but Jake was not. She could not bear to see Takashima hurt him.

"N-n-nothing, I swear." She could not keep her voice from trembling.

"Joro!" He did not believe her. Viciously he slapped

her. Chisako put her hand to her cheek as a red flame began to color the side of her face, but she did not cry out. She stood her ground, defying him.

Takashima grunted his displeasure. There was no sense in questioning her any further. She was more dangerous to his plan of revenge now than before her betrayal. She would be useless to him from now on. She obviously had strong feelings for this American. No sword could sever such a bond.

He had but one recourse left.

He took one long hard look at the woman who had shared so many nights of pleasure with him. She must uphold her responsibility to him. He felt no emotion as he ceremoniously washed his hands of her with the wet towel handed to him by his Yakuza.

"Minoru-san, you have your orders," Takashima said as he nodded an okay to his chief bodyguard. "Begin."

Chisako had no time to react as two more Yakuza entered his office and grabbed her by the wrists, pulling her so abruptly that she could feel her arms tearing from the sockets. Her head snapped back and she felt herself falling swiftly into a swirling black madness. Her long dark hair came unbound and flew around her like the frantic fluttering of raven's wings.

No, no! she screamed silently, no words coming from her throat. Her eyes widened in horror as she watched Minoru raise his hand. His gold tooth glinted in the light as he smiled down at her while holding a long sword in his hand. She drew in her breath, her heart beating wildly as she closed her eyes and prayed. Then with one savage cut the Yakuza sliced through her dress. He then ripped it from her body.

Chisako silently endured further humiliation as Minoru ripped off her silk bra and panties; then he cut her garter belt from her waist and tore her stockings down her legs, cruelly scraping the pale white flesh of her thighs with his rough fingers. When would this end? she wondered.

She closed her eyes tightly, but she could still feel Takashima's eyes devouring her nakedness with some sadistic pleasure she did not understand. She would not give him the pleasure of seeing her cringe from his stare. She opened her eyes, and through the mask of her unspent tears she looked at him in silent appeal as his Yakuza went through her clothes until they found the thin gold box of opium.

"You will have no further need of this pleasure," Takashima said calmly as he took the gold box from Minoru.

She struggled to free her arms from the Yakuza's grasp, but they held her tighter.

"My pleasure will always live in my heart. You cannot take that from me!" she cried out, daring to raise her voice to the master. She looked at him strangely.

He clenched his fists, crushing her gold box of opium in his hands. "You leave me no further choice, Chisako-san. You are no longer a woman in my eyes."

Nodding, Minoru ceremoniously handed him his sword, its steel shaft clean. With a loud grunt Takashima stepped forward and looked deeply into Chisako's eyes, searching for some resemblance to the creature he had once taken to him. But all he saw was the fire of a she-devil who had dared to defy him. Smiling cruelly, he grabbed her long hair in his hand, then raised the sword and began chopping it off swiftly, until it lay in a pile at her feet.

For the first time, she wept.

Takashima ignored her tears. His voice was calm and deadly. " 'Duty is heavier than a mountain, while death is lighter than a feather,' " he said, repeating the code of the Imperial Rescript to soldiers. "You have betrayed me in your duty, Chisako-san. Do not fail me in this, your final debt."

He clapped his hands. Another Yakuza appeared, holding a white kimono in his hand. It was the color of death. He threw it at her. The Yakuza released her and she fell to her knees.

Her words came in short breaths in a cry for justice, not for mercy. "Takashima-san, I beg of you, I do not deserve the honor of joining my ancestors in their sacred rest. *Dozo*, allow me to wear the unholy kimono instead, stained with the color of my blood."

He looked at the woman in wonder. The red kimono was worn only by the lowliest of murderers and thieves. She obviously had more courage than he had believed. Or perhaps she was trying to make a fool out of him.

"Please, I will live out what remains of my life as a woman without honor. Each day I will suffer the memory of what I have done," she said, making a final appeal to him.

Takashima had not expected this. She asked to be banished.

This was the equivalent of the living death.

For several moments he considered her request, his body straight, his eyes never blinking. Finally he relaxed and bent over to lift up her face.

"So be it, Chisako-san, your karma shall be to live as you request," he said calmly, smiling with a secret pleasure. Now her soul would always be his.

He next picked up the white kimono, tossing it aside as he gathered up her tattered blue dress and wrapped it around her shoulders to cover her nakedness.

Tears of her lost youth mixed freely with those of her sins, rushing down her cheeks and wetting her trembling lips with the salty taste of repentence.

"*Domo arigatō gozaimashita*, Takashima-san." She could barely speak the words of gratitude as she bowed, her forehead touching the ground.

Takashima nodded farewell to her, then quickly turned away. He heard her again utter her cry of thanks.

He did not look back as the Yakuza dragged her away.

* * *

The black Mercedes drove up the winding road off Sunset to the foot of the Hollywood Hills and parked in front of the bungalow at Chateau Marmont, a residence hotel where the famous and the infamous often retreated to hide their sins from the outside world. Takashima had leased this quaint dwelling as a possible retreat, but he never before had had an occasion to use it.

Under the shadow of twilight, a small entourage of several Yakuza carried Chisako quickly inside. The breeze of the warm winter night filled the room, along with the subdued din of traffic from the boulevard below. The once-luxurious duplex was now only a dusty memory of a glorious past. A flattened-out mattress lay in the middle of the room where the sofa and end tables were usually placed. The Oriental rugs scattered on the floor were faded and ragged at the ends. The kitchen cabinets were covered with cobwebs. The only light in the living room came from a lone streetlamp filtering through the fifty-year-old louver window that creaked as one of the Yakuza opened it.

Chisako, pushed onto the floor, heard only the beating of her telltale heart. Dressed in a plain dark kimono and with no shoes on her feet, she did whatever the Yakuza told her. Unconsciously she kept pulling at her shorn hair, as if that would help to bring back her long tresses.

She stood quietly, dusting herself, as she clasped her hands to her breasts. Her eyes were dry; all her tears had been spent while the Yakuza had gathered up the few belongings Takashima had allowed her. They had been hurriedly dumped into a pillowcase.

She was to spend the night in this dungeonlike room before her return trip to Japan tomorrow. *"Joro,"* one of the Yakuza shouted as he abruptly shoved her and her pillowcase of belongings against the side of the kitchen cabinet.

Chisako felt a lump in her throat as she saw her few

possessions fly out the open end of the pillowcase, scattering all over the floor. Quickly she got to her knees and tried to gather up her things—some jewelry, some scented soap—but two of the Yakuza, having some fun, grabbed her by her short hair and teased her mercilessly with their jeering. She cowered before them.

As she looked frantically for the rest of her things, she did not hear Noda quietly entering the room. His eyes were very sad as he watched her. He did not approve of Takashima's treatment of people, especially women. He had kept his thoughts to himself all these years, as was the protocol, but when he saw the Yakuza abusing her, he could no longer stand it. The woman had been humiliated enough.

"Leave her alone, *now*. Wait for me outside!" he shouted, adjusting his glasses on his nose. "I have given you an order, now obey me!"

One of the Yakuza took a step toward Noda, then changed his mind when he saw the insistent look on Noda's face. Instead he bowed and left. The other quickly followed.

Chisako gave Noda a small awkward smile of thanks. She had never paid much attention to Takashima's quiet protégé before. Mumbling to herself, she began stuffing her few possessions back into her pillowcase.

"My bracelet, where is my bracelet?" she mumbled, frantically looking for her solid gold rope bracelet until she found it. She held it up to her chest, grateful for a fond remembrance.

"And my combs, they've taken my combs from me." Her voice was small, childlike, and sad.

Noda hated to see anyone, especially a woman, look so pitiful. Her face was drawn and pale from crying, her eyes sunken from the withdrawal effects of her opium. "Wait, I'll help you," he said, bending down on his knees to look. Almost immediately he spotted twin glints under the dusty kitchen table: two slender hair ornaments in the shape of ginkgo leaves.

As he reached to grab them, Chisako called out, "My combs! You found them!"

Happily he fetched the combs and handed them to her.

As he watched her look at them, a sudden chill from an approaching storm swept into the room. Remembering himself, Noda shut the window and looked at his watch. It was getting late. He should leave now before the Yakuza become too impatient.

As he walked to the door, she called out to him, "Noda-san, are they not the most beautiful combs?" She held them up to her hair. They were hand-carved and studded with perfect black pearls from the South Seas.

She tilted her head from side to side, pressing them into her hair, now too short to hold them. But they made her feel regal again, something she needed very badly. And to Noda's surprise, she danced around the room, feeling the pearl combs as they glimmered like drops of night rain. His stomach started fluttering. He had once seen a woman prance about like that, with twin black combs flashing in her hair . . .

Seeing the strangely rapt expression on his face, Chisako slowed to a halt. "Noda-san, should I tell you something no one else knows?" Her eyes grew wide like a child intent on telling a secret, even if no one wanted to listen. And this was a particularly horrible secret.

"There was a geisha who owned the combs before me. She was young and beautiful, and she was Takashima's favorite for a time—until he accidentally discovered she had a child."

He took a lunging step toward the woman, "You must put them away immediately!" he yelled, his voice choked with emotion.

"Come, Noda-san, surely you do not believe that old wives' tale about it being bad luck to pick up an old comb?"

Noda did not answer, for his heart was thundering

in his ears as a strange but familiar smell filled his nostrils. The strong scent of ginger incense still lingered on the old combs, filling the room with its pungent odor. He was reminded of another room—small and with a low ceiling, but decorated with tall screens and lacquered furniture. In his mind he saw the delicate figure of a woman kneeling in front of a mirror and fastening the combs into her hair. She hummed softly, tilting her head from side to side. Noda knew who she was: his mother. When he was a small boy she had often allowed him into her room as she dressed.

"Do you know what happened to this geisha?" he asked cautiously. When she did not answer right away, he pressed further. "I must know. My mother had combs like these," he said, his voice quavering as he spoke.

Chisako suddenly turned pale. Was Noda speaking the truth? Yet she was certain she had nothing to fear in telling him. Her destiny had already been decided by Takashima. He would never go back on his word. This would be her final moment to make certain he would never forget her.

She began slowly. She had carried the burden of Takashima's secret for so long, it was difficult for her to speak. "She had a young child before she came to the house of Takashima-san," she said, "but she kept the child secret from the master. When he discovered this, he insisted she could no longer remain in his house as his geisha."

"Because she had a child?"

"That is correct. When a woman comes to Takashima-san, she must be a virgin," she said slowly. "It is his way."

As she spoke, Noda stared numbly at the combs in her hand. And when she finished, he heard another voice, one from far away, echoing in his head: "Are they not beautiful combs, my child?" His heart leapt into his throat. It was his mother's voice—and these were her rare combs. "There are no other combs like them in the whole world." Yes, she had often said that.

Deathly pale, Noda grabbed Chisako by the shoulders. "What happened to her? Tell me!"

Feeling the unearthly sway of his dread, she continued, faltering, "She was murdered by Takashima-san ... tortured on the water wheel until she could no longer draw a breath. Takashima-san is clever—he made it appear as if she had committed hara-kiri by her own hand. Her death was accepted by the police as a suicide."

Noda's hands dug deeper into her flesh. "You are certain of this?"

She nodded. "Takashima-san often boasted of this to me when we were alone. He took pleasure in gloating of his power over everyone, especially women."

Without either of them realizing it, he had taken the combs from her hands. Now he looked at them, turning them this way and that in the light. So that is why Takashima has always shown me such favor, he mused. The man who had given him everything, as a father would, had also taken the life of his beloved mother. . . .

"My combs. Please, may I have them back?" Chisako asked quietly.

Noda looked into her sunken eye sockets. He laid the combs back in her hands, certain that the restless soul of his mother would continue to protect Chisako from any other harm.

Then he grabbed a dirty planter resting on the counter and violently threw it across the room. It shattered into a hundred pieces.

His face was hard as he turned toward the door. A madness had overtaken him. His thoughts were interrupted by the Yakuza banging on the door. "I will be right there," he shouted to them.

He then walked confidently out of the room, certain

of what he would have to do. The ties of *giri* had been broken.

As Jake looked out the paned glass window of his office, a strong Santa Ana continued to blow. His face was grim. It had been a miserable twenty-four hours.

He closed his daily studio log for the last time, then put the red leather book with Constellation's logo, embossed in gold, back into its protective box. He continued to stare out the window, watching a low-hanging branch from the weeping willow bang noisily against the wall.

He saw scenes of his past flash by him: Bunky driving him up his namesake street in his 1954 Mercedes; Bunky giving him his first camera, then telling him not to come back until he had shot the whole reel of film; Bunky getting him a little drunk after Constellation had won an Oscar for Best Picture in the early sixties.

Suddenly the pain became too much. He put his hands to his head and shrieked with agony.

"You okay, Dad?" Mistica asked, looking up from the floor, where she was stacking Jake's personal files. She was wearing her torn-at-the-knee jeans and a UCLA sweatshirt. Her hair was pulled back in a long ponytail.

"Yeah, sure, sweetie." Jake looked down and smiled at her. "Just letting a little of my anger out."

"I don't know why we have to do all this packing so soon," Mistica commented angrily. "I asked Stephen if he was going to get his stuff packed and leave with us, but he didn't say anything. He just said he was too busy to talk to me."

Jake stiffened. He still hadn't told her about Stephen turning traitor. She would find out the truth about his betrayal in due time.

"Hey, what's this, Dad?" she asked, confused, as she picked up two pieces of iron sculpture about a foot high with no particular shape.

Jake laughed. "Awful-looking, aren't they? Your

Aunt Beattie on Stephen's side bought those bookends in an antique shop on the Left Bank when she went to Paris to find herself. That was before you were born, Mistica." He remembered his eccentric sister-in-law fondly. "She always claimed they were 'genuine' Picasso reproductions. Every time she took a trip, I could expect something different from her."

That gave Jake an idea. "How would you like to go away for a couple of months on a vacation?"

"Are you kidding? Where?"

"What about Barbados? We can lie on the beach all afternoon, dance all night, then sleep all morning . . ."

His happy mood was swiftly deflated as his office door opened without anyone knocking. It was a menacing-looking Yakuza along with a couple of mysterious-looking electricians. The two Asian men in coveralls with their faces hidden started immediately rewiring the office.

Jake was outraged, but he knew there was nothing he could do. He wasn't in charge anymore. He turned his back to them and just continued talking to his daughter as if they were still alone. In fact, he spoke louder and more slowly, for their edification. "It doesn't matter where we go, even Tokyo, as long as we're together, right?"

"Right. Hey, look what I just found." She began to read from a small book with ragged corners, its yellowed pages filled with faded writing: " 'To my pal Jake, Mickey Rooney.' " She turned the page. " 'Remember, Jake, perseverance is the key to open any locked door. Best always, Orson Welles.' "

"Let me see," he said, reading over his daughter's shoulder. " 'Love, Kisses, and Lollipops, Shirley Temple.' " Jake turned the page. " 'Memo to Jake Baron: If you want to be a success, learn to write memos. D. O. Selznick.' "

There was a knock on the partially closed door and Rose Kaufman poked her head inside and waved a stack of pink phone slips. "Are you guys allowed visitors?" she asked, giving the stern-faced Yakuza a dirty look.

"Come in, Rosey," he said, closing the door all the way, shutting out the Jap goon.

Rose was openly upset. "I've got to talk to you, Jake. I just don't know how to begin."

"Calm down, Rose. What's the problem?"

She chewed on her reading glasses nervously. "The calls haven't stopped coming in, Jake. The whole town wants to know what you're doing next. I don't know what to say."

Jake smiled broadly, looking at Mistica. "Tell my friends that I'm disappearing for a few months. It'll be a good way to clear my head." He moved across the room and piled up a couple of boxes, then turned back to Rose. "And as for any other questions, just give the usual 'No comment.' "

Rose peered over her half-glasses; she wore them more for effect than anything else. "Here," she said as she handed him two telephone slips. "Both of these calls might lead to something." One message was from Jake's friend Sir Richard Attenborough, the renowned English director, and the other was from Victor Kaufman, Columbia's CEO in New York. "Just to satisfy my own curiosity, when are you really planning to come back?"

"I don't know, probably after the Oscar show," he answered nostalgically. "This year I can miss all the pre-awards hoopla. Maybe the change of scenery will be good." But suddenly he stopped to reflect. Nothing seemed to be going right in his life now: Kelly . . . the fire . . . the Italian . . . Stephen . . . and even the invasion of Takashima.

Biting her lip, Rose looked around the large executive office, searching for a reason not to run off. She felt Jake's uneasiness; after all, he had been a winner for so many years, and now . . . "Jake, can I help you with some of the packing?" she asked quietly as she wiped her glasses clean before she put them back on.

He shook his head with a polite "No."

But there was something else on her mind. She looked at him with tears in her eyes. "Jake, will you be all right?"

He smiled in reply. "What? You mean financially? Believe it or not, I have some rainy-day savings hidden in some old shoe boxes that I didn't pour into Constellation."

With her lower lip trembling as she tried to smile, she grabbed him and did something she had never done in all her thirty years at the studio. She kissed him on the lips, clinging to him emotionally. "Jake, I . . . I don't know what I'm going to do without you. You've been like a son to me."

Jake, too, fought to keep control of his emotions. This wonderful lady—who was only a few years older than he was—was the closest thing he had ever had to a mother. His mom had died when he was five.

"It's never good-bye between us, Rose," he said softly as he kissed the top of her head and held her close. "We're family, and don't you ever forget that."

She nodded, too choked up to say anything more. She managed to give him a smile; then, with a quick squeeze of his hand and a wave to Mistica, she was gone.

Jake stood silently for a few minutes. It had been like that all day, saying good-bye to everyone on his staff. It's like a goddamn funeral, he thought sadly.

Mistica, seeing the torment her father was going through, strode toward the door. She had to get him out of there, and right away.

"You coming, Dad?" she asked, coaxing him. "Let's tell them they can load the boxes now."

"Sure, honey, I'll be right with you."

He wanted to take one last look around his office. Everything he needed was now packed up. But somehow, he knew this wasn't the final act. He reflected on what his dad used to say: "Remember, son, until you see the curtain drop all the way to the floor, the show's not over yet."

"Jūran shazetsu!" the Yakuza shouted to the curious spectators gathering around the main gate of Constellation Studios. "No visitors!"

The master's limo continued on its way, then stopped in front of the executive office building.

When Takashima and his group entered, all heads turned around in curiosity.

Numerous secretaries and production assistants whispered among themselves as the Yakuza hustled them back into their offices. They couldn't believe that this quick transformation was for real. They wondered how they would learn the new keyboards with Japanese characters for the computers they had been told they would soon be getting.

When the Asian Octopus and his associates got into the elevator, the other occupants weren't sure what to do. Two men immediately got out. A young receptionist said hello, but an overly exuberant mail boy was quickly ousted when he failed to move after the Yakuza indicated to him that the left-rear corner of the elevator was the *kami za*, place of honor, for Takashima.

After the *wa* had been restored, the elevator went straight to the top floor without stopping.

So far, the day had gone as planned. Takashima was very pleased. As soon as he entered one of his new offices, he placed only one phone call: overseas to Tokyo.

He sipped a cup of tea as he listened to his old friend Akio Morita, chairman of Sony, rant and rave for several minutes on the other end. Morita had been just as determined to be the first Japanese entrepreneur to run a major Hollywood studio. This had become a personal battle between these two billionaire competitors, but Takashima had beaten him. He had no doubt that his rival would have his day soon.

As he hung up the phone, he laughed. He sat quietly and gathered his thoughts. Morita-san had boasted that Sony's future plans would be more elaborate than his. Takashima pretended to worry out loud to his visiting Japanese journalist friends, allowing them to believe how serious he was about running a Hollywood studio. Little did the journalists or Morita know.

Takashima, still full of energy, stood in the middle of the studio's main quadrangle, watching Constellation undergoing an overnight face lift. The visiting Japanese journalists snapped pictures of anything that moved. They were equally excited.

Nearby, the veteran guards at the main gate had already removed their caps and badges and handed them over to the Yakuza, who would be taking their places. Takashima had personally fired them, even though some of them had been on duty at the studio gates for more than thirty years.

Everybody had been busy doing something, including Noda, who supervised some of the workmen putting up survey sticks for the new Shinto shrine. It would be built in the burned-out area of the back lot.

Some of the waitresses stared curiously out of the large picture windows of the commissary. They still couldn't figure out the changes in the menu ordered by the new owner, especially some of the Japanese dishes that no one had ever heard of before.

The flagman waved the black Mercedes limo with Takashima and the journalists inside to a halt as the sign reading "Bunky Boulevard" came crashing down in front of it. A new sign went up: "Hiroshi Avenue."

Exiting the limo, Takashima now turned his attention to the flagpole. The master's supreme moment had come. The entourage all stood at attention.

He nodded a signal to the Yakuza on his left. Minoru gave the order as he said: *"Nippon no kokki!"*

Slowly, deliberately, the Stars and Stripes came down as the Japanese flag of the Rising Sun began to ascend.

Takashima smiled broadly. It was now time to change Hollywood.

PART TWO

PART TWO

10

Over the next few weeks, Hollywood was rampant with rumors. With the acquisition of Constellation, Takashima had acquired not only the studio and all of its facilities but also its forty acres of land, every current project either in development or in production (including *Criminal Intent*), and the biggest prize, the studio's library of twenty-five hundred films, including many award-winning classics. This opened up many questions as to what his plans would be.

Takashima was just the latest foreign investor to claim a stake in the show-business capital, even if he was the first Japanese. And, as had happened when other offshore buyers arrived in Hollywood—such as Australian tycoon Rupert Murdoch when he purchased Twentieth Century-Fox—a hungry media gave Takashima the same rough grilling. The questions only accelerated when he began to "No comment" everything thrown his way:

"Will you confirm that you will turn the studio into condos with a Japanese motif?"

"Will you hire only Asians to succeed the Americans in executive positions?"

"Aren't you quietly thinking about raiding Warners of their two hottest producers, Guber and Peters?"

But the primary difference between Takashima and the other big guns like Murdoch was that he enjoyed all the confusion he was generating. The more confusion he spread about his real plans, the happier he felt. After all, this was a part of his scheme of revenge.

Ensconced in his leather executive chair, Takashima leaned back after the latest of the wearying media calls and closed his eyes. A few minutes of meditation were what he needed. Then he could charge back into the fray renewed.

He did not find the peace he was seeking, though. As had happened more and more frequently over the past few weeks, he was overtaken by a scalding vision from his past, one that had scorched his soul forever.

Takashima had been a boy of nine when the *pika*, the great blinding flash, came.

It was late morning, and he had gone for a swim in the river outside Nagasaki. The water was cool, still sweet from a fresh rain. Then he heard the plane coming. An American bomber flew over his head. Quickly he dived deeply into the dark waters.

As he swam deeper, the whole river seemed to be turned upside down, like a giant turtle on its back. Takashima began to swallow water as he fought his way back to the top. Just when he felt his lungs would burst, he made it to the surface. What he saw next frightened him far more than any fear of drowning. A pillar of white smoke curled high into the morning sun, like the long neck of a sea serpent reaching out over the city nearby and lapping it up greedily with its fiery tongue. Terrified, he dived into the river again, this time praying it was all a bad dream.

Takashima shivered and began to sweat. He could not shake the sickening feeling that came over him every time he allowed himself this journey into the past. And now the memory was more vivid than ever: the burning flesh, the cries for merciful death, the slow poisoning from radiation. He had survived the bombing unscathed, but when he returned home he found the charred wooden sticks that had once been his house scattered over the burned-out fields, the gaping hole leading to hell where he and his family had once prayed to their gods, the broken bodies of raw flesh that had been his mother and sisters. Yet he did not weep. He scoffed at those who prayed to the Emperor for forgiveness for losing the war. Instead he prayed to the Emperor for revenge.

Because of that day, Takashima missed his childhood, that time when childish games, individual freedom of self-expression, and complete abandonment of duty reigned supreme. These were the most cherished moments of a Japanese boy's life, especially as he would grow older and take his place in the rigid society. Takashima had been deprived of knowing any of this.

When the Americans came to liberate, he had, as had the thousands of homeless children scouring the garbage cans to survive, been forced to take any work the hated conquerors had to offer. He started by running errands for the American Army officers quartered at the Omura Japanese Naval Hospital. He carried blood plasmas, which he occasionally dropped or casually misplaced. He took messages, loaded medical supplies. But inside, the fire was beginning to ignite.

Soon after, he was assigned to the sergeant in charge of the projection room. Many nights he brought coffee to the fanatical southern military man with the foul-smelling, liquor-laden breath. He was forced to watch many times over the stupid American movies he never liked or understood. He did not appreciate the humor of the silly-looking three men hitting each other on the head with sticks, nor the scenes of men and women kissing in public. And he especially hated the combat films that showed the Americans winning every battle.

He had promised himself that one day he would destroy the Americans. Forty-three years he had waited. Over that time his hatred had grown to an obsession. And now he had the power to destroy the very thing Americans loved most: their movies. In fact, he wanted to destroy everything that was Hollywood—from burning down the studios to ruining the film labs, to busting the unions, to even kidnapping and harming many American movie stars. He intended to leave a real void that would affect the American people for a long time.

Bolting upright in his chair, Takashima chided himself for allowing the past to overtake him again. There was much work to do now, today. Quickly he reached for the file lying in the center of his desk.

His Ronin group, who had recently set up their headquarters in Century City under the cover of darkness, had recommended that his best first step—and a very high-profile one—would be to steal a powerful insider who would front as the head of his studio. This suggestion mirrored what Murdoch had done when he purchased Twentieth and hired away Barry Diller from his position at Paramount.

After carefully evaluating some of Hollywood's top talent—people such as MGM executive Richard Berger, independent producer Ray Stark, superagent Michael Ovitz—Takashima had decided that his big catch was going to be the Academy Award-winning producer Lawrence Evans, who was currently under a five-year, first-look deal at Universal. *Daily Variety* had headlined Universal's immediate response: "NO WAY IN HELL." The powerful studio was adamant that they would not allow a tremendous piece of manpower like Larry Evans escape without a major legal fight. And that was exactly what Takashima was hoping for.

Even after direct appeals from studio president Sidney Sheinberg and a few phone calls from legendary chairman Lew Wasserman of the parent company, MCA, the most influential executive in Hollywood, Takashima still did not waver one bit. In fact, he upped his offer to Evans. It was so lucrative that many top agents phoned Takashima pitching other high-powered executives. He loved every moment of it. Already he was sowing seeds of discord in the industry.

Universal and MCA quickly hired two famous Washington attorneys renowned from Watergate to file mega-lawsuits against both Evans and Takashima, as well as the Takashima Group and Constellation Studios.

The town was abuzz. From the Hollywood trade papers to the *Wall Street Journal* to the *Tokyo Shimbun*, even to the nightly network reports from Rather, Brokaw, and Jennings, the ongoing Japanese-Hollywood dogfight was being written and discussed as one of the major stories each and every day. In fact, a *New York Times* lead editorial stated that the outcome of the legal mess could affect already fragile business relations between the Japanese and the Americans. In a poll conducted by *Newsweek* as part of a cover story on Constellation, most Americans surveyed thought that the purchase of the last privately owned studio by a Japanese group was a bad thing. And nearly all of them had the same opinion about Japan's continued economic growth: it bothered them more than the Soviets' military power. As one farmer in Iowa put it: "It scares the shit out of me."

Thousand of miles across the Pacific Ocean, many Japanese business executives were disturbed as well. Takashima was openly agitating the American system with his controversial attempt at luring away the much-sought-after producer. This was contrary to the traditional philosophy that it was always better to make changes quietly and slowly. As the day-to-day media coverage increased in Tokyo as well, many members of the Takashima Group were summoned to various *ad hoc* meetings. And in every case the powerful group members were pressured to persuade Takashima to immediately desist in his tactics. If not, they all stood a chance of losing face with the Americans.

"I most solemnly disagree with my distinguished group members," said a chagrined and apologetic-looking Takashima.

It had been a long, tiresome meeting, conducted via his newly installed two-way floor-to-ceiling tele-screen hookup in his 1901 Avenue of the Stars office suite.

The members of the Takashima Group had held an emergency luncheon meeting at a secret location in a prefecture outside of Tokyo, and had agreed unanimously to disapprove of Takashima's overly aggressive moves. What would they do, Takashima wondered, if they also knew he had vowed to make Universal his next target for ruination?

Noda, who had been taking notes across the conference room—out of camera range with Minoru—motioned to his master to read a message he had just finished writing and was holding under his chin. Takashima glanced at his heir apparent, rubbed his cheek as an okay motion, then quickly turned to his group on the large screen.

"Gentlemen, with your permission, I would like to take an important telephone call and reconvene this conference in, let us say, fifteen minutes."

The group, in unison, agreed with this request. With the proper respect, they all bowed their acknowledgment to Takashima while remaining seated around their board table. He returned their bow and pressed a red button on his console. The large screen went black.

During the next few minutes both Noda and Minoru huddled with Takashima, discussing options. Takashima must save face with his powerful group members but at the same time push forward.

As fast as the two associates tossed out ideas, Takashima rejected them. Finally, to Takashima's surprise, Noda excused himself and politely said he would return in a minute or two. As Noda strode from the office, he gritted his teeth in rage. It was all he could do to keep from grabbing his mentor by the throat and accusing him of his mother's murder. *Gaman*, he told himself, you must wait. He had much work to do before his trap would be sprung.

He returned with a black leather notebook he had borrowed from the Ronin leader down the hallway. Inside this confidential manual was the rough draft that he had intended to discuss fully with Takashima at his next meeting with his propagandists, but under the circumstances, Noda had decided to unveil it right away. "Under the topic of 'Leadership Succession,'" he said as he read from the Ronin notes, their research suggested that Hollywood leaders were constantly capricious. "They quickly forget any misfortune that befalls one of their own," he quoted before going on to cite some recent examples.

Takashima was not interested in any lectures, however. Looking at his watch, he realized that he would have to recommence his meeting very soon. "*Dozo*, Noda-san, you must learn to come to the point. I must continue immediately with my group." Takashima then walked over to his high-backed black leather recliner.

He was about to press the buttons to continue the meeting when Noda said in an uncharacteristically raised voice, "Please wait, Takashima-san." The Asian Octopus paused, surprised by this breach of decorum. Smiling inwardly in satisfaction, Noda hurried on: "In conclusion, master, you need a very strong person to act as a magnet. This person must not only give Constellation employees a sense of security but also enable the studio to reestablish itself as a fertile creative ground where box-office talent, as well as agents and filmmakers, will want to do business. Otherwise, you are in danger of being dismissed as a major player." Noda paused, eyeing his mentor nervously for a moment before he continued. "And the first suggestion on their list is someone currently available and without a contract somewhere else. That person, master, is Kelly Kristopher."

Takashima was taken aback. His Ronin advisers had selected a woman? Women were for fetching or fucking. The more he considered the idea, though, the better it seemed. His Takashima Group would applaud such a move, especially now with the women's movement in high gear in Tokyo. What's more, this Kristopher woman had had the guts to stand up and defend herself—and before all of her powerful peers, he recalled. She would make a perfect cover for his subterfuge with the American enemy.

With his shoulder twitching, Stephen paced his office reception area on the thirty-third floor of the exclusive Fox Plaza, only one floor below the recently leased offices of the Reagan Foundation for the ex-President. The clients of his firm were the superstars of Hollywood and they expected to be treated as such. He was successful because he understood that.

All of the offices in Stephen's suite were personally decorated with a different designer's touch, but each had an Early American theme: mahogany writing desks, beveled glass mirrors, exquisitely polished highboys, and other priceless antiques. The only modern touches were soft plush furniture in the anteroom for easy conversation, and a refrigerator, in a private room, stocked with the finest champagne and wines from around the world.

Ambience had always been important to Stephen, as well as to his three associate lawyers. He had a theory that every client liked to believe there was a touch of Thomas Jefferson in the attorney he hired: wit, intelligence, versatility.

But the attributes of the third U.S. President weren't on Stephen's mind today as he walked around the spiral staircase leading up to his private office loft. He had been despondent over the past few weeks. First his stepfather had denounced him as a "goddamn traitor," then a majority of his clients defected with one of his colleagues to a new firm, and now the Vegas bookies were closing in again.

Stephen ignored the stares of his two receptionists, surprised at seeing Mr. Resnick roaming around the reception area in shirtsleeves. "Good morning. Law offices," one girl said as she continued, sneaking a glance at Stephen. "Right away, Miss Hawn, I'll see if he's in."

He observed the time on the stately two-hundred-year-old grandfather clock near the entrance to his reception area. Twelve-twenty. The loud tick-tocking was driving him crazy. It was almost as if a time bomb were ready to explode at any minute. He felt like smashing the glass face on the clock, but that wouldn't solve anything.

He climbed the spiral staircase into his private office and locked the door behind him. He glanced at his Harvard law degree hanging on the wall and remembered how happy Jake had been when he passed the bar on his first try. Jake had felt that he was going to be something special when he helped him start his first law practice.

Yeah, I'm something special, all right, he thought miserably. He was up the creek with gambling debts. He constantly lied, to the point he didn't even know when he was telling the truth anymore. And now he had sold out his own stepfather.

Suddenly the guilt of all that he had done was too much for him. He took out a small key and pulled open the bottom drawer. He looked at the locked metal box inside. He placed it on top of his desk and opened it. Twitching, he stared at the loaded Smith & Wesson. He had bought it a year ago, thinking he might need protection if he were ever trapped in his office by thugs from Las Vegas. Increasingly, however, the snub-nosed revolver had become a kind of eerie lure for him. He would take it out and stare at it for long minutes, wondering if he had the courage to kill himself. He would write a letter to his dad begging forgiveness and place it under his In box so that the blood would not . . .

Stephen was startled as his intercom buzzer pierced the stillness. Hurriedly slamming the cover of the box, he reached for the button. "Yes?" he asked in a faint, quavering voice.

"Mr. Resnick, Mr. Takashima is on the line. Shall I say you're in?"

"Uh, I . . . yes. Yes, put him on."

Moments later, Stephen found himself listening to a remarkable offer.

". . . I understand, Resnick-san. When you lose face the way you have, it must be very difficult to continue to deal with your colleagues and your associates. I am also truly sorry to hear that many of your clients have decided to leave your firm," Takashima said as he pretended to express his deep sympathy.

Until Noda had read to him the Ronin findings, Takashima, like most other people in Hollywood now, had no more use for Resnick. Once Takashima had secured the studio, he had wanted to keep only Japanese personnel around him. But with his new plan—overwhelmingly approved by his Takashima Group—Resnick once again had become his key operative in this latest acquisition.

Takashima realized that he would have to move rapidly to lure the American woman into his fold. According to the Ronin report, she had been considering recent offers to join such studios as Paramount, Orion, and Fox as an independent producer. She had also been offered a key management position with Disney. Every offer she had received was very lucrative, with numerous perks and a great deal of autonomy attached—something that creative people cherished. But Takashima knew that his offer would be the most attractive ever made to any executive in the entertainment business, and, no less, to a woman. And Kristopher-san could hold the highest executive position that a woman had ever held in Hollywood—that of CEO of a major movie studio.

"Resnick-san, I have recently been updated that you have lost a lot of money in Las Vegas once again and that the gamblers have given you a very short time to repay your debt. And if you do not, they have threatened, as is their way, to 'make you pay.' Is this not true?"

"Takashima, it's true. I need a pile of cash to pay back some people. Maybe when I pay everybody . . . I will be left alone . . ." Stephen replied, stammering.

Takashima growled at the hesitant voice on the other end of the line. He would never have contacted the weakling if he had not had a use for him. Finally he said, point-blank, "If you can convince Kelly Kristopher to run my new studio, I will pay you, in cash, a half-million dollars. Are you interested?"

Stephen was momentarily dumbfounded. The idea seemed almost funny. The person who had ruined his reputation now wanted to use his talents again. If I wasn't so out in the cold with everyone, he thought, I'd tell him to go fuck himself on the first flight back to Tokyo. Besides that, would Kelly even listen to his offer from Takashima? And if he didn't agree to help Takashima, or if he failed, would he be fucked anyway? There didn't seem to be a lot of choices left.

Gathering up his courage, he responded, "For one million dollars, I will deliver Kelly with bells on her toes to your doorstep . . . and not a dime less."

Takashima could not believe his ears. How dare the traitorous worm double his offer? he thought angrily.

"Resnick-san, what if I refuse to pay you what you want?"

"It's very simple, Hiroshi," Resnick said, sounding cockier than ever. "I'll tell the newspapers how I stole confidential papers from my dad's office to help you in your acquisition of his studio. Then, my good friend, how long do you think you will have left in this town?"

Takashima could not believe his ears. Was this American scum actually threatening to blackmail him, the Asian Octopus? With the greatest concentration of effort, he calmed himself. Already he had decided that Stephen Resnick had run his last errand for him.

"Resnick, you have one week to deliver the woman to me."

Stephen wiped his forehead with the back of his hand. Shit, he had to get a grip on himself before they arrived. It wasn't going to be easy working out this deal, but he figured he'd have a better chance of making Takashima's offer work if he met Kelly on neutral ground. Robert had even agreed, especially when Stephen had given him a clue as to how big the deal would be.

As he took off his jacket, Stephen looked around the trendy Pacific Palisades restaurant with sawdust on the floor. Most of the patrons at Gladstones 4 Fish were dressed in a casual style. He didn't give the crowd around the bar a second glance. He was too busy worrying about what he had to accomplish tonight.

He grabbed a handful of peanuts from the bowl on the bar and started nibbling while he sipped a glass of water. It was warm for a winter evening, even at the beach, he thought as he tugged at his shirt collar, staining it with peanut oil.

Leaning against the counter, he closed his eyes. His life was going nowhere. Because of his own gambling sickness, Stephen was now ruined. To make matters worse, his stepfather had left town before he had a chance to explain. He had tried to contact him several times, but it was always the same. His stepfather would slam the phone down in his ear without saying anything, or shout "You're no longer my son!" and then slam down the phone. Sometimes, Stephen thought, maybe it would be better to end it all.

"How about a drink, sir?" the tanned cocktail waitress asked, a big smile lighting up her face.

Stephen shook his head—he had his free glass of water. He walked toward the front door again. "Where the hell are they?" he mumbled, the frustration in his voice evident as he looked at his Rolex.

"Hey, Resnick," called out a fellow lawyer, "how are things over at Constellation?"

Stephen stopped, then smiled weakly to himself. It was the most frequently asked question in Hollywood these days.

"It sure is different, Bertram. That Jap's got everybody hopping—everything from morning exercises to weird food in the commissary," Stephen complained, but he was careful not to say too much.

He excused himself when he finally saw Kelly and Robert park their Wrangler Jeep and enter the restaurant. They both seemed to be smiling. So far, so good. He walked over to greet them.

Robert immediately spied Michael Douglas and Danny DeVito dining over in the corner. Acknowledging Stephen with a nod, he told Kelly he'd join them later. Stephen liked that idea. He wanted to be alone with her.

It was now show time.

The beach was surprisingly calm for an early-February evening. The flood of starlight lit up the ocean like uncut crystal, making a pathway for Stephen and Kelly as they walked along the rim of the beach. The two former colleagues had been talking for almost two hours about Takashima buying the studio and the incredible offer that he had made for her services.

After Stephen's phone call, Robert, as agent for Kelly, had put on hold the various offers he had been considering on behalf of his wife until this mega-offer was fully explored. No other studio offer had come close to a three-million-dollar annual salary with huge perks.

"I don't understand why Takashima sent you to ask me. Why didn't he send one of his own people?" she asked, somewhat confused.

Stephen grinned, feeling important for the first time. "I'm still the studio's attorney as well as the only one he can rely on to get the job done."

Kelly kicked up some sand with her shoe, choosing her next words carefully. "Have you heard from Jake?" She had received only a brief call from him before he left for Barbados, and he had seemed distant, chatting with false merriment about finally being able to take a vacation. It was as if they were merely acquaintances thrown together at a cocktail party.

Stephen looked at her sharply. "No . . . he hasn't called yet."

"But he knows you're working for Takashima."

Stephen was hesitant. "Yeah, sure, he knows."

Kelly and Stephen continued walking in awkward silence, and after a few moments she zipped up her deep-pink hooded sweatshirt to keep out the chill. All she could think about as they strolled down the beach was Jake. How would he feel about her working for the Japanese mogul? Would he hate her? Or would he want her to do what was best not only for her career but also for the future direction of Constellation? If she took the position, then she would have a controlling voice in how the studio was run; that meant keeping Constellation a top studio in town. She owed that much to Jake.

Or was she deceiving herself? Did Jake care what happened to Constellation now that he no longer was infusing it with his life's blood? Maybe all she was doing was making excuses to herself to justify becoming CEO. No, she realized, I would never do that to him.

Finally she said, "I'll think about the offer, Stephen. I'm still not sure."

He shook his head in frustration. He had to convince her to take this offer. "Kelly, he's making you a multimillionaire with all the power that goes along with it. What's there to think about?"

His attitude made her angry. "Fuck you, Stephen," Kelly responded. "I don't care about the money. Jake paid me a million. What I really care about is preserving a Hollywood landmark . . . and your dad's family heritage. Your family heritage, in case you've forgotten."

"I'm telling you, Kelly, Mr. Takashima is in a position to make you the most powerful woman exec ever in Hollywood," Stephen urged, his voice insistent. He saw her face light up. She was weakening. "Shit, Kelly, this guy's offering you the biggest deal this town has ever seen."

"What about the scandal with the judge?"

Stephen shook his head. "That means nothing to him."

"By the way, Stephen, if it wasn't for you, I wouldn't

have had all the headlines with the judge in the first place. After all, he was your good friend."

"Let's forget the past, Kelly."

She thought about it for a minute, then looked directly at him. "I'm not sure," she said, raising her hand for him to keep quiet until she'd finished her thought. "But before I respond to your proposal, I have one condition that has to be met, or there's no deal."

"I'm listening," he answered, trying to keep calm.

"If I accept Mr. Takashima's offer to come back to Constellation, Robert comes on board as my studio president."

"What?" Stephen's voice leapt up a few octaves. He was sunk. Takashima would never agree to that. He had to talk her out of it. "Robert give up his talent-agency partnership that he built from scratch? Shit, no way."

"You're wrong, Stephen. After you arranged this meeting, I asked Robert if he would join me at Constellation and he agreed it could be a fantastic opportunity for both of us."

"Kelly, you're insane! A husband-and-wife team running a studio? It's never happened before."

"A Japanese studio owner never happened before either, Stephen."

He bit back the retort on his tongue, quickly regrouping his thoughts as he played with his shirt collar. This was something he hadn't expected. So that's why Zinman was so cooperative about this meeting tonight, he thought.

"Sorry, I don't think Takashima will go for it."

Kelly was firm. She hoped that making Robert part of her team at Constellation might better hold their marriage together. "That's my only condition, Stephen. It's both of us together or nothing at all. End of discussion."

Kelly turned and walked up the wooden stairway to the cliff and the restaurant.

Stephen had to think fast as he followed her. He remembered his last call from Takashima: "I want her at any cost, Resnick."

"All right, Kelly," he yelled after her. "I'll give Takashima your condition. We'll let him decide."

Robert, finishing a drink, was leaning over the bar when he saw Kelly and Stephen come in. He could tell by Stephen's expression that Kelly had outlined their plan to him.

As she greeted Robert with a hug, he said over his shoulder to Stephen, "Remember, Resnick, Kelly has lots of other offers that I'm considering." He then put his arm around his wife and they went out the front door.

Stephen headed back down to the beach. He stared out to sea, ignoring the waves lapping at his shoes.

"Shit, shit, shit."

He felt himself sinking faster than the sand.

11

It was getting late, about nine-ish. The smell of a new spring was alive in the evening air. Inside the Shrine Auditorium, the Sixtieth Annual Academy Awards telecast was concluding. In moments, the mob of movie stars would be hurrying out to the cavalcade of limos stretched around the block, only to be grazed by the paparazzi and the crowds of fans waiting behind police barricades.

Kelly was anxious to beat the crush. She quietly said good night to her seatmate, a smiling Tom Cruise, as she motioned to Robert to follow her through the wings. As Robert slowly picked up his program, Kelly tugged on his arm to hurry as Cher announced to the live SRO crowd as well as to the worldwide televised audience of over one billion: "And the winner for the best picture of 1988 is . . . *Rain Man!*"

As producer Mark Johnson ran up the aisle to thunderous applause to accept his Oscar, hundreds of reporters and photographers were already backstage in various press rooms, questioning or photographing the night's other winners. Several reporters spied the Best Actor winner as he sneaked out the side exit doors with his wife, Lisa. Kelly and Robert followed behind them.

"Follow us, Dustin!" Kelly said, grabbing his arm as they came to a blocked exit.

Smiling, Dustin said teasingly, "I'd follow you anywhere."

With Kelly in the lead, the foursome ran the other way and, unfortunately, into the hundreds of excited fans waiting for a glimpse of any movie star outside.

"Dustin, Dustin!" they yelled, pushing and shoving as they tried to get past the police security to get a closer look at the celebrated Oscar winner.

Dustin turned to his wife, the corners of his mouth turning up impishly as he grinned, squeezing his Oscar in his hand.

Robert was getting agitated. He hated large crowds. He tried to smooth out his new Versace tux, badly wrinkled from sitting for more than three hours, but there was no room to breathe. He just wanted to get away from here.

"How about sharing our limo?" Kelly asked Dustin and his wife. They nodded.

"Kelly, stay here with Dustin and Lisa while I get our limo," Robert shouted over the noisy chanting of the crowd. The excited fans were becoming more unruly, but Dustin continued to wink and smile for pictures.

"Dustin . . . oh, Dustin!" several women in baggy sweats and dirty-white running shoes continued shouting, holding up posters bearing his name and the words "West L.A. Loves You, Dustin!"

Kelly leaned over and whispered in his ear. "How would you like to not only star in but also direct a film for Constellation?"

Before Dustin could answer, a woman carrying a sign broke through the police barricade and ran up to him, pleading for his autograph.

"Oh, Mr. Hoffman, you were so wonderful in *Mississippi Man*," she said as Dustin signed her book. Then she turned to Kelly and looked her up and down. Kelly looked glamorous in her black velvet off-the-shoulder Armani gown and bold diamond-studded earrings. "Are you anybody?" the woman asked curiously.

Kelly didn't know what to say, so she started to laugh. Dustin, at his most serious, said, "Is she anybody? She's only the first woman CEO to ever run a Hollywood studio."

Kelly looked slightly embarrassed. Less than two months had passed since she had accepted Takashima's offer, but she still hadn't gotten used to hearing her new title.

The woman shook her head, not quite understanding what he had just said. "I didn't see the picture," she said disappointedly. As a policeman pulled her away, she called out, "Hey, wait, when's it coming out in video?"

Kelly couldn't help but be amused at Dustin's quick response. "So much for my fifteen minutes of fame," she said to him and his wife.

As the stretch limo pulled up to the curb, Robert jumped out. "C'mon, everybody, let's go."

As they took off for Swifty Lazar's Oscar party at Spago—only the most important members of the entertainment community were invited—Dustin leaned over and whispered in Kelly's ear, "Now, about your idea . . ."

"At the top of our eleven-o'clock news," Paul Moyer of *Eyewitness News* announced, "the key word around Hollywood tonight is Oscar . . . who won, and who didn't."

Click.

"It was no surprise when Dustin Hoffman took home the Best Actor Oscar tonight, but quite a surprise for Best Actress winner Jodie Foster."

Click.

"An estimated audience of one billion, including for the first time the Soviet Union, watched the embarrassing opening production number featuring a squeaky-voiced Snow White singing a duet with Rob Lowe."

Click.

"*Rain Man* took home a total of four Oscars."

Click.

Takashima leaned forward in his high-backed swivel

chair, deep in thought in the still darkness of his studio office. All four television monitor screens were now turned off.

He let the cool silence wash over him, preparing his spirit for the ordeal ahead. He closed his eyes, but he was still troubled. Such trivia, such hype, he thought. The American awards show did nothing but showcase exposed female anatomy and reflect American male stupidity. What he was planning was much more interesting and deadly.

He was pleased that Kelly had settled into the day-to-day operation of running Constellation. This was Takashima's well-designed subterfuge to buy him the time he needed to have his men infiltrate the Hollywood landscape and get ready for his next attack.

However, with the multitude of theories abounding as to which direction his studio would go, many in the Hollywood creative community—on advice of their agents—had become somewhat reluctant to work for Constellation. In fact, most had adopted a wait-and-see attitude.

Clapping his hands, he summoned Noda. "Quickly," Takashima instructed him, "assemble all the Ronin. I want their most recent intelligence reports on the major Hollywood studios."

Finishing their tea, Takashima and Noda, in shirtsleeves, sat around the dimly lit conference table with the Ronin group, wearing their traditional black suits and gray shirts. They had updated him on MGM/UA, Columbia, Disney, Fox, and Paramount. Now Takashima awaited the report on MCA-Universal as he nodded to each of the Ronin around the room to begin.

"Honorable master, the target date for our newest revenge scheme is next Friday," the first Ronin reported.

"We have set our sights on the newspapers, television, the wire services, radio."

"The best base of operations is the New Otani Hotel in the downtown area."

"We will leak the information that Sony Corporation once again is in the process of purchasing MCA-Universal."

"The giant MCA entertainment corporation is unaware of our revenge plot against them. We will eventually firebomb the MCA executive black tower building at a time when everyone is busy somewhere else."

"When the Nikkei and the American stock exchange open on Monday, speculators will enhance their earnings with fast-paced acquisitions of the stock."

"There will be great damage to the reputation of your rival, Sony."

"And, as it has been written," the Ronin said in unison, "we obey only you, master." They bowed slightly toward Takashima.

The master nodded back, saying, *"Yoi desu."*

Takashima concluded the meeting with a favorable reaction to all the Sony rumors in the daily newspapers. However, he was adamant that under no circumstances could his men err now. Sony's Morita must not be permitted to become a major player in Hollywood at this time.

Takashima had become paranoid and sensitive to any comparison from the media or the creative community about how he and Morita conducted their operations. He did not want the creative community to become exposed to Morita's ethical ways. After all, Morita only wanted to buy into Hollywood for legitimate business reasons.

Standing and slowly looking around the board table, Takashima, after checking his watch, admonished his spy group that they must continue to make the Hollywood people believe that all Japanese did business in only his evil way. He then abruptly adjourned the meeting.

"Gentlemen, please wait here until I finish some

private business. Then I will allow you to partake of the evening's entertainment." It was a tradition for Takashima to accommodate his men after their secret meetings.

As he quickly summoned Minoru, Noda looked up in surprise. It was most unusual for the master to suggest private business without his knowledge.

Bowing low, Noda said, "Takashima-san, as you have instructed, I have also brought the scorecard with me tonight. I have listed and updated all the current payoffs to our friends in the ruling party."

Takashima nodded several times. "Fuji-san is waiting for you in Minoru's office. He has my specific orders to leave later tonight for Tokyo with the scorecard in his possession. He will deliver our secret ledger to Asano-san, who will lock it securely in our safe. Take it to him immediately," he said, dismissing him.

Noda could not hide his surprise as Takashima ushered him out while he closed the door behind him. Something did not seem right. Why was Takashima shipping off the one piece of incriminating evidence that—placed in the wrong hands—could burn him?

When he was certain Noda was gone, Takashima sat down at the long table, where Minoru waited patiently. "You have your instructions and the briefcase for Resnick-san?" Takashima asked calmly.

Minoru bowed low, holding the leather briefcase under his arm. "*Hai*, Takashima-san."

He grunted back his pleasure. Takashima had Minoru cryptically instruct Resnick to be in his law office at midnight. "Finally, tonight, we will pay our debt to the enemy's son . . ." he said, smiling, his voice trailing off.

Takashima had learned from the Ronin that Resnick had already forked over his new Jaguar as a goodwill down payment to the Las Vegas gamblers, but that his time with them was quickly running out. Resnick would have to pay them in full soon, or they would come after him. And that could be at any moment.

In a conversation earlier that afternoon with the desperate attorney, Takashima had been amused at Resnick's agitation. What Resnick did not know was that he had intentionally stalled his payment until this specific night. This was something he had planned to happen. In fact, during the seven weeks Kristopher-san had adjusted as his CEO, he had purposely kept Resnick dangling like a hungry dog for the million-dollar fee. After all, he felt, the traitorous enemy should sweat for his reward. Tonight, the night of the Academy Awards, when all of Hollywood was celebrating, he had decided, would be the most appropriate time to resolve this debt.

Takashima now ordered his chief Yakuza, *"Go!* And send Noda back in here."

Minoru bowed again, then hurriedly left.

Moments later, the younger man appeared.

"Noda-san," Takashima said. "Please bring in our entertainment."

Noda lowered his head. "I . . . I would prefer not to be a part of this tonight, Takashima-san."

Takashima stood up angrily. "What? You cannot defy my order. What kind of man are you, Noda-san? Go at once, and bring in the American whores!"

Noda did not move. "Please, Takashima-san."

"You will obey my order at once!"

Noda bowed respectfully, but inside he was seething. First Takashima ignored him with some secretive business, and now this.

The master knew how much Noda disliked his perverse sexual activities. All the same, he must not arouse Takashima's suspicions by disobeying him. Takashima must not have any doubts.

He walked quickly down the hall to an office where an argument was going on in English.

"What the hell are you doing with my garters?"

"Hey, those are mine."

Noda opened the door, keeping his head bowed

low. "We invite you to come join us now," he said in English.

"Okay, okay, honey, we're ready," a sexy redhead said, straightening her black satin bikini bottom. The other girl, wearing a pink teddy trimmed in white lace and white stockings, followed.

The sexy girl in the black satin bikini was getting impatient. She readjusted her straps, pushing up her cleavage. "C'mon, Emperor, we only get paid for showing it, not talking about it."

"I am also ready, Noda-san," a soft voice said.

Noda raised his head. Kakue!

He grabbed her and pushed her behind the screen as he swallowed hard. "No, no, you are not to come, Kakue-san, not tonight." The master had requested only the hired women. Pillow-geisha, as they were called in Japan.

"Go home, Kakue-san, now!" he said.

She looked at him, not understanding. "But I am here to serve Takashima."

"Not tonight, moon face. Now, go!"

Noda closed the door behind him quickly, forcing her to obey him. Then he led the two women down the hallway.

He did not remain long. He needed only to see the redhead tied to the post by her wrists before he managed to slip away, unnoticed by the partying men inside.

The woman, naked from the waist up, her big breasts glistening with sweat, tried to wrench free, but the leather straps binding her hands together tightened each time she struggled. This was something she had not agreed to be paid for.

A Ronin grabbed her by her red hair and pulled her close to him until her hard nipples brushed against the rough black material of his coat. Her eyes stared back at him, begging him to stop. But he threw back his head and laughed, then cracked a slim leather riding crop over her quivering ass, cleanly slicing off her black satin bikini panties.

When the redhead finally slumped her head down in submission, Takashima yelled: "*Banzai!*" smiling with lustful satisfaction.

Another Ronin brought forward the other girl, now stripped naked except for her white stockings and garters. She cried out in fear of her life as her wrists were also tightly bound and a gag stuffed into her mouth.

She could offer no protest as two of the men laid her on her stomach on top of the table, her arms spread out in front of her. They held her down as Takashima pulled apart her legs and inserted his hard cock and began to fuck her.

This was Hollywood's biggest night to celebrate. It was also Takashima's.

As Jake got out of the blue-and-yellow LAX Super Shuttle in front of his Beverly Hills mansion, he noticed the neighbors peeking through their window shades. As always, when he stared back at them, the louver shades quickly snapped shut.

Damn nosy neighbors, he thought.

Mistica jumped out of the shuttle while Jake helped the driver unload their luggage. "Wait for me! I'll be right out," she called back to her dad as she ran into the house to make a quick trip to the bathroom.

"Here, buddy," Jake said as he opened up his wallet and tipped him five dollars. Wearing a pair of old jeans with a Barbados souvenir T-shirt, he felt like a beach bum after their few months away in the beautiful tropics. He and Mistica had soaked up the sun, gone scuba diving, dug for clams, and forgotten the world.

There were no phones, no newspapers, no anything on the tiny island. That's just what he had needed. He was sick of hearing about this Japanese or that Japanese buying up this or buying up that, and especially he was very tired of hearing any mention of Constellation.

As he picked up the bags and started toward the house, he noticed a Los Angeles patrol car parked across the street. He didn't give it a second thought, even though it was unusual. This was the Beverly Hills area, and from what he knew, the cops were very territorial.

Then the car doors opened and the two cops got out. As they headed toward him, the tired, drawn look on their faces caught his attention.

"Mr. Baron . . . Jake Baron?" the first cop asked politely.

"Yes, I'm Jake Baron. What can I do for you?" Jake tried to smile; then all of a sudden it hit him. He realized that even though Constellation was adjacent to Beverly Hills, the Century City property was considered Los Angeles. "Gentlemen, I'm sorry, but I no longer own . . ."

The second cop shook his head, playing with his gun holster nervously. He always hated this part of his job. "No, Mr. Baron, it's about your stepson, Stephen Resnick."

Jake's eyes narrowed. "What's he done now? Is he in trouble again? I've warned him a number of times—"

The first cop put his hand on Jake's arm. "Please, Mr. Baron, let's go inside."

Jake nodded and ushered the policemen into his house. He dropped the luggage in the entryway, then started toward the kitchen. "Coffee, gentlemen? I'll have my housekeeper brew some in a jiffy," he said. Stephen was in deep trouble, he just knew it.

"Mr. Baron, please sit down."

Growing even more apprehensive, Jake took a seat. The policemen continued to stand. One began talking from notes on his pad:

"The department has made repeated efforts to reach you over the past few days. However, we understood from a Rose Kaufman that you were traveling incognito and couldn't be traced." The cop paused to get his breath, but it was his buddy who picked up the ball:

"We're sorry to give it to you like this, Mr. Baron, but according to our preliminary investigation, your stepson, Stephen Resnick, committed suicide a few days ago."

Jake went numb as a cold shudder passed through him. Stephen dead?

"How . . . how did it happen?" he asked, too stunned to realize he might not want to know.

"From our preliminary investigation, Mr. Resnick attended Swifty Lazar's Academy Awards party at Spago on the night of March 27. According to several people who saw him there, he left before midnight. At approximately eight-thirty the next morning, he was found slumped over his desk at his Fox Plaza office by his secretaries, with a single bullet to his brain. A thirty-eight-caliber snub-nosed revolver, registered to your stepson, was found beside him."

"Oh, no," Jake uttered harshly, his voice cracking as he buried his face in his hands. He started shaking. My God, poor Stephen, he thought. Should he have seen it coming? "Are you certain it was suicide? Did he leave a note?"

The second cop responded, "The prints on the gun match Mr. Resnick's, and the powder burns near the wound indicate it was fired at close range. The trajectory of the bullet makes it seem that the victim fired the shot. No, Mr. Baron, I'm sorry, there was no note."

Jake, not completely satisfied with their explanation, was too overwrought to pursue the matter any further now. He would, of course, make preparations for the funeral. It would be private, just the family.

"See you later, Dad," Mistica said, bouncing down the stairs and swinging her Century City Health Club gym bag over her shoulder. She had changed into a sheer white-and-pink Danskin leotard outfit. She planted a quick kiss on his cheek and smiled at the two policemen. "It's nice of you guys to check to make sure we're home."

"We'll see ourselves out, Mr. Baron," the first cop said quietly, then motioned for his buddy to follow.

"I've talked to Josefina about dinner. She's—" Mistica rattled on before Jake stopped her. He took her hand and led her over to the couch.

"Sit down, honey, I have something to tell you."

Even hours later, Jake couldn't relax, no matter how hard he tried. He kept reading the same stories in all the newspapers over and over again about Stephen's death. It had made the headlines: the *Los Angeles Times*, the *Herald Examiner*, and of course the Hollywood trades. The story even went out over the AP wires.

He sat back in his chair and pulled the lamp closer to him. His eyes were tired from reading so long. He sipped the hot chocolate his housekeeper had left for him before she went to bed. He felt so responsible. If only he could have spoken with Stephen, then maybe things would have been different.

But maybe not, he thought, putting down the cup. He could never have forgiven Stephen for selling him out.

Mistica had taken the news of Stephen's death badly. Screaming and shaking, she had cried in Jake's arms for hours. She blamed herself, confessing to her father that she knew how much in debt Stephen was, but she hadn't done anything about it.

Finally she cried herself to sleep. Jake had lifted her in his arms and carried her upstairs, then kissed her good night on the forehead. She was still his little girl.

As Jake finished his hot chocolate, the old clock in the corner began to strike, its chimes reminding him of the passage of time. There was never enough of it. . . .

Somehow he had to get his mind off Stephen, at

least for a little while, or he'd crack up. Aimlessly choosing several outdated Hollywood trade papers his housekeeper had put aside for him, he skimmed through them. Same old stuff: box-office figures, executives playing musical chairs at various studios . . .

"What?" he yelled as he looked at a *Daily Variety* from a couple of weeks ago. The headline read: "KELLY'S BACK AT HER OLD HAUNT." According to the lead story, she was now CEO of Constellation and working for Takashima.

Jake stuffed the paper into his back pocket. He couldn't believe it. He felt his blood pressure rising. It just wasn't possible that Kelly was now working for that Jap. What had gotten into her?

Jake felt his world collapsing around him all over again. It was too much for any man to endure. Kelly working for his rival—he felt confused and hurt.

He had to get out of the house and get some air.

It was late in the morning as Jake looked around the trendy Italian restaurant off Melrose Avenue. This had always been one of his favorite spots for a power breakfast. By now most of the breakfast powwows had already broken up and the various movie and TV executives had already left for their offices.

Jake had not stood still after learning about the lack of a suicide note. He had raised hell down at police headquarters, but to no avail. However, several hours later that day, he had received a surprise call not from the police department but from the Department of Justice. When he had asked what in the world was going on, all they had said to him was to pick a meeting place and they would explain to him in person.

As Jake reached into his coat pocket, fumbling for his cigarettes, he heard someone behind him say:

"Smoke, Mr. Baron?" A man snapped open a leather-covered cigarette case.

Jake noticed that a tall man who carried a portable phone stood impassively while his partner offered him a good old-fashioned American cigarette, not one of those disgusting French ones used in so many of his former crime films. His mind had been wandering. He hoped this meeting was just a bad dream.

He smiled as he took the cigarette and lit up. "I guess you are the agents from the Justice Department?"

Agent Jim Donaldson, a no-nonsense type, kept his frozen look and began his story. "Since your son's death, our office has been getting anonymous tips indicating that we should keep a close eye on Constellation, although ordinarily we wouldn't get involved in such a sale."

Jake sat impassively as he nodded.

Donaldson continued: "Since Constellation had been sold as a private studio and has remained that way, it wasn't subject to the usual scrutiny from the Securities Exchange Commission. And outside of the IRS keeping a close tab on things, everything else should have been routine."

Jake flagged down his waiter. "More black coffee. The strongest you have."

"Sì, signore."

"However, after the mysterious alleged suicide of the studio's principal counsel, with no note left behind . . ." Donaldson paused, allowing Jake to drink some of the freshly brewed coffee. "Someone in our office back East did some routine checking on the new owner of Constellation, Hiroshi Takashima. That's when we discovered through our computer system some of Takashima's questionable background. The Attorney General's office became somewhat suspicious of any possible motives he might have and ordered an investigation of him. Between his ownership of a Beverly Hills bank and, now, his Hollywood movie studio, Takashima has established a very strong foothold in the community."

Jake continued to sit quietly. He had been drained of his own emotions over the past days.

"Mr. Baron, we believe that Mr. Takashima's bank

might actually be a front for him to wash clean, that is, to make legal, his vast cash flow in and out of the United States."

"You mean Takashima's involved in a money-laundering scheme?" Jake asked, a glint in his eye. "Please, keep talking."

"It's quite intricate, Mr. Baron," Donaldson responded. "However, since our investigation, along with that of the IRS, is ongoing and far from being conclusive, I am not at liberty to discuss those details with you. However, I will say that our preliminary investigation has indicated that your stepson was involved in heavy gambling. If he didn't kill himself, as some do believe, then we have two theories: he was killed either by organized crime in the Las Vegas area or by Takashima's organization. And if Mr. Resnick's death turns out to be homicide by a foreign national, our friends at the FBI will be brought in pronto."

"The Jap did it?" Jake thought out loud. "I just know it!" He ran his hands through his hair while slowly putting out his newly lit cigarette. Then he looked at the agents with a hard cast on his face. "How can I help you?" There was no mistaking the emotion behind his words.

"That could be very dangerous, Mr. Baron, but we were hoping you would volunteer to work with us. The Yakuza bodyguards that Takashima surrounds himself with are killers who are just as effective as Mafia hit men." The agent paused a minute as he looked over at his partner, and then continued. "We have plenty of trained men in the field working against organized crime, but maybe you could help us with our investigations of Mr. Takashima. However, let me warn you again to be extremely careful. He's definitely no stranger to strong-arm tactics."

Jake smiled wryly. He had his mind made up and there was no changing it. "I'm ready—"

"Remember you'd be putting yourself at great risk.

If they discovered you were assisting us, they might kill you."

Jake laughed uneasily. "You don't know the movie business, gentlemen. Just when it looks like the wagons are surrounded by the Indians, in comes the cavalry to save the day."

12

Kelly looked around the posh dining room in the Bel Air Hotel, the power breakfast "in" place for every important CEO in Hollywood. It was not only *de rigueur* for her to be seen here by the most important people in town, but this was also one of her favorite places to dine. The hotel's beautiful grounds, complete with sweeping lawns, a walking bridge, and graceful swans, brought fond memories of a time early in her marriage when Robert had first suggested an evening cocktail in the fireside library.

It was nearly nine-thirty. Most of the regular crowd had already finished up and were off to their next meeting. It was time for Kelly herself to get going. She took out her credit card and laid it on the white linen tablecloth as she continued to chat with her good friend Wendy St. John, who had just returned from another one of her whirlwind trips on behalf of the environment. This was the first opportunity the two women had had to get together since the award luncheon for Kelly.

"I'm glad we had a chance to catch up on the latest . . ." Kelly's voice trailed off as she suddenly remembered that terrible day. She had so appreciated all of Wendy's unwavering support. And like any other scandal in Hollywood, with the passing of each new season, it faded away. Or, as Robert had reminded her: "Show business has no memory."

Kelly and Wendy noticed that the restaurant still had a few of Hollywood's heavy hitters. Michael Eisner, for one, was still nursing his coffee over in the corner with some of his Disney executives, while Barry Diller, the Mr. Everything at Fox, caught Kelly's eye and waved as he and some director stood up to leave.

She also spotted several Secret Service agents discreetly checking out the sunny dining room. This had become a usual occurrence now that the Reagans had moved to Bel Air. Nancy would probably be arriving soon for an early brunch, she thought. Ronnie must be sleeping late again.

"By the way, Wendy, I'm honored you asked me to co-chair the network special on Earth Awareness Day and round up some talent. I've already committed Ovitz to helping me with some of his superstar clients," Kelly said, smiling as she continued to gaze around the room.

"Your bill, Miss Kristopher," the waiter interrupted, laying down an ornate leather folder with the crest of the hotel emblazoned in gold in front of her.

Kelly opened the folder and quickly scanned the check. "Let me know what you *don't* get for your birthday," she joked, signing the bill. As Wendy smiled in response, Kelly noticed that her friend was preoccupied with watching a man across the room sitting on a small sofa.

"Kel, see that man over there?" she whispered, indicating the stately-looking gentleman with a sway of her head as he tried to hide behind the *Wall Street Journal*.

Kelly nodded.

"It's that English actor," said Wendy, "you know, the one who does those crazy detective movies. Inspector Something-or-other."

"Are you sure?" Kelly asked, trying to get a better look. She really wasn't sure who he was, but it was obvious he was interested in them, for he kept glancing over his paper in their direction. She noted his elegantly cut gray wool flannel suit and monochromatic shirt and tie. But his hair was too blond and stiffly curled, his eyebrows too bushy to be natural. He also wore dark, expensive sunglasses that kept sliding down to the end of his nose. A gray fedora rested on the tiny lamp table next to him.

"I'm certain that's him," Wendy insisted. "He's known for his funny disguises—that hairpiece, for instance. And those socks!" She couldn't help but smile as she subtly pointed to the loud black-and-white-striped socks peeping from underneath his cuffed pants.

Kelly still wasn't convinced. Something about the way he kept squinting at her over those awful dark glasses made her feel uneasy. And as they left the restaurant, she felt his eyes boring into her back. She quickly put him out of her mind as she chatted with Wendy about some of the changes at Constellation since Takashima had taken over. Kelly said good-bye to her friend, who went into the tiny powder room while she decided to take a short stroll in the outside garden before getting her car from the valet.

She breathed in deeply. The air was a trifle cool, but it did have that wonderful smell of spring flowers. She needed this moment of tranquillity before heading into the usual chaos at the studio.

"Don't say anything. Just keep moving," a man's voice behind her ordered, pushing her forward into the garden and away from the hotel. Startled, she sensed he was tall and strong by the pressure she felt on her back. She tried to turn around, but he forced her to keep walking straight ahead.

"Who . . . what do you want?" she whispered, trying to keep her tone hard, even though her pulse was racing so quickly she couldn't think clearly.

"Lady, just keep walking until we're out of sight," he said, keeping his voice disguised.

Not knowing if he was going to rob her or what, she forced herself to keep talking; he probably had a gun pointed at her back. "Listen, you can't get away with this. There are Secret Service men everywhere," she said as they entered a circle of tall oak trees, away from prying eyes.

"I know, Kel," the man said, dropping his disguised voice.

Kelly turned around, shocked and angry as she saw Jake Baron take off his dark glasses and smile crookedly at her. "Sorry I had to scare you, Kel, but it was the only way."

"Jake Baron, you're one damn sonofabitch!" she said, trying to act outraged, but she couldn't keep a straight face. Jake looked hysterical in that blond wig and phony eyebrows. Not to mention those awful sunglasses and fedora askew on his head. No wonder she hadn't recognized him. She started to laugh. "I thought you were that English actor," she said through her giggles.

"I should be. These are from some British detective movie." He laughed back, touching his hat and suit jacket. "You should have seen me yesterday. I was an Arab sheik. In fact, one of our favorite agent pals, Billy Haber, and his partner, Sidney Sheldon, lent me enough wardrobe from their newly purchased Western Costume to last for five days—and, Kel, this is day number four. If you hadn't shown up today, I would have probably been forced to repeat the cute little tennis outfit again on Monday," he said, taking off his hat and pulling up the blond wig while scratching his head. "Damn, this fuckin' thing itches."

Laughing hysterically, Kelly shook her head and affected an English accent. "Oh, Blake . . . I mean Jake"—Kelly paused to wipe her tears—"what are you doing here? It's a trifle early for high tea."

"Waiting for you!" Jake laughed with her.

Kelly, trying to compose herself again, looked surprised. "Come on, Jake, I know you better than that. You could have called me at the studio."

He turned serious. "I know I could have called, but after I lost Constellation, I . . . I—"

Kelly silenced him with a finger to his lips. "Please, Jake, I'm just as much at fault. I should have phoned you, but I was so afraid you wouldn't understand why I decided to take Takashima's offer. I believed then, as I do now, that it was the right thing to do for Constellation . . . and for . . ." She lowered her head, unable to finish.

She continued to look at him in his getup. He looked so silly—yet so wonderful.

"Okay, I give up, Jake. You want to be an actor, and this is a private audition, right?" But the time for bantering was over, she realized. So she said simply, "I'm glad to see you, Jake."

"Me too, Kelly," he answered, taking her hand. His was cold, not from the morning chill, but she sensed from something else. Damn, why wasn't I there when he needed me the most? she thought.

She had to find out what was wrong. "You wouldn't want to keep your identity so secret if something wasn't troubling you. Now, tell me, what is it?"

Jake hesitated a moment as he cranked his neck around. This was the part he had been dreading. It still wasn't easy for him to talk about it. "It's Stephen, Kel."

Kelly gripped his hand tighter. "Jake, I feel your loss deeply."

"Thanks," he said, nodding absently. Then he blurted, "Kel, I have been led to believe his death might not be a suicide."

"What! Says who?" she asked, startled. "Then . . . are you saying it was . . . ?"

"Murder."

Jake gave her a moment to absorb the harsh news. "It looks like someone wanted Stephen dead. And obviously they accomplished what they had set out to do."

"Oh, no," she cried softly, too shocked to answer. As she held on to Jake for support, he led her over to a small stone bench in the middle of the trees. The budding green leaves formed an umbrella over them, shading them from the rays of the sun as they sat down. He gently placed his arm around her, which she accepted gladly. In fact, it felt good to both of them.

"Are you really sure, Jake? Stephen was far from perfect, but who would want him dead?"

Jake chose his words carefully. "Well, he had major gambling debts, so there's the distinct possibility that it was a hit by organized crime. However, I believe it was Takashima's dirty work."

Kelly felt her head reeling. She swallowed hard, trying to keep her words from sticking in her throat. "That's crazy, Jake. Where did you get such an idea?"

Rambling, he told her in strictest confidence about the Justice Department's investigation. Kelly listened intently, sitting very still. She knew Takashima had a reputation for ruthlessness in his business dealings, but murder? She still couldn't believe it.

"Why are you telling me all of this anyway? What can I do?"

"If you can get me employed with an ongoing project, I'll be able to snoop around the lot for the feds. When they came to me, they emphasized, loud and clear, just how dangerous this might become, but if Takashima had something to do with Stephen's death, I want to help in getting him."

"What would you do then?"

"I'm not sure yet." He tried to smile, but his face was tense with worry. "Besides, someone's got to watch out for you, Kel. I don't trust that Jap one fuckin' bit."

"Listen, Jake Baron, I'm a big Texas girl, remember? I'll be all right. Besides, he wouldn't dare touch me." She hesitated a second, then said, "You forget, Robert now works with me."

"You had to remind me."

Kelly didn't pull away as he drew her closer to him. She felt protected in his arms.

"What do you say, Kel? Can you help me?" he asked, the plea in his voice tearing at her insides.

Slowly Kelly nodded.

* * *

Kelly was still thinking about her unexpected meeting with Jake as she drove along Olympic Boulevard late that same morning. She had decided to take the longer route back to the studio, needing some extra time to think things out. She was more aware than ever of a nagging ache inside her that even her fancy new title and her enormous salary couldn't cure: she couldn't get the warm feeling of Jake's arm around her out of her mind.

There was no way that Takashima would willingly hire him. She'd have to devise a plan to force his hand into taking Jake back.

Just then she saw a billboard advertising a soon-to-be-released film. Of course, that's it, she realized. Why didn't I think of it sooner? She remembered her recent memo to Takashima about letting her complete work on all films that were in production before he purchased the studio. There was one project Jake would be perfect for.

She turned left onto Century Park West, then left again at Constellation Boulevard and into the studio, trying hard to ignore the flag of the Rising Sun.

"Good morn-n-ning, Kristopheru-san," the Yakuza guard at the main gate said, greeting her with a polite bow. She had to summon up a smile in return. She missed Scotty, the veteran guard of twenty-five years.

She checked the digital clock on her Mercedes dashboard. Ten-fifty. She had to hurry now. Takashima had called his first major meeting of all the studio VP's for eleven-thirty. That would be too soon to mention her idea, though. Instead she would prepare her plan over the weekend and present it to Takashima at Monday's general meeting.

"Get your filthy hands off me! Don't you know who I am?"

Kelly stepped on the brakes as she looked over her shoulder and saw a commotion going on to the side of the main gate. Several men were scuffling around a car she recognized, parked alongside the entrance lane.

Robert was surrounded by a horde of Yakuza searching him as well as his Ferrari. They made him open the trunk, then the hood.

"What the fuck are you doing?" he screamed. "Stop this immediately!" he continued to yell as they emptied his pockets. "This is an outrage! Wait until Takashima hears about this!"

Kelly couldn't help it; she started to laugh. Robert looked so funny being manhandled by Takashima's strong-arm guards.

She got out of her car. "What's going on?" she asked as she strolled over to them.

"Dammit, Kelly, these assholes are ruining my suit."

She grabbed her cellular car phone and punched a few buttons. "Get me Takashima. Tell him it's Kelly, and it's urgent." As she waited for him to get on the line, she raged inwardly: Robert is the studio president, for Chrissakes. It was bad enough that people had been fired left and right without harassing those who still worked there. ". . . sign, what sign?" she asked aloud into the phone.

A Yakuza, overhearing her, pointed to the front gate. Kelly read the new sign with surprise: "ALL WHO ENTER THIS AREA ARE SUBJECT TO SEARCH AND SEIZURE."

Search and seizure? Kelly couldn't believe her eyes. This was plain harassment.

Kelly tried to calm herself. This time Takashima had gone too far. She hadn't said anything about the morning exercise classes, or the funny Japanese music being blasted everywhere, or even the strange-looking food in the commissary, but turning his thugs loose on her employees and their visitors was going too far.

Before the Yakuza could stop her, she tore down the tin-plated sign and threw it into the back of her car. "Boss's orders," she said smugly as she pointed to herself.

Takashima's new mandate was no longer amusing.

"Yamada-san ohayo gozaimasu."
"Gokigen ikaga desuka . . ."

"Anatano kasoku wa genki desu . . ."

Takashima's department heads were speaking their usual Japanese gibberish. Kelly had no idea what they were saying, nor did she care. She had been doodling with her pen, waiting for them to include her, but they didn't stop talking. Even when they tried to speak English, or "Japlish," as she coined it, she didn't understand them. She looked helplessly around the table. Among the group was the studio's new legal counsel, who had been recruited from Osaka to fill Stephen's position. As hard as she tried, she just couldn't get used to seeing the Japanese lawyer with the huge overbite replacing Stephen, especially now. She'd had her problems with Stephen over the years, but she couldn't bear the thought he was dead—possibly murdered.

With a lot on her mind today, she became very restless and couldn't stand all the pigeon talk any longer. She closed her notebook as she got up from the table. To her surprise, the men seated around her bowed without rising. She bowed back to them as she left the conference room. She smiled openly, but cursed under her breath.

She had to learn—and fast—how to play hardball with them.

Outside, she put on her sunglasses, then unbuttoned her Anne Klein suit jacket. Maybe Robert was right to skip these meetings. As he would say: "Kel, they don't mean sushi to us. Sayonara, and fuck you too." She began to laugh to herself before she remembered there were more of "them" now and fewer of "us."

Other things were also bothering her. As if it wasn't bad enough already that the Japanese flag now flew alongside the Stars and Stripes—after she had staged a major argument with Takashima, he had allowed the U.S. flag to rise over the studio again—the signs on the bathrooms were now written in Japanese characters. On top of that, she had daily memos sent to her from various department heads—all typed in Japanese.

Frustrated, Kelly pushed her hair away from her face and looked up into the sun. This wasn't turning out the way she had wanted. She was expected to answer every Japanese reporter's inquiry through an interpreter, but when she asked a question of a department head or of anyone else who was Japanese, the person never said a word in response. She learned through the interpreter it was called communicating through *maku satsu*, putting ideas across without words. She shook her head in disbelief: movie makers putting ideas across without words?

Suddenly, as a truckload of teamsters drove by her with big hellos and waves, she heard music blasting from the studio's public-address system:

> Rise above the sands of time,
> Give today all your joy and strength,
> Blossoms of our youth give way
> To new fruits of our endeavors.
> Around the world hear our cry,
> Constellation! Constellation!

No need to look at her watch. The Constellation *shaka*, or corporate hymn, was heard twice every weekday—in the morning at exactly seven o'clock, and twelve noon. Everyone—from the commissary to the wardrobe department, from production to post-production, to the back-lot reconstruction team, to even the attendants in the rest rooms—was required to stop what he was doing and listen instead to Takashima's propaganda song.

It was just one more thing getting on Kelly's nerves. In an attempt to escape the music, she poked her head into the sound booth on the Foley stage. She had always been fascinated by the skill of the technicians who added sound effects to film.

"Hey, Sid, how—"

"Excuse, Kristopheru-*san*?" a heavily accented

voice questioned from the darkened stage. The man was standing silently out of respect for the hymn.

Kelly stepped back, startled. For a moment she had forgotten that her old friend Sid Cameron had quit. He had been on the lot for years, but like so many other employees, he had discovered that working for the new Japanese owner was terrible. Many others had either been fired or left of their own accord after being demoted to lesser-paying jobs. The fun and the camaraderie under Jake's regime were now gone.

She smiled at the Japanese technician. If she had learned anything from Takashima, it was not to say anything in an embarrassing situation. Just pretend it never happened.

She took off her jacket as she wandered into an empty stage. Number 8. She had a lot of things to reflect on.

On the one hand, since she had become the industry's most powerful woman executive ever—and she and Robert were Hollywood's first husband-wife team to run a major movie studio—she had become the subject of many nightly news stories. Besides the media's constant inquiries, agents were also phoning her, and in droves, setting up meetings on behalf of many of their talented writers and directors, hoping to sell their ideas to the new Constellation. That was terrific and exciting, she felt. In fact, she realized that no woman executive had ever had the money and power together that she now enjoyed.

But on the other hand, it hadn't been long before she had realized she wasn't going to have quite the authority or control she had expected. She had been promised—first by Stephen, then by Takashima—a place on the new board; but Takashima did not follow through. Instead, he had followed the tradition of many Japanese company heads of disallowing a foreigner a seat—even with a USA-based company. He probably assumed that he would be perceived in an embarrassing light back in Japan, especially if he gave her a seat. As far as she was concerned, she was still just good news to the Japanese women, and great public relations for Takashima and Constellation.

As she looked around the stage curiously, her attention quickly turned to the ski-lodge interiors from *Criminal Intent*—they were still intact. Talk about ghosts. Stage 8, like some of the other large stages, hadn't been used since Takashima halted production months ago. She bent down and picked up some of the plastic snow and let it fall through her fingers.

Suddenly she heard the squeal of a racing motorcycle. A blue-suited Yakuza drove right into the soundstage and screeched to a halt only inches from her. Kelly's heart nearly stopped, but she kept her composure. "What are you doing here?"

"*Dozo*, Kelly-san," he said as he politely bowed from the cycle. "Takashima-san wants to see you. Now!" he ordered firmly.

Kelly put on her jacket. "Okay, tell him I'll be right there— "

He shook his head. "Now!" he said as he picked her up with one hand and put her on the back of the motorcycle.

"Hey, what are you doing? Get your hands off me!" she screamed. "I can't ride on this thin-n-n—"

The Yakuza did not understand "no."

The cycle took off like a rocket, out of the soundstage and through the lot. She held on tightly, her hair flying while her legs banged up against the wheels.

She didn't dare let go.

"A billion dollars?"

Takashima nodded, never taking his eyes off Kelly. He was pleased at her reaction. He was even more pleased with the sight of the beautiful woman with hair the color of a butterfly's cloak. She was dressed simply but elegantly in a form-fitting blazer and skirt, and her low, sexy voice perfectly accompanied her shapely body. The more he met with his useful "tool," the more he itched to bend her to his will and possess her.

Kelly didn't notice that Takashima was watching her with such scrutiny, for the incredible amount of money he had just mentioned took her breath away. She even forgot her complaint about being snatched by the Yakuza.

She paced up and down Takashima's office, her mind ticking so fast she couldn't even remember how many zeros there were in a billion dollars. With that kind of money they could hire the best writing teams, get the top directors, the star performers. Wait until the industry reads these headlines in the trades, she thought.

"What the hell's going on here?" yelled a voice in the hallway. "What's the big hurry?"

Kelly smiled weakly at Takashima: Robert. She turned as two Yakuza escorted him into Takashima's office, holding him up by his elbows.

He marched over to Takashima's desk. "How come your fucking gorillas don't know me, Takashima? Tell them to buzz off."

Takashima nodded to his Yakuza, and they bowed and left.

"Forget them, Robert," Kelly said, jumping right into her news. "Listen, Mr. Takashima has budgeted a billion dollars in development money over the next four years."

Robert's eyes opened wide. He was more than impressed. After he had sold, with some reluctance, his share of his Worldwide Artists Agency back to his two partners, he had been hoping this new gamble would pay off. He believed that he and Kelly would be the hottest couple and the most powerful team in today's Hollywood. He rubbed his hands together greedily. It looked like it might start to come together.

"Well, well, no wonder you're tightening up security around here." He leaned over Takashima's desk, his voice dripping with phony charm. "Good idea. We indeed have to be more careful. By the way, this isn't some kind of belated April Fool's joke?"

Takashima was not amused by the brash American's humor. Robert was a man of only one face—the right one for the moment—and Takashima could barely tolerate him. He was patiently awaiting the day that he would take the beautiful Kelly-san away from her loud-mouthed husband. Actually, that day was not so far off, since he was sending Mr. Zinman on a long trip.

"I am glad you approve, Mr. Zinman," Takashima said wryly, purposely avoiding the Japanese honorific *san* after Robert's name. "However, there is more work ahead for all of us."

He outlined his master plan: Robert would be in charge of all project development, including the overseeing of thirty new scripts per calendar year . . .

"Excuse me, Mr. Takashima, but every other studio in town has at least a hundred projects in development at a time." Robert leaned over the desk and cocked an eyebrow at Takashima. "Warners has about two hundred projects in the works."

What Takashima was not telling Robert was that his Japanese managers would simultaneously begin development on many more scripts—all with radical Asian themes. Robert would make the creative people in Hollywood think that Constellation was still doing business as usual. Takashima turned to Kelly as if Robert had never said a word.

"Kelly-san, you will continue to oversee all production as you did with the former regime. I have decided to allow you to continue production on all projects that had been started before I bought the studio. No new film that you oversee will be allowed to exceed twenty-five million dollars in its budget. Have I made myself clear?" he asked with a slight smile.

Kelly, very pleased, nodded back.

"Now, Robert, you will also be in charge of advance publicity for our new look at Constellation as well. I want you to leave immediately, as Constellation's envoy, on a tour through the capitals of Europe to talk up the studio as well as look for potential projects."

Robert looked at Kelly in surprise. She was equally taken aback, so he realized it was Takashima's idea. But the more he thought about it, the better he liked it. It was a great opportunity to be a big shot in Europe. Maybe he'd make an appearance at Cannes. After all, he was now one of the elite Hollywood studio presidents, with an impressive business card and all the other trappings that went with the important title. And that included lots of babes who would be meeting him. Wouldn't his buddy John be envious.

"Well, Mr. Takashima, it appears that you have very big plans for Constellation. That sort of money is going to make the studio a serious competitor. And that's great. But all of these plans will take some time," Kelly said.

"We have nothing but time, Kelly-san," Takashima replied in a caressing tone, as if there were no one else in the room but the two of them.

Squirming, she had the strange feeling that he was undressing her behind those glasses of his. Putting down her pen and looking up at him from her legal pad, she breathed easier. He wasn't looking at her. Maybe she had only imagined it.

"So what about this Europe idea?" Robert said irritably. He hadn't missed Takashima leering at his wife.

"Hey, I've got a great idea!" Kelly said suddenly. "Instead of just telling everyone in town through the typical trade-paper announcements, let's show them by staging a spectacular press party—on the back lot! We'll turn the studio into a small city for the night, with neon lights, shooting fountains, skyscrapers, music, food . . ."

Takashima eyed her with new respect. "That is an

excellent idea, Kelly-san. But we must make the city Tokyo, recreated all over our Constellation lot."

Kelly smiled broadly as she turned to Robert. Even he seemed to like the idea. "Perfect, Mr. Takashima," she said. "The town won't stop talking about us for months."

Takashima beamed, charged up with the idea of being able to see every important movie star before he slowly began to eliminate them. They would all want to attend this spectacular event. "We will build skyscrapers, a manmade lake, pavilions, stages," he said, now rambling on with a glassy look in his dark eyes. Everyone would be treated as royalty as part of the ruse. "No cost will be spared. I am very pleased with your idea, Kelly-san, very pleased." He gave Kelly's shoulder a friendly pat of encouragement.

At his touch, she turned away, unable to stop shivering. Was this the man who had killed Stephen Resnick?

Jake and Mistica entered a hi-tech elevator in the Beverly Center, where the rich and famous shopped. Jake was casually dressed in Nike sweats and Reebok tennis shoes, topped with a Dodgers cap. This Saturday morning he had decided to take his daughter out, for Mistica had been worrying him lately. Since Stephen's death, she had been listless. She made few calls to friends, preferring to stay in her room and watch television alone. He hoped that by taking her shopping, he could perk her up.

As they ascended, Jake looked at his pretty daughter and smiled. She was really something, he thought. Dressed in stone-washed blue jeans with more holes than denim, a tight pink tank top, and high-heeled cowboy boots, she was busy cracking her chewing gum while listening to her favorite George Michael tape on her Sony Walkman. She didn't even notice her father's scrutiny or the cute guy about two elbows away, checking her out.

When they got off the eighth floor, Jake lifted one of her earphones and said, "Sweetie, how about splurging with me on a hot-fudge sundae?"

"Yeah, sure," she answered, frowning, as if she were doing him a big favor. She turned off her tape and put the earphones around her neck as they headed for the Vie de France, the festive Parisian confectionery shop over in the huge food arcade.

Jake mentally patted himself on the back. Was he imagining it, or had he just opened the door with her?

Minutes later, Mistica licked her spoon, sitting silently. Then a cloud passed over her face and she turned to her father. "Do you remember how much Stephen hated chocolate syrup?"

Wincing at her continued preoccupation, Jake nodded. His stepson used to break out so much when he was a teenager, he had never touched the stuff again. Mistica had often teased him about it.

"You know, Dad, I really miss Stephen," she said, choking with pent-up emotion. Her eyes started to tear and she sniffled. "We didn't help him enough. I mean, he was such a jerk most of the time that I just ignored him."

Jake reached out and lightly clasped her wrist. Her lower lip was quivering, and chocolate was smudged on her chin. He took a big breath. He wasn't sure if he was doing the right thing, but he had to tell her, for her own peace of mind. "Honey, it wasn't a question of doing enough . . . or anything at all."

She looked up at him, puzzled. "What? I don't understand."

"Look, Mistica, I had a breakfast meeting with some federal agents. They think that Stephen might not have killed himself." He put his arm around her shoulders for added comfort now, holding her tightly. "They believe he could have been murdered."

She stared back at him in surprise. Then she started to shake with suppressed sobs. "Who would do such a thing?"

Jake sighed. He had gone too far now to hold back, and besides, she had a right to know. "They think that either the mob or Takashima's thugs killed him."

Mistica sat very still for a moment. Then her lips tightened with new resolve as she said, "But they're not certain."

Jake shook his head. "No, but they've asked me to help out with the investigation. I spoke yesterday with Kelly, and she's trying to find some way for me to get back on the lot to snoop around Takashima."

Her eyes flickered with alarm for a moment, and Jake was sure she was going to beg him not to do it. But then she firmly pushed away her empty dish. And when she looked up at him, her mouth was set in an ugly grimace. "Then you're going to have to let me help you."

"Good Monday morning, Mr. Zinman. How was your weekend?" The cute production assistant smiled cheekily as she zipped past him in the hallway.

"Terrific. Read four scripts at the beach," he said, stopping abruptly as he turned his head all the way around to catch her rear view. Her skintight short denim skirt left little to the imagination, he thought. Thank God for the return of the miniskirt.

He forced himself to turn away. He was late getting in today. He'd had an important breakfast meeting with actor Michael Keaton and his agent, and it had gone on longer than expected.

As Robert breezed into his office, his secretary handed him his airline tickets. He checked them quickly. Ten cities in four weeks, he thought. Not a bad itinerary.

If his schedule permitted, he'd have some time in each city for a little R&R with the local talent: blonds, brunettes, redheads, etc. He was dead set that his philandering was justified. At least over there, Kelly would never find out, he figured. He didn't feel guilty in the least. Why should he?

After all, he hardly saw her anymore, except at staff

meetings. She was usually holed up all day with either Takashima or the shoguns. With everything he had done for her, she had now become too damn powerful, as well as too damn busy, especially for the one person who had put her there. In fact, he was lucky if she had more than a few words for him at night. She usually fell asleep before he could turn her on.

However, neither one of them would admit there was a strain in their marriage. They would carefully cover up their marital problems when they were out in public, not wanting to tarnish their professional images and end up on the sleazy covers of the trash tabloids.

Smiling with anticipation, he couldn't wait to get going.

Late-afternoon sunlight streamed through the old latticed windows into the studio's conference room, where founder Bunky Baron had often raised his voice as well as his blood pressure.

The room had recently been painted a pale earth color, and the gigantic oak table, rumored to have belonged to William Randolph Hearst, had been polished to a mirror shine. Even the high-backed eighteenth-century chairs had been reupholstered.

Takashima entered the room precisely on time with Noda and his Yakuza. Kelly and Robert were already waiting, along with the Japanese managers. No one dared to sit down. They waited for the signal. This was the respected way of doing Japanese business.

Without a word, Takashima passed out a *manga,* or comic book, of instructions that he wanted his managers to give to all of their employees. He wanted to continue the same work ethic he and his other Japanese business leaders had used in Japan with their workers: the "team-oriented" plan. The pamphlet helped in outlining the work ahead, and by using illustrations, complemented Takashima's strong approach to discipline. It was very traditional.

Next, Takashima slowly walked around the room, greeting each member of his new team. All the Japanese men who stood around the large table bowed in succession when he asked about the welfare of their families.

Impatient as usual, Robert whispered to Kelly, "C'mon, what are you up to?"

"What are you talking about?"

"Don't play games with me, Kel. Ever since our meeting with the Japanese emperor about this so-called big press party, you've been keeping something else from me. What's the big secret?"

"Shh, you'll find out soon enough."

Robert was nervous—he didn't want to be left out of any loop, especially Kelly's—as he began flipping through the comic book. Soon he was muttering softly, "Can you believe this shit? We're supposed to bow fifteen degrees to colleagues and forty-five degrees to top execs." He laughed loudly at the antiquated diagrams. "No fucking way."

The Japanese department head for wardrobe sitting next to him cleared his throat. He tried to keep from looking at Robert, but it was obvious from his clenched teeth that he was not pleased at the American's lack of *gaman*.

Noticing the man's discomfort, Robert flashed a big toothy smile. He had learned that trick from Takashima.

Takashima took the seat at the table farthest from the door, as tradition dictated. The others continued to stand.

"Dozo okake kudasai," he said. "Be seated."

Once the incessant prattle of Japanese started up, Kelly lost interest. Instead she went over again and again in her mind the argument she had had with Takashima moments before the meeting. She had told him that she was sick and tired of the way he was treating the employees. Also, she was annoyed at the way the other Japanese *kacho* refused to listen to her ideas and lacked respect for her position as studio CEO. One man had even gone so far as to ask her to copy documents for him.

Her only friend on the Japanese side seemed to be the accountant, Noda, who confided in her that the Japanese thought very lowly of American women, "as a third sex." In time, he had promised Kelly, as a way of reassuring her, they would all start to be more relaxed with her. He would help with that process. "Please have patience for now."

For now? Kelly thought. It couldn't get any worse. Both Cynthia Ortega and Rose Kaufman, along with many other women executives, had been fired, and the only women left on staff were those in clerical positions.

However, Kelly was determined not to back down and to continue to persevere. She had to choose the moment to present her plan.

It came soon enough. Takashima turned and looked directly at Kelly as he announced:

"I have decided on an important change that will be implemented immediately as a part of studio policy. As of today, all teamster-union drivers on the lot will be replaced by my nonunion Yakuza. In six months all other union personnel will be completely eliminated from Constellation. There will be no more unions on my studio lot."

Robert jumped up and banged his fist on the table. "Mr. Takashima, excuse me! You can't do that, no damn way." He looked at Kelly for support. "Dammit, Kel, you tell him he can't do that."

Kelly was strangely silent. This might be the very bargaining chip she needed to put her own plan into action. It was worth a try.

"Yes, Robert, he can," she said loudly.

As all the assembled men glanced up in surprise, Robert looked stunned. Both Takashima and Noda were baffled as well, but they did not openly show it.

She stood up, staring at Robert. For the first time since she had been back at Constellation, she knew she had the upper hand.

"Robert, if Mr. Takashima believes that by eliminating unions, he can make better movies, then he has that right. This is his studio." She paused. This idea, contrary to what she really believed, was hard to swallow. She was now surprised to hear the Japanese whispering among themselves.

"However, Mr. Takashima, you may never get that opportunity if Constellation doesn't have a major hit in release soon. Your success in Hollywood will be judged solely by our box-office numbers in both the domestic and international marketplaces."

Takashima was wise enough to know she spoke the truth, from her years of experience. And he knew that he should not disrupt his outer appearance of pretending to run a studio. "What do you propose we do, Kelly-san?" he asked politely. He was becoming more and more intrigued by this beautiful woman who had the courage to stand up to him. She represented a challenge he had never known before.

Kelly took a big breath. This was the moment she had been waiting for.

"As we will now try to complete production of some of our stalled films, please be aware that our biggest potential for a box-office hit is *Criminal Intent*. We need only four more weeks of principal photography, plus two months for postproduction," she continued.

"It's a guaranteed hit, especially with the names of Terry Taylor, Harrison Ford, and Michelle Pfeiffer attached. But we must be able to gather all these people together again or the picture won't ever be completed. It will be the best opportunity Constellation now has to get its name out in front of the public as well as in Hollywood . . . once again."

She paused to see if he was going to comment, but he did not.

She smiled brightly as she finished: "Mr. Takashima-san, there's only one person who can pull everything together, including our big stars and director, and maintain our budget. And for the moment, he's still available. That person, Mr. Takashima, is my former boss, Jake Baron."

Takashima winced while Robert looked stoic.

13

"And according to our reports, the rumors about Sony taking over MCA-Universal are just that. Rumors."

Takashima switched off the VCR in his master bedroom, extremely pleased with the television newsman's report, and drank some warm *sake*.

The Ronin no Zaibatsu had created another perfect false story that everyone from Hollywood to Wall Street had initially believed was true. So believable were the persistent rumors that local KNBC-TV business reporter Doug Kriegel had devoted a complete segment of his Channel 4 broadcast to the phony stories of the Sony buy-out.

Takashima poured another drink to further celebrate his latest victory. In addition to the confusion, he had made a fortune in Japanese yen on the sale of MCA stock because of the speculators' panic. He loved every moment of his deception; after all, MCA had blocked his deal with producer Larry Evans, and in doing so, upset his *wa* with his Takashima Group. Now he had partially paid back the embarrassment he had experienced.

As he set the tiny porcelain cup back down, he felt content. He next took off his glasses and removed his short-waisted kimono while he walked naked to his bathroom. After he quickly washed himself, he would be ready for his evening relaxation.

"Takashima-san, do I not please you?" Kakue asked

timidly minutes later as she rubbed his back with her small hands.

Her master was not listening. As the hot waters of the bath flowed over his muscular body, he looked out at the panoramic view from the corner glass window of his Mulholland hill. Between the majestic trees that surrounded his home, he could see the Pacific Ocean out in the distance. This thousand-square-foot bathroom had become one of Takashima's favorite places in his mansion. He had decorated the entire bathroom with black marble from Carrara, although as tradition dictated, the tub itself was made of cypress. Artificial moonlight from overhead added to the ambience that made him feel at ease.

He wanted only to close his eyes and breathe in the sweet fragrance of the many flowers blooming all around him. He meditated on the serene sounds of the water, trying very hard to bring peace and harmony to his inner thoughts. It was no good, however. His troubles would not leave him alone.

One issue that gnawed at him was his decision to allow Kelly to bring Jake Baron back to Constellation. True, the thought of having his enemy on his payroll—doing what he wanted him to do—had amused him. But all the same, Baron had once owned the same studio, and it was not good to have workers looking up to two masters. He would have to publicly humiliate Baron, and soon. That would settle this problem.

Takashima squeezed his eyes in irritation, when suddenly he felt the hard nipples of Kakue's breasts press against his back. As her tiny fingers began to expertly massage the pressure points on his neck, he grunted in contentment. Ever since the mixed baths of his boyhood, when he had seen his first glimpse of the nude female body, he had associated baths with sexual desire. Letting himself relax at last, he felt his penis getting hard as his geisha reached even lower. She began to gently play with his balls.

"Kakue-san!" he whispered hoarsely, but she did

not stop. She simply giggled, for she was already learning the pleasures of giving sex.

He slowly eased himself out of the hot water onto a black marble settee. As he leaned back, she sat in front of him on the cold marble floor and put her warm lips around his elongated penis. He wound her long black hair aimlessly around his hands while she licked and sucked him until he reached a climax.

With his lust satisfied, he put his house kimono back on and lay back on a soft chaise longue. Quickly, with her eyes cast downward, Kakue fetched a hot towel for her master. As she tended to him, he tried to relax, but already he had become restless again. He needed something else to soothe his nerves.

He looked at her, still naked and wet from the bath. He picked up his bottles of paints lying nearby. "Kakue-san, it is now time for your art lesson."

As she had been taught, Kakue lay down on the soft tatami mat and waited. Her slim young body provided a pleasing canvas on which Takashima could practice his art. Methodically he began by carefully selecting the right colors from his palette. He dabbed a rainbow of colors in brushstrokes across her breasts. Spreading her legs apart, Kakue giggled, hiding her mouth behind her hand as she moved her legs. She tried to lie still, but the brush hairs tickled her fair skin.

"Hold still, Kakue-san. You are disturbing the symmetry of my painting," Takashima ordered, dabbing more yellow paint on the inside of her bare thigh near her pubic hair.

Sometime later, he put down his paintbrush and scrutinized his work. Not bad, he thought, However, the circular designs on Kakue's breasts would have been in perfect harmony if she had not squirmed. To correct his painting, he picked up his brush and added a bright blue dot to the middle of her right nipple. Finally he dabbed his brush in red paint and stroked two stylish characters on her stomach that read *fukushū*, revenge.

* * *

Neither of them noticed that Noda was nervously pacing over in the corner. He had been summoned by Takashima after the master received a disturbing fax from his group.

"*O-jama shite sumimasen,*" Noda said as he bowed apologetically. As he raised his head, he could not bear to look at Kakue, her nakedness as fragrant to his senses as the first breath of the cherry blossom. "I am sorry to disturb you, Takashima-san, but you said you had an urgent message from Tokyo."

"I must leave alone for our homeland immediately!" he said firmly to Noda, hurrying to pack for the trip. "Noda-san, while I am away for the few days, the Ronin will brief you on the destruction they are planning for every Hollywood film and tape lab. You must also continue to see that Constellation maintains my militant course of action. You alone will be in charge. No exceptions to any of my rules. Kristopher-san must report all business to you."

Somewhat alarmed, Noda wondered why Takashima had been recalled and what it meant. He bowed politely to Takashima, acknowledging his command. The master had caught him off-guard. However, he thought, Takashima's absence could be beneficial for his own plan of revenge.

The sellout crowd at Korakuen Stadium was on the edge of their seats as they watched the next player step into the batter's box. He was the Takashima Dragons' cleanup hitter. If he could make contact with the ball and get a run across the plate, the game would be tied. The Japanese preferred to end their games with a tied score so no one would lose *kao*, face.

Takashima stared through his dark glasses. His mind was not on *besuboru* today. He was tired and he felt the strain of the long flight from Los Angeles. He was still trying to compose his thoughts. There was important business at hand: he must convince his group members that he would run the studio in compliance with their wishes.

He gratefully accepted the warm, moist towel offered by the serving girl. He barely glanced at her shapely figure, revealed by her tightly fitting bra top and thigh-high cut shorts. Instead he wiped his face, noting the various members of his Takashima Group seated around him and watching the game with intensity. Obviously they were cheering for their group-owned team.

The members not only enjoyed the pleasures of beer and whiskey inside their luxurious sky box overlooking the field but also had sleeping accommodations, a wet bar, and a bathroom. Their attention shifted back and forth between the field and the muffled sounds of the play-by-play announcer on the overhead giant TV screen.

No one spoke as the American pitcher completed his wind up and threw the first ball. A strike.

Takashima was getting impatient. He wanted to respond to his members quickly. He debated whether or not he should first question them, but some inner wisdom quieted his emotions and he remained silent. He had no desire to wait until the game was over, but he did not want to upset the *wa* of his group.

On the drive into Tokyo from Narita Airport, he had learned from two of his members that the entire group was disturbed over the daily local news stories of the Japanese bribery scandal known as Recruit, named after the company in the center of the trouble. The scandal centered on the question: When does a gift of money or a donation become a bribe? Several prominent politicians, including Prime Minister Takeshita, were currently under criminal investigation as well as heavy media scrutiny.

The group members were also upset with the new three-percent consumption tax that went into effect on April 1. After thirty-four years of the LDP in power, the Takashima Group now worried that opposition parties might begin to start chipping away at the ruling party's power. If the LDP lost enough seats in the Diet in the forthcoming summer elections, they feared that the scandal might blossom out of control and they would all be at a disadvantage.

"Strike two!" shouted the umpire.

Takashima urged his group to listen to his side of the story, and also to hear his fabricated story about the progress at Constellation. However, they merely smiled and gave him the silent treatment.

Takashima fumed over their reaction as he took the Asahi beer offered by the serving girl.

Crack! The batter hit the ball and ran to first. All eyes were on home plate—except for the Asian Octopus.

Forty minutes later, after a long reprimand that had begun in the top of the fifth inning and was now coming to its conclusion during the seventh, Takashima squirmed in his plush seat as he continued to listen to the group member: "And finally, Takashima-san, since you are both one of the prominent contributors to our ruling-party politicians and a close friend to our Prime Minister, we urge you at all cost to be very careful in your dealings from now on, especially with your running of the Hollywood movie studio. You must keep your controversial ideas out of the news as much as possible, or we will all suffer. Remember, we will continue to support your plans only if you continue to cooperate with us."

"*Banzai! Banzai!*" the group cheered as the new batter hit a home run. The fans in the stands below as well as the group members stood and screamed in a wild frenzy. Takashima remained seated.

The game had long been over as Takashima continued to sit quietly in his seat, completing his meditation. It was becoming more and more difficult for him to continue as part of a group.

He now questioned the validity of keeping with

tradition and working within this group process. Even though he was an old-time pragmatist at heart, he was still very much an individual. But he realized that this group system was still his best bet. He decided, at least for now, he would not break with tradition.

"Aren't they cute, Dad," Mistica said to her father as she watched two little tiger cubs scrapping with each other in their cage.

"Yeah, sure they are," Jake said with a chuckle in his voice, throwing a peanut into the cage. He had to admit even he wasn't immune to the animals as they walked through the Los Angeles Zoo. He looked down at his watch. There was more on his mind than cute animals.

"They should be picking us up any minute now, Mistica. Let's go."

Jake looked at his daughter. She looked so pretty and happy today in her slim jeans and lime-green overshirt, he wished he didn't have to drag her away from the animals. She was still taking Stephen's death very badly.

With a last look at the cuddly cubs, Mistica walked with her father out the front entrance. They tried to look nonchalant as they waited around the assigned place near the parking lot, but Jake was getting impatient. Why the hell they wanted to meet here was a mystery, but he couldn't argue the fact that Griffith Park offered thousands of acres of picnic areas and hiking trails where they could get lost among the tourists and picnickers. Jake certainly fitted that picture in his khaki pants and plaid flannel shirt, complete with an Instamatic camera hanging around his neck.

"Dad, is that them?" Mistica asked in a low voice as they saw a long black Lincoln Town Car slowly circling the parking lot.

Jake wasn't sure as he squinted into the sun. "We'll soon find out."

As the Lincoln pulled up to the curb, the back door

opened quickly and a voice called, "Please get in, Mr. Baron."

Without a word, Jake helped Mistica inside the car first, then took a seat next to her. Even before the door shut, the car slowly took off up into the hills surrounding the park.

Jake tried to keep his attention on the two men as Agent Donaldson drove the big luxury car higher up into the hills, but it wasn't easy. The interior of the Lincoln was like a miniature radio control center with numerous phones, gadgets, even a fax machine. He was amazed by all the technical wizardry.

"Thank you for coming, Mr. Baron, Mistica," Donaldson said in an even but cordial voice.

"What's up, Donaldson?" Jake asked quickly, noticing the quiet, tense-looking man in the front passenger seat popping a cough drop into his mouth.

"Mistica and Jake Baron, this is Len Hyatt, Internal Revenue Service. We wanted to give both of you a last-minute update before you begin your producing chores on the movie. From then on, we will have to be very careful with our communications."

As Hyatt turned around, Jake saw that he was friendly but all business. "Mr. Baron," he said, acknowledging Mistica and him with a curt nod.

"We hope to nail Takashima on a money-laundering charge. However, at the moment we haven't gathered enough evidence," the IRS agent said.

Donaldson pulled the car over to the side of the road and let the engine idle. He turned around and leaned over the front seat. "We're still getting anonymous tips from an inside source at Constellation who we now believe is a ranking Japanese executive in Takashima's organization."

"No shit," Jake uttered in amazement. So there was a turncoat in his own camp. "How can you be sure this isn't just a trick?"

"The informant has been feeding us substantial information that checks out. We have also confirmed the reports that Takashima's secret intelligence organization has been sneaking into the United States through Hawaii. This delegation of spies may even be more dangerous than his Yakuza bodyguards. We wanted you to be aware of this unit, Mr. Baron. You must be extremely careful."

As the agent's word sank in, Jake looked out the car window as Donaldson drove the Lincoln back onto the road. He thought of Kelly working so close to that monster. Whatever the danger, he wouldn't turn back now.

"What do you want us to do?"

Donaldson continued to explain: "In order for the government to nail Takashima, we need evidence of concealment of assets and sources of funds. But be aware, like many Japanese, he operates on a cash basis. That's where you and your daughter come in, Mr. Baron.

"All we ask is that you both keep your eyes and ears open for any suspicious accounting procedures regarding the movie production. In addition, please advise us of any unusual visitors to the production locations or to the studio."

They both nodded.

"You've got it," Jake said as Donaldson brought the car to a stop in front of the zoo.

"Thanks, Mr. Baron, Mistica," the agent said, smiling, hardening his voice as he shook Jake's hand. "But don't forget that Takashima's a very dangerous character. Don't *ever* trust him."

"Hey, you, stop or I'll . . ." the elderly private security officer yelled, his hand on his unloaded gun. He had his sights on a man half-hidden in the shadows, sneaking out of the side entrance of the mansion and carrying a box.

"You'll do what, Sam? Shoot me?" the man answered glibly as he put the box down gently and stepped into the sunlight.

"Oh, it's only you, Mr. Baron. Sorry."

Relieved, the officer holstered his gun. "We had quite a scare yesterday when some guy tried to walk off with Mrs. Grimes's silverware."

"You're doing a good job, Sam. You can't be too careful with a setup like this. Just don't shoot your foot off."

Jake, smiling over his little joke, looked around at the massive undertaking needed for the day's location shoot. He always marveled at how a film company created a world unto itself.

Two long blocks of movie trucks lined the quiet streets in the luxury neighborhood of Hancock Park, just around the corner from the home of Los Angeles Mayor Bradley. Numerous makeup people, their cosmetic boxes strapped to their sides, were constantly on the run, applying powder or fixing a ruined lip job. The electricians and grips were laying additional cables and dolly tracks, that is, when they weren't raiding the M&M candy jars. The camera crew had already set up their equipment in front of the Grimes mansion for today's shoot and were now enjoying their pre-dawn doughnuts and coffee.

Several off-duty Los Angeles policemen in uniform were diverting traffic from the secured area.

Jake scratched his head in amusement to Sam, who followed behind him, as he saw some extras sitting on the grass and playing "spin the Coke can."

"Too bad, Sam, the camera isn't running." Jake bent over and picked up the small pile of scripts, placing them in a box.

"Let me help you with that, Mr. Baron," the security officer immediately offered.

"Thanks, but I'm all finished, Sam," Jake said, walking over to the row of blue canvas director's chairs inscribed in flowing script with the names of the stars, director, and producer.

Jake sat down in his chair with his new title, executive producer, and began skimming through his three-inch-thick *Criminal Intent* production notebook filled with the shooting script as well as casting sheets, call sheets, and production notes, not to mention numerous phone numbers and location addresses.

Jake felt the blood kicking up in his veins. Shit, he thought, it was great being back in the movie biz again.

He loved it all: the five-thirty-A.M. calls, the hours of getting the lighting just right, the briefings with the director, the wardrobe people fighting with the first A.D., even the crazy bunch of film students from UCLA that were hired as extras—following him around, asking a million questions.

He was especially gratified when he found out that most of the original crew, the two stars, and the director had all agreed they would return only for him.

His face turned serious for a moment as he thought of the man above them all: Takashima. The one problem with this location shoot was that he had little opportunity to snoop around the studio, which was his primary objective. Well, that would come soon enough, he mused. The most important thing now was to set up his cover.

He had a few minutes before the first shot of the day got under way, so he lay back in his chair and put on his shades as the sun finally put in an appearance. As the rays flooded his body with warmth, he found himself thinking about Kelly and the way he had held her at the Bel Air Hotel. Afterward he had realized that she must not have been fucked for a while by her weasel of a husband, for that glow of contentment that only lovemaking could give had been missing from her face.

Jake shaded his eyes from the hot, blinding sun, thinking about making such passionate love to her . . .

"Dad, are you okay?" Mistica asked. Startled, he looked up and found her sitting next to him in Terry Taylor's director's chair.

With a guilty smile on his face, Jake said, "Just

taking a snooze with my eyes open. Your old man's not getting any younger, honey."

She smirked. "Who are you kidding? I saw those two college girls throwing themselves at you yesterday. And I'm sure you noticed that neither one had a bra on."

He pretended that he wasn't flattered. "Oh, is that what they were doing? I never really noticed."

Exasperated, Mistica snapped, "Dad, they couldn't have been more than nineteen."

"Really, I . . ." he mumbled, still pleased. As he looked at his daughter, he noticed with satisfaction that she was dressed conservatively in blue jeans and a long flannel shirt. Her hair, too, was pulled back. After the incident in Aspen, he had insisted that she change her look when he hired her this time as his executive production assistant.

And so far, so good. She had been working hard, getting her hands dirty, doing whatever he needed to be done.

"Now, don't forget, Mistica," he joked as he pinched her on the cheek, "I'm *Mr.* Baron to you when you're on the set."

She smiled back mischievously.

"Sure thing . . . Dad."

"I'm sorry, Jake, but that's the way it is," Terry Taylor said, pouring Jake another cup of coffee. "We have to stop production. Immediately!"

Jake didn't touch his coffee. Today was only the third day of his revised shooting schedule, and already another headache. "Terry, you gotta be kidding."

Taylor shook his head. "Jake, look, we're old friends, so let me level with you. We put up with the driver problem as much as we could yesterday, but my production keys met last night and decided they won't accept nonunion drivers anymore, especially those Japanese bullies. They've all agreed to stand tough with the teamsters. Unless this matter is cleared up right away, every department head has agreed to put a halt to production." He showed Jake a letter signed by the entire company. "There's no other choice, Jake."

Jake looked over the letter, downing his coffee in several big gulps. Of course, it was all Takashima's fault. Rumors that he was officially getting rid of the unions had been rife when Jake arrived, but it had come to a head yesterday, when someone leaked information that the Yakuza were going to replace the teamster drivers immediately.

He pounded his fist on the Formica tabletop, spilling coffee all over his shooting script. "Dammit, Terry, I don't know what's going on, but I'm getting hold of Kelly now!"

Taylor looked out the side window. "Jake, come here . . ."

Jake couldn't believe what he saw outside.

The three Yakuza drivers of the previous days had now grown to a dozen today. A couple of the local teamsters were now taunting the Japanese bodyguards. One teamster even took a swing at one of them, but the only thing he hit was the ground after a well-placed judo chop to his back.

"Shit, I've got to stop this." Jake picked up the phone and dialed quickly.

"Geoffrey, get Kelly on the line." His blood was boiling, but the only indication he gave was the clenched fist at his side. "Kelly, what the fuck is going on? Takashima's Yakuza are all over my set, and the department heads are refusing to work without union drivers . . . Say that again, Kelly. I've got Terry sitting next to me and I want to let him know also." Jake held the phone away from his ear as he repeated to Taylor: "Takashima flew to Tokyo a few days ago." He spoke again into the phone. "So what do I do now? . . . . Sure, that little Jap Noda, I remember him. . . . Okay, talk in two minutes."

After Kelly called back, Jake quickly related to Taylor what she had said to him. She would be meeting with Mr. Noda—if Takashima didn't return in time—and Randy Peterson, the newly elected president of Teamsters Local 399, at eleven o'clock sharp.

As Terry muttered something about the shooting time they were now losing, Jake left the trailer and walked around the perimeter of the set. He had to find Mistica and send her over to the studio pronto, with the production company's letter and noon ultimatum.

Mistica, tucking her shirt into her jeans, looked around the office as she waited for Geoffrey to get off the phone. She just wanted to give him the letter and get out. She shifted her weight from one foot to the other, the thick heels of her cowboy boots tapping loudly on the floor. She felt ill-at-ease being back at Constellation.

She noticed the photo on the wall, not realizing it was of the new Japanese Emperor, as well as the strange-looking paintings of hills and valleys. Nothing from the old days was left. She was glad her father had not come himself; he would have been heartbroken.

She felt that the changed atmosphere of the studio did something to her as well. For the first time in her life she felt a strong sense of wanting something so badly she'd do anything to get it back. It wasn't like wanting a new dress or a car, but something bigger.

Infuriated, she stomped her boot down, not realizing she'd made such a loud noise. Two young Japanese secretaries working for Kelly stuck their heads out from their office cubicles in surprise. But the more she thought about what had happened to her dad, the angrier she got.

She had already been convinced by him that Takashima had been responsible for Stephen's death. She wanted to do whatever she could, no matter what, to assist his efforts.

"Hi, Mistica. Be right back," Geoffrey said as he

hurriedly ran by her on his way from one office to another, where the phone was ringing off the hook.

"Yes, operator, I will accept. . . . Yes, Mr. Zinman, I have every word," Geoffrey said while he checked Kelly's morning mail: an invitation to the upcoming Women in Film luncheon; an announcement of the new CAA building, several invitations to speak at various charity events, her trade papers. "You're leaving Milan tonight for Zurich. . . . You'll phone her back in a day or two? Excellent. . . . What's that? . . . Great, I'm sure she'll be happy to hear that everything is going well. . . *Ciao* to you too."

Timidly Mistica approached his desk. "I have an important letter for Kelly."

Geoffrey looked at her in puzzlement, then at the wall clock. "Letter? Ohmigod, quick, follow me!"

"Wait, I'm just supposed to leave . . ." She couldn't finish her sentence as Geoffrey grabbed her by the hand, and together they ran through the old halls where the Marx Brothers had once chased a wild pig.

"Stop, Geoffrey," Mistica said, nearly out of breath as they entered the newly decorated executive office that had once been her father's.

Takashima looked up as she came in. He had arrived moments earlier, and after his private jet had touched down, he had phoned Noda from his limo and learned about this emergency meeting. With his Takashima Group's strongly advised warning still in his mind—not to make waves—he knew that he had to resolve the union problem. Cosmetically, he would look very conciliatory to everyone, but before the enemy knew it, he would catch them off-guard with another strike.

Mistica felt his eyes on her. He frightened her more now than at the party. She wanted to spit in his face as she lifted her chin in defiance, determined not to let him see her fear.

"Mistica, give me the letter!" Geoffrey whispered urgently.

When she handed it over, he waved it at Kelly, trying to get her attention as she spoke, but she motioned to him to wait until she was finished.

". . . and as Mr. Peterson has just outlined, Mr. Takashima, neither he nor his drivers are willing to accept any change in their current contract. The union can't ink a separate deal with you or anyone else."

Randy Peterson, the union head, along with a couple of his driver captains, nodded to each other as she spoke, but the Japanese men around the table remained silent and motionless.

Exasperated, Kelly wiped the perspiration off her nose. *Maku satsu.* Here we go again, she thought, time for the long maybe, as she now called it. It wasn't a definite no, nor was it a definite yes. And all she could do was wait.

She motioned for Geoffrey to approach and give her the letter. Turning, she said, "Thanks, Mistica. You can please wait for me in my office." She smiled at her, realizing how difficult it must be for her to be in the presence of her father's enemy.

"No, the young woman stays here," Takashima ordered, interested in discovering who the pretty blond in the blue jeans was.

Reluctantly, Kelly didn't countermand his order. She had no choice. She read the letter immediately—she wanted to cover her embarrassment—then took a drink of ice water before going into her final argument. But the contents of the letter seemed to be more relevant than her own ideas; this would become her final stand.

"Mr. Takashima, you must listen to me carefully. According to this letter, signed by the entire cast and crew of *Criminal Intent*, they will walk off the set at noon if this isn't resolved." She paused to check her watch. "That's about twenty minutes from now." She handed the letter to Noda, who quickly passed it to Takashima. "Also, according to Mr. Baron, it will cost

Constellation over a quarter-million dollars each day, whether or not the cameras roll.

"I need your answer. Now."

Takashima did not look at the letter. It was his final moment of defiance, like the great Japanese warriors who faced the enemy before him. Instead his eyes turned toward Mistica. He had not seen this sexpot around the studio before, but somehow she looked very familiar. As he peered at her, he could not make out her figure; her beautiful face was mesmerizing. Angelic, like the Madonnas he had so often admired in the paintings of the masters. Pure and untouched. He must have her.

Uncomfortable, Mistica was perspiring as she rubbed her hands together. She wanted to run out, but her feet wouldn't move. Takashima was making a fool of her. Her heart was beating so fast, she thought it would burst through her chest any second. It was now obvious to everyone in the room he was watching her.

She carefully stole a glance at him. His dark looks and powerful aura frightened her, but she sensed a strange magnetism that she had remembered feeling at the party. She looked away from him, determined to show him her lack of interest.

Takashima did not display any anger, but he clenched his fists under the table. Her coolness toward him only made her more appealing.

Kelly, now becoming impatient, wanted Mistica out of this meeting. She was only distracting him now. She looked at the clock on the wall: eleven-fifty-two. She had to resolve this matter now. She had one card left to play. She prayed it would work as she interrupted his reverie:

"Mr. Takashima, I'm sure you realize that the teamsters and Constellation have always enjoyed a harmonious relationship in all these years. However, by not acknowledging their contract to work on our projects, you are upsetting the *wa* of the other studio employees."

Randy Peterson and his men looked at Kelly curiously, not following her Japanese reasoning. Noda, however, smiled and regarded her with new respect. Even the group of Japanese managers was impressed by her logic.

But Takashima ignored her, knowing it was a ploy. With his eyes still focused on Mistica, he quickly bowed to the teamsters, then left the meeting. He pretended he needed time alone to think, but this was more of his charade. His answer had already been decided.

No one dared to bother him until he returned with his decision.

"You have begun to learn our ways, Kelly-san," Takashima said, once again taking his seat at the table, mindful of the time. No one moved as they awaited his decision. The wall clock showed eleven-fifty-eight. "As we say, you are selling face, that is, displaying respect and friendliness in a time of crisis, which is most admirable."

Kelly looked at Takashima, scarcely believing that he was actually complimenting her. She tugged at her earrings, then quickly stopped. She must keep up her show of manly resolution.

"You leave me no choice in this matter," he said slowly. "You may continue with the film . . . with your teamsters."

Then he got up from the table and without any further discussion exited with Noda and the Yakuza. This time he did not bow.

14

As Robert walked through the lobby of the Savoy Hotel in London, he spied a delicious-looking redhead sitting at a cocktail table in the American bar. She smiled back at him, but he kept walking. He had no time now for extracurricular activity. He was scheduled to meet with English producer David Puttnam for a high-power tea, the popular British afternoon ritual, to talk out a business deal. He didn't even notice the portraits of Fred and Ginger and Bogart and Bacall hanging on the wall in the bar.

The hotel, which still retained its elegant art-deco look, had been a favorite haunt with visiting Hollywood movie stars and executives through the years. Located in the middle of the theater district and close to the hub of London business activity, it was the perfect place for Robert to meet his English contacts. He had always felt at home there, realizing that he could line up his evening's entertainment while still doing business.

He walked into the Thames Lounge and looked out at the view of the famous river. He did not take a seat near the window, but one closer to the busy bar, where he could watch the pretty cocktail waitresses bouncing around in their short, frilly petticoats and tight low-cut tops.

"Robert, good to see you," David Puttnam said,

walking quickly over to him and extending his hand. "How's the trip going?"

"Looking good," Robert said with his phony charm, noting that Puttnam looked happier and healthier since his tumultuous exit a year and a half ago from running Columbia studios. Admiring his beard, Robert ran his hand over his smooth chin, thinking, as he had often before, that maybe that was what he needed to look more the part of the distinguished executive.

"Well, I've been through four countries so far, and I've had offers galore from every major foreign production company or studio I've talked to about setting up co-production deals," he lied.

"How is your wife, Zinman?" Puttnam asked.

"Oh, you know Kelly, she always does the best she can. I'm the one who's basically calling all the shots now."

Robert, feeling important in his new lofty position, leaned against his wing-back chair as a very pretty tall waitress came up to take their order. He listened to Puttnam telling him about his new film *Memphis Belle*, while Robert looked the waitress up and down a few times, flashing his handsome smile.

"David, Takashima hopes I might be able to persuade you to do a picture or two with us," he said while eyeing the girl's breasts. "We would love to have a *Chariots of Fire* picture at Constellation."

Puttnam smiled but made no comment. He waved to a man just entering the lounge. "Excuse me, Robert, there's Andrew Lloyd Webber. He's in the middle of rehearsals for his new play. I want to say hello; I'll be back in a minute."

After Puttnam excused himself, Robert signaled for the waitress to come back over.

"Yes, sir, is there something else you would like now?" she asked in a refined accent.

Coyly Robert took a business card out of his pocket, flipping it back and forth between his fingers. "I was just wondering: if I push the red button in my suite, I get the maid. If I push the green button, I get the valet." He paused, then eyed her mischievously. "Which button do I push to get you?"

"The right one, sir," she answered with a cool smile, but the fire in her eyes told him to keep talking.

"I'm sure you can help me find it," he said, writing his room number on his card. He then slipped the card onto her tray, along with a fifty-pound tip. Looking her up and down one more time, he thought: She's worth it.

And after all, it was Takashima's money, anyway.

One of the two Department of Justice agents, perched on the roof of the Bullock's Department Store on the corner of the Century City Shopping Center, about a half-block away from Constellation's main gate, was peering through his binoculars. All morning long they had taken turns, watching a steady stream of trucks flowing into the studio, bringing in props, costumes, lumber, sets.

" 'Bigger than the parting of the Red Sea. More spectacular then the chariot race in *Ben Hur*. More opulent than Cleopatra's entrance into Rome,' " the other federal agent read from the gold-engraved invitation to Takashima's spectacular press party that Jake had slipped to them.

The agent, with his binoculars draped around his neck, turned to his left with a grin. "Shit, I wonder if they're going to have some of those geisha gals too. I remember a time in Kyoto—"

"Cut the jokes, Murphy. Donaldson only has us here to make a report on what goes in and out of the studio." He picked up the press release as he continued to read: "Says right here: 'No expense will be spared in this two-million-dollar extravaganza to entertain our guests in the spiritual and pleasurable delights of both old and new Japan.' "

"Forget it," Murphy said dryly. "We're not invited anyway."

* * *

"Noda-san, we have a problem," Minoru said, looking very perplexed.

Noda looked up as Minoru approached with a couple of Yakuza holding on to two men and a woman. More reporters, Noda thought, grinning. They had probably tried to crash the gate by hiding in one of the delivery trucks.

Since Takashima had let the word out about the gigantic press party, every overzealous reporter had tried to get to Takashima for an exclusive interview, but he had given strict orders that only Japanese journalists would be allowed to enter the studio in advance of the party. However, every reporter with proper credentials would be admitted the night of the gala. No exceptions to these commands!

"What shall we do with them?" Minoru asked, grabbing one of the men by the collar, nearly choking him in the process.

The other two reporters remained silent. Tales of the cruelty of Takashima's Yakuza had become well known around town.

"Exactly what we did with the others," Noda answered, smiling wryly. He looked directly at the reporters and said tongue-in-cheek, "Cut off their heads if they do not leave right away."

The reporters looked startled for a few seconds; then they took off, not turning around until they were well past the gate.

Noda left for his afternoon briefing with the master in the other direction.

"Takashima-san, I have prepared the notes for your luncheon meeting with Kelly-san," Noda said, handing him a set of printouts from his computer. "I also have your mail, and Henry Cordova is here to trim your hair."

"Good. Ask Mr. Cordova if he will wait until after my lunch."

Takashima then read over the notes, highlighting

the excerpts from the latest press release prepared by the Ronin regarding the slate of films Constellation was planning for the future. He would change the facts every few weeks just to keep the media confused. Then he saw something that did not please him.

"What is this?" Takashima asked, frowning as he rolled up his shirtsleeves. He pointed to a new separate press release regarding a twenty-minute trailer showing the highlights of *Criminal Intent*.

Noda became concerned, knowing this was a touchy subject. "Baron-san is working many hours to complete the film clips for the press party. And Kelly-san said we must promote the movie at this party."

"Tell her it must wait until another time."

"But, Takashima-san, the press and all of the creative people in Hollywood will be most interested in seeing what Constellation has to offer."

Takashima was still not convinced. "We must be careful. Baron-san is a very powerful man. Like an imperial falcon, we must clip his wings so he can fly no farther than the palace gates."

Noda, pushing up his glasses higher on his nose, realized that he must carefully support Baron. "*Hai*, Takashima-san, but is it not true that it is the *master* of the falcon who receives the Emperor's praise? Why not let Baron-san present his film? The glory will still be yours."

As Takashima weighed his protégé's words carefully, he was not aware that someone was listening outside his office door.

Mistica had put her ear against the door. She felt her stomach turn over as she listened to her father's name being bandied about by the two men. Here, Takashima was talking about screwing her dad with his film, and at the same time, she had been receiving gifts of jewelry, a new leased car at her disposal, as well as a letter of credit at his Beverly Hills bank for up to one hundred thousand dollars, interest free. And she had been on his payroll only for a week.

After Takashima had noticed her at the emergency board meeting, he had requested she meet him privately in his office. For her father's sake, she had gone along. And when he had found out she was Jake Baron's daughter, he took her hand in his and said, "It would be my greatest pleasure, Mistica-san, to have a representative of the Baron family on my team full-time. It would be most appropriate to continue the legacy that your grandfather began. We Japanese are very pragmatic people. We believe in completing the circle of *on*. That means debt."

Something in the way he said that word made her blood turn to ice in her veins. She would have to be very careful around this man.

Standing in the hallway, she swallowed deeply. She had run over from the wardrobe department with a crazy scheme in her head, and now she had to go through with it. On one hand, she would try to keep Takashima interested in her; on the other, she had hoped to have the opportunity to look around his office.

Takashima had placed her in charge of purchasing the costumes for the press party. The sample geisha-girl kimono that she was modeling for him was on loan from her dad's friends at Western Costume Company.

Gathering up her courage, she tapped lightly on his door, then sashayed into his office, shooting him a pretty smile. "Excuse me, Mr. Takashima, sir," she said sweetly. "I'd like to show you the costume the geisha girls will wear at the press party."

Takashima merely nodded in reply.

Mistica tried not to shiver as she fingered the thin silk of her short kimono. She had nothing on underneath but her bra and lacy bikini briefs.

Noda, eyeing the seductive blond, was worried. Baron's daughter could get herself into trouble. She did not possess the sweet curiosity of Kakue-san. She used her body in a dangerous way he had occasionally seen before. He feared for her safety if she remained alone with Takashima.

As Noda quietly walked out, he left the open file of mail on the desk near the door. Curiously, he glanced back at Mistica for another look. He was embarrassed to see that her sapphire-blue kimono was very revealing.

"Utsukushii desu ne!" Takashima commented, his dark eyes piercing through the soft folds of silk around her breasts. "Beautiful."

Mistica continued to smile. "We also have pink, the color of my lining—"

"Show me," Takashima ordered, standing up and walking past his four color TV monitors and over to her. Before she could protest, he untied her sash and slid her kimono off her shoulders and down to her waist.

He stopped to appraise her. She had an incredible body, he thought. The gods in heaven would give up their place to possess her.

Hyperventilating so fast she felt that she might pass out, she thought: This is insane. But she couldn't stop now. She turned her back to him and reversed the kimono, then slipped it back on, the pink side now showing. She turned around to face Takashima. His eyes had not left her.

"Well," she asked, her voice barely a whisper as she wrapped the sash around her, "which do you like better? The blue or the pink?"

Takashima smiled broadly and said, "I would like to see the blue again."

Mistica froze. She couldn't do it again. She couldn't stand him gawking at her like that; it made her feel so unclean. Plus, she was afraid of what would happen if he took off her kimono again.

But before she could make a move, Noda returned. He bowed as he interrupted the master. "Takashima-san, you must leave for your luncheon. Mr. Cordova has agreed to wait." Noda bowed again, and then he was gone.

Tightening her kimono around her, she couldn't forget her mission. She must look around for any incriminating ledger files. She looked up at Takashima and asked nervously, "May I do something to help you?"

He purposely avoided giving her a response. Instead he straightened his tie and put on his suit jacket. He began to collect some loose files still spread out over his desk from an earlier meeting. By design, he put all but two of these files into a side file drawer, then turned the key. He pulled on the locked drawer as a double check, all the while knowing that Mistica was watching his every move.

"*Domo arigatō*, Mistica-san, I am sorry but I am late for a luncheon meeting with Kelly-san. But you may stay. I will return around two-thirty. Then you may continue with your fashion report."

He led her over to a comfortable-looking leather couch and sat her down.

Takashima walked back behind his desk and picked up a heavy coffee-table book. At the same time, he pressed a button on the side of his desk—out of Mistica's view—that immediately activated two hidden video cameras. He planned to record her every move to test her truthfulness and loyalty. If she was to continue to work in close proximity to him, he wanted to know if he could trust her.

Handing her the book on the ancient art of Japanese flower arrangement, he bowed politely and said, "Please, relax and enjoy this book." Then he left for lunch, smiling to himself.

Pretending to look through the book, Mistica began to breathe easier for the first time since she had made her unannounced visit to his office. After a few moments she laid the book down and peeked out the door. No one was in the hallway. Good. She carefully approached his desk and leafed through the two open files.

They could be important, she decided, putting the

sheets into an interoffice studio envelope and stealing across the hall. She scarcely took a breath as she made copies of the ledger sheets on the large copy machine. She didn't want to think about what would happen to her if anyone found out what she was doing.

Then very carefully she replaced the ledger sheets in the files on Takashima's desk. After checking the hallway once again, she closed the door behind her as she quickly left, the envelope neatly folded and safely concealed in the sleeve of her kimono. She hoped Donaldson could use these papers to arrest the monster who had killed Stephen.

The Constellation commissary was filled during the lunch hour with mostly Japanese employees, while the other workers, especially the few Americans still on payroll, either came with brown bags or went off the lot. Takashima and Kelly were dining alone in a newly decorated private tatami room.

"Are you telling me there's poison in this fish?" Kelly asked as she sampled her first taste of *fugu*.

Takashima glanced over at his *gaijin* executive, admiring the outline of her breasts straining against her tight aqua suede dress. However, his gaze drifted down to her legs as she awkwardly shifted her weight. She wasn't used to sitting on the floor. He smiled; she was exposing a great deal of her slim thighs.

"All the poison is removed before cooking," he said tactfully as he continued to eat.

Still not convinced, she decided to tackle the *suno momo*, cucumber-and-shredded-carrot salad. In another moment Kelly put down her chopsticks in frustration. The idea of eating poisoned fish had turned her off eating at all, even though she was still very hungry. Looks like I'll have to send out for pizza again, she thought.

"You are not hungry, Kelly-san?"

She smiled weakly, trying to cover up her embarrassment. "I've been so busy working on the press party, I lost my appetite."

"You have sent out all the invitations." It was more a statement than a question.

Kelly nodded. "The calls haven't stopped coming in. The town is buzzing about our spectacular. And every agent in Hollywood worth his ten percent will be there, along with their biggest clients."

Takashima, finishing his meal, reached for his tea. "I am very pleased." Everything was going according to his plan.

In fact, his personal, hand-delivered invitations to Akio Morita, Marvin Davis, Robert Daly, Sid Sheinberg, Frank Mancusso, Dawn Steel, Rupert Murdoch, Ted Turner, and Richard Berger, as well as Peter Guber and Jon Peters, had all been well received. And except for Morita, everyone on his VIP list had confirmed.

Takashima noticed that Kelly appeared to be unhappy, when she should be overjoyed. "Tell me, Kelly-san, why do your eyes cry without tears?"

She didn't respond.

He decided to try an American approach to make her respond: a joke. "Let me guess. You have nothing to wear to the party, correct?"

Kelly tried to smile, but she didn't succeed. "I just heard from Robert. He's decided to stay abroad and attend the Cannes Film Festival. He says he wants to concentrate on the foreign distributors from the Asian countries."

Takashima raised his eyebrows. This was news. A trip to the film festival was not on Zinman's original schedule. But he was not displeased. It simply meant that her stupid American husband would not be here for his gala party.

"Perhaps Robert wants to open a branch office in Thailand," Takashima joked again.

"Who cares?" Kelly responded sarcastically.

She felt that while Robert had been away, all the problems with their marriage had become more focused. Maybe she had been wrong to bring him to Constellation. After all, she had been successful all these years on her own. And her career was now more important than ever before. Also, seeing him every day as often as she did had become a deterrent at home. There was nothing left to discuss at night. Maybe it was time to stop pretending that she loved Robert; because she *didn't*. The sparks just weren't there. Their relationship had definitely faded. But she hoped they could still be professional friends.

But for now, she wanted to get some good old American junk food.

". . . and only after the most exciting chase scene ever filmed in an action-adventure movie—against the backdrop of the spectacular Aspen Mountains—will the surprise ending of *Criminal Intent* be revealed," Jake said, exhausted, as he completed rereading aloud his script. The final mix for the preview trailer was just days away, and then the big press party.

With pride swelling in his head, Jake pondered over what he had just watched in the editing room. The almost completed film trailer looked good, and it would be even better with the temporary music track that they were going to lay in.

He ran his hands through his hair, then over his face. He needed a shave. He had spent hours—or was it days?—hunched over the Kem editing machine.

Funny, a few months ago he never would have thought that he would see this day so soon. With the delayed completion of principal photography for *Criminal Intent*, Jake had had no choice but to take over the cutting of the trailer from Terry Taylor when the director realized that he had to leave for Europe immediately to begin prepping a previously contracted Orion picture.

"You've really got something to be proud of, Jake," said Howard "Happy" Berstein, Jake's editor, slapping him on the back. "Looks great."

"Yeah, not bad for an old man," said his assistant, full of admiration for Jake.

"Thanks, guys," Jake said, turning on the overhead lights. He was pleased by their praise. These two seasoned film editors had seen many films go through these CFI labs, and they knew what was good.

Jake had insisted to Kelly that the trailer, as well as the entire picture, not be cut in Constellation's editing rooms, for he didn't want any direct Japanese interference.

He pulled out a pack of cigarettes: empty. He didn't care. He was flying high on his can of film.

In some ways, it had been a new beginning for him. He loved the hands-on control only a director had with an editor. In the private world in their darkened room, the entire film belonged to them and no one else. Only the rattle-clapping sound of the editing machine could be heard along with the mental clicking of his brain as the scenes fell into place. With all the turmoil with Takashima, this had become good therapy for his nerves. Maybe when the Takashima investigation was resolved, he'd go back out as an independent producer, or maybe he'd even try directing.

But for now he couldn't wait to show off to the town what his team had done.

"Jake, how about joining us across the street at the slophouse for a few burgers?" Happy said, looking for his coat.

"Sounds good to me, Hap," Jake responded as he noticed the time on the big wall clock. Nearly midnight. "Damn, you know, we haven't stopped since lunch . . . yesterday." He shook his head in amazement.

As Jake reached to turn off the lights in the lab, they heard the front door open.

"Anybody hungry?" a woman's voice called out.

"Yeah, what are you offering?" Happy responded, not knowing who was asking.

"It's okay, guys," Jake said, grinning widely. "Guys, you know our boss, Ms. Kristopher?"

"Hi, fellows," Kelly said with a big smile at Jake as she handed a large pizza box to each of the editors.

Hap's partner opened his box and sniffed the aroma floating through the room. "Ummm, pepperoni, sausage . . . and anchovies," he said as he headed, along with Hap, to the lunchroom. Happy opened the door, then turned to Jake and Kelly. "You two want a beer?"

Kelly responded, "No, thanks. Jake?"

"I'll pass too. I'm a bit pissed off that I didn't get a pizza," he said, tongue-in-cheek, to Kelly.

When they were left alone in the dimly lit hallway, he eyed her tight green leotard jumpsuit and smiled. "What a nice surprise to see you tonight . . . boss. I know the guys appreciate the food. After all, we've all been working around the clock. So what brings you down here on a Friday night? And how come no food for me?"

"Well, I had nothing better to do," she said, winking. "If you're a good boy, I'll take you over to Musso and Frank's for a midnight snack."

"How good a boy?"

They were standing so close now, Kelly didn't know what to say. She swore she could hear his heart beating. His rugged face was flushed, and he was breathing faster. He looked so good to her in his tight jeans and cut-off sweaty black T-shirt, exposing his well-developed biceps. Suddenly she ached to kiss him. "You know, you don't look too bad for an older man working such long hours," she teased.

"Thanks," he said, also vibrantly aware that their bodies were almost touching. "You want to fool around?" he asked, teasing her right back with a crooked smile.

"Here, in the editing room?" She feigned surprise.

"Sure. Look, we'll close the door, then I'll put on the radio—"

"Mr. Baron, you're incorrigible," she said, laughing.

Overcome for the moment by his need for her, he took her into his arms. "That's why you love me."

She immediately stepped backward, no longer smiling. He hadn't meant to say that, but he wasn't sorry he had. He let her go.

"Kelly, I'm sorry."

She put her finger to his lips. "It's okay, Jake," she said, quickly picking up a newspaper and pretending to look through it. "Look, I don't have a date for the *Indiana Jones* premiere. Robert has extended his trip. How would you—?"

Jake didn't wait for her to finish. "Well, let me first speak with my social secretary. I might already have a date."

Kelly grinned, thinking: What a lovable big shit he is.

And at that moment she realized that she had never stopped loving this big shit.

Takashima sat on a tatami mat in the middle of the floor in the darkened hidden vault located behind the main vault of his Beverly-Rodeo Bank, surrounded by stacks of paper money. The large steel-walled room was dimly lit by three strategically placed lamps hanging down from the ceiling, casting a greenish glow on the money.

With his eyes closed, his head low, his palms resting on his knees, and facing outward, Takashima continued to meditate for the success of his newest venture: diverting the money he skimmed from his many Tokyo pachinko parlors and laundered through his Beverly-Rodeo bank on to his various shell corporations throughout the world, then eventually deposited into various foreign bank accounts. He had been amused with his latest scheme.

He was praying to Inari, the fox god, to safely speed his couriers tonight on their trek to various parts of the world: Switzerland, Colombia, the Netherlands Antilles, even the Fiji Islands.

In addition to his ritual of offering special prayers to the god messenger, he had prepared gifts of bean curd and rice, since food offerings were a vital part of the ceremony. But should the fox god not be pleased, he had been known to turn the tables and falsely deliver a message to the other gods, which could result in business failures. Takashima was always careful not to displease him.

After his Ronin intelligence had informed him that the U.S. Department of the Treasury had stepped up their investigations of wire transfers of large sums of money to foreign banks, Takashima had decided to use only couriers to throw off any trace should there be a future investigation regarding his money laundering through his new Beverly Hills bank. Although the current U.S. law required that any deposits of ten thousand dollars or more be reported, no bank was required to tell the government when any part of the money was wired abroad.

Suddenly he grunted loudly, and his voice echoed off the high ceilings of the vault. It was not just the sounds that made the atmosphere eerie. In the murky light, only Takashima's face could be seen. He wore a soft black cashmere turtleneck sweater, black pants, and black socks. He had left his shoes outside the vault, where several Yakuza stood guard.

Noda entered very quietly as Takashima continued praying. He was also dressed in black pants and sweater, his hair falling over his eyes as he bowed. Some inner instinct made Takashima open his eyes and acknowledge Noda's presence.

"You have disturbed me, Noda-san. I trust you have important news," Takashima said irritably, his voice cracking as he tried to speak. For some reason he could not explain, he had more difficulty than usual coming out of this deep trance.

"Takashima-san, they are here," Noda said simply, then pushed a button on the wall. Several hidden panels slid open simultaneously to reveal a wall of secret surveillance TV screens monitoring the outside of the bank. Takashima was extremely paranoid about this laundering operation. No one, including his heir apparent, Noda, was privy to Takashima's entire operation. And Takashima kept the one key to the hidden vault.

Takashima got up quickly from the mat and checked the screens. He carefully monitored the activity going on outside. He grunted, pleased with what he saw: Japanese tourists with cameras, a couple of fashionable Spanish ladies, several Indian businessmen, even an elderly American couple, were all being led in a preselected order into the bank through the triangular courtyard at the gold-and-marble back entrance.

Each of these bagmen would receive a specified amount of cash in an elegant suitcase or a locked pouch, complete with personalized bogus initials, for his trip abroad. None of them were U.S. citizens, so if they were caught, they would not have to face American courts or testify against Takashima. Moreover, most of their trips were on direct flights. One couple might fly to Las Vegas first, then take a train to Chicago before driving on to New York for a flight to the Netherlands. Another would fly directly to Paris, then take several trains before reaching their final destination in West Germany. Another would spend a couple of weeks in Florida before boarding a cruise liner through the Panama Canal. It was a most ingenious plan. And all were being paid very well.

"Noda-san, I will drill each of them personally before their departure," Takashima said as he opened the vault door.

Noda nodded as he followed Takashima into his private bank office, where the first courier awaited them. He shuddered involuntarily as he bowed to Takashima. He prayed to the spirit of his mother that she would forgive him for continuing to comply with Takashima's wishes. Preparing a trap in Japan took time, for none of Takashima's employees could suspect him until the time was ripe. And that time was approaching, Noda comforted himself. Now that the political scandals were mushrooming in Japan, he needed only exercise *gaman*.

A few hours later, Noda decided to drop some papers off at his 1901 Avenue of the Stars office. But instead he walked up the street, stopping in the middle of the Olympic Boulevard overpass. He leaned over the railing and looked toward downtown L.A., ablaze with lights in the far distance.

For some time, he watched the spectacle of lights flickering on and off. Every human life, he thought, was as brief as that. His breathing became more shallow as he realized that his own life was now as fragile. If Takashima found out about his betrayal, he would dispose of him instantly. Therefore, he had to make absolutely certain that Takashima would get caught before he was discovered.

He walked back down the block to the deserted ABC Entertainment Center and found a pay phone. With a steady hand he dialed the now familiar direct number to the Department of Justice. When the party at the other end answered, he put his handkerchief over the mouthpiece, as he had always done before, and began to speak softly, slowly, and without a pause.

"This is the concerned Constellaton employee with some more information about illegal transfers of money to foreign countries. Are you interested? . . . Yes, it concerns the studio owner, one Hiroshi Takashima." He continued, giving specific dates and places, enough that could be checked out to verify its authenticity.

"Yes, I understand, you would like my name." As Noda paused, he remembered the ceramic lion-dog animals he had often seen as a child. They were placed on the roofs of houses to ward off evil spirits. He could use some of that same protection. It was finally time to give some identification.

"Please know me by the name of Lion Dog. I will continue to contact you again with more information."

* * *

"C'mon, Kelly, we'll be late," Jake said, looking out at the crowd as they got out of their limo in front of the Mann National Theater in Westwood. Big banners proclaiming *Indian Jones and the Last Crusade* were hung above the marquee as well as on both sides of the red-carpeted, canopied runway.

"Jake, relax. The movie doesn't start until Spielberg says so, and you know he'll be late," Kelly said, laughing as she took Jake's arm. She smiled at the photographers taking their picture from every angle.

"Damn paparazzi." Jake scowled, looking like he was ready to slug a couple of photographers who got too close.

Kelly held him back. "This is a premiere, Jake, not a boxing match. Please relax."

He looked over at her and smiled. "You're right, Kel. I guess I'm just a bit uptight, that's all." He bent down and whispered in her ear: "But whoever heard of making contact with two agents from the Justice Department at a movie premiere?" He patted the left breast pocket of his black tux to make sure the envelope—that Mistica had passed to him—was still there. He breathed easier after making sure it was.

The teenage girls yelling and screaming in the bleachers as they waited for the movie's stars to arrive were disappointed when they saw Jake and Kelly approaching. Who were these people? Nonetheless, Kelly received quite a few whistles from the guys in the crowd, as well as several loud cheers when columnist Army Archerd, the premiere's MC, announced Jake and her over the loudspeakers.

Indeed, none of the men could take their eyes off Kelly. Wearing a floor-length slinky emerald-green sequined gown with long sleeves and an off-the-shoulder neckline, and with her strawberry-blond hair piled high on her head, she evoked the old-time glamour of stars like Carole Lombard and Rita Hayworth.

Jake held her tighter as they walked farther. "Do you see them, Kelly?"

"C'mon, Jake, let's go inside."

"Wait," he said as he looked over at a small crowd gathered outside near the far entrance. Smirking, he saw Takashima. As usual, the sonofabitch was holding court with some of the town's biggest executives, including Spielberg and Connery as well.

Takashima did look the part of a studio owner in his elegant evening clothes. The beautiful young geisha, Kakue, wearing a sapphire-blue velvet gown with big angel-wing bows on her shoulders, was right at his side.

"Let's take the scenic route, Kel," he said. Before she could protest, he led her past Takashima and his entourage. "Smile," he said, grinning widely and waving hello to Takashima and the Yakuza around him. Kelly did the same, gritting her teeth.

"You're insane, Jake Baron," she said out of the side of her mouth. "Don't push your luck with him. He's no one to kid with."

Once they were inside, they sat in the back of the theater. Jake scrutinized everyone, trying to locate the federal agents. "I wonder if it's those two guys over there in the white jackets."

"Stop it, Jake, they'll find *you*."

"Look, here comes Spielberg with Ford and Connery. The show's going to start any second."

Then Jake saw Takashima with Kakue walking past them down the aisle. A late entrance, Jake thought. The bastard was learning how to be big-time. No sooner did Takashima take his seat than the lights went out and the theme music came up under the credits.

"Mr. Baron," whispered someone behind him.

Jake stiffened in his seat. He felt the hairs on the back of his neck stand up. He started to turn around.

"Don't turn around. Agent Donaldson sent us. Continue watching the film."

"Sure. Whatever you say."

"Slide the envelope along the right side of your seat and let it drop."

Slowly Jake removed the envelope from his breast pocket. Out of the corner of his eye he could see Kelly helping an elderly lady next to her take off her jacket, thus keeping her turned in the other direction. With fumbling fingers he carefully slid the envelope through the slit between the theater seats. He waited a couple of seconds, not even breathing, but he didn't hear it drop.

He whispered, "Did you get it?"

There was no response. He turned around. They were already gone, just like in the movies.

15

"From Manhattan to Tokyo, they call him the 'Asian Octopus.' But here in Hollywood, they call him the new emperor of the film industry," began Mike Wallace as he taped his opening segment for a forthcoming *60 Minutes* story. The segment, called "The Tokyo Exchange," would focus on the Asian influence now permeating Hollywood.

"Recognize the bright lights of Tokyo's Ginza behind me?" Wallace continued, gesturing behind him as he walked along with the throngs of invited guests. "Well, we're not in Tokyo, but on the back lot of Constellation Studios in Century City, California . . ."

All decked out in a thousand-dollar tuxedo, Hiroshi Takashima leaned over the railing of his three-thousand-dollar-a-night suite on the thirtieth floor of the Century Plaza Tower and gazed on his make-believe world. It was exactly as he had planned.

Giant klieg spotlights lit up the Century City sky, while a long line of limos inched their way through the heavy traffic to the front gate. Inside the studio grounds, a ribbon of neon lights slithered through the alleys and streets of his recreated Ginza district with its pachinko parlors, glitzy shops, and traditional geisha houses.

But he was especially pleased with his showstopper: twenty-foot-high gold-plated doors patterned with prowling jeweled tigers, accentuated with ruby and sapphire eyes, and golden dragons snorting incense smoke. All five thousand invited guests would enter through these magnificent portals.

Hollywood had not seen anything like this since Cecil B. DeMille's wrap party for *The Ten Commandments* in 1956. Some reporters already speculated it was going to be even bigger than Mike Todd's *Around the World in 80 Days'* Madison Square Garden party. With just the amazing logistics alone, the party was being termed "colossal," "spectacular," "overwhelming":

Special tactical police units that totaled hundreds of uniformed and plainclothes men and women; more than two thousand waiters, valets, attendants; every available parking space in the nearby Century City Shopping Center reserved for the party; every hotel room in the Century Plaza—both towers—reserved for his VIP guests; more than a hundred chefs to prepare the food, and enough French champagne to fill a small lake.

The crowd of fans behind the barricades was going crazy. Each limo pulling up contained the most important stars in all of show business: Michael Jackson, Sinatra, Stallone, Diana Ross, Madonna, Kim Basinger, Streep, Streisand, Redford; the list went on and on. Even the special squadron of police had a difficult time keeping fans from jumping over the temporary wooden fences. They had been lined up for days waiting for the event that all the newscasters had called "The Hollywood Party of the Century."

For the first time in many years, Takashima felt no urgency. A late entrance would be most appropriate. He wanted to savor the anticipation of this grand feeling tonight: to see all the movie stars that the American public worshiped before he set out to harm them.

He raised his arms high in victory, feeling the west wind blowing in his face. He looked into the heavens, speaking to the moon: "Was this how the gods felt when they watched the first flower blossom? The first bird fly?"

He smiled. Even the stars, the spies of the gods, made an early appearance tonight to bear witness to this prodigious event. "In memory of the honorable Emperor," Takashima said, bowing low as he made a proper tribute.

It was now time to make his grand entrance.

"The master's coming. You have your instructions."

From inside the sophisticated communications van, Noda watched as a double line of uniformed police on motorcycles escorted the gold stretch limo, followed by five platinum stretch limos with VIP's. He closed the window draperies, turning to the men and women seated in the back who had been recruited by the Ronin for this special assignment tonight. It would be their responsibility to see that the massive lights and sounds were all operational, at all times, as they had rehearsed.

They all nodded.

"Good." Nervously Noda peered through the draperies again, hoping all would go as planned tonight, especially for Baron-san.

As the gold stretch limo came to a stop in the main quadrangle, it glowed like a golden sun.

Takashima was the first to get out. He stood proudly like an emperor displaying the wealth of his kingdom. He smiled at everyone in the crowd, making sure they all recognized him. Photographers began snapping away, while the reporters with notebooks or mikes in their hands raced toward the Asian Octopus.

"Takashima-san, what is your involvement with the current political scandal in Tokyo?" a reporter from Japan's NHK network yelled in Japanese.

"Are you glad that you didn't get your first choice for CEO . . . Larry Evans?" a CNN reporter shouted to him.

Takashima ignored those questions as well as the

many others shouted out to him. Instead, with a big broad smile, he waved to the mass of fans. After all, he was the biggest of all superstars this night. Then he helped his very special companions out of his limo.

Mistica—encouraged by Jake to accept Takasima's personal invitation—smiled and waved to the crowd like she had been born for this role, even though she was apprehensive about being part of his personal entourage. She wore a long gown made of the sheerest black silk embroidered with thousands of precious black pearls. Next came Kakue—somewhat shy with all that was going on around her—with her long black hair covering her bare shoulders. She looked like a delicate blossom in her white lace gown with rare white orchids in her hair. She smiled sweetly and blinked several times as the bright flashes exploded in her face.

The reporters couldn't get enough pictures of Takashima and the two women.

"Mr. Takashima, how does it feel to be the richest and most powerful man in Hollywood?"

". . . and the luckiest?" another reporter asked, still trying to get him, at best, to respond to one of their questions.

"Hey, look, there's Ted Turner!" yelled a reporter as the maverick cable-station owner got out of one of the platinum stretch limos in the entourage. He waved and flashed his famous grin at the squealing crowd.

"Good evening, Mike," Kelly said, full of energy and grace as she gave him a peck on the cheek. "How's everything working out?"

Kelly and Jake were standing in front of a traditional teahouse. Kelly, as usual, looked gorgeous in her Bob Mackie red-sequined gown with a train of luxurious red and white plumes especially designed for her. Her hair was pulled back from her face, and the only jewelry she wore was dramatic ruby-and-diamond earrings in the shape of a fan. Jake, as usual, wore the same old tux he had worn to Stephen's New Year's Eve party.

As Jake shook hands with Wallace, he pulled subconsciously at his tie. "Good to see you again, Wallace. Haven't seen you since we played in the Kennedy Tennis Tournaments . . . mmm, a few years ago."

"You're right, Baron. It's been a long time between sets." He turned toward Kelly. "Kelly, you look beautiful tonight. And I assume things couldn't be any better: this is a great crowd. Hopefully your Mr. Takashima will give us a few words later. . . . Jake, old buddy, I hear you're a big part of the festivities later tonight?"

"Yeah, you know how it is with us Hollywood legends," Jake said, laughing. "Seriously, we're previewing Constellation's soon-to-be-released—and soon-to-be-a-hit—*Criminal Intent*."

"We'll look forward to seeing it later. Gotta go now," Wallace said, then looked into the camera with a nod to start taping. His crew followed him from location to location. "Tonight's gala has been billed as the biggest press party Hollywood has ever seen. Let's look now at a real Shinto purification rite.

". . . and a Shinto priest has also been flown in from Japan especially for the purification rite that is important to the opening of any new company. Several festivals are going on simultaneously around the Ginkaku-ji, the Silver Pavilion, including the Dance of the Golden Dragon and the fire ceremony.

"A maze of small streets—none with names, as it is in Tokyo—beckon the colorfully dressed party guests. The aroma of ginger from a cooking grill and the seductive scent of incense blend together to tempt the guests to forget everything else and find *wa*, harmony, here in Takashima's Tokyo.

"Thousands of fresh cherry blossoms flown in from Japan decorate every corner, along with hundreds of miniature bonzai trees. Outdoor Kabuki actors in long flowing lion costumes play out the drama of life and love lost on an outdoor stage in the Ginza district. Gigantic advertising panels are lit up with flickering neon lights. Fortune-tellers read eager palms, while street vendors sell—with play yen money—meat on skewers, along with souvenir samurai dolls. Even the Yoshiwara, old prostitution district, has been recreated, with erotic prints predominantly displayed in the houses.

". . . but even the cherry blossoms can't compare with the beauty of Constellation's CEO, Kelly Kristopher." Wallace stopped momentarily, then relaxed as he lowered the notepad that he had been glancing at. Next he said to his audio and video operators: "Let's cut for a few minutes. We'll insert the sit-down with Kelly here. Let's follow that crowd and get some reaction shots."

Kelly grabbed Jake's arm. "I've never seen as much press coverage as I've seen tonight, Mr. Baron. And wasn't it you who once told me to use all the free publicity you can get today, because tomorrow the price might go up?"

"Yeah, I did say that, I guess," Jake agreed, pulling on his tie. The thing was driving him crazy. "I'm getting nervous, Kel."

"Don't worry so much—"

"Oh, there you are, Kelly, dear." Jackie Collins suddenly ran up to them, her long hair flying behind her. She looked gorgeous in a long leather trench coat the color of a golden sunset. "I've got lots of questions to ask you."

Jake looked at Kelly and mumbled, "What gives?"

"Oh, didn't I tell you, Jake? Jackie's doing a new novel, Lady Boss, about a woman studio owner. She wants to interview me. She's already spoken with Sherry, Dawn, and, I believe, Marvin Davis."

Jake grabbed Kelly's hand tightly and said, "Jackie, why don't you interview both of us? If there's anyone who knows how to run a studio, it's yours truly."

                        *   *   *

"Your garden is so very beautiful, Mr. Takashima," an exquisite Elizabeth Taylor, gowned in her favorite purple, said as the Japanese mogul showed her around the elegant grounds. "But why are there no flowers?"

Takashima reflected for a moment. The truth was that there are no flowers in Japanese gardens because they draw excessive attention to themselves, which is against the Buddhist philosophy. Instead he said to his guest politely, "I prefer to adorn my garden with living blossoms of beauty. Like yourself."

Miss Taylor laughed. "You certainly have a way with words, Mr. Takashima."

"And with women," Malcolm Forbes added as he caught up with his best friend, Elizabeth. "This is quite a bash, Mr. Takashima," he said with some envy. "However, wait till you see my seventieth birthday party in Tangier in a couple of months. You'll come, won't you?"

Takashima merely smiled as he left the twosome to speak with *Rich and Famous'* Robin Leach.

"Mr. Takashima," Barry Diller said, walking over to him. Michael Eisner was at his side, trailed by a crew from *Inside Edition*.

Takashima recognized the Disney chairman who was with Diller. He had some of his Yakuza raise their arms to block the television crew while he greeted them. "I am pleased that men with your creativity would honor me by enjoying the peace and spirit of my garden."

But as the aggressive tabloid reporter strained his neck under the bodyguard's hulking arms to see what was going on, he yelled out to the three studio moguls, "Are any of you taking any additional precautions for security in light of the firebombing tonight at Universal?"

Takashima, looking at Diller and Eisner and pretending to be surprised, quickly responded, smiling over the report, "Please, these are my guests and we all have 'no comment.' " Takashima began to walk his guests away from the nosy reporter, silently celebrating another one of his victories against Hollywod until he heard the newsman add:

"Universal must have been tipped off; their security doused the fire before there was any major damage."

Takashima kept walking, but his face turned stone cold.

Eisner, like Diller, was startled by the report, but didn't respond. Instead Eisner was very awed by Takashima's big extravaganza. "Mr. Takashima, I'd be honored if you'd come down to Florida and see how we've recreated Hollywood at our new Disney-MGM theme park."

Takashima nodded with delight.

With some of the most powerful people at his side all night, he thought, he was truly in the middle of the Hollywood community now.

"Jake, are you crazy?" Kelly shouted, exasperated as the two of them stood behind one of Noda's communication trucks. "Takashima has Yakuza all over this lot tonight. And don't forget what I've been hearing through the grapevine about all of his hidden surveillance cameras."

"Listen, Kelly, Takashima might be King Shit tonight, but the last thing that he or any of his Jap henchmen would be worried about is somebody breaking into his office. If I get caught," he began, laughing while he teased Kelly, "I could always say that I was homesick for the nighttime view from my former office."

Kelly smiled, but she wasn't very amused. Jake had been antsy about Takashima's locked desk drawer ever since Donaldson let him know that the papers Mistica copied off Takashima's desk were only petty-cash allocations for clerical staff. Now Jake wanted to try to open the locked drawer Mistica had described to him to see if there were any incriminating documents inside.

"Well, Jake, I always wanted to be a lookout for a burglar."

Looking at her Piaget watch, Kelly cautioned Jake that he had less than twenty minutes before the fireworks announced his part of tonight's presentation. He would have to hurry.

Slowly panning the pocket flashlight around the strange-looking placement of antiques and Oriental furniture, Jake held the elongated beam on each object just long enough to recall what he had had in that same spot over the many years of his occupancy. It all seemed so different now. The only reminder of the past was the same pane glass windows, now partially hidden behind bamboo shutters.

"Ouch!" he groaned, banging into an end table. It figured that the Jap would stick a piece of furniture in front of the back office door, Jake thought. He realized that he must be very careful. Kelly's warning made sense. It would be more than embarrassing if he got caught tonight.

After finding Takashima's desk, Jake got down on one knee and scanned the area with his light. As he spotted the locked drawer, he noticed that the lock was not the standard furniture type.

Damn, this would be a motherfucker to try to jimmy, he realized, feeling the lock with his finger. Suddenly a thought came to him. He remembered something from one of his detective movies that his buddy Richard Widmark had starred in as a burglar. There was not much time left; he knew he had to rush now.

Jake quickly took out his cigarette box and peeled the inside foil. After rubbing his pen over the paper—smack against the lock—he had a clear impression that he could give to Donaldson.

It would be interesting to see what kind of Dick Tracy the Justice Department agent was, Jake mused as he gently closed the back office door.

The crowd was getting restless as the last fireworks display exploded into a golden chrysanthemum in the night sky. It had been a long evening for Kelly and a beaming Jake who was inwardly pleased with his successful break-in. After he left Takashima's office, he and Kelly had hurried around the back way to cover his tracks. Out of breath, they had just crossed over the bridge from pretending to have visited the Silver Pavilion constructed in the middle of an artificial lake with tiny islets.

Suddenly every neon advertising panel in the Ginza, every painting in Yoshiwara, and every mirror in the pachinko parlors began to light up with a hypnotic red glow. Millions of dots began to vibrate; then slowly they began to take shape, until everyone recognized the beautiful face of Kelly Kristopher smiling down at them from the hundreds of video monitors. Noda and his communications team were right on time, as was expected by Takashima.

"Ladies and gentlemen, good evening," boomed Kelly's voice across the Constellation lot. "Through the power of our Japanese electronic technology, I am pleased to present to you, on the hundreds of monitors, the man who will now lead Constellation Studios and all of Hollywood into a new era. Ladies and gentlemen, may I present Hiroshi Takashima."

The monitors now slowly dissolved into a blue glow as Takashima appeared. "*Konban-wa*. Good evening. I would like to thank our most beautiful CEO, Kelly Kristopher . . ."

From inside his communications van, Noda, with binoculars around his neck, closely watched some of his field technicians stationed around the large stage. So far, so good, he thought. Everything seemed to be on schedule. While glancing at some of the twelve monitors in front of him, he gave the "standby" signal to his senior techs, who were ready to project the twenty-minute *Criminal Intent* trailer.

Jake, standing near Kelly behind the lectern, fidgeted nervously. During the few weeks that he had been completing the preview trailer, Takashima had purposely avoided running into him. But now, listening to Takashima addressing the throngs of celebrated people about *his* Constellation Studios—that upset Jake more than if the Jap had been looking over his shoulder in the editing room. He threw his cigarette to the ground. Playing out this game with the Jap was sometimes more than he could endure.

Takashima continued: ". . . in addition to making ten to fourteen pictures a year, my Takashima Group has agreed to invest a billion dollars over the next four years for the development of very special kinds of films under the Constellation banner."

This pronouncement drew loud applause from the audience from all over the lot.

"Of course, we have some very tough competition, but we are all very confident that Constellation will make the films the American public wants to see . . . and that you, the members of this prestigious industry, will support our sincere efforts. It was a pleasure to have seen all of you tonight. *Domo arigatō*. Thank you."

Before Kelly walked back to the lectern, she grabbed Jake and gave him a quick kiss. "For luck, honey."

She smiled, then squeezed his hand.

She moved to the mike. "Thank you, Mr. Takashima. We are all very excited about the future of Constellation . . ."

Jake straightened his tie. He was ready. In a few minutes, he would introduce to the industry their first preview of *Criminal Intent*. Funny, he thought, this movie had first cost him the loss of his studio, and now would represent his return to Hollywood as its executive producer.

". . . and tonight we'd like to show you part of that future," Kelly continued. She turned toward Jake as he joined her behind the lectern, looking into the closed-circuit cameras.

"I'd like to introduce a man most of you know well: the former owner of Constellation Studios and the executive producer of our exciting new film, *Criminal Intent*. Ladies and gentlemen, your good friend Jake Baron."

As Jake took the mike, he received thunderous applause and a volley of cheers. He looked out into the crowd but was too choked up to speak. So, they hadn't forgotten him after all. He looked at Kelly, clapping and smiling too. He'd never forget this night.

Takashima's smile vanished. He had not expected the audience to be so enthusiastic. But it did not matter. He was ready with his surprise.

He gave a nod to his disguised Ronin, standing ready by the side of the stage—he had been pretending to be one of Noda's senior techs—near where the heavy audio cable wires were piled.

"Thank you, everybody," Jake began confidently. "Tonight I . . ."

Suddenly his mike went dead. He tapped the head of the microphone, but there wasn't a sound. He couldn't believe it. "What the fuck is going on?" he shouted furiously, turning to Kelly.

Kelly was frantic. "I don't know, Jake, all the equipment was checked out during rehearsal."

Noda panicked, screaming to all his senior technical people on the two-way radio. He couldn't understand what had happened to the American's audio. Would the master blame him? he wondered, when all of a sudden, Japanese music began blasting throughout the lot. He immediately realized that the Ronin had cleverly sabotaged his system. Takashima, he thought, must be enjoying Baron-san's humiliation.

"What the hell is that?" Jake asked Kelly. "I'll kill that fuckin' Jap bastard for setting me up like this."

"Calm down, Jake. The feds will get Takashima soon enough."

A highly incensed Jake started looking in the crowd for Takashima. But he and his Yakuza had already left.

* * *

". . . yeah, that's right. Jake Baron was just launching his speech when the mike went dead," Army Archerd said into the pay phone. He wanted to make sure the press-party story made his tomorrow's *Daily Variety* column. "Some Japanese music started playing—I think it was their national anthem—then the party went on like nothing had ever happened. We never did see the preview trailer."

He paused as he thought a minute, watching the last of the crowd leaving the party.

"And add this tag: 'A strange ending to the strangest party Hollywood has ever attended.' "

Sitting in his Constellation office a few days later, Takashima read from the various newspapers that had been piling up in the center of his office. He smiled with delight at Art Buchwald's closing comment on the press party: "We're quickly on our way to making English our second language."

Takashima was highly amused by all the continuing publicity. The aftermath of the party was nearly as exciting as the party itself. He put down the paper and picked up the cup of hot tea his secretary had prepared for him. But he changed his mind and put it down. Like a small boy who could not get enough of his new toy, he wanted to enjoy more of his publicity.

He punched a couple of buttons on his remote, turning on his VCR machine to review some of the TV news highlights of his smash success.

". . . and according to the latest reports, the new Japanese owner of Constellation still has no comment about what is being called 'The Jake Baron Incident.' "

Takashima continued to watch the TV monitor, flipping through the myriad stories. Even though several were not very complimentary, he loved all the controversy that he was stirring up. In fact, several reports were on the current bandwagon of Japan-bashing, but Takashima was not disturbed. He thought it was great publicity and perfect for his plan of disrupting Hollywood. He was even amused when he found out that Ron Smith's newest celebrity look-alike would be one of himself.

Takashima turned off the VCR and quietly finished drinking his tea. He needed to meditate. He had a new problem to deal with now.

He summoned Noda. "What is my schedule today?"

Noda, still inwardly furious at being tricked the other night, fumbled nervously through the master's desk calendar while sneaking a glance out the window.

There was little activity throughout the studio. Noda had heard earlier that Takashima had received some advance information from the Ronin about a secret union meeting on the back lot sometime later in the day. And judging by the empty sidewalk along Hiroshi Avenue, it must be true.

"Noda-san, I have asked you a question," Takashima reminded him.

Embarrassed, Noda quickly continued to flip through the black leather calendar book. "You have a luncheon with that new German producer. Then cocktails with the commercial people you spoke with yesterday morning. Then dinner later at Spago with that young actress you met."

Takashima gazed straight ahead, tapping his forefingers together. He was not pleased. Who were these people? Nobodies. There would always be a hungry producer willing to let him pick up the tab, a gorgeous woman who called herself an actress, but whose real talents were in faking a performance in a bedroom. These were small players in a town where he had proved himself to be on top. This was not good. Harming the enemy could only be accomplished by being seen with their true leaders.

He snatched the calendar book from Noda's grasp. "What happened to my dinner with Diller-san at Morton's? And why has not Eisner-san's invitation to the new Disney-MGM studio party in Florida arrived?"

Noda knew what was happening, but he would not

speak. Whatever his personal feelings were for Takashima, he could not allow Takashima to lose face. He had to remain loyal to him.

"Norou!" Takashima cursed, skimming his secretary's notes in his book. The appointments had been canceled, as had several others for future dates.

Takashima did not have to ask why. He was beginning to get the picture. Since he had shown his muscle at the press party, and Baron had complained to the media that he was a fanatic, they were avoiding him. Hollywood's top executives and their superstars would all pay dearly for this.

Highly agitated at this backlash aimed at him, he took out a cigarette, but did not light it. How dare these fools think they could snub him? He would not tolerate it. He tore out today's page in his calendar and ripped it up, then poured his tea over the torn pieces of paper.

"Summon the Ronin!" he ordered Noda.

16

"Monsieur Robert, encore, si tu veux," the woman purred through her full lips. *"J'en ai besoin."*

Robert smiled, twisting his newly grown mustache with his fingers. Why not screw the black bitch again? That's what she wanted. He was up to it. Even after six exhausting weeks of traveling through Europe, he wanted to make his farewell fuck last as long as possible.

He had taken the best suite in the Hotel Plaza Athenée, made a few more business phone calls, then settled down to some relaxation. This was his last stop of what had been a good trip.

With his usual charm he had convinced various foreign distributors that this year's planned Christmas release of *Criminal Intent* was going to be the big box-office hit of the season. He also made sure that everyone knew that the new Japanese owner wasn't going to change the studio's policy of making the best films possible. In fact, Robert had said, the new owner would make bigger and better movies than Baron did.

"Okay, baby, you asked for it."

Robert ripped off the girl's frilly panties, then turned her over on the bed and began fucking her through the back way. Reveling in her creamy, soft skin, he let his hands roam all over her, squeezing her breasts, then up and down her hips.

She was a French Moroccan actress he had met in the hotel bar. Well, she said she was an actress. He didn't ask to see her SAG card, nor did he care if she washed floors. She was another gorgeous piece of femininity.

Since Robert had been away, he had fucked Swiss chambermaids, knapsack-carrying college students, English waitresses, Thai hookers, rich playgirls from South America—what the hell? he thought, smiling. As long as they had beautiful pussies, he jumped right in and fucked their heads off.

"Hang on baby," Robert cried out. "I'm going to come in you nowwww . . ."

He shot his load into her, pushing and thrusting with an urgency he didn't know he possessed. "Oh, shit, you're so beautiful! You're so fucking beautiful!" he shouted over and over again, not meaning a word of it.

Minutes later, he was singing in the shower: "California, Here I Come." Soaping up his cock, he glanced down at it. He was always amazed at the way it just kept on rising. Too bad the chick had fallen asleep, he mused.

Suddenly the phone rang.

As it kept on ringing, he looked around for a towel. Who the hell could be calling him anyway? he wondered. He had already sent his wife a wire that he'd arrive home sometime tomorrow evening. Probably it was just the night maid or the front desk.

"Repondez, telephoné," he called out to the naked girl in his bed.

The girl stirred and finally woke up. Without pulling up the sheet, she picked up the phone. *"Allo?"* she said breathlessly.

"Is this Robert Zinman's room?" Kelly asked at the other end.

"Mais oui, but 'e eez in shower."

A long silence followed. Kelly couldn't believe what she was hearing. A woman was in his room, saying, "He's in the shower"?

Kelly breathed deeply, unsure of what to do next.

Her mind was racing ahead of her, her thoughts tangled in confusion. She didn't know what to say. All she had planned to tell him was the good news that she had finally gotten that Guber-Peters project in turnaround from Warners over to Constellation.

"Hello," Robert said, grabbing the phone.

"You sonofabitch," Kelly growled. "We're through, you bastard!" she yelled into the phone.

Robert's mouth dropped as he recognized her voice. This couldn't be happening, not after such a great trip. He had to talk to her, explain that it was the maid who had answered the phone. He yelled, "Kelly, Kelly!" over and over into the phone, but it was dead.

Still holding the phone, he looked down.

Shit, he thought, my future now looks as limp as I do.

"No, stop . . . what do you want?" Kelly cried out in her sleep. She kicked the bedcovers onto the carpet, then turned over onto her stomach. She grabbed the pillow and held it tightly to her chest, trying to shake the nightmare. Perspiration poured from her body, and her long hair stuck to her face.

Moments later, she pulled herself out of bed. Her jaw hurt from clenching her teeth so tightly during the night. She shivered, remembering the terrible feeling of being so completely helpless. It had all seemed so real that she felt drained. Putting on her robe, determined to wipe the nightmare out of her head, she walked over to her bedroom picture window. The morning was overcast, with deep gray clouds lingering low over the dunes. She shook her head in dismay. She felt so alone. Not even a sea gull cut through the mist. Thank God for Saturday; no work today.

Kelly opened the sliding glass door and breathed in the salt air. She loved to hear the sound of the crashing surf, but this morning the ocean waves were merely whispers on sandy velvet. The only sound was the constant tune of her windbells reminding her that life never stood still.

She went back inside and strode to the kitchen. After putting on a pot of coffee, she wandered around her downstairs, watering the plants, dusting here and there, and finally sinking into her favorite armchair and picking up a crossword puzzle in the paper. Anything to keep busy. Anything so she wouldn't have to think about Robert. Or Takashima, for that matter. She felt like she was in the middle of a lot of battles and she was losing on all fronts.

It was becoming harder and harder for her to pretend that everything was normal at the studio, especially since Takashima had refused to acknowledge what had happened to Jake onstage.

"*Sumimasen*, Kelly-san, I do not know what you are talking about," he would say, then smile and continue with his meeting.

She threw down the newspaper in disgust and stared coldly at the surf breaking outside her picture window. Just below her line of sight she noticed the open telegram sitting on the marble coffee table. Looking down, she reached for it and scanned the short message again. Robert would be arriving home tonight.

She got up and poured herself another cup of black coffee. Staring into the steaming liquid, she mused over the phone call to Paris. She had added a lot of things up—the canceled dinners, the inexplicable delay at her award luncheon, the nights spent at John's. How long had Robert been cheating on her? "Well, one thing's for sure," she muttered to the empty house. "I know about this one, and one is more than I'll stand for."

As she fumed, an idea began hatching in her brain. She drank her coffee slowly, savoring its flavor. Checking her watch, she realized she didn't have much time for her big welcome-home surprise.

Robert got out of the airport limo and walked up the

driveway. He looked handsome and confident as he twisted the ends of his new mustache. Home, sweet home . . . and Kelly, he thought, frowning. He shifted a bouquet of roses in his hand. Then he breathed in the sweet fragrance of the flowers. They were Kelly's favorites.

Come on, he told himself, Kelly will understand about the girl. They hadn't been married all these years for nothing. Besides, Kelly was a woman of the eighties, a new breed. She'd understand when he explained that with all the stress they were both under at the studio and the long time he was away . . .

Shit, he thought, maybe the truth wouldn't work. The chambermaid story was still the best one. He momentarily practiced his forlorn look, then smiled confidently. He'd tell her over and over how much he loved her and missed her. That was what she wanted to hear anyway.

Quickly he walked up to the front door. It was still early enough in the evening that she probably wasn't asleep yet. In fact, Kelly was probably in bed, just lying there, waiting for him. He smiled as he felt himself getting hard.

Humming under his breath, he took out his keys.

The key didn't fit. He tried it again, trying to force it into the lock. It was too wide. He must have the wrong key.

A strange notion—Kelly had changed the locks—hit him, but he dismissed the idea right away. She wouldn't do that, would she? Nah, she'd been angry before, but in a few days she was always fine again.

He kept trying the key, until he finally had to admit that he was locked out of his own house.

"Kel," he yelled, banging lightly on the door. "Open up this door! I'm home, honey . . ."

No answer.

He started banging harder on the door. "C'mon, Kel. If you're there, please open up this door . . ."

"Go away, Robert, I don't want you in this house

ever again," Kelly responded in a subdued tone from inside.

Robert was shaken. "Kel, you don't mean that."

"Either you leave now, or I'll have the Malibu sheriff take you away," she said, trying not to break into sobs.

Robert stepped away from the door, trying to calm down. He knew Kelly would do it. She was never one to make idle threats. Damn, why didn't I send her some expensive jewelry or something? he thought. And why did I let that black bimbo answer the phone?

He laid the flowers carefully before the door. This was no time to storm the fort. He had to make other plans. A few phone calls telling her how much he loved her, dozens of roses, a story about how much he needed her. All she needed was a little time and she'd be begging him to come back.

And besides, his role at the studio was vital for her continued success.

Robert smiled coldly as he walked off the porch. He'd show her who was boss.

He opened the garage door and started up his Ferrari. He raced the engine a few times, then tore out of the driveway before taking off down PCH with his radio blasting. He headed down the coast toward town. He'd hole up for a few days with his good buddy John.

Robert smiled to himself and fingered his mustache. What the fuck? he thought. At least now my chances of getting laid tonight are good.

Jake held his breath as he clicked on his flashlight, its yellow arc penetrating the darkness of his old office. The whole building was so quiet, he could hear only the slight rustle of a warm Santa Ana breeze blowing outside. Holding the shutter ajar, he looked out the pane glass window. Fortunately, there was no moon tonight.

Without making a sound, he walked over to Takashima's desk, grateful that the Jap had covered the aged hardwood floors with plush carpeting. Hell, everything was in perfect order, he noted wryly, not even a paper clip out of place. Hopefully that would make his job easier. This time he was determined to get into the locked desk drawer and secure as much evidence as he could find.

He had to stop a moment and catch his breath—he had run all the way from the back lot after climbing up a steep hill below the reconstruction of WestTown.

Then it was only a matter of keeping in the shadows and using a passkey to get into the executive office building. Once inside, he had simply waited until the Yakuza security guard went in the other direction. Then he ran up the steps to the top floor.

He knew he didn't have much time. The guard was certain to check this floor.

Carefully he knelt down in front of the locked drawer and focused his flashlight on the unusual-looking lock. Hopefully, he thought as he pulled on the drawer, the Jap forgot to lock it. But it wouldn't budge.

In frustration he banged his hand on the side of the desk without thinking; the loud wooden sound, however, startled him. He looked over the desk, half-expecting to see some hulking Yakuza breaking through the door. Nothing. He breathed a sigh of relief. The only thing he did hear was his own heartbeat. If Kelly knew I was here again, she'd kill me, he thought, directing his attention back to the lock. But somehow, thinking about her made his job a little easier.

He fumbled through his jacket pocket and pulled out the ring of skeleton keys Donaldson had lent him. He was careful not to let them clink against each other. Then, one at a time, he tried each key. There's got to be one here that works, he prayed. After he gave the fed the impression of the lock he had made from his first visit, Donaldson had assured him it was a standard lock and that one of these master keys should do the trick.

"Shit," Jake muttered out loud, breaking the stillness around him as he pinched his finger. So far, nothing. Only a few more keys left, he noticed, not even taking a moment to rub his aching finger. He stole a glance at his watch. Twelve-fifty-five. It wouldn't be long before the Yakuza guard would find his way onto this floor.

"C'mon, baby . . ." Jake muttered as he held up another key. "This is the one . . ." he said, trying to fit the key into the lock. *Bang!* Jake dived onto the floor. His flashlight rolled under the desk, leaving him in the dark.

Jake peeked up at the door but saw nothing. The room was pitch dark except for the ray of light coming through the crack in the bamboo shutter and beaming a grotesque shadow on the wall.

"What the . . . ?" he sputtered under his breath, realizing the wind had knocked a heavy branch from the sycamore tree against the window. "Damn tree," he cursed, retrieving his flashlight and focusing his attention on another key in the lock. "I should have cut the sonofabitch down years ago.

"Damn, it works!" Quickly he unlocked the drawer and opened it.

Peering inside, he saw several files stamped "Confidential." He shuffled through them, noting that some of the itemization was in Japanese but the numbers were all written in English. This could be the evidence Donaldson needed in order for the government to prosecute their money-laundering case.

Suddenly Jake froze. Heavy footsteps were coming down the hall toward him. They were getting closer. Shit, he had to get the hell out of here—pronto.

As he shut the drawer and switched off the flashlight, the front door burst open and the overhead lights went on.

Jake squinted into the light. He could feel the two men staring at the desk. His mouth dropped. Nothing to worry about, he thought; the files and all the papers were still locked in the drawer.

As one of the men walked toward him, Jake abruptly stood up, holding his arms high in the air, trying to make light of the situation. "I've got nothing in my hands—see!" The Yakuza guard quickly drew his gun, while Noda eyed Jake. But to his surprise, Takashima's protégé told the Yakuza to put his gun back into his holster and leave the office.

"I demand an immediate explanation, Mr. Baron," Noda said quickly and loud enough so the Yakuza waiting in the hall could hear him.

"Listen, Mr. Noda," Jake tried to explain, smiling. "Well, you see, I lost a watch in here when I was moving my things out. It, uh, belonged to my father and it means a lot to me . . ." Jake struggled with the words, knowing he wasn't making any sense.

Ignoring him, Noda walked over to the locked drawer and surveyed the messy finger marks all over the polished locked drawer.

"I suggest, Mr. Baron, that for your own safety you leave down the back stairs immediately," Noda ordered firmly.

Jake looked hard into the man's eyes. It was obvious he knew he was lying, but the young Jap was giving him a break. For whatever reason, he was letting him go.

Without another word, Jake quickly left the office.

"If we don't stand together now and fully support our union brothers and sisters in the Teamsters, not only will all the unions at Constellation disappear, but it'll happen on every other studio lot in town," the man in a T-shirt and jeans said to the crowd of remaining American studio workers that gathered in front of him. He stood on a small platform constructed on the large soundstage.

"You said it, man," one person cried.

"We're not taking this shit," shouted another.

As the crowd cheered, Takashima watched the secret meeting in his office on one of his monitors. A tall

Ronin who sat nearby with his back to him operated the secret remote-camera hookup. Another Ronin in disguise was stationed at the scene, watching who was participating.

Now that *Criminal Intent* was in the final editing stage, Takashima had decided to push forward with his plan to get rid of the union drivers as a first step to deunionize Constellation. He took a long drag on his cigarette as he kept his eyes focused on the screen. The problem was bigger than he had anticipated, but he was only slightly upset by this show of solidarity. Let the lazy Americans walk out, he thought. He would immediately replace every one of them with his inexhaustible supply of nonunion Japanese workers.

More important, though, was the ripple effect that a strike would have all over town. He was well aware of the union-busting sentiment that had taken over America. Soon other studios would throw out their union workers, he thought. All over Hollywood, work would stop. And that was exactly what he wanted.

"Well, what do you say? Do we walk off in support?" the leader yelled out, holding his fist up high.

The crowd yelled a unanimous "Yes."

"Wait, everybody," a woman yelled from the crowd.

Takashima leaned closer to the screen. He was not really surprised to see Kelly make her way up to the stage. After all, she had been pestering him for weeks about this situation.

"Listen, please," she asked, trying to quiet them down. There were a few dissenters who didn't want her to speak, but finally they listened. They had great respect for her.

"A strike is not the answer," she said.

"Then what is, Kelly?" a grip yelled out. "We have to feed our families."

"And make our car payments," another guy said.

The crowd laughed, but everyone realized the seriousness of the situation. No one wanted to strike, especially after the six-month Writers Guild strike the year before, which had affected everybody. Nonetheless, many felt they had no choice if Takashima did away with the Teamsters. They would be next.

"All I'm asking of you is to stay cool while I work out the problems," Kelly said, trying to maintain a pleasant smile. She scanned the crowd: the men and women who painted the sets, drove the trucks, sewed the costumes. Every one of them was important.

"Constellation was built on new ideas, independent thinking, and a lot of sweat," she continued. "We can be a great studio again, but only with your help . . . and your patience."

She decided to go out on a limb. "All I'm asking is that you give me ten days while I try to work out the Teamster problems for all of you with the owner. If at the end of that time I'm unable to come up with a favorable contract, then you'll be free to go . . . and with a strike bonus. That I'll guarantee. Ten days, that's all.

"Remember, Constellation belongs to you, the men and women who make our movies. Without your love and creative input, this studio will not survive."

Kelly gathered up her remaining strength and gave it her all. "Well, what do you say? Will you let me try?"

No one had to think twice. Kelly's word was good enough. She'd never let them down before. And she wouldn't now.

"Okay, Kelly, we're with you!"

The rest of the crowd cheered her on. There was not one dissenting vote as people started to mill around her.

Takashima signaled the Ronin to turn off the remote as he sat thoughtfully in the darkened room for several minutes. He was no longer troubled by the missed appointments or the threat of a strike. He had a bigger problem: Kelly's power.

If he fired her, he would destroy all semblance of keeping Constellation as a major studio. On the other hand, if he retained her, he would have to immediately figure out a way to stop her.

How dare the American whore do this to him? Feeling his anger building, he grabbed a marble paperweight. With all his might, he hurled it across the room through the bamboo shutters, shattering the window on the other side. The Ronin dived onto the carpet as the crash resounded throughout the office.

With their guns drawn, three Yakuza immediately broke down the master's front and back office doors. The first ran toward Takashima while the other two instinctively overpowered the Ronin before he could react.

But the three Yakuza stopped in their tracks, watching a crazed Takashima climb on top of his desk. They could not help but wonder—as he jumped up and down, grunting and screaming—what had happened to cause the master to lose all of his *wa*.

"It's Robert again, Kelly," Geoffrey said distastefully as he put him on hold.

Kelly shook her head. "Tell him that unless it's about Constellation, he can talk to my lawyer."

As she continued by Geoffrey's desk, she noticed the big basket of yellow roses and carnations waiting on her desk. "Robert?" she asked Geoffrey, pointing to the flowers, even though she already knew.

Geoffrey nodded, then shook his head in disbelief. "That's the second basket today. I'll send this one over to the switchboard operators as well."

"Thanks. And then you can tell him for me that either he stops or else he will have a much more serious problem with me."

As Kelly walked into her office, she heard Geoffrey give Robert her message. She had no sooner closed the door and sat down at her desk than her phone buzzed. She pushed down the button. "If it's Robert, tell him—"

"Kelly, Mike Ovitz is on your private line. Also,

Barbara Walters and her crew are waiting for admittance at the front gate."

She turned to her calendar. "Oh, shit, I forgot that Barbara's interview was today."

She told Geoffrey to make sure they let Barbara and her people pass through right away. She already knew what Ovitz wanted to discuss: Dustin Hoffman. She'd get to him in two seconds.

"Tell me, Kelly, what really happened between Mr. Takashima and Jake Baron at your gala press party?" Barbara Walters asked inquisitively as the cameras began taping. The award-winning interviewer had just asked the question all America wanted answered.

Kelly, looking very much the successful CEO in her two-piece Ungaro charcoal-gray suit, squirmed in her chair even as she continued smiling. She had known this question was bound to come up when she had agreed to do a taped interview for an upcoming *Barbara Walters Special*. She had her answer already prepared.

"Whatever I say, everyone will have his own opinion," Kelly said seriously, "but I do want to say one thing: Mr. Baron was prepared to speak on behalf of our studio, and he was denied that opportunity. There is nothing more I want to say."

Barbara Walters raised her eyebrows, pleased with this dignified reply even though she was sorry she didn't get a more detailed answer. How well she understood the mind of the public, especially since the "Jake Baron Affair" was on the covers of all the supermarket tabloids.

Walters had to admit Kelly was a smart woman, inviting her to interview her here in her office at Constellation instead of her Malibu home. She had already taped the other two personalities for this special, Jack Nicholson and Glenn Close, and both at their respective homes. Kelly, on the other hand, had hoped that she could keep the two-hour interview focused mainly on her studio work and not on her personal life.

Barbara folded her hands on her lap, then continued, "With the new Japanese regime at Constellation, what can the public expect in the way of future films?"

Kelly thought for a moment about how she should, or *if* she should, respond to any question about Takashima. Why not? Maybe Takashima would then realize how adamant she was about her points of view.

"Well, Barbara, Mr. Takashima has agreed to let us complete a half-dozen or so mainstream films, but we're all ready in the . . ." Kelly paused a second. Damn him, I'm not going to pussyfoot and protect him any longer.

"However, permit me to change the topic. Right now we are in the middle of a union problem at Constellation. Before we can even think of completing any films, we have to get our house back in order. Hopefully, we will work out a fair agreement and remain a fully union studio . . . and avert a possible strike—"

"What strike?" Walters quickly pounced. She hadn't heard about this problem. She might have a scoop on her hands.

"Honto desuka?"

"Watashi-wa shiri-masen."

Two Ronin, wearing headphones and recording the interview, suddenly became very agitated. They were sitting in low light in what had once been the wine cellar, directly underneath Kelly's office.

". . . besides turning out good films, that is my biggest goal as the new CEO of Constellation," Kelly finished, realizing that she still hadn't caught up with Jake in the past two days. She hadn't told him the latest on her plans to file for divorce.

Barbara noticed her producer giving her the wrap-up sign, and smiled broadly at Kelly. "And finally, Kelly: Speaking of good films, can you tell us what will be the first major release of Constellation under its new regime?"

Kelly smiled easily. "Hopefully—if no more plugs are pulled—*Criminal Intent*."

"*Hai,*, I have all the information," Takashima said into the phone to his Ronin leader. "You have done your job well." As he hung up the receiver, his hand was shaking with anger.

He had remained home again today, contemplating both of his problems: the unions and Kelly. They continued to make him uneasy. But now . . .

He tore through his living room like a madman, kicking furniture, shoving vases onto the floor, and throwing pillows every which way.

Finally, out of breath, he stopped. He sat down exhausted on the marble floor and buried his face in his hands. He had to settle the score with Kelly. He would have to make her pay for her disobedience. She had broken a very important rule by speaking to the woman interviewer about their internal problems. It was as if she was working against him at every turn.

Minutes later, Takashima cupped cool water into his hands, then splashed it into his face. He looked up into the bathroom mirror. He drew back in shock. He grabbed on to the sink to steady himself.

In his eyes he saw the ancient demon-dragon now turning its heads in different directions.

He picked up the telephone and made the arrangements.

"How is Takashima-san?" Noda asked gravely as he peeked inside. He had never seen Takashima like this before. He had been sitting in seclusion for hours, taking no food, no drink.

It was almost midnight, and Minoru silently stood sentry to the master's indoor garden adjacent to his private office at 1901 Avenue of the Stars. Takashima had been sitting cross-legged on a tatami mat near the rocks in the running stream. He had been too frustrated to stay at home tonight. He stared straight ahead, aware of nothing but one rock in front of him. He meditated on its purity of form, its texture, its shape, concentrating with all his strength to merge with it. He must again discover Zen wisdom if he was to solve his surmounting problem: Kelly.

"I must speak with him, Minoru-san."

"That is impossible, Noda-san," Minoru said firmly. "He cannot be disturbed."

"But he wanted the closing numbers on the Nikkei as soon as they—"

Minoru shook his head, then ushered Noda away from the peace and tranquillity of the garden. Takashima's orders were that no one should disturb him.

Kelly's strength had surprised the Asian Octopus. Like the many humble rocks in his garden: the most beautiful things lie about without ever being noticed. So was the strength of Kelly. He had seen only what his selfish eye wanted to see: her beauty.

He kept his mind on one level—that of consciousness. He must concentrate to see *satori*, enlightenment. First, he must cleanse his mind of *go*, the burden of ignorance and evil, to find guidance on how to deal with her.

As he had not done for many years, he got on his knees and recited the prayers of his youth.

Was there anyone he could trust anymore? Noda-san seemed to be scared all the time, as if he was hiding something. He even smelled like the American enemy, with the stinking after-shave he now wore. Other frightening thoughts raced through his mind: the Ronin might be double agents selling his secrets to the American CIA; the Yakuza might kill him by suffocating him with a pillow one night while he was in a deep sleep; his cowardly Takashima Group might turn him in to the Japanese authorities as their contribution to resolve the current political scandal; Kakue might even be stealing from him. And last, the shattered screams of his mother constantly calling his name—after the enemy dropped their atomic bomb—was more than he could endure.

As he slowly lifted his head, trying to regain some control over his constant paranoia, he realized he was sweating profusely. He contemplated completing his revenge plans immediately: every major movie studio would be torched simultaneously on the enemy's Memorial Day holiday; unsuspecting major movie stars would be kidnapped and tortured during the next few weeks; and the Yakuza would destroy every Teamster truck. Smiling, at the same time he would also continue to strike his personal revenge against Baron where it would hurt him the most: with his women.

Like the heroic kamikaze pilots during the war, he would now devastate the American enemy severely without any worry to himself. "In the memory our late Emperor—*Banzai!*"

17

As Kelly sipped her wine, she glanced around the posh restaurant. Jimmy's wasn't crowded yet, for it was only late afternoon and most show-biz regulars were still wrapping up the day's work.

Seated across from Kelly were Geoffrey and a visiting Rose Kaufman. Kelly toasted them silently, glad Rose had insisted they join her for a cocktail. Kelly looked at her watch as Rose—who sensed her nervousness—placed a reassuring hand on her wrist, jangling her armful of bracelets. Kelly appreciated her moral support. It was no fun working at Constellation anymore.

"Thanks, Rose," Kelly said, grateful as she scanned the extensive menu quickly, wondering if she should order for Jake. She longed to ask Rose to come back to Constellation full-time, but they both knew that was impossible, considering Takashima's attitude toward women.

The waiter approached. "Are you ready to order?"

Caesar salad sounded good to Kelly. Although she was tired and wanted to get home early, she wanted to talk to Jake—whom she'd invited for dinner. She closed her menu, smiling. "I'll have him," she joked when she suddenly saw Jake enter the dining room and head toward their table. She got up and met him halfway.

"Kel, I'd have been here sooner if there hadn't been a tie-up on the freeway."

Kelly laughed. He always looked so cute when he was annoyed.

He looked around. "Do you think anyone will mind if I kiss you?" he breathed into her ear.

"Well, since I'm closer to becoming a free woman again, kiss me first, then we'll ask." Jake's face lit up at her comment.

Geoffrey and Rose smiled at each other. "This place is getting too crowded . . . and much too steamy for us," Rose said, grabbing her coat and oversize purse.

"I agree," Geoffrey commented as he helped her on with her coat. "How about we head up the road to the Stage Deli?"

Rose nodded and the two of them quietly left the restaurant, ignoring the disgruntled look on the waiter's face.

Jake and Kelly didn't seem to see them leave.

Kelly never took her eyes off Jake. She couldn't even remember when the waiter had lighted the candle on the table.

They had finished their meal an hour ago, but neither of them was ready to leave. Jimmy's was now filled with diners as well as several happy-hour patrons still lingering at the bar. She had talked out the details of her impending divorce, examined the ramifications of the Walters interview, and now had turned to Takashima and Constellation.

"And you say that Noda dismissed the Yakuza immediately?" she asked, trying to picture the scene in her mind—Jake having a gun pointed to his head.

"Funny, I can't figure that Noda guy out. He acted almost as if he was trying to help me." Jake let the words dangle. He couldn't help but stare at her pretty face. As he leaned over, he brushed the side of her cheek with his lips. "Let's forget Noda and the gun. Let's forget Takashima and his henchmen. Let's just talk about us."

Kelly lowered her head. She wasn't ready to rush

into anything yet. "Jake, there are some things that we should talk about—"

But he cut her off. "Not now." He looked around the restaurant as he took her hand and squeezed it. "We've got the rest of our lives to talk; I've got other plans for tonight."

Kelly tried to smile, but couldn't. She had to make him understand. "My divorce from Robert will take a number of months before becoming final . . ." She paused to look into his handsome face, hoping for understanding. "I'll need some time, Jake . . ."

Jake was clearly disappointed, but, biting his tongue, he merely said, "I understand, Kel."

He took out a cigarette, stared at it, but didn't light up as he mulled over her thoughts. "Okay, Kel. I guess I'll just have to wait."

Robert winked at the stunning blond giving him an eyeful from the bar as he walked through the restaurant, grazing with his pal John.

"You know her?" John asked hopefully.

"Not yet," Robert answered, checking out the rest of the room. He recognized some of the patrons, but none of them looked as good as the shapely blond. "Let's go back to the bar."

"You know, Robert, old pal, you haven't paid off our Super Bowl bet. What 'bout we head down to Little Tokyo and get one of those geisha gals that ugly Yakuza told you about? I bet they have a different slant on things." John snickered.

Robert shook his head. Leave it to John.

"Forget it, John." He was about to go back to the bar when he saw Jake and Kelly sitting together at a table. The color drained from his face. They're holding hands, he realized. What the fuck is Baron doing here with my wife? Robert glared at the two of them, his face darkening with anger. At that moment he didn't consider the fact that Kelly had thrown him out of the house and filed for divorce. All he knew was that they were still legally married, and until the papers were final, Jake Baron was not going to put his hands on his wife.

"Excuse me, John, but I've got some unfinished business," he said hurriedly, stalking off.

"Sure, buddy," John said, turning his attention to two hot dollies giving him the eye. Robert was on his own.

"What are you doing with this old has-been?" Robert asked sarcastically, stopping at their table. "It's bad enough that you avoid me at the studio, but to be seen with this asshole in public . . . what's with you, Kelly?"

"Robert, please," she begged, hoping he wouldn't make a scene. Instinctively she pulled away from Jake.

But Jake had no intention of backing down. "I don't think it's any of your business, Zinman."

"My wife is my business!" Robert challenged. "I don't take too kindly to watching you fondling my wife in public."

That did it. Jake stood up and pointed a finger at Robert. "Now, you listen, schmuck, I'll pretend I didn't hear that if you leave right now."

Robert raised his chin in defiance. "Stay the fuck away from her, Baron."

Jake advanced quickly until they were nose-to-nose. "I don't take orders from you, prick," he snapped back loudly.

Neither of them realized that everyone around them had turned to stare, but Kelly did. "Stop it, you two!" She was close to tears as she pleaded with Robert. "There's no reason for this. You and I are finished."

"I don't give a shit, Kelly. You're still legally married to me," he answered hotly.

"I'm asking you to leave. Please don't make a fool of yourself any further," Kelly responded, trying to keep calm.

Finally Jake backed off, realizing that Kelly was being humiliated by the public scene. He casually threw a couple of fifty-dollar bills on the table, never taking his eyes off Robert. "Get into your limo, Kelly. I'll join you in a minute."

"Jake, please—"

"Really, this won't take a second. Just go."

Reluctantly she looked at Robert. She couldn't believe what she saw. His eyes were now full of hate, not just for Jake, but for her as well. She started to say something, but realized it was useless. She didn't know him anymore. Turning away, she grabbed her purse.

"Good-bye, Robert," she said, brushing past him.

"You goddamn sonofabitch!" Robert said, taking a swing at Jake.

Jake ducked it easily, though, and said, egging him on, "Forget it, Zinman. You couldn't hit a blind old lady."

"Fuck you!"

Robert took another swing at Jake as two waiters rushed up. One grabbed each of the men and pulled them apart. "*Please*, gentlemen, not here!"

Jake looked at Robert. "He's right, Zinman. I'll take you on outside."

Robert pulled back, remembering his position at the studio and noticing that all eyes were now on him. As he smoothed down his jacket, he also recalled that Baron had always had a reputation as a brawler. Even last year he had taken on a man half his age.

"She's not worth this, Baron," he said as he turned his back and left before Jake could get in a final word.

Robert didn't have to look back to know that Jake Baron had just made a fool out of him.

As Kelly stepped into her studio limousine, parked by the side of the restaurant, she didn't notice there was a different Japanese chauffeur. She didn't give him a second glance when he slammed the door behind her, then got into the front seat and spoke in hushed tones on his phone. She was too overwrought.

Suddenly the limo lurched forward, took a screeching right, and zoomed down little Santa Monica Boulevard.

"Hey, wait!" she called out. What was going on? As she leaned forward, tapping the studio Yakuza driver on the shoulder, the car made a fast left and she slid to the other end of the seat. Kelly winced as she bumped her knee. She had become accustomed to the Yakuza's crazy driving, but this character was roaring down the road like he'd never stop.

"Hey, what's going on?" Kelly yelled louder. "I told you to wait for Mr. Baron. *Tomatte kudasai!* Stop, please!" she yelled to the driver, trying as much Japanese as she could remember. But the Yakuza driver kept looking straight ahead, paying no heed to her pleas.

Kelly looked outside as the limo sped through the Beverly Hills traffic. There must be some mistake. She tried to roll down the window, but it was now locked. She tried the doors. Finding them locked too, she sat back in the sedan, her arms folded in front of her. She was scared. Something was terribly wrong.

"What do you mean, that white stretch limo with the pretty lady just pulled away in a hurry?" Jake shouted at the young valet.

"Yes, s-s-sir," the boy stammered.

Perplexed, Jake looked down the boulevard where Kelly's limo had disappeared. Why did she run off like that? he wondered. Did this mean he'd have to start all over again?

He shook his head. Something didn't add up. He didn't believe she'd just leave him high and dry.

Jake wasn't finished with the valet. "Who was driving that white stretch limo?" he asked in a more civil tone, pulling a twenty-dollar bill out of his pocket.

"I don't know, sir, I didn't see his face," the valet said, eyeing the money. "But I heard him talking to the driver he replaced . . . in Japanese."

* * *

Kelly pressed her face up against the window as the limo turned into a long, winding driveway. Her heart skipped a beat when she recognized the address on the lighted mailbox: it was Takashima's mansion.

She wiped the beads of sweat from her forehead. The night air was humid, but she was perspiring from fear. What kind of stunt was Takashima pulling? Was he kidnapping her? Had he become aware of the Justice Department's investigation?

She held her breath, calculating how to proceed now. She was determined not to show any fear. The one thing she had learned from Takashima was never to back down from anyone, especially from him. That only made him more incensed.

As soon as the car came to a stop, the door locks popped and she jumped out, carrying her jacket. "What's going on here?" she demanded hotly as a trio of Yakuza immediately surrounded her. They seemed to come out of nowhere.

She kept her chin up, refusing to let them see any fear in her. "Where is Takashima? I demand you take me to him. *Now!*"

One Yakuza bowed respectfully. "*Dozo*, come."

Kelly flinched as the other two bodyguards flanked her on either side. She felt her skin crawl, even though they didn't touch her. Just the way they marched step by step with her, she knew there was no escape.

As they entered the luxurious mansion, Kelly looked around the spacious front hall. This was the first time she had been there. She had seen many beautiful homes in the Hollywood Hills, but there was something horribly majestic about this one. A twenty-five-foot ceiling with an intricate border trim gave the place the cold feeling of a Gothic cathedral. Everywhere she looked were rare antique pieces of furniture, all from different eras. Nowhere did she see the traditional Japanese she would have expected.

"Kelly-san, *konban-wa*," Takashima said, appearing

out of nowhere. Kelly stepped back in surprise as he bowed graciously. "I am pleased you came."

Even though she was shaking, she snapped, "I didn't have any choice."

Takashima smiled, challenging her with his eyes. "No one forced you into the car. Please relax."

"Why did you bring me here?" she asked, refusing to allow him to have the upper hand.

"I intend to honor you with a special dinner."

What? she thought, growing angry. These damned Japanese never said what they meant. "I've already eaten and you know it. What do you want?"

"I want to teach you a simple lesson, Kelly-san. Sometimes the bird must be caged before it can be taught to fly in a new direction."

She looked at him irritably. After being humiliated by Robert, she was in no mood for Eastern philosophy. "I'm very tired. Please have your man take me home. We can talk about it tomorrow. At the office," she added pointedly. As she walked toward the door, one of the Yakuza quickly blocked her exit.

"I regret that I have other plans," Takashima stated flatly.

Kelly whirled around quickly, for the first time showing her fear. "What do you mean by that?"

Takashima, noticing her discomfort, smiled, then slowly clapped his hands. Immediately Kakue walked softly into the room, her head down, her hands folded across her chest.

Seeing her dressed in Japanese fashion—wearing a flowered silk kimono tightly tied at her waist by a sash and her long hair bound at the nape of her neck— Kelly couldn't help but think how out of place her presence was in these Western-style surroundings.

With a wide gesture, Takashima turned to Kelly. "Go with Kakue-san, *kudasai*," he said pleasantly. "She will prepare you for the evening ahead."

Feeling goose bumps spread down her arms, Kelly stood her ground. "No! I wish to leave now."

Takashima continued to smile at her, but his eyes looked darker than ever behind his tinted glasses. She was defying him, and that he would not allow. He must show his employee how foolish it would be to challenge him.

He picked up two matching Sèvres urns with miniature portraits of Louis XIII and Louis XIV. "Beautiful, are they not?" he asked, smiling.

Kelly didn't respond. Even her untrained eye knew they were priceless.

Suddenly she was very frightened of this man. There was something sadistic about the way he inspected the vases carefully, turning them over and over in his hands. She could see the cruel lines around his mouth hardening as his smile widened. But it wasn't a smile: it was an expression of hatred. She shivered. Did he feel that way about her?

Takashima ran his fingers over the necks of the vases. "And so very fragile." He looked directly at Kelly, his eyes flashing like two iridescent black pools; then he deliberately let them both fall to the floor with a loud crash. They broke into tiny pieces on the hardwood floor, their beauty lost forever.

Stunned, Kelly looked up at Takashima's face. It began to contort with fury. In that moment she wondered if he was going mad.

She didn't dare breathe as Takashima stopped before her and ran his hand up and down the side of her cheek. The touch of his fingers burned her skin like white heat.

"The most beautiful things are always the most fragile."

He continued stroking both sides of her face for several seconds, but Kelly couldn't move. Her eyes were wide with fear.

Suddenly Takashima turned and said something in Japanese to his Yakuza. They bowed, then picked up the pieces of porcelain. Eyeing Kelly menacingly, they crushed the pieces in their hands, mindless of the sharp fragments cutting into their palms and fingers. She felt her stomach heave as trickles of their blood dripped onto the floor.

Takashima clapped his hands twice, startling her. "Go now, with Kakue-san," he ordered.

Respectfully, Kakue bowed to Kelly. When she looked up, her eyes begged Kelly to follow her. Simultaneously the Yakuza closed in on her. She had no doubt they were just waiting for a signal before grabbing her.

"I will go," she said firmly. She didn't look back at Takashima as she followed Kakue upstairs.

"*Dozo*, put this on, Kelly-san, quickly," Kakue begged, holding out a light blue silk *yukata*, a house kimono. Kelly took it but defiantly threw it on the bed. She tried the door. Locked.

In desperation, she turned to the Japanese girl. "You've got to help me, Kakue," Kelly said, checking the room for a way out. Noting the window, she ran over and looked out. The room faced out over the cliff side. A sheer fifty-foot drop was below her.

Kakue politely kept her head bowed low, but she couldn't keep her voice from quavering as she said, "*Dozo*, you must do as Takashima-san asks."

Kelly shook her head. "I can't, and I won't."

Kakue cringed. She had seen many times what her master had done to Chisako, and she feared she would also receive a severe beating with his bamboo stick if she did not make this proud American beauty obey.

Kakue clenched a small vial of powder in her hand. She knew she had no choice. Not only for herself, but for the beautiful lady. They would both pay a dear price if she failed to do as Takashima ordered.

"You will feel your spirit refreshed with a bath," Kakue suggested in her lightly accented English as she slipped the vial of powder underneath the lace doily on a nearby tray. "I will take you."

Kelly couldn't take all the phony politeness anymore. She grabbed Kakue by the shoulders and shook her. "What's wrong with all of you? Why do you obey him without question? Have you no will of your own?"

Kakue looked at her, her young eyes honest as she spoke. "He is our master. We know no other." Kakue looked away for a moment, disgusted with this rude woman who did not know her place. "You must do as he asks, Kelly-san. If you do not, he will become terribly angry. No one is safe when he is like that. *Dozo*, I speak the truth." Then she turned away and covered her face, fearful she had said too much.

"I don't believe you. You're all working for him," Kelly yelled out, heading for the door. "I'm going to bang on this door until someone lets me out!"

"Wait," Kakue called fearfully. She quickly picked up a small cup and with shaking hands poured some tea from the warm pot. As she emptied the white powder into the cup, she prayed for forgiveness from the beautiful lady. She must understand this was the only way to save her.

"Ocha," she said, smiling weakly.

Kelly shook her head. "No."

"Please, it will give you courage."

Kelly weakened. This girl didn't mean any harm. She was no doubt scared. With a weary sigh, that was the closest she could come to politeness, she took the tea and sipped it slowly. Surprisingly, it tasted good. Very sweet. Slowly she began to feel warm all over, at peace.

She closed her eyes and let the warm feeling envelop her. She started to feel sleepy, but her inner voice kept telling her to fight it off. She couldn't sleep . . . she had to leave.

But she couldn't fight any longer. As she dropped the cup, her body began to sway lazily and her head felt heavy. Dazed, she protested as Kakue slipped her jacket off her, then unbuttoned her sheer blouse, damp with sweat. The young Japanese woman continued her duty, removing her skirt and the rest of her clothes until Kelly realized she lay naked on the scarlet satin brocade coverlet. She didn't understand what was happening to her, but she no longer cared. She just wanted to relax and let this glowing pleasure wash over her. . . .

Strong tattooed arms picked her up; then someone wrapped something soft and cool around her and laid her back down on the bed.

"Please . . . help me . . ." she begged in her semiconscious state, but she fell asleep before her head touched the pillow.

Takashima entered and looked down at her, smiling with pleasure as he carefully pulled aside the gossamer cover and began to stroke her. Her lesson was just beginning.

He began to massage her temples, her neck, then her shoulders. Kelly lay completely still as he gently played with her naked breasts, flicking his tongue over her nipples until they were hard. As his fingers moved to the warm flesh between her thighs, Kelly moaned, "Please . . ." not knowing what was happening to her, knowing only that she didn't want it to stop. It was such a lovely floating sensation.

Meanwhile, Jake pulled his car over to the side of the road and turned off the lights. He had already driven by Kelly's house in Malibu to make sure she wasn't home before he had decided to pay an unannounced visit to Takashima.

He got out of his car and carefully made his way up the hill toward the lighted mansion. He noticed that the place wasn't surrounded by anything more threatening than a tennis court and swimming pool. As he eased himself over a five-foot stone fence surrounding the house, he was surprised how easy it was to get onto the grounds. Perhaps with his bodyguards, Jake reminded himself, the Jap doesn't worry about burglars.

Bent way over, he raced toward the tall French windows. Without a sound he flattened himself against the wall and peered inside. He strained to see through the sheer curtains covering the window. There he is, Jake realized, standing in the middle of the room.

Takashima was gesturing to a young Japanese girl preparing a low table with small bowls and plates. She bowed many times as he indicated the placement of the dishes.

Jake leaned back against the wall, breathing deeply. Takashima was merely preparing for an evening meal, and Kelly was nowhere in sight. Maybe he was wrong after all . . . but where the hell was she?

Suddenly he heard a rustle behind him. He turned around just in time to see two hulking Yakuza stalking toward him with raised fists.

"Oh, shit," he muttered under his breath. Then he made his move. Jake hit the first one on the chin, causing him to stagger backward, but the second launched a lightning-quick blow to his face. Taking the brunt of it, Jake stayed on his feet, but he realized he was no match for these two gorillas.

Before he could move, a third man came up behind him and grabbed his arms, pinning them behind him. Jake yelled out as the Yakuza he had punched hit him in his midsection, once, then twice. Jake doubled up in pain as he fell to the ground. The last thing he remembered was a bright flashlight shining in his face.

Moments later, Takashima spat on the unconscious man lying on the ground. He smiled wryly. If Baron only knew how close he had been to discovering that his woman was here with him.

"Get the American enemy out of here," he ordered the Yakuza. He had no further use for him.

Returning inside, Takashima reached for his *sake* cup and drank the warm rice wine slowly. He still had a most pleasurable evening ahead. He then eyed the beautiful woman seated across from him at the low table.

Kelly looked more beautiful than he had ever seen her, dressed in the sheer blue *yukata*. Her full breasts and hard nipples were visible through the gossamer material and her strawberry-blond hair flowed loosely around her shoulders. He breathed in deeply. She was indeed worthy of him. However, she must be taught a lesson instead.

He smiled as the drugged woman quickly ate her meal. "I am pleased you enjoyed the meal, Kelly-san."

Kelly looked up blearily. "Yes, I did." She was still dazed, even though she was recovering. She was also a bit uneasy, for the first thing she remembered after she had passed out was Kakue toweling her off. She had taken a bath. And what else had happened?

She was careful to keep the wrap closely tied around her. She didn't like the way Takashima kept leering at her.

Takashima picked up two drinks from the tray next to him. "Now, Kelly-san, you must join me in a drink to the new Constellation."

As he handed it to her, she looked at it with distaste. "What is it?" she asked, turning her face away from the strong smell.

"*Shochu* cocktail," he said, smelling its fragrance. "It is made from *sake*. To Constellation," he said, raising his glass.

"To Constellation," Kelly said, reluctantly repeating the toast. She drank it down slowly. It burned her throat, her tongue, her whole insides. Her head began to sway and her vision blurred as she began to feel the effects of the highly concentrated alcohol almost immediately.

Takashima put down his empty glass and smiled. She would soon be in a submissive mood again.

"You are a very intelligent woman, Kelly-san, but you have acted foolishly," he said.

Feeling extremely groggy once again, Kelly put down her drink. "What are you talk . . . ing a-bout?"

"I am not pleased." Takashima stood up, then walked behind her as he spoke, making her dizzy as she twisted her head around to follow his movements.

"You did not give favorable comments during your interview with Walters-san." He bent down low, speaking into her ear. He took her long kimono sash in his hand.

Kelly rubbed her forehead, trying to clear her thoughts. How did he know that? Unless he had a large network of spies. The show had just been taped yesterday.

"And you also publicly embarrassed me by speaking about our private problems with the unions at Constellation. I am most distressed."

Takashima playfully pulled on her sash as he walked back around her the other way.

Kelly was too woozy to fight back. "You're . . . wrong," she argued weakly. She tried to pull her sash closer around her, but Takashima refused to let go of it. "I . . . I didn't mean to embarrass you—"

Takashima cut her off. "You are merely to follow my orders!" he shouted, pulling her sash completely away from her body. Her sheer kimono fell open, partially revealing her breasts.

Kelly tried to cover herself, but Takashima grabbed her kimono and pulled her up to him.

He held her tightly. "You must apologize. Now!"

Kelly tried to think clearly, but couldn't. "What . . . ?" she asked.

Takashima, out of control now, threw her to the floor, then whipped the long sash at her. *"Norou! Joro!"* he screamed. Then he tore the thin kimono from her shoulders, uncovering her breasts completely. Kelly instinctively crossed her arms in front of her as she cringed.

"I will show you who is master!" Kelly listened to his words in horror. This was insane. She must get away from him. He was mad. Absolutely mad.

She tried to get to her feet, but she was still too groggy. "Please, listen," she begged, trying to push herself up by leaning on the low table.

"Dozo, Takashima!" Minoru yelled out, running

into the sunken living room and bowing slightly. "Come, quickly. Urgent news," he whispered.

Takashima did not take his eyes off Kelly. Even her feeble attempt to escape him enraged him.

"What is it?" he barked.

Minoru said something in Japanese. Takashima's eyes grew wide and his hands started shaking.

He threw her sash on the ground at her feet, then left without looking back. She no longer mattered. His world back in Japan was starting to crumble.

Sometime later, Kelly heard two men whose voices she recognized arguing in the next room.

Because they were speaking in Japanese, she had no idea what they were saying, but she heard her name mentioned several times, and by the sound of their voices, it was obvious that Noda was challenging Takashima. She was astonished at this unexpected change. He always did everything his master said without a murmur.

The door flew open and she remained sitting on the floor, hugging a large pillow to her chest for protection.

Noda, bearing her clothes, entered along with Minoru.

"*Dozo*, Kelly-san, Takashima-san asks that you understand," Noda said in his usual calm manner. "He cannot return. Please get your things together, *kudasai*." He then placed her clothes at her feet.

Kelly was shocked as she noticed the wetness on his cheeks. Had he been crying? Then she also noticed the sadness on Minoru's face. Whatever the reason for their sadness, it had saved her from a madman's rage.

What a strange people, she thought, pulling the kimono around her. Such violence, then such emotion. She would never understand them.

As she got to her feet, she pretended she did not see his tears. "What is it?" she asked. "What has happened?"

Noda stumbled over the words, his voice cracking

with strong emotion. He and Minoru turned their backs as she changed into her own clothes. "Our Prime Minister has just announced his resignation. He was forced out of office."

18

Jake rolled over on his bed, gritting his teeth to keep from yelling out in pain. His ribs hurt like hell, and he wasn't sure if that Jap gorilla had cracked a couple of them. At least he'd had the satisfaction of hearing the crack of the Yakuza's jaw breaking when he smashed him with a right cross.

He looked over at the digital clock-radio on the nightstand. It was after five in the morning. He must have been unconscious for a few hours. He didn't remember anything after being roughed up by Takashima's goons. Somehow he had made it into the house after they probably dumped him off outside. Mistica hadn't heard him come in, and he didn't want to disturb her. She'd probably panic and insist on taking him to the hospital. He'd get fixed up first thing in the morning by one of his doctor pals who knew how to keep his mouth shut.

He pulled himself out of bed, ignoring the pain racking his body. Then he remembered Kelly. He reached over to the nightstand, quickly picking up the portable phone next to the radio, and punched in her familiar numbers.

"Shit, her machine is still on," he mumbled loudly to himself. "Ye-o-o-ow!" he yelled, holding his ribs as the pain shot through him. That wasn't important now, though. Where the hell was she? He thought about calling the police, but he had no hard evidence that she was now or had been at Takashima's house. Besides, they'd ask a lot of questions when they got a look at him in his present condition. And he was certain the feds downtown would sideline him from the investigation if he got the local police involved. And that would probably spook Takashima, which nobody wanted now.

He dragged himself into the bathroom, one step at a time, and took some aspirin to ease the pain. Then he lay back down in bed and lit a cigarette. As he took a long drag, he mulled over Kelly's disappearance. Maybe he had the whole thing wrong. She might have decided to take a room in a hotel for the night to think things over after the scene Robert had made at the restaurant. Maybe she had been afraid to go home . . .

After a few minutes he leaned over and put out his cigarette in the ashtray. Every bone in his body ached. He turned out the light and lay on his back, thinking he should try to get some more rest. He would find out later what had happened to Kelly.

Daylight was just breaking when Kelly, cold and shaken, stumbled through her front door, clutching her shoes and purse in her hand. All she wanted was to block out the whole incident. She reached for the staircase for support, and then cringed as she heard the black limo pull out of the driveway and onto the highway. Thank God, she thought, I'm home safely.

Kelly put her things down on the kitchen counter, keeping the lights off. She sat on the back patio for a long time, listening to the surf beating against the shore. The sound dulled her senses, but not her emotions. She tried to cry but couldn't. Instead, she kept replaying the night over and over again in her mind: the kidnapping in the limo, Takashima's phony politeness, his fondling of her. She felt violated and dirty.

She buried her head in her hands. My God, what am I going to do now? Go back to the studio and act as if nothing has happened?

She lay down on the patio lounge and closed her eyes. She remained lying there for what seemed like hours, searching for an answer. But the more she tried, the more confused she became.

Slowly the shock began to wear off. Even as the morning sun warmed the air, Kelly broke out in a cold sweat and started shaking all over. Her teeth chattered and her heart beat so quickly she felt faint. She tried to shake the feeling, but it only became worse.

Jake was sleeping soundly when a constant hammering started in his head that wouldn't stop. It sounded like cannons going off. What kind of pills did my doctor friend give me, anyway? he wondered. After he had checked him over earlier and assured him he only had a couple of badly bruised ribs, which he taped up, he had insisted that Jake take some pain pills and get some rest. Now Jake felt like a war was starting in his brain.

He sat up with a start. It took him several minutes to realize there was someone pounding on the front door. Suppose it was more of Takashima's Yakuza returning to finish the job?

Ignoring his aching side, he got out of bed and rummaged through his closet until he found a baseball bat—personally autographed by Mickey Mantle. Armed with it, Jake carefully made his way downstairs, thankful that Mistica was already gone for the morning. He looked out the front window, but didn't see any suspicious cars outside. Slowly he unlocked the front door, with the bat raised.

"All right, what's . . . ?" he said, opening the front door. His mouth dropped. "Kelly!"

She rushed in, grabbing on to him like her life depended on it. "Jake, please, hold me. I've got to talk to you," she sobbed, tears streaming down her face.

He held her tightly, stroking her hair. "It's okay, you're safe now," he said tenderly.

341

He didn't have to ask her: she *had* been at Takashima's.

He picked her up, grimacing with his own pain, and carefully laid her down on the living-room couch. He noticed that she was still wearing the same silk suit from their dinner last night, but it was terribly wrinkled. Her face was dirty, her makeup smeared. There was no sign of blood or bruises, though. "Kel, what happened?"

She shook her head. She couldn't explain the horror of what she had gone through. Not yet. "Please don't ask any questions," she begged. She looked up at him, her green eyes filled with longing. "Just keep holding me tight."

They held each other for a long time. Jake knew she would tell him what had happened when she was ready. He looked at her pale face and bloodshot eyes. Maybe some food in her stomach would make it easier to talk.

"How about some breakfast?" he asked, holding her away from him just enough to see her face, but not letting her go completely.

Kelly nodded and he kissed her gently before disappearing into the kitchen. She heard him making a lot of noise; then the smell of bacon frying tempted her to join him.

She walked into the sunny kitchen nook and sat down at the round table. She let the tantalizing aroma of the food fill her nostrils.

Jake watched her anxiously. He hadn't asked any questions, but he couldn't help but blame himself. If he hadn't stayed behind to show Robert up, none of this would have happened.

Kelly abruptly pushed away her plate and looked up at Jake. He was still silent, but she could see the questioning look in his eyes. "Jake, I . . ." She stumbled for the right words, but she didn't know where to begin.

"Kel, take your time," he said reassuringly as he sat down next to her.

"It was . . . it was . . ." She tried to say his name, but couldn't. She was too ashamed to look into his eyes.

He tried to control his rage as he spoke. "When I left Jimmy's, I wasn't sure where you had gone. First I drove around Malibu; then I staked out Takashima's mansion, but I didn't see you inside. Actually, I didn't have much time to look," he said, trying to laugh as he held his midsection.

Shocked, Kelly grabbed his sweatshirt, hiking it up to reveal the tape holding his ribs steady. "Jake, you're hurt."

"Who, me? It's nothing much. Just a couple of bruised ribs," he said, pretending they didn't hurt. "Don't worry, I'll be all right. I'm getting better as we talk."

But Kelly quickly turned her thoughts somewhere else. Her eyes grew cold. "He's going mad, Jake, I'm frightened."

She glanced out the window. In the late-morning sunshine, the daisies and violets in the garden looked so pure and fresh. But as Kelly pushed back her straggly hair, the smell made her nauseated. She realized it reeked of incense.

As she tried to button her stained, wrinkled blouse, she discovered some of the tiny buttons missing. She also noticed a large brown stain on the sleeve: tea. She must have spilled it. Slowly she touched her arm, her face. Her skin tingled slightly from the effects of the drug.

She pulled down her blouse, feeling dirty all over. She turned to Jake, crying softly. "Jake, what am I going to do?"

Jake put his arms back around her and cradled her head next to his chest. "It's okay, Kelly, it's okay," he murmured, stroking her hair.

"Do you want to tell me what happened?" he asked

softly, taking both her hands in his. He looked into her eyes. "I want to know."

Kelly looked into his face, his cheeks ruddy from the sun and his beard stubbled with gray. But it was his eyes that held her. Gray with familiar flecks of brown. They had never looked more caring.

She began slowly, looking directly at him. "Takashima had a Yakuza substituted for my driver . . ." She continued, telling him about the abduction to his house, about the drugged tea Kakue gave her, then the terrible accusations Takashima had made, and finally the near-rape.

"What happened next? Why did he stop?" Jake asked, trying to keep the anger out of his voice for her sake. He grabbed the coffee and filled her cup.

"He received news about the Japanese Prime Minister's resignation," she finished, picking up her coffee cup.

Jake shook his head in disbelief. "Shit, you mean to tell me that this guy's about to rape you and he stops just because some jerk-off leader in Japan can't keep his act together? I don't fuckin' believe it."

Kelly sipped her coffee before answering him. "I believe he had close ties with the Prime Minister. He always mentioned him."

"Fuck Takashima! And fuck his Prime Minister too!" Jake said, banging his fist down on the table, rattling the dishes. "Damn, I'll cut his fuckin' balls off for touching you."

"No, Jake, please," she pleaded, grabbing his arm. "It won't do any good." Kelly squeezed her eyes shut. Her head was pounding. There was only one way out of this. "I'm resigning my position." She hadn't made up her mind until now.

"What?"

"I'm not going back, Jake. He's too crazy to work for any longer."

Jake grabbed her and held her close to him. As she buried her face in his chest, he groaned inwardly. The last thing in the world he wanted was for her to go back to the studio, but at the same time he knew that if she quit, Takashima might go after her again. For keeps this time. It was apparent that she was the only reason the Hollywood creative talent was working for Constellation.

He kissed her on the cheek. "Look, we'll talk later, after you've had a chance to get cleaned up," he said good-naturedly as he pushed her toward the bathroom, gently patting her ass.

"Thanks, Jake," she said, turning around and smiling at him. "If you hadn't come back into my life again, I . . ."

As she disappeared into the bathroom, Jake picked up the phone and dialed a now-familiar number. As he waited to be connected to his contact, Agent Donaldson, he mulled over Kelly's courage. A lot of women would have folded under those circumstances. A lot of men too, he thought.

Finally he heard a voice answer in even tones, "Department of Justice. Donaldson here."

"This is Baron. Listen to this," he said, a lot calmer than he felt. He related the whole nightmare.

Less than an hour later, Jake had turned on the sauna and convinced Kelly to join him. Immersed in the hot, therapeutic heat, she had already shown signs of calming down.

She sat next to Jake on the redwood bench with white fluffy towels wrapped around them both. Jake continued to bring Kelly up to date on what was happening with the investigation of Takashima. "Donaldson says they've been tailing him regularly. Even his Yakuza can't shake off his federal guys."

"Any more anonymous calls?" Kelly asked as she wrapped the oversize bath towel tighter around herself, tucking it in over her breasts.

Jake nodded. With beads of sweat glistening over his body, he carefully bent down—feeling the tape restricting his movement—and turned up the dry heat; then he pulled his towel tighter around himself. "The Justice Department says the caller appears to be a native Japanese who uses the code name Lion Dog."

Kelly laughed for the first time that morning. "Lion Dog? How weird. Jake, maybe we should call 007 for his help." She looked at him significantly, her eyes sparkling with determination. "You know, sweetheart, I was thinking it over in the shower. I've got to go back to the studio. There are a lot of union people depending on me to stand up for them." Her eyes flashed with anger as she went on: "God knows, our studio president won't. He'll do whatever it takes to keep kissing Takashima's ass for more power, even if he has to sell out every union worker."

Jake winced at the idea of her going back, but he knew she was right. "Kel, just forget that slimeball husband of yours," he said huskily. Then he grabbed her and hugged her tightly. No other words needed to be said.

After a few moments he pulled away and stood up on the wooden slats. "I'll get your things for you," he said, heading toward the guest room.

"Not so fast, Mr. Baron," she teased.

To his surprise, Kelly, wrapped only in her white towel, her long hair pasted to her cheeks and forehead, like a sea nymph tempting any man who listened to her call, stood in the way, blocking the door. She looked ravishing. He breathed in deeply, trying to ignore the erection beneath his towel.

With his hands on his hips, Jake challenged her. "Kel, it's getting late," he said slowly, trying to read the expression on her face. She didn't look like the same person who had helplessly fallen into his arms a few hours ago. This was a determined woman, one who was no longer afraid.

"Jake," she whispered, then smiled devilishly at the man who had meant so much to her. He never flinched, never gave up. Her heart went out to him. He was *her* man, and she couldn't leave without letting him know it.

"I'm certain a few more minutes won't matter," she said, grinning as she dropped her towel onto the wooden slats.

He couldn't take his eyes off her. Her beautiful naked body was glistening all over with sweat. She glowed with desire. He wanted her now more than ever.

"We've got all the time in the world," he agreed, smiling, then lifted her up into his arms. "Starting now."

"Starting now," she happily repeated, snuggling up to his hairy chest, her arms around his neck. She had never felt so close to anyone before as he carried her into the master bedroom and laid her down on the brown velvet coverlet spread over his bed.

He took his time as he touched her soft skin and played with the wet wisps of strawberry-blond hair sticking to her cheeks. She was his alone.

He kissed her lips first, then her breasts, then slowly roved over her entire body. Feeling his lips and tongue probing the inside of her thighs, she moaned. Her head was spinning, but she didn't want him to stop. She was feverish with desire.

She responded by exploring his body with her beautiful long fingers. His muscles were hard and taut, his body lean. "Jake, darling," she whispered. Her breath came hard and uneven as she tugged at the small terry-cloth towel still covering his midsection.

He gently pulled her head back by her long hair and stared longingly at her. He wanted her now, but he wanted to give her all the love he'd been holding back for so long.

"Oh, Jake, I love you," she called out as she put her arms around his neck and pulled him closer to her.

He held her so tightly, she couldn't breathe as they began passionately kissing each other, letting their tongues slide deep into each other's mouth.

Then she felt his hardness inside her. She moaned over and over again as they became one, vowing that no one would ever separate them again.

"Wow! That's a sensational outfit, Mistica," Josette said, whistling as she picked up a bright turquoise leather jacket from the bench. Nearby, Mistica was finishing dressing after playing an hour of tennis, then taking a hot shower. As was usual for a late Wednesday afternoon, the women's locker room in the Century City Health Club was filled with chattering females coming in for a workout after a long business day.

Mistica finished zipping up her matching leather pants, then took the jacket from her friend. "Thanks, Josette. It's a present from my father for helping him on his film."

"You mean you didn't get fired this time?" Josette asked snidely.

Mistica ignored her friend's comment as she put on the jacket and looked into the full-length mirror. She was smiling with a brightness in her eyes that had been missing recently. She had to admit she felt good about herself and the job she had done for her dad. For the first time since Stephen's death, she was actually going out on a date tonight.

Why not? she thought as she slipped on her high heels and grabbed her purse. She had just met this new hunk and he had asked her to meet him around the corner at Hy's Restaurant for a drink.

"Did I tell you about Donna and that good-looking married lawyer—?"

"Sorry, Josie, I'm in a big rush. Gotta dash," Mistica said, already out the door. She knew Josette was dying to dish her all the latest dirt about her husband's new secretary, but she didn't have the time to listen.

Excited about her date, she walked briskly through the ABC Entertainment Center, oblivious of the admiring as well as envious stares of passersby. She took the escalator down to the underground parking, where she had left her VW Rabbit convertible.

As she walked to her car, her high heels echoed loudly. The parking area, normally empty at this time of the afternoon, had a few extra automobiles. She looked down at her watch. Five-thirty. She wanted to leave before it got crowded. The business people would be running to their cars any minute now.

Mistica spied her car over in the corner, parked between two dark-colored vans. As she opened her purse for her ignition key, suddenly someone grabbed her from behind, pinning her arms behind her back. Before she knew what hit her, her purse fell from her hands, the contents spilling out onto the ground. "Aaaagghh . . ." she started to yell, when someone else stuck duck tape over her mouth to silence her.

Panicking, she shook her head back and forth and tried to kick the man holding her. He only laughed at her feeble efforts as the other man pulled out a slender knife and with a swift movement slashed through her jacket, revealing her white bra. Then he quickly sliced off the bra's shoulder straps.

She nearly passed out when next he slashed her pants with his sharp knife, coming close to touching her skin. She tried to kick him, but it was no use.

As she continued to struggle, the tattooed man threw her into an oil spot on the concrete floor. She tried to roll away, but couldn't. She felt sore all over.

As she wiped the oil off her face with her sleeve, she heard them get into their vans. With a Japanese accent, one of them yelled back to her, "No one cheats and steals from the master and gets away with it."

Then with loud screeches of burned rubber, they were both gone.

For the third time in the past hour, Jake emptied the ashtray full of cigarette butts in his living room as he heard the antique clock chime the early-evening hour.

He was more than worried; he was frantic. After Kelly's harrowing experience, he had agreed with her: Takashima was really crazy now. Next time, he might try to kill her.

He wandered into his trophy room, trying to decide whether to watch a video or read a book. Whatever he chose, he needed to lose himself in some obscure fantasy or he would start to go crazy as well. Maybe I'll watch some wrestling, he thought.

Looking through the *TV Guide*, he decided instead to watch a movie on HBO.

Holding a cold can of beer, he stretched out on his leather recliner and punched the buttons on his remote.

Suddenly the phone rang. "Yeah?"

"Dad?" came a small, weak voice.

"Mistica! Honey, where are you? Are you okay? I thought you had a date tonight."

"I'm fine, Dad . . . now," she said. He could hear a cry in her voice. She sounded like she'd burst into tears any minute.

"Tell me where you are and I'll be right there," he said, balancing the portable phone and the beer can under his chin.

"No, Dad, please. Just listen," she begged, her voice insistent. "I'm okay. Just shaken up."

"My God, were you in a car accident?"

"No, it was . . ." She started crying softly. Jake could also hear a woman's voice in the background comforting her.

He almost yelled into the phone, "Who's there with you, Mistica? What the hell happened? Just tell me you're okay."

"I'm at Josie's place. I'm fine, really," she answered.

Jake breathed easier. She was okay, that's all that mattered. Then it hit him. "Mistica, was it Takashima?" he asked slowly, trying to keep a grip on himself.

"No . . . I mean, yes. I . . . I was all dressed up in my new leather suit, when—" She began sobbing as the humiliation of the situation hit her full force. "They cut up my jacket . . . then they threw me into the oil slick."

Jake nearly crushed the beer can as if it were made of paper. "Damn fuckin' . . . Did they touch—"

"No, they left, shouting at me. I ran back to the club then, and Josie took me to her house."

Thank God for that. He was damn grateful that his daughter didn't seem to be hurt. Shit, first Kelly, now Mistica. When was the Justice Department going to stop this madman?

"Listen, Mistica, stay over at Josie's for a while. I don't want you alone."

"Okay, Dad," she mumbled weakly. "I love you." she said in a small voice.

"I love you too, baby," he said more calmly than he felt, and hung up. Even before he heard the dial tone, he was punching in Donaldson's number.

He didn't have to wait long to hear the familiar voice of the federal agent at the other end. ". . . and at the beep, clearly leave your name and number and we'll get back to you. Thank you. Beep."

"Dammit, Donaldson, this is Baron. It's happened again," Jake stammered, carrying the portable unit from room to room, almost expecting to hear his response. Shit, why couldn't it be tomorrow morning already.

Jake rubbed his forehead as he depressed the phone's connection. He felt the blood rushing to his head, making his temples throb madly. He couldn't take any more chances. Fuck that Jap. He never should have let these Justice Department guys talk Mistica and him into this fuckin' mess.

He flipped on the television and turned to CNN *Headline News* by mistake. Once again, for the umpteenth day in a row, another updated story on the Jap's government. Who the fuck cared about their crooked politicians?

Jake followed the man in overalls into the big downtown office building. Donaldson had finally allowed him to come down to his L.A. headquarters. "No more restaurants or zoos," Jake had insisted, "only offices from now on."

Jake noticed that the man would constantly look over his shoulder and from side to side. He decided to glance all around as well. No one in sight. He shrugged his shoulders.

As they entered a locked office, he watched the man tap the right side of the large mirror in the dimly lit unused reception area. Jake was amazed to see the mirror suddenly rise upward, high enough for them to bend under and walk forward.

Jake blinked a few times, adjusting to the bright light behind the two-way glass. As he looked around the open office, he was amazed to see a whole world in there: secretaries and clerks scurrying back and forth, men in suits, some in jeans and sweatshirts, cleaning people, even a sophisticated communications center.

"This way, please, Mr. Baron," said another man in a dark suit, approaching him as he moved ahead. Jake nodded.

He followed the man into a standard-looking office with standard worn-out government-issue furniture, where Agent Donaldson sat waiting for him. A middle-aged secretary entered behind him, ready to take notes.

Donaldson began by repeating some of the department's latest findings in their investigation.

"Takashima is now running scared," Donaldson continued. "We have just intercepted one of his couriers as he was ready to depart from JFK. Our inside informant marked some cash for us. We're betting this is laundered money he has been funneling in from Tokyo."

"What does this mean?" Jake interrupted.

"It means that we may finally hit some hard evidence—"

"Does this mean you'll be able to indict him?"

Donaldson rubbed his head. "We're hoping we can, Mr. Baron."

"So what the fuck are you waiting for?" Jake demanded, not attempting to keep the anger and frustration out of his voice. He wouldn't be responsible for what he'd do to Takashima if he ever touched Kelly or his daughter again.

"First things first, Mr. Baron. We are in the process of sealing off his bank; any attempt by Takashima to do any financial transactions would be a direct violation of our laws. Both the IRS and the FDIC have strict rules and will be monitoring the situation. If we can convince Takashima that we have enough evidence to indict him, then, we believe, he might try to skip out of the country."

"What! What good will that do?" Jake wasn't happy with the idea of seeing Takashima get off scot-free. He lit up another cigarette. "Why don't you just walk in and pick up the sonofabitch?" he asked.

"That's not so simple, Mr. Baron. Our informant believes that since Prime Minister Takeshita's resignation, Takashima might split from his own financially rich Takashima Group and bail out to a third-world country, where he would set up a new power base in asylum. It also means that he wouldn't want to return to Tokyo, where he's up to his ass in deep financial and criminal trouble as well."

Jake was outraged and confused. "I don't understand this thing about the Prime Minister. Why wouldn't Takashima stay here?"

"Their Prime Minister was forced to quit because of his involvement in accepting bribes. Takashima supposedly has been a leading contributor in this political-bribery scandal. If he's indicted by the Japanese government for his part, he knows if he stays here, Japan would try to extradite him from the U.S. With our informant's cooperation, we are now painting him into a very tight corner. If he stays, we'll get him; but if he runs, they'll get him."

Before Jake could ask any more questions, Donaldson stood up, signaling that the meeting was at an end. The federal agent had other headaches to attend to. "Please try to relax, Mr. Baron. We're doing the best we can."

The man in overalls suddenly appeared in the doorway. Jake started to say something, but it was obvious he wasn't going to get any more answers.

Silently Jake followed the man outside into the bright spring sun. He noticed that the air temperature was hot, but his hands were ice cold.

The tires of Robert's red Ferrari squealed as he whipped around the corner and into his parking place in front of the executive tower at Constellation. He was unaware that Takashima almost raped Kelly. All Robert cared about was his appointment to speak with Takashima regarding the unions. Somehow, he felt that Takashima might not understand where his loyalties lay. Once and for all, he would convince him that they were definitely not with his wife. If Takashima decided to fire her, Robert had to make sure he would be saved.

"You are late, Mr. Zinman," Takashima said, looking at him. He was already seated, his men around him.

"I am sorry, Mr. Takashima-san. I got caught in traffic." Robert looked at the smiling Japanese *kacho* seated around the table and returned their smile. "May I speak with you alone, *please*?"

Takashima was surprised. It was not like Zinman to show such respect. Curious about this unexpected change of behavior, Takashima snapped his fingers twice. The *kacho* all rose at the same time, bowed low to Takashima, then to Robert, and left.

"Now, Mr. Zinman, what is on your mind?"

Robert didn't notice Takashima's cool smile or the tapping of his forefingers: sure signs of strained relations. Instead he jumped right into his speech, charm oozing out of him. "Mr. Takashima, because of my wife, you're still having union problems. Now, please understand, Kelly and I are in no way on the same side in this matter." He paused as he grinned slyly at Takashima. "I'm sure that with the right incentives, I could bring this situation under control. Now, here's what I can do to help you turn Constellation into a nonunion studio," he began, a greedy smile lighting up his face.

Carefully monitoring their conversation were the Ronin, Minoru, and some of his Yakuza. The master had already decreed an end to this two-faced American. The Yakuza were already scheduled to inform the weak American in an appropriate way that he was no longer welcome at Constellation or anywhere else in Hollywood.

"Her-r-r-e-e-e-'s Johnny."

As the familiar late-night TV theme played loudly inside the fashionable town house, a voice shouted, "Hey, Robert, turn the television down, I have neighbors. And by the way, we're out of vodka."

Robert looked up at his buddy John, busy fondling a newly arrived actress from Miami in his water bed in his upstairs loft.

"I'll check the cabinet," Robert shouted back, lowering the television volume. He was wearing cut-off jeans and a T-shirt that said: "Life is a bitch and then you die."

"Show me some more tit, Sandra," he said, putting down the camera. He had been in the middle of taking some Polaroids of the pretty UCLA brunette he'd met earlier at the beach. Opening the liquor cabinet, he found it was empty except for a few cans of warm Diet Coke.

"How's this, Bobby?" she asked, unhooking her bra and slipping it off. Robert almost forgot about the vodka; he couldn't take his eyes off her big firm breasts and hard nipples.

"Great, honey, great, Wait a minute."

He was feeling terrific, more certain than ever that he would be able to convince Takashima to give him more power, and maybe even take over Kelly's position as CEO. Not to mention a raise in salary after he supported the Yakuza drivers. But he knew he'd have to be very careful.

Robert called up to his friend, "Hey, John, I'll run down to the liquor store before they close and pick up a couple of bottles." Then to the girl he said, "Don't move, Sandra. I'll be right back."

Whistling to himself, he grabbed his jacket and walked out of the town house. He'd also buy some extra film. He intended to see a lot more of Sandra before the night was over.

No sooner had Robert walked outside than a couple of huge guys jumped him.

"What the hell?" he said, struggling as he tried to see who had grabbed him. But they were wearing stocking masks over their heads.

One of them pinned his arms behind his back while the other punched him in the ribs. "Aaaaggghhh!" Robert cried out. What did they want? Money? Credit cards?

"My wallet's in my—" he said, reeling with pain. The bigger guy just snarled, then punched Robert again in the ribs. As Robert yelped, both men hoisted him up and carried him to his car. Unceremoniously they slung him into his open convertible. Robert landed with a loud thud, his head hitting the steering wheel.

As he put his hands up to his head, the big thug leaned over into the car and slit open his jeans and briefs with a long knife. Then he grabbed Robert's shriveled-up dick and flashed the cold steel blade in front of his eyes. "Leave town immediately, or we'll cut your balls off and feed them to you," he growled ominously.

Robert almost choked on his saliva, barely able to nod his head up and down several times. He had no doubt they'd do it.

Then, just as quickly, the thug let him go and walked away. But it wasn't over yet. "What the fuck?" Robert yelled out in desperation as he saw what was coming.

But it was too late.

Robert only had time to close his eyes as the two monster gorillas hefted a nearby trash dumpster and turned over the smelly garbage right on top of him and his car.

Robert remained perfectly still for a long time as he wondered who had done this to him. Had the union boys somehow learned already of his betrayal? Or was it Takashima's Yakuza? This second possibility sent a chill down his spine. They didn't make idle threats.

If it was the Japanese, it was time to split town. And fast.

19

As Noda fed the documents into the fax machine in Takashima's 1901 Avenue of the Stars private office, he kept looking at the clock ticking away. It was nearly three in the morning. He was perspiring profusely even though he had made sure he was absolutely alone.

But Noda smiled in spite of his nervousness as he thought of Takashima's prime operative in Tokyo, Asano-san, who was on the receiving end of this fax. As soon as the Prime Minister had resigned, Noda had placed a call to Asano. He had little difficulty convincing him that Takashima was now legally vulnerable and prone to arrest. After he explained to him that Takashima would no longer be able to protect either of them, Asano agreed to help him expose Takashima to the Japanese authorities. "When the ship starts to sink, all the rats scurry from their holes," Noda muttered softly.

As he finished faxing the last few pages of the real scorecard—the complete files on all of Takashima's illegal business dealings, including his money-laundering scheme—he began to collect the many scattered documents. The master had no idea that he secretly kept the scorecard up to date. Nor did Takashima realize that he had been duped by his heir. He thought that the scorecard Noda had prepared for him—that Takashima had his Yakuza hand-carry back to Asano—was the real one. If the master only knew it was a phony . . .

Noda looked again at the gold-plated sunburst clock above the entryway. The time had not changed. Suddenly everything opulent and grand made him sick to his stomach. How could he have been so blind all these years? Why had he not seen what was really going on long before he learned of his mother's murder? Takashima was an evil monster to everyone but him.

Deep within, though, his steely resolve had not changed. He realized it would be impossible to make Takashima pay for the murder of his mother, or all the other hideous crimes he had committed over the years. Too much time had gone by. Also, his Yakuza, who had committed most of the crimes, would rather die than betray their master. And Chisako, who had witnessed many of Takashima's crimes and had every reason to betray him, was now exiled to a Buddhist temple. But whatever it now takes, Noda thought, I must and will bring the master to justice.

As he turned off the lamp on the desk and headed to the back elevator, he reflected uneasily. Of course, I, too, took part in these activities. He was no better than a *bunraku*, a puppet, whose every movement and gesture was controlled by the black-cloaked puppeteer. He bowed his head low in shame. And now, without regret, he was also a traitor.

Noda waited until the next afternoon to drop the bombshell on his master: Takashima was about to be indicted on multiple federal U.S. banking violations. At any moment, and certainly before the week was out, U.S. Marshals would be moving in to shut down his Beverly Hills bank.

As Takashima peered over his sunglasses in shock, looking out of his penthouse office, Noda tried desperately to keep calm. He went on, saying that an old Wharton classmate of his, now a high-ranking authority with the IRS, had tipped him off. "I believe he meant for me to flee, master, to save my own skin. B-but he does not understand that *giri* is more important to me than anything else," Noda stammered, praying that Takashima would mistake his nervousness for fear. "As it is for anyone who works for you."

Takashima exploded. "How can this be? How could the American government have found evidence for an indictment?" He lurched to his feet and began pacing around his office. "And how is it that the Ronin have not learned of this?" he bellowed at his cowering protégé.

"I . . . I do not know," Noda said, feeling sweat pour down his face. "All I know is what Mr. Elliot told me."

Noda was so frightened that he hardly felt any satisfaction that his master was snapping at his bait just as he had planned. He knew that his plan depended on luring Takashima to Tokyo, but he had not dreamed that betraying his foster father would be so hard.

Finally Takashima stopped pacing and glared at Noda malevolently. "You. You must summon the Ronin right away. Right away, do you hear?"

Shortly thereafter, Takashima scanned the faces of the men gathered before him. He spoke quickly, while keeping his voice emotionless. "I have brought all of you here to announce my revised plans. Our stay in the United States has ended. We are being hunted by members of the enemy's law-enforcement agencies. We must leave tomorrow."

He then launched into a tirade that baffled his team of Ronin spies. Was this what he was paying such huge sums of money for? That he should have to run like a beaten dog? Noda had spoken of multiple indictments, and that meant the feds must have proof of money-laundering. But how had they gotten it? As Takashima angrily looked from one to the other for a culprit, his men blanched in fear.

All except one. Eyeing Noda suspiciously, the Ronin leader rose to his feet.

"You are being deceived, honorable master," he challenged. "We are not aware that the American authorities have discovered any financial discrepancies in their investigations. Our international money-laundering system has worked exceedingly well."

Takashima quickly fired back: "You are forgetting that one of our couriers did not show up at the appointed bank in Luxembourg."

"But, Takashima," the Ronin leader said, but suddenly stopped when he saw Takashima put his hand up.

"Enough," said Takashima firmly. "I know full well that you have never liked my chosen successor. He is all that you are not: honorable, straightforward, and *trustworthy*," he hissed violently. Turning to Noda, who was staring intently at his toes, Takashima finished: "Come, we have much to do before we leave."

The Yakuza, in black shirts and pants, using the disguise of darkness, silently packed up Takashima's priceless antiques and works of art and carefully loaded them into the limos.

Ignoring any thought of sleep, Noda kept the men working through the night. He must keep them moving and make sure that Takashima's plan was carried out. There were too many people involved now for anything to go wrong.

They began their clandestine journey from Takashima's Hollywood Hills mansion down to Sunset, then took a snakelike path over the surface roads to his Palisades home.

Even the hookers on Sunset Boulevard were curious when the same motorcade of limos traveled down Laurel Canyon for the third time. The streetwalkers, all waving, lined the curb in their tight minis and high-heeled boots, hoping one of the limousines would stop.

As Jake and Kelly walked along the Santa Monica

Pier, hand in hand, they were dressed like the other early-morning joggers running below on the sandy beach. Kelly, wearing a creamy rose sweatsuit, looked soft and pretty. Jake, as usual, had simply thrown on a pair of baggy gray sweats and a T-shirt with his Dodgers jacket and matching blue hat. They both knew it was getting too dangerous to be seen openly now, so Jake suggested they meet at the pier. Hopefully, nobody would recognize them there at the early hour. They didn't realize how wrong they were.

During the past few days, since Kelly had returned back to the studio—she took a few vacation days to regroup herself—Takashima had totally ignored the fact that he recently tried to rape her.

Kelly had swiped some confidential information about Takashima's finances yesterday that she wanted Jake to give to his federal friends. She unzipped her sweatsuit and took out a plain envelope. She held it tightly between her fingers before handing it over to Jake.

Finding Takashima's office in disarray, she had decided to take advantage of the opportunity when he was suddenly called away from his desk. Making sure no one saw her, she carefully checked through the scattered files on his desk. When she had seen some key names and figures, she quickly stuffed the papers into her attaché case. Almost totally afraid of her own shadow now, she didn't want to think about what would happen to her if she were caught.

As Jake peered into the envelope, Kelly coughed uncomfortably. She had to show him one of the papers. "Jake, there was also something I spotted on Stephen."

She thumbed up the top paper and handed it to Jake. He scanned it quickly, then paused to read it thoroughly. Takashima had been paying Stephen a bonus of ten thousand dollars a week to do his dirty work. The paper also contained Stephen's long list of IOU's to different bookies in Vegas.

As he looked up at her, she knew what he was feeling. Somehow, after Stephen's death, Jake had hoped that he might have been confused about his stepson's true role with Takashima. But this proved his worst fears: Stephen had been a traitor after all.

"My God," Jake whispered, his breath erratic. He couldn't think straight as he looked out to sea through the morning mist.

He looked around the wooden pier, feeling miserable, noting the few early-morning walkers and a couple of weathered fishermen. "C'mon, Kel, let's get some breakfast," he said as they started to walk silently.

Kelly held his hand tightly in hers as they entered the restaurant at the end of the pier. She couldn't see his face very well since the wind had blown his hair over his eyes, but she was certain she saw tears glistening on his cheeks.

A figure in a black sweatshirt continued his vigil from his vantage point high across the rocks on Pacific Coast Highway. The long-range lens on his videocam enabled him to tape everything, including Kelly passing the documents to Jake. He smiled slowly, baring the gums above his stained teeth. As Takashima had suspected, the *gaijin* with the sun-red hair had taken the all-important file.

"More coffee?" the fat, middle-aged waitress offered Jake and Kelly as they completed a light breakfast in the pier's famous coffee shop.

"No, I'm fine, thank you," Kelly said, not looking up from Robert's resignation letter she was reading to Jake. In it Robert had written that he believed his life was in danger, so naturally he was leaving town. And for good.

Kelly bit her lower lip as she read aloud the end of the letter: " '. . . and don't forget to give my regards to your sugar daddy, Baron. Tell him that the next time I run into the old fart, I'll break off his limp dick.' "

"That fuckin' little shit—" Jake stopped short, shrugging irritably. It wasn't worth commenting on.

Kelly folded the letter and put it back in her pocket. "I still can't get over Robert running off to England like that, although I'm not surprised." She rested her chin on her hands, momentarily reflecting on her years with him. "I don't know why it took me so long to see through him." She tried to laugh, but it wasn't very convincing. "Imagine him getting some cocktail waitress pregnant and going back to her."

"I feel sorry for the kid; some father Robert will make. But what I can't believe is that he is so fuckin' naive as to think Puttnam will give him a job with his production company." Jake snickered. "Wait till I speak to David."

"You never know, Jake. Robert can usually talk his way into anything . . ." she answered, her voice trailing off.

Looking out the window, she just wanted to forget him completely. She concentrated on an old man removing the tarp from his souvenir stand. Right behind him was the carousel, its high-stepping animals trapped in frozen movement until the music would bring them back to life.

She smiled at Jake, suddenly stirred by an old memory. "Jake, do you remember our first date? Our *very* first date?"

Jake scratched his head, trying to think back. "No. . . . Only kidding, of course I do," he said, snapping his fingers, then pointing outside. "It was right there, at the carousel."

They both smiled as he reached over and took her hand.

Kelly looked at her watch suddenly. She could sit here forever with Jake, but Takashima would be suspicious if she was late for his morning managers' meeting. "I've got to go. I have a lot of work to do today.

Takashima wants me to spend some time with our new Japanese studio president."

"Be careful, Kel. Takashima is very dangerous now. I wouldn't be surprised if the dumb motherfucker doesn't wind up committing hara-kiri one day." Jake smiled at his thought, but he felt his heart racing faster now as he let go of Kelly's hand. He wanted to hold her close to him and protect her. He knew she had taken a great risk by stealing Takashima's confidential papers. "I don't trust him, Kel. You might be better off not going in at all." Any false move on her part, and there was no telling what might happen.

She couldn't let Jake know that she was now terrified to be anywhere near Takashima. Trying to smile, she said, "Don't worry, I'll be all right. I won't take any chances. As Donaldson has been telling you: 'Just a little bit longer, and then, bingo, we got him.'"

"That won't be soon enough for me," he answered hotly.

Kelly grabbed his hand and squeezed it. "C'mon, cheer up. I'm going to see you at twelve-thirty for lunch."

They left the pier and walked down to the beach. Underneath, in the shadows, they hugged and kissed, then left in separate directions.

They never realized that Takashima's Ronin observer had taped their every movement.

Walking quickly, Kelly glanced in the direction of the Bunky Theater—now officially changed to the Odori Theater—and frowned. She would have a long afternoon ahead of her, previewing clips from the old Constellation movie classics. Under normal circumstances she would have enjoyed seeing some of the films and their stars again, but during this morning's meeting with the new studio president, Takashima had informed her he now wanted to remake several of the classics with only Asian actors and locales. He hoped that this would be more infuriating to the Hollywood community than what Ted Turner had done when he colorized some of the black-and-white MGM classics.

Kelly, of course, wasn't aware of Takashima's motive. She checked her watch: almost twelve—just enough time to get over to Beverly Hills and meet Jake at the Bistro Garden.

She unlocked the door to her Mercedes convertible and was about to get inside when she heard the screech of a car braking behind her. Turning, she was surprised to see Takashima's gold limo come to a complete stop. She stood silently and watched as the blackened-out passenger window slowly glided down.

"Kelly-san, please," Takashima called out from inside the limo. "I must speak with you a moment."

She felt her pulse racing as she walked over to the limo. Whatever I do, she told herself, I'm not going to get waylaid. I'm already late for lunch.

"Mr. Takashima?" she said, leaning down to the partially open window.

"Please, Kelly-san, I need just a brief moment of your time," he said, opening the door and motioning for her to get inside.

"What is it?" Kelly said warily, bending down far enough to see the Japanese tycoon. But when she saw his face, she instinctively drew back. He was leering at her with the same sadistic smile she remembered so vividly from that night at his mansion.

Suddenly someone pushed her forcibly from behind into the limousine.

"No!" she screamed as she landed head-down on the seat, hitting her chin. She looked up to see Takashima still leering at her.

She desperately tried to scramble backward out the door, but at that moment two hands gripped her tightly under the armpits and shoved her up and over Takashima's lap. A moment later the door slammed shut. As the car slowly started up, the Yakuza's hands grabbed her again and roughly moved her to a sitting position.

"You have betrayed me, Kelly-san," Takashima growled. "You took what was not yours, and you gave it to my enemy, Baron-san. Now I will take what is his."

He then nodded to Minoru, who was leaning over the front seat.

The hulking Yakuza chief grabbed her around the neck with one huge hand and held her so tightly she couldn't catch her breath. With his other hand he ripped off the left sleeve of her jacket and blouse. The Yakuza driver then handed Minoru a hypodermic needle.

She could barely glance around. "*No!*" she screamed as he squirted out a few small drops of liquid into the air. He then jammed the needle into the bare flesh of her arm.

"No! No!"

Then, in a big hurry, Takashima's gold limo left Constellation through the seldom-used back gate. He wanted to catch up with the other two limos that had left moments ahead of him.

They all had an important flight to catch.

"Yes, that's right, Kelly Kristopher . . . yes, I'll hold," Jake said irritably as he waited by the pay phone. He paid no attention to the crowd of chic lunchgoers wandering off the valet lot into the restaurant's rear entrance. The Bistro Garden, one of the "A" places with Beverly Hills society, had been a favorite of Jake's for years.

Jake was starting to get worried when Geoffrey's voice came on the line. "Geoffrey, where's Kelly?" Jake said hurriedly into the phone. "She left the office twenty minutes ago? Are you sure? Well, she hasn't shown up yet." Jake started to panic as Kelly's assistant tried to calm him down. Something was terribly wrong.

A moment later, Jake was phoning for help.

"Donaldson."

"We've got no time to waste," Jake said. "I'm frightened. Kelly's missing. She didn't show up for lunch."

20

"Takashima-san, everything is ready," Minoru said, bowing as Takashima hurriedly climbed aboard his private jet at Los Angeles International Airport.

"*Yoi desu*," Takashima replied. "There will be no further delays. Alert the captain that we will be ready for takeoff in a few minutes."

"*Hai*, Takashima-san," he said, bowing. Then he left him alone with Noda in his cabin.

Takashima looked around the first-class cabin of the private 727-stretch jet. The aircraft was well supplied— his best champagne, his favorite Japanese foods . . . and his special entertainment—all ready for the long escape trip.

He snarled as he sat down and took off his shoes. Punishing a beauty had once been a ritual he relished, but now it seemed a paltry victory in the face of his crowning defeat. He had failed. Hollywood would go on. And he? He was fleeing like a common criminal.

"Takashima-san, *kon-nichiwa*," Kakue said, bowing respectfully as she entered his cabin. She had been driven to the plane in one of the other limos, and as she lifted her head, Takashima noticed how pretty she looked in her white-and-red-striped sundress. She wore a pink rose in her hair, and her wide-brimmed sunhat had a long, trailing pink chiffon scarf. By the look on her sweet, smiling moon face, it was obvious she was very happy to be going home.

At the moment, however, Takashima had no interest in her blossoming womanhood. "How is she?" he asked sternly.

Kakue nodded, bowing. "She is safely secured, as you have requested, in the back of the plane, Takashima-san. She is still unconscious . . ." She paused, not understanding why Kristopher-san had been brought on board. She also did not understand why the Yakuza had tied her securely to the struts; she would not awaken soon with the drug that Minoru had injected into her. It had seemed unnecessary to Kakue. There were so many women who would gladly come along with her master. Like herself.

Takashima breathed in deeply, remembering his many recent pleasurable nights with Kakue. She had served her purpose, though. There would be many others like her available to him: fresh, unspoiled virgins.

"Kakue-san." His voice was suddenly cool, impersonal. "You will stay behind. Noda will give you money for a taxi. I will contact you with further orders."

Kakue looked up in fear. She wanted to ask many questions now, but she remained silent. Her eyes met Noda's and she saw uneasiness on his face. She smiled and bowed as she took the cash from Noda.

She then picked up her suitcase and left the plane. She did not look back. She did not see Noda's goodbye wave to her.

Standing on the tarmac, she watched the 727 take off into the bright afternoon sun with its black-and-silver body soaring straight into the yellow ball of fire, taking everything that had been her life far away.

Takashima dozed occasionally as the aircraft reached its cruising altitude of thirty-seven thousand feet. He needed all his strength for what lay ahead. He unbuckled his seat belt and picked up the rice wine on the tray next to him. He gulped it down.

As he got out of his seat, he looked over at Noda

opening his briefcase. He could see by his red-rimmed eyes and slumped posture that his heir apparent was very fatigued, but he never put himself first, never shirked his duties. He was proud of Noda.

Walking to the washroom to change his clothes, he smiled to his Ronin members seated on one side of the aisle, and his trusted Yakuza on the other side.

Kelly finally opened her eyes, but everything she saw was a blur. Her head felt heavy and her throat was raw. She had been unconscious for hours. She tried to cry out, but there was a silken gag tied over her mouth. When she moved, her body ached all over.

"Kel . . . ly . . ." his voice called out from somewhere in the distance. Kelly raised her head, becoming slightly more alert. She strained, but she couldn't hear the voice clearly. There was a dull roar in the background.

Slowly regaining her senses, she realized she was crouched on the floor with her arms extended over her head and tied securely above her. She tried to move her legs, but they were tied together at the ankles. She was helpless.

She felt a soft coolness, as if from an air conditioner, caressing her skin. Suddenly she stiffened. She was completely naked.

"Kelly," his voice called again. Closer now.

She had to get help, to call out to the voice. She tried to bite through the gag, but it was useless. Kelly felt tears sting her cheeks as she furiously blinked to see clearly. She was more frightened than she had ever been in her life.

"I am over here, Kelly," she heard the voice say. She turned her head quickly in the direction of his voice. Her eyes were still blurred from the effects of the drug, and the dull roar continued to buzz in her ears. Damn, she thought, where am I?

"Are you not afraid?" His voice was closer and more distinct.

As he bent over her, she saw Takashima's face, his dark eyes. He was not wearing his glasses or one of his custom-made suits. Instead he wore a black karate outfit and he had a black kerchief tied around his forehead with Japanese characters scrawled on it in bright red and white.

Kelly's eyes widened in terror. He must have gone completely mad. Her heart beat wildly, her breasts heaving up and down as the sweat of her fear poured from her body. Where was Jake? Was he coming to her rescue?

She tried to speak, but couldn't. She begged him to remove the gag from her mouth.

"I know what you want, *kirei na*, but not yet. First, you must see what I have for you."

He picked up something from a table nearby. Kelly could see that he held a long slim object in his hand. With the other hand he stroked it slowly, lovingly, like he was caressing the body of a beautiful woman.

Kelly kept her eyes on him, watching, waiting, always mindful of that sickening smile of his. That frightened her more than anything.

"Do not be so curious, Kelly-san, you will soon discover the way of the bamboo splint."

Then, without warning, he raised his arm and struck her across the back. He hit her again on the arms, shoulders, legs. Methodically he made the circuit again and again.

Kelly tried to shield her naked body from his blows, but the long, ancient instrument of pain found its mark again and again. She yanked feverishly at the straps holding her arms above her, but they cut into her wrists, inflicting more pain.

She could now feel the trickles of blood slowly running down her arms and mixing with the blood from the gashes on her back.

The pain scorched her body like ripples of fire. The gag was so tight over her mouth that her screams came out as muffled groans. She prayed he would stop, but he didn't. She realized that he would kill her soon.

Kelly looked at him, but she couldn't see his face. She saw only the action of his arm again and again as the bamboo smacked hard against her defenseless body. After several minutes more, she could no longer tolerate the torturous pain. She became woozy, and then, blissfully, she lost all consciousness.

Takashima did not notice that Kelly had slumped over, motionless. "*Buriburi!*" he yelled over and over, repeating the ancient chant from the days of the harlot quarters of the Yoshiwara district. He kept hitting her and did not stop until he had spent his wrath. But even then he was not finished.

As he cut her down from the overhead luggage rack, she fell by his feet. He sliced through the rope around her ankles, then turned her over onto her back.

The time for the final humiliation had arrived. He zipped open his pants, pulled out his penis, and urinated all over her.

When he had finished, he stared down at her, unmoved by her pretty face or her beautiful naked body. She was only a low-class American whore who had been subjugated to his power.

Hours later, Kelly lay still, fearing to show she had awakened. The gag had been removed from her mouth and someone had draped a sheet over her. Finally she tried to stand, but she slumped back in pain. Her back was on fire. She didn't know it, but the juice of a chili pepper had also been rubbed into her open wounds. She could smell the stench of dried urine . . .

Suddenly she saw light coming through tiny cabin windows. She finally realized: an airplane.

Then that unbearable earlier scene with Takashima came back to her. Fear and disgust gripped her again. She pulled her knees up to her chest. The pain no longer mattered. At least she was still alive. But for how long? Would she ever see Jake again?

She closed her eyes and prayed. "Dear God, help me," she whispered, her cracked lips now oozing with sores from the tight gag.

"Your God has abandoned you," Takashima said, reading her lips.

Kelly's eyes flashed with hatred. She hadn't lost her courage. He could never take that away from her.

"You're truly the devil," she shouted.

Takashima laughed. "And you are the devil's mistress." He pulled down the sheet from her shoulders, revealing the ugly red welts on her body. "No man will ever again be fooled by you."

His words chilled her. There was no doubt now; he meant to kill her.

Summoning her remaining strength, she pulled the sheet over herself, feeling the soreness in her arms. She wasn't going to die without a fight. "Why are you doing this to me?" she asked, beginning to cry.

Takashima looked at her with a twisted smile. "My little beauty, your secret was discovered. I do not tolerate traitors."

"Are you going to kill me?"

Takashima, with his shirt now removed, did not hesitate to answer. "You and Baron are the symbol of all that I have hated my entire life. You and your American people have always had everything, while I had nothing. Did you know I am a survivor of Nagasaki?"

Takashima looked past her, as if he was seeing that terrible day once again in his mind.

"Your people will never understand what they did to my country on that day. It was a hot summer morning, the air so thick you could hardly breathe. We had heard air-raid sirens before we had time to eat our morning rice, but when we realized it was only a false alarm, I begged my mother to let me go for a swim in the river . . ." His voice trailed off as he remembered that was the last time he had seen his mother. "Then, before the sun rose into the noonday sky, the plane came and dropped the bomb. I survived by diving deep into the river.

"When I returned home, I found our wooden house flattened to the ground. Everything I touched was burning hot, but I did not stop trying to find my family. Underneath the shapeless rubble of scorched wood, I discovered the charred body of my mother, lying protectively across my baby sister, also dead. I noticed a funny smell that seemed to suffocate me. I found out later it was magnesium.

"I searched for my older sister and found her not far away, gasping for breath. She was not as badly burned but was cut and bleeding from the slivers of glass embedded in her skin. I helped her into my small two-wheel cart and pulled her all the way home. But by the time we got there, she, too, was dead."

Kelly was silent. She was afraid to speak.

Takashima continued, still looking past her: "Everywhere I went, I saw people I once knew now merely walking sticks of burning flesh. There was not a living thing left untouched, not even a blade of grass."

As Kelly watched him in horror, she saw that his eyes had taken on the demonic cast of a lunatic.

"Those who did survive were not always so fortunate. My grandmother died from radiation poisoning." He suddenly paused a moment, thinking about his next statement. "I, too, have been diagnosed to have radiation poisoning."

He looked down at Kelly, not seeing a woman brutally beaten by his own hand, but instead the symbol of a whole nation.

"But now, we have won," he said softly. "The twenty-first century belongs to us in the Pacific Rim. And your people are too blind and too stupid to know that we are taking it from you.

"However, before I can join my ancestors, I must first be worthy." He bent over her. His voice was caressing. "You have helped me to do that, Kelly-san. I have now regained my honor."

"I . . . don't understand," she said, starting to sob.

"Okane yori kao ga kiku," he said slowly. "Face is more powerful than money."

He opened the door leading to the main cabin of the aircraft.

"Wait!" Kelly desperately called out, wrapping the sheet closer around her. "You can't leave me like this. Where are you taking me?"

Takashima looked back at her, smiling.

"Paradise."

As the plane taxied over to a private runway on the island of Viti Levu in the Fiji chain, Takashima had just finished listening to Noda's suggestion that he return to Tokyo and become better acquainted with the new Prime Minister, Uno. Noda had also informed him of the final plans for Kelly. Not wanting to dirty his hands with the American whore, Takashima had asked that his trusted aide finish her off.

"A helicopter will take Kristopher-san to one of the outer islands. Do not worry, master, everything is arranged for her disposal."

Takashima grunted with pleasure. "It was she who gave all the information on my financial activities to the American authorities. She will now pay the ultimate price for her treason." Having pronounced this conviction, he turned with a serene smile that sent a chill through Noda.

"Now, Noda-san, have you administered the sedative injection?" Takashima asked impassively.

"*Hai*, Takashima-san," Noda said, bowing. "I have administered the final dose of the drug . . . excuse me, I . . . I mean the sedative. She will be dead and buried, out of sight, before I leave her on the tiny outer island of Kabara."

Takashima recoiled with sudden suspicion. Noda seemed terribly ill-at-ease. Was he losing his nerve?

After all, this was the first time he had asked his heir to murder anyone. Maybe I should not take the chance of him failing, he pondered carefully.

He quickly summoned Minoru and, gazing steadily at Noda, said, "You must go along to make sure the deed is done.

"Noda-san, if you need to contact me, I will be on Castaway Island, where I will reside until tomorrow. I will be on a survey with my Fijian construction team, checking the blueprints of my golf course and private club."

This was Takashima's latest business venture. With golf the number-one pastime for his fellow Japanese, the Asian Octopus had decided to capitalize on the craze. With no more available space in Japan, and with Hawaii so overcrowded, the still-barren Fiji Islands were perfect to develop year-round paradise golf clubs. He knew that he would quickly sell out annual memberships to his golf-crazed countrymen at the going rate of one million dollars per person.

As the 727 finally completed its long taxi, Takashima, followed by Noda, left the plane and was met by a Fijian native dressed in his traditional grass skirt. The man presented Takashima with a basket filled with coconuts, ginger root, and taro.

"*Bula*," the native said, greeting Takashima and Noda with a slight bow.

"*Bula*," Takashima and Noda replied. Takashima then breathed in the pleasant aromas of the gift. The fragrance of the sweet-smelling fruits and spices revitalized him, making him forget the recent smell of revenge on his hands.

He snapped his fingers and one of his Yakuza appeared, carrying his luggage. Takashima then turned to Noda. "I will return here tomorrow. At that time, Noda-san, I will decide whether or not we stay here or fly to Tokyo or to another safe haven. Remember, do not fail in your duty."

As the native led Takashima to the waiting helicopter that would transport him to nearby Castaway Island, he smiled pleasantly with approval as he looked at the native's primitive long skirt. This was a new land, unspoiled by greed, war, and Americans. A place where they still respected tradition. This would be ideal for my new base of operations, he thought. He was easily becoming at peace with himself.

Noda smiled and waved to Takashima as his helicopter took off, but inside he was very troubled. He went back to the private jet to secure Kelly, his steps faltering as he climbed up the stairs. He saw Minoru, as Takashima had commanded, waiting for him at the plane door.

This challenge to his loyalty by the master made him very tense and uneasy. Minoru would ensure for the master that Kelly would be killed. Noda realized that he would not be able to abandon his *giri*. There was not much time left. They had to ready the American beauty for her final journey. Their helicopter would be ready any moment.

Inside his grass-thatched hut, Takashima thrashed around on his hammock, finding no peace in his sleep.

He cursed the tropical typhoon that had come up suddenly and spewed its angry torrents on his unsuspecting survey party. He wondered how his Fijian team were faring, huddled together in the smaller, less-sturdy huts nearby. He looked up, dismayed at the small steady stream of rain that began to leak through the roof.

He lay back in the hammock. As it lazily rocked him, he closed his eyes. The sounds of the winds and rain continued to echo in his head as he slowly drifted into sleep. . . .

All he could see in the blackness was an ugly serpent with three frightening heads: those of a grisly dragon, a sleek panther, and a sly lion, all snarling at him through their blackened fangs. The serpent guarded a magnificent box shimmering with precious stones, each one possessing a secret of the universe.

Takashima tried to run from the serpent, but the scaly creature grabbed him with its sharp, pointed claws and dug them into his flesh. He looked down, but no blood spurted from his wounds. He cringed as the serpent's hot breath burned his face.

"You will be my prisoner for two hundred years," the serpent shouted, laughing as his claws dug deeper.

Then suddenly the serpent dropped him and he felt himself falling down, down into a deep purple cloud of smoke. But before he hit bottom he was propelled up into the mushroom cloud by a mysterious unseen force, then thrown to the ground. He pulled himself up; he was shaken but not hurt.

He began crawling on his knees over warm sands until he struck something sharp, half-hidden in the sand. It was the serpent's forbidden box. He smiled greedily as he cried out in glee. It was his at last.

As he opened it up, whirling sands, as light as the wind, escaped. Takashima fell to the ground, shaking with convulsions as the sands began to cover him from head to toe. He felt the hair on his face growing into a long, graying beard. He looked down at his hands: the skin wrinkled up like bamboo paper, and his bones cracked through the skin like dry wood. He felt his muscles shriveling; he was so weak he could not stand up.

He had aged two hundred years in seconds. . . .

Takashima awoke screaming. Immediately he looked down at his hands. They had not changed. Still in the grip of the nightmare, he rummaged through his belongings for a mirror. His face looked the same.

He yanked off his wet cotton kimono and threw it on the dirt floor. His body was dripping with sweat.

He grabbed a towel and walked to the window, pushing aside the flimsy covering of large banana leaves. Outside he saw the large coconut trees surrounding the tiny circle of grass huts swaying dangerously low as the trade winds tried to tear them from their roots. It was still dark. The fierce rain was still coming down hard.

Lifting his eyes upward, he fell on his knees and prayed. He was certain the dream had been a warning. He felt trapped, as if some horrible apparition from his past was haunting him with the reality of his future. He welcomed the stinging pelts of rain that bit at his face, making him feel alive once more.

He would not be foolish. He knew what the dream had meant. He should never return to his homeland.

Takashima took his helicopter back to the main island at dawn. And when he saw the other helicopter land on the tarmac, he was pleased. He waited for Noda and Minoru to descend the portable steps.

"Noda-san, I have decided your suggestion to return to Tokyo is not a good one," he said. "Instead we will stay here and establish our new base of operations."

Taken aback by this sudden turn of events, Noda fidgeted with his glasses, then wiped his sweating palms on his rolled-up shirtsleeve. The private jet was almost ready for takeoff. Surely his plan to lure the master back to Tokyo could not be changed now.

"But why, Takashima-san?" he challenged.

"It is not safe," Takashima said firmly. "Send word to the captain that we will not be taking off."

Noda wrung his hands in frustration. He could not allow his plans to be changed. Everything he had prepared depended on their arriving in Tokyo at the appointed time. He must break with tradition once again and speak his mind.

"Takashima-san, it is most important you return to Tokyo for other reasons."

His master looked up and grunted loudly, clearly annoyed by Noda's outburst. "I have already made our decision."

"But, master, you have forgotten the most important reason for your return at this time." As Takashima eyed him coldly, Noda pressed on: "Takashima-san, your records. The scorecard, all of the payments to the politicians from your pachinko parlors, all the records of tax evasion, are recorded in this ledger book."

Seeing Takashima nodding thoughtfully, Noda added, "Also, master, you realize that Asano-san may not remain faithful to you if he is the only one arrested. He could lead the authorities to our safe. We *must* secure these vital records immediately, and in person. This is for your continued safety."

"Takashima-san," the Ronin leader interrupted, overhearing the conversation. He vigorously disagreed with Noda's reasoning. "Our intelligence clearly indicates that now is not the time to return to Japan. Due to the political unrest, many prominent business leaders like yourself are targets for arrest. I am afraid I must inform you that the supreme public prosecutor has issued a warrant for your immediate arrest."

"But, master, that is not true. I phoned the supreme public prosecutor earlier this morning." Takashima stared matter-of-factly at this sudden revelation. "It is done, Takashima-san," Noda said. "No indictments will be filed against you."

"You are sure there is no mistake, Noda-san?" Takashima did not show his nervousness, but he had to be sure it was safe to return to Japan.

Noda bowed, and his eyes did not meet those of Takashima or the Ronin leader. "I have been *personally* assured."

Takashima was satisfied. He nodded his approval. The prosecutor had been well taken care of over the years and would be again in the future. Like all members of the Ministry of Justice, he was under an obligation to respect *tatemae*, the accepted way of doing things.

Noda said nothing more. He knew now was the time to let silence win his argument.

Takashima stood quietly for several minutes, mulling over Noda's words. But, he mused, maybe he had been too hasty with the Ronin leader. His heir had a strong argument, but the Ronin intelligence was also something he relied on.

"Noda-san, although what you say is true, the Ronin leader is also correct. It is still very dangerous to return now. I was a big contributor to the Prime Minister. No, my decision has changed. I will send you back alone—"

"Takashima-san," interrupted a perplexed Noda nervously, "I would gladly perform my duty and retrieve the ledger book myself. But, master . . ." He paused. "The safe can be opened only with both our thumbprints. Remember when we left Tokyo, we left the safe open and instructed Asano-san to lock it only upon receiving your instructions. And when you sent back the scorecard with the Yakuza, you then instructed Asano-san to close the safe. But the authorities would have a way of opening it,"

Takashima hesitated, shaking his head. That is true. However, the weight of his Ronin leader's intelligence and his dream still rested heavy on his mind. "I cannot return, Noda-san. I could be risking everything I have if you are wrong."

"But the ledgers must be burned, Takashima-san," Noda insisted, almost pleading his final argument. "Do not trust Asano-san with his knowledge of this most important book. He can easily be persuaded to save himself from any involvement by the authorities."

Takashima removed his tinted glasses and rubbed his eyes. He knew they were bloodshot, with deep circles underneath. His whole body was sluggish from the long flight. He felt completely drained of energy and could not think clearly.

He sighed heavily. He realized he had no other choice. He must ignore the warning in the nightmare and choose Noda's opinion over that of the Ronin leader.

"I will take your advice, Noda-san. We return to Tokyo immediately."

He had started up the stairs to the jet when he decided to turn around. He summoned Noda.

"Noda-san, please tell me, did the final solution for Kelly-san go as planned?"

Noda nodded, bowing. "*Hai*. It is done," he said fiercely.

21

"Baron, I'm warning you, please, for the last time, let us do our job," urged a frustrated Agent Donaldson after hearing another outburst.

"But, Donaldson, you don't understand," said Jake as the two men stood on the tarmac at Edwards Air Force Base, waiting to board the government plane now loaded with supplies.

"Please, Mr. Baron, try to relax. We're almost ready for wheels-up." Donaldson had given a ten-minute warning to the two teams of federal agents.

Jake nodded as he put a cigarette into his mouth. He cupped his hands together to light it with his lighter. He said nothing more; he knew that if he pushed his luck, Donaldson would make good on his threat and wouldn't allow him to go along with the rescue party.

After a long afternoon of pleading with Donaldson at the downtown office, Jake had finally been granted his request to come along, but under specific guidelines. He would be allowed to accompany the hastily put-together Medivac rescue party, while Donaldson would lead the capture group in another direction. Jake would have to follow *every* instruction or he couldn't go. There were no exceptions.

Jake took a long drag on his cigarette before dropping it to the ground and stomping on it with the heel of his boot. As he waited to board the plane, he

384

couldn't help asking himself: Is Kelly still alive? Why the hell didn't I talk her out of returning to the studio?

It had been a horrible twelve hours. He had been told that once Donaldson had confirmed that Takashima had left LAX, and allegedly with a kidnapped Kelly Kristopher, he had immediately called an all-out alert.

Now that Takashima had seemingly committed specific criminal acts accountable to the United States government, Donaldson could act. To ensure the government's case, Donaldson had decided to also take along a federal prosecutor from the U.S. Attorney General's office.

Before joining up with an entire elite government team of specially trained federal agents—FBI, U.S. Marshals, DEA, and ATF, who were all prepared to respond quickly in a crisis situation—Agent Donaldson had asked the FBI to decipher a cryptic phone call from Noda. Barely audible, Noda had whispered: "Fiji, girl," then hung up. That was all Donaldson needed to hear before going ahead.

When Jake had been informed of this on the phone, he didn't waste any time. He threw his shaving kit and a change of clothes into an overnight bag, then had a teary-eyed Mistica drop him off at the Federal Building in Westwood, where Donaldson had him picked up in a government chopper for the trip to the California Air Force base.

He looked around the sprawling airstrip. Located on the western end of the Mojave Desert, it was filled with jets. Edwards, best known for the NASA space-shuttle landings, was one of a few "hot" bases that the government had designated as a staging area for the western region of the U.S. for any crisis in the Pacific Rim.

"C'mon, Baron, let's go," mumbled Donaldson.

Narita Airport was crowded with businessmen, tourists, students fighting to get through Immigration and Customs quickly.

Once inside the fortified gate, all arriving passengers were greeted by police in full riot gear, who stood guard, ready to examine any suspicious-looking visitor. Never-ending lines and security checkpoints frustrated even the most seasoned traveler.

Takashima and his entourage strode quickly into the immigration area, even though they were fatigued from the ten-hour flight. They ignored the confusion around them. Takashima was in the lead, his heels clicking off the steps like seconds on a clock. Noda followed him. The Yakuza and the Ronin members brought up the rear.

When they came to the clearing section, Takashima looked around for his usual contact with the Japanese immigration department. His well-paid man was not there. What is going on? he wondered. He was always processed without any delay. This was most unusual.

He lit a cigarette, then tossed it away impatiently. He was not used to being kept waiting. Especially now. He had only one thought on his mind: to destroy his incriminating ledgers and pay a final visit to his family shrine, then leave the country immediately.

Nervously he checked around the arrival area. Everything seemed to be quite normal. Arriving passengers were showing their passports for inspection while the uniformed inspectors asked routine questions. No one made a move to welcome him.

Tapping his forefingers together, Takashima now looked at Noda accusingly. "Noda-san, where is our contact? Have you failed in your *giri*?"

Noda could barely answer, for his fear of Takashima choked him. "I do not know, Takashima-san," he said simply.

Noda began searching for their contact while the Ronin leader leered at him. He walked around the perimeter of the immigration area, while the Yakuza stayed close to Takashima.

Takashima noticed several people staring at them. They were beginning to attract a crowd of curious onlookers, especially tourists, who were probably not used to seeing the menacing corps of Yakuza in their flashy business suits.

It was then that Noda noticed a well-dressed man walking briskly toward them. He did not recognize him, but his instincts told him this was the man he had been looking for.

The man walked directly up to Takashima and stopped in front of him. He politely bowed and said: "Takashima-san, *kon-nichiwa*."

Takashima returned the friendly greeting, bowing slightly. He smiled at the official. Perhaps he had been worried for nothing.

"Follow me, *kudasai*," the man said quickly.

As Takashima and his entourage accompanied the friendly stranger through the airport, he noticed the official was leaving the immigration area. He was suddenly on guard. "Where are you taking us?" Takashima demanded.

Not pausing, the official turned around and said, "Excuse me, Takashima-san, but we have recently instituted a new rule for special businessmen like yourself."

Takashima turned to Noda. "Why was I not informed of this?" As Noda looked at him blankly, Takashima became even more alarmed. Something was wrong. He had never known his heir apparent to be caught unaware in any situation.

"New rule?" Takashima questioned the official brusquely as they all entered a private lounge area.

The official nodded. "It will take but a moment. Please hand me all of your passports, and I will have them quickly stamped. Then we will proceed on to Customs."

As Takashima, Noda, the Yakuza, and the Ronin handed the official their passports, they were all cordially invited to take a seat while the official went into the next room.

Takashima, instead of sitting down, stared furiously

around the lounge to see who else was marked for this treatment. His eyes widened as he noticed a beautiful Eurasian girl wearing a very short skirt, sitting across the room from him at the bar. She smiled in return.

Takashima bowed back in her direction, smiling. She could be an interesting addition to his one evening here. He would send Minoru to find out who she was.

Takashima took his eyes off her only for a split second, but it was long enough. The beautiful girl jumped off her stool and pointed an Uzi at his head. "Takashima-san, I regret you are under arrest."

Shocked, Takashima froze. Had he heard clearly? he questioned as his eyes looked around for his Yakuza. They had already assumed poised karate stances and were starting to surround her on all sides.

Then it was all over.

"All of you, freeze!"

They were immediately surrounded by uniformed Japanese police as well as several *keiji*, the elite Japanese detectives. Their guns were drawn and pointed at everyone in Takashima's party.

Takashima faced straight ahead, keeping his shoulders squared back. He refused to allow fear to invade his mind. He listened silently as the *keiji* advised him of his right to counsel. Then he turned to one of the detectives and smiled. He knew he had no reason to panic. He was too powerful.

"I believe you have made a mistake," he said confidently.

"No mistake, Takashima-san," a man said, entering the lounge.

Takashima spun his head around. He recognized Toshio Makimoto, the Tokyo district public prosecutor and head of the Special Investigations Division. He was a man with a reputation for honesty and immunity from outside pressure, including that from businessmen like Takashima.

"You are now within our Japanese jurisdiction," he said calmly, "and you are under arrest."

"What are the charges?" he barked back to the chief prosecutor.

Makimoto's eyes never left Takashima as he spoke. "Tax evasion, bribery, money-laundering, violation of securities laws, as well as other crimes." He paused, accenting his next words with a firm conviction. "Perhaps even murder."

Takashima laughed. This made no sense. He had paid off too many people in high places to prevent something like this from happening. His participation in the recent political scandal had been carefully covered up. There was nothing to worry about.

He quickly turned to his protégé. "Noda-san, please phone my Tokyo attorney immediately and have him arrange for our bail." He paused, smiling wryly at the Tokyo district public prosecutor. "Then we will go free."

The prosecutor merely nodded to one of his detectives, who came forward, bowed to Takashima, then pulled a set of handcuffs from his pocket.

Takashima was not disturbed as he was being cuffed. This was simply a police formality. There was nothing they could do to him. After all, he was the Asian Octopus. He merely stiffened his shoulders, then turned to Noda as the policemen started to handcuff the others, including the Yakuza and the Ronin.

But to Takashima's amazement, Noda and Minoru were singled out and were not handcuffed. He looked at them, but neither looked him in the eye. Takashima felt the strength draining quickly from his body, but he refused to back down. He must not show weakness.

"What are you waiting for? Noda-san, you have my instructions," he ordered loudly. "Contact my attorney."

Noda did not look at Takashima. Instead he glanced over at Makimoto and smiled broadly.

Takashima glared at his heir apparent. "Noda-san!" he commanded.

"*Dozo*, Takashima-san," a *keiji* said politely, urging him on with a light tap on the shoulder.

"Wait," Takashima requested. The police detective looked at Makimoto. As was the custom, Makimoto allowed *ninjō*, compassion. He signaled for the *keiji* to wait. An invited Associated Press photographer suddenly flashed a quick photo of Takashima during this lull.

"Noda-san, I have given you an order," Takashima screamed, noticing that neither Noda nor Minoru had yet been handcuffed.

With a stern face Noda looked directly at Takashima through his glasses. "No, I have chosen not to obey. Not now or ever again." He bowed respectfully to Takashima for the last time.

Takashima was too shaken to speak. Noda had never said no to him.

"I believed in you all these years," Noda stated softly. "You were the father I never had. But you deceived me, Takashima. You murdered my mother." He then spat in Takashima's face.

Takashima flushed with anger. "That is ridiculous. I did not know your mother."

Noda shook his head. "*Hai*, but you did know my mother. Her name was Midori-san. She was your geisha before Chisako-san. And when you discovered she had a child, you had your men torture her until she died."

Takashima kept his face expressionless, but now all the blood drained from it. Indeed, he remembered the shy, beautiful woman called Midori. Many times he had cursed the spell of the full moon that had seduced him into taking the whore—a homeless maiden drenched from the storm—into his house.

"I know nothing of this woman," Takashima lied convincingly. "You cannot prove anything." He refused to admit that he had known that Noda was the son of the woman. When he had discovered the existence of the young boy, he had been angry. But then he had decided to raise the boy as his own. It was his one chance to be a father and live out his own boyhood through Noda. And now that boy had taken everything from him.

Takashima's attitude only angered Noda more. "You are lying," he said, grabbing Takashima's lapels with clenched fists. "When you ordered Chisako-san banished to a life of exile, she showed me the combs that had belonged to my mother and told me the story of the mystery that surrounded her death—how you murdered her and made her death appear to be suicide."

Takashima searched Noda's eyes; he was telling the truth. He turned away. He should have known that whore Chisako would say too much. He should have had her tortured to death as well.

"I can never bring back my beloved mother, nor her kind words, nor her warm arms, but I can make certain that you account for your crimes."

Noda then backed away from the man whom he had always known as his father. He continued to stare at Takashima, spitting out his hatred as he slowly circled him. "I knew that one day you would be here, chained with the sins of your own greed." He paused, trying to compose himself. "Asano-san has given the authorities every document—including the real scorecard—which will put you away for a long, long time. You will now pay for your sins."

Outraged by this betrayal, Takashima felt his blood racing madly through his brain. As Noda began to walk away with Minoru and one of the detectives, Takashima yelled after him, "Stop him! He is the guilty one." His dark eyes raging like a madman's, Takashima turned to the prosecutor.

"A *gaijin* is dead!" he cried, raising his handcuffed hands in protest. "And this man murdered her yesterday in the Fiji Islands after he administered to her a lethal dose of drugs. Then the two of them," he yelled, pointing his finger at both Noda and Minoru, "buried her on the island of Kabara!"

"That is not true, Takashima-san," Noda said calmly,

and Minoru nodded agreement. "The girl lives," he said, a triumphant glow in his clear brown eyes.

Takashima glared back at Noda, then at Minoru, stunned. "What . . . what do you mean? She's dead. You and Minoru killed her."

To Takashima's further surprise, Noda told him that he had convinced Minoru to help him keep Kelly alive. In exchange for Minoru's complete testimony against him, the chief prosecutor would be asked to be lenient with the Yakuza during the court proceedings.

"Takashima-san, your fate is now sealed," the public prosecutor said. He then signaled his men to move Takashima along.

As they started to march Takashima through the swinging doors, two men, out of breath, suddenly entered the room: Agent Donaldson, carrying a handheld cellular phone, and a U.S. federal prosecutor. Donaldson flashed his badge to Takashima.

"Mr. Takashima," Donaldson said, "in addition to any Japanese charges against you, our U.S. arrest warrant here"—he paused, pointing to the envelope the prosecutor held under his arm—"includes kidnapping as well as attempted murder. And we're still completing numerous indictments of racketeering, money-laundering, and income-tax evasion. Also, there's our ongoing investigation of the Stephen Resnick so-called suicide."

Makimoto smiled at Donaldson's comments while the federal agent turned to a tired-looking Noda and shook his hand.

"Noda," Donaldson began, "on behalf of the United States government, please accept our very special thanks for leading us"—he turned and nodded to Makimoto—"in the apprehension of Takashima." Turning back to Noda, he said, "It was your phone call from Takashima's plane that gave us the necessary data we needed."

"Thank you, but please tell me, how is Kelly?" Noda asked, concerned.

"She'll be okay. We have already, with Mr. Baron by her side, medivacked Kelly to Honolulu, where a team of doctors is treating her. In fact, a little while ago, Baron phoned me on the plane, saying that she appears to be in good spirits and will make a complete recovery. He wanted me to thank you for both of them."

The chief prosecutor cleared his throat to interrupt this complimentary exchange, bowing to Noda. He wanted to add to Donaldson's praises: "I must congratulate you, Noda-san, especially on your bravery. With our recently appointed new Prime Minister and the roundup and capture of ruthless businessmen such as Hiroshi Takashima, a new day begins to dawn for our people and Japan."

Moving closer to Takashima, Donaldson watched him lower his head in defeat. "Mr. Takashima, I don't know how long you might spend in a Japanese prison, but if you ever do get free, the U.S. government will be waiting for you." He grabbed the federal prosecutor's envelope containing his arrest warrants and shoved them into Takashima's face. "We'll make it our business to extradite you back to the good old U.S.A. and put you on trial there."

Takashima grimaced, contorting his face into a murderous stare. He then nodded to the *keiji*. "Please, I am ready now."

As the phalanx of guards surrounding Takashima slowly moved him through the double doors, he could think only of Michio Noda: the boy he had raised as a son was now a man guilty of betrayal. He suppressed a groan from deep within him. He had never felt such sorrow.

He suddenly remembered his dream about the three-headed monster. It had been Baron, Kristopher, and Noda all along. He had been warned by the gods, but he had failed to listen. He smiled remotely. He deserved to be punished now. Somewhere in the deep secret parts of his mind, he had known this day would come.

He then turned to Noda one last time. He stared at him coldly, showing him the face he wanted him to remember forever; his eyes staring, never blinking, as in death, but with a hatred so alive it would never die. Noda quickly turned his back.

But Takashima could not resist one parting shot against the American enemy, directed at Donaldson: "There will be more of my kind who will invade your country—rich Japanese businessmen full of hatred and revenge. Just you wait and see. And as in any war, you will not be able to catch all of our noble warriors. You can be sure of that. *Banzai!*"

As the swinging doors closed behind him, Hiroshi Takashima's plan for *fukushū*, revenge, came full circle.

Epilogue

"Jake, did you see the front page story in the Sunday *Times*?" Kelly, still with a lingering sore throat, called out as she pulled the bedcovers up to her chin. She lay back on the pillow, grateful that most of her pain, after the weeks of hospitalization, had subsided. Her wounds had now started to heal nicely. She would be as good as new physically in a short time, even though she and Jake both knew that her mental scars would never heal completely.

Hollywood trade papers, along with newspapers from the past month, were spread all over the bed. All of them related the shocking story of Takashima's background, his revenge, his anti-Hollywood sentiments, as well as Kelly's kidnapping and attempted murder, his arrest, and so on. It was all there for the whole world to read. Many of the headline stories included a wire photo of a subdued Takashima being led away in handcuffs.

"Kelly, I'll be right up," Jake shouted from the kitchen.

As she continued to peruse the article she had been reading, she smelled something cooking. She wrinkled her nose. It smelled good, whatever it was. "Jake, what are you up to now?" she yelled out.

With a devilish smile on his face, Jake entered the bedroom and looked around with pleasure. It certainly was cheery. Mistica had helped him place many of the pretty get-well flowers and plants all over the room, along with the hundreds of cheerful cards pinned up everywhere.

"Wouldn't you like to know?" He wore only a chef's apron and held a tray piled high with blueberry pancakes, a bottle of champagne with two tall glasses, and a single red rose in a wineglass.

Suddenly they heard the doorbell chiming downstairs.

"Who do you think that is?" Jake asked, furrowing his brow.

"I hope it's not any more reporters," Kelly sighed, closing her eyes. She was exhausted from all the interviews.

"Well, I'll find out," he said, going downstairs. He was surprised to see Mistica standing outside, going through her purse.

"I can't find my key, Dad," she said, embarrassed. As she followed her father into the house, she started to giggle. He wasn't exactly dressed for Sunday brunch. But she decided not to say a word, although she discreetly turned her eyes away from his bare posterior. He probably had forgotten how he was dressed.

"You won't be needing your key," he said, holding her hand. "I've booked you a room at the Century Plaza for the next few days, honey. I just had the Platinum representative at American Express pre-approve any charges you make. How's that for a surprise?" he said as he motioned his head, winking an eye, toward the upstairs.

Mistica grinning, winked back at this sudden treat from her dad. As she hugged him, she said, "Sure, Dad. Give Kelly my love." Then she was gone before her father could change his mind.

Kelly was still reading the Sunday paper as Jake sat down on the bed next to her. "Sounded like Mistica," she said.

"Yeah."

"Mistica's really been an angel over the past few weeks," she said, then picked up another newspaper and changed the subject. "Oh, I almost forgot. Larry King wants us on his CNN show, Cindy Adams called three times for any new updated items, and Arsenio Hall wants me to talk about my kidnapping experience."

Jake grinned. "We'll have Rosey do us a favor and respond to them and all the others in a few days. Look, this is only your second day home and I don't care if George Bush wants to shake your hand at the White House or Geraldo Rivera wants you to do a theme show on battered CEO's, the answer is no! You are all mine for the next forty-eight hours," he finished as he nibbled on her ear.

Kelly pushed him away playfully. "Later, Romeo. I want you to see this." She pointed to a trade story in *Daily Variety*. He read it aloud over her shoulder. " 'Robert Zinman, the former president of Constellation Studios, has been sued for three million dollars by Israeli investor . . .' "

Jake dropped a more positive article on top of Robert's as he laughed. "Serves the bastard right. Here, Kelly, listen to this: 'Constellation has been placed into federal receivership, with a group of private investors already intending to buy it. The probable chances are that it will go public when the deal is set . . . that the unions will be welcomed back . . . word is that the first film release will be the recently completed *Criminal Intent* . . . and the whole Hollywood community is relieved to see Takashima go.' "

"That's quite a mouthful. Here, try this . . ." Kelly said, stuffing a pancake into his mouth as she picked up Friday's *Hollywood Reporter*. She smiled, but she couldn't help but notice the sudden cloud over his face. "Jake, what's wrong?"

"I'm sorry, Kel. My mind just started drifting again. While you were recuperating at Cedars, Donaldson phoned me. He said he took a statement from Minoru about Stephen's death. According to the Yakuza, Takashima did send him and a second henchman to snuff out Stephen, but he claims that Stephen surprised them by killing himself. Supposedly, Stephen was holding the gun when they arrived, then panicked when he opened up the Yakuza's briefcase and found it empty of any money. Then he blasted himself away."

Kelly grabbed Jake's hand tightly, then kissed his cheek. She knew he needed her support now, probably as much as she needed his. Maybe if she quickly changed the topic, he'd perk up.

"Hey, did you see our hot item in Robert Osborne's column?"

"What?" Jake mumbled as he chewed on a pancake. Then he grabbed her hand and put it on his hard penis. He growled contentedly. He was himself again.

"Jake, stop it . . . wait a minute," she said, smacking his hand away. " 'According to reliable sources' "—Kelly pretended to clear her throat—" 'Kelly Kristopher will become Mrs. Jake Baron.' And you and I are the odds-on favorites to run the newly revitalized Constellation."

"I'll drink to that," he laughed, pouring a glass of champagne.

"What, that I'll marry you?"

"Mmm, we'll see," he said, taking a sip of the bubbly. Then he looked back at her, his eyes bright and shining. "Have I ever told you how beautiful you look in the morning?" he said, pulling down the sheet and running his hands carefully over her breasts. He knew he had to be very gentle. Her body had been scarred by Takashima's savage beating.

He held her close to him, the warmth of her flesh melting into his own. There was nothing he cherished more. He wanted her to be with him always.

"Jake, please," she begged with a smile in her voice. Suddenly the phone next to the bed began to ring. "Oh-oh, I'll bet that's Michael Douglas again. He wants to do a film about my ordeal. He says Oliver Stone is interested in writing and directing . . . and would you believe that he's already thinking about casting Meryl Streep." Laughing, Kelly continued, pinching his arm. "And Michael already sees Gene Hackman playing you, Jake."

Jake picked up the phone, then quickly hung it up again. He took it off the hook before pulling it out of the wall. "I don't hear any ringing," he muttered. "Listen, Kel, there'll be plenty of time to think about films and book deals. We'll let Ovitz handle that," he whispered, caressing her shoulders tenderly. "But first, what'll it be? Champagne or . . . ?" he asked, biting her earlobe.

Kelly smiled as she tenderly wrapped him in her arms, pushing the plate of pancakes onto the floor. "Why don't we just keep everybody wondering about us?" she teased, grinning.

"Kel, I love you so much," he said as they both sipped champagne from his glass before disappearing under the covers.

If we act like the American occupying Army in postwar Japan, we would be bashed; but if we keep Columbia totally American, everything will be fine.

> —AKIO MORITA, Sony's chairman,
> after buying Columbia Pictures,
> September 27, 1989

I just have a feeling that maybe Hollywood needs some outsiders to bring back decency and good taste to some of the pictures that are being made.

> —Former President RONALD REAGAN
> in a taped interview broadcast
> in Japan, October 25, 1989,
> regarding Sony's $3.4-billion
> takeover of Columbia Pictures

About the Authors

JINA BACAAR is a freelance travel and television writer who has worked extensively with the Japanese.

ELLIS A. COHEN is a television movie producer and former Hollywood publicist. Both authors currently make their homes in Los Angeles.

⊘ SIGNET (0451)

NOVELS TO REMEMBER

☐ **ABSENCE OF PAIN by Barbara Victor.** "Humor, romance and tragedy in a memorable novel about finding love.... With her quirks, courage and vulnerability, Maggie Sommers is an endearing heroine."—*Publishers Weekly* (162153—$4.99)

☐ **MISPLACED LIVES by Barbara Victor.** Gabriella Carlucci-Molloy returned from Paris to a home she thought she had left forever and faces new love and betrayed dreams. "A lovely, touching novel about love that tugs at the heartstrings."—Barbara Taylor Bradford (169719—$4.50)

☐ **SHE WHO REMEMBERS, a novel of prehistory by Linda Lay Shuler.** Kwain's blue eyes made her an outcast in the tribe that raised her, but they made her one Chosen of the Gods in the Eagle Clan, and named her She Who Remembers, because she taught young girls the ancient secrets only women know. "I loved this compelling story of love and adventure." —Jean M. Auel, author of *Clan of the Cave Bear* (160533—$5.99)

☐ **NO REGRETS by Fern Kupfer.** A wry, poignant novel about love, loss and marriage. "Wise and reflective ... reveals honest insights and simple pleasures."—*Kirkus Reviews* (165705—$4.95)

☐ **THE THREE SIRENS by Irving Wallace.** World-famous anthropologist Dr. Maud, his beautiful young wife and son had come to the Polynesian islands as observers and are forced to confront their own deeply entrenched fears and sexual taboos.... (159403—$4.95)

☐ **MAIA by Richard Adams.** The Belkan Empire. It is here that the fabulous Maia is sold into slavery, an innocent young peasant girl, beautiful beyond belief and gifted with a rare erotic talent that will open to her all the strongholds of Belkan power. "Extraordinary."—*The New York Times Book Review* (168119—$6.95)

Prices slightly higher in Canada.

Buy them at your local bookstore or use this convenient coupon for ordering.

NEW AMERICAN LIBRARY
P.O. Box 999, Bergenfield, New Jersey 07621

Please send me the books I have checked above. I am enclosing $_____
(please add $1.00 to this order to cover postage and handling). Send check or money order—no cash or C.O.D.'s. Prices and numbers are subject to change without notice.

Name_____

Address_____

City _____ State _____ Zip Code _____

Allow 4-6 weeks for delivery.
This offer, prices and numbers are subject to change without notice.

ⓞ SIGNET BOOKS (0451)

HAUNTING PASSION

☐ **DARK WINDOW by Linda Crockett Gray.** When Barbara Ashcroff's wonderful husband, T.J., suddenly died, Barbara found that desire had not died in her. But the two new men in her life had a rival for her passion and possession. For desire had not died in T.J. either. (169824—$4.99)

☐ **THE GIRL IN A SWING by Richard Adams.** "Astonishing...sublime eroticism and gruesome nightmare...an absolutely terrifying ghost story, as gripping and psychologically penetrating as anything in James or Poe. Richard Adams has written with marvelous tact and narrative power, a strange, beautiful, haunting book."—*The New York Times Book Review* (163060—$5.95)

☐ **THE MIRACLE by Irving Wallace.** Natale Rinaldi, a ravishingly beautiful, tragically blind Italian actress, becomes lost in a maze of dark lust and mysterious love... as people from around the world are drawn together at one extraordinary moment in time and caught up in a miracle whose true nature you will never predict.... (158962—$4.95)

☐ **PEARL by Tabitha King.** After arriving in Nodd's Ridge, Maine, to claim her inheritance, Pearl Dickenson becomes involved with two men whose rivalry explodes into violence, and threatens the fabric of everyday life in the small community. "Powerful...truly masterful."—*Washington Post Book World* (162625—$4.95)

Prices slightly higher in Canada

Buy them at your local

bookstore or use coupon

on next page for ordering.

ⓈSIGNET

DRAMA & ROMANCE

(0451)

- ☐ **FLOWERS OF BETRAYAL by June Triglia.** Tiziana D'Eboli risked everything to free herself from a ruthless mafia bond. Here is a novel of passion, shame, deceit, and murder—and the stunning woman who took destiny into her own hands. (402472—$5.99)

- ☐ **BOUND BY BLOOD by June Triglia.** Two beautiful sisters overcome brutal pasts to become successful and prominent women. From Pittsburgh to Paris, from Manhattan to Milan, Angie and Nickie learn just how far they can go. "Masterful storytelling that will keep you turning pages!"—Fred Mustard Stewart (401832—$4.95)

- ☐ **VEIL OF SECRETS by Una-Mary Parker.** In this sizzling novel of mystery and seduction, Una-Mary Parker vividly interweaves the *haut monde* with affairs of art and finance, giving full reign to three beautiful women who become tangled in a triangle of love, passion and greed. "A glitzy romp with the rich and famous."—*Booklist* (169328—$4.99)

- ☐ **DOCTORS AND DOCTORS' WIVES by Francis Roe.** Greg Hopkins and Willie Stringer, two powerful and dedicated doctors, find their friendship shattered by personal and professional rivalries. A masterful medical drama, this novel vividly portrays the lives and loves of doctors and their fascinating, high-pressure world. (169107—$5.50)

Buy them at your local bookstore or use this convenient coupon for ordering.

NEW AMERICAN LIBRARY
P.O. Box 999, Bergenfield, New Jersey 07621

Please send me the books I have checked above. I am enclosing $_____
(please add $1.00 to this order to cover postage and handling). Send check or money order—no cash or C.O.D.'s. Prices and numbers are subject to change without notice.

Name_____

Address_____

City _____ State _____ Zip Code _____

Allow 4-6 weeks for delivery.
This offer, prices and numbers are subject to change without notice.